PRAISE FO

"Keyes mixes cultures, religions, in
the rewards [are] (
Publishers Weekly **(starred review)**

"Here is a high fantasy novel that has the grit of secular combat and
the heart of one of the great romances."
Fantasy and Science Fiction Magazine

"Recommended… Keyes's talent for world crafting and storytelling
make this series opener a strong addition to fantasy collections."
Library Journal

"Keyes takes all the genre's conventions and, while never overstepping
their boundaries, breathes new life into them."
Kirkus Reviews

"Keyes is a master of world building and of quirky characters who grow
into their relationships in unexpected ways."
Booklist

"Greg Keyes has always been both a skilled storyteller and fine
writer of exciting tales."
Terry Brooks, author of *The Sword of Shannara*

"Starts in the realm of normalcy and quickly descends into the favorably
bizarre and surprising… there was not one character that was
uninteresting. The world building is epic."
Koeur's Book Reviews

"Strong world building and superior storytelling."
Library Journal

"[A] sophisticated and intelligent high fantasy epic."
Publishers Weekly

"A graceful, artful tale from a master storyteller."
Elizabeth Haydon, bestselling author of *Prophesy: Child of Earth*,

"The characters in *The Briar King* absolutely brim with life…
Keyes hooked me from the first page."
Charles de Lint, award-winning author of *Forests of the Heart*
and *The Onion Girl*

ALSO BY GREG KEYES

THE
BASILISK
THRONE

GREG KEYES

TITAN BOOKS

The Basilisk Throne

Print edition ISBN: 9781789095487
E-book edition ISBN: 9781789095494

Published by Titan Books
A division of Titan Publishing Group Ltd
144 Southwark Street, London SE1 0UP
www.titanbooks.com

First edition: April 2023
1 3 5 7 9 10 8 6 4 2

A CIP catalogue record for this title is available from the British Library.

Printed and bound in the United Kingdom by CPI Group (UK) Ltd, Croydon, CR0 4YY.

For Sandra Baxter

THE BATTLE
OF THE EXPIRY

988 E.N.

"HARD ABOUT!" Captain Salemon shouted, as half of their prow disintegrated into a cloud of wooden shards. Sailors fell screaming as splinters pierced them. As Alastor watched, his friend Danyel covered his eyes with both hands, stumbling as blood leaked through his fingers.

The *Laros* rocked under a second impact, so jarring that Alastor nearly lost his grip on the rigging. Flames erupted, spreading across the deck like a liquid.

"Christ of Ophion," Jax yelped. Alastor saw his fellow navior holding on by one hand, dangling twenty feet above the deck below. He reached out and grabbed Jax by his shirt, pulling him closer so he could double his grip.

"Captain, if we turn, we cannot engage," Lieutenant Captain La Treille snapped. "Our orders—"

"We are two hundred yards from being at the outside of our

range," Salemon returned. "We'll be fish food long before we cover the distance."

Even Alastor, as green as he was, could see the truth in that. Every ship on their line had been hit, and several were sinking, while the Drehhu vessels remained untouched in the distance. Whatever demonic weapons they were using, they had a far greater range then the spear-flinging quilaines with which the *Laros* was armed. The fleet was being chewed to pieces, and they hadn't yet fired a shot.

"They *are* demons," Jax said.

"Come on," Alastor said. "We've got to get the sails up."

They were going against the wind, so they had dropped sail and put the rowers to work. The ship was turning, but very slowly.

"Ah, merde," Jax said. "The captain's put us broadside."

The mainmast exploded in flame; what was left of it went up like a torch. The ship lurched as her babord side was slammed repeatedly by the invisible weapons of the Drehhu. La Treille twisted at the waist and kept turning, as his body tore apart and caught fire at the same time.

"We're done," Jax said. He groaned, and Alastor saw his friend had a splinter of the mast as long as an arm sticking out of his chest. Then Jax let go and plummeted to the flaming deck.

As the ship foundered, Alastor clung to the rigging. When it tipped to the side, he let go and fell into the sea. The Drehhu flames ran across the surface of the water. Swimming furiously as the fire swept toward him, he felt heavier with each stroke as the woolen clothing that had kept him warm during their cold passage to this battle became a sodden weight pulling him down. His breath rasped in his chest. His arms and legs stopped burning with exertion and began to grow numb for the chill in the water.

Alastor's head dipped below the surface and salt stung his nose. If not for the many hours of his boyhood spent swimming, he would already be sunken in the gray depths. These were not the warm, sunny waters of the Coste de Sucre, however. He had escaped the fire, but even so he knew he didn't have long to live.

He spied some floating wreckage and bore toward it, grasping with fingers he could no longer feel, and pulling his arms around it. It wasn't much, not enough to pull himself fully out of the water, but it kept him afloat. He rested a moment, eyes closed, drawing in breath before opening them once more to look around.

IN THE distance, it looked as if the whole fleet was burning. Forty-five ships of war, turned to scrap in under an hour. Against all odds, a few had managed to come into range before succumbing to the enemy weapons, but so far as he could see, not one of the Drehhu vessels had been damaged. He was hardly surprised. They had no masts and were armored in metal.

The fleet of Ophion had never had a chance, here on the open sea.

The flames on the waves flickered and died away until only a few ghostly blue vapors remained. It was strangely beautiful, and then they too were gone, leaving only the iron-colored swells.

Another survivor began swimming his way.

"Do you mind?" the fellow asked, gasping as he drew near. He was a freckle-faced man with auburn hair.

"Come aboard," Alastor said. "I'm Alastor Nevelon, from the *Laros*." He helped the man find his grip on the flotsam and then waited for him to gather enough air to speak again.

"Henri Vallet," the other navior finally said. "Late of the *Delphis*."

"Charmed," Alastor said. "With the two of us pushing this thing, we might be able to join up with that bit of debris over there." He gestured.

"Ah, and have a proper boat," Vallet said. "I'm for that." They set out, kicking hard and navigating their piece of wreckage, and had some luck. Their prize was part of a mast that had some rope on it. It seemed like hours before they managed to lash together enough of a raft that they were able to draw themselves out of the water, and the overcast sky was little help in telling time. Once above the life-leaching sea they both sat silently, rubbing swollen hands. Alastor had torn out three nails, but didn't feel it yet due to the cold.

"Where from, Nevelon?" Vallet asked, after a time.

"Mesembria," he replied. "A place called Port Bellship."

Vallet nodded. "On the Coste de Sucre. Nice little place."

"And you?"

"Ophion Magne," the man said. "From the city. Not the nice part of it, though."

They fell silent. Other survivors could be seen, and more could be heard. Alastor turned his head slowly, surveying the horizon in all directions. The Drehhu ships were visible amongst the ruins of the center of the fleet, but none yet headed their way.

To the west, there was no horizon, only a strange grayness, like a wall of cloud.

"That's it, isn't it?"

"The Expiry," Vallet confirmed.

"We never had a chance," Alastor sighed. "What madness drove the admiral to this?"

"This wasn't the plan," Vallet said. "You must know that. The plan was to slip up into their port of Agath, and launch the assault in the harbor. We would have had twice their number, plus the advantage of surprise. That's why we swung out so far—so close to the edge of the world—to avoid being noticed until we were there. But the Drehhu found out and met us here, with our backs to the Expiry, so we had no choice but to fight."

"I hadn't heard any of that," Alastor said.

"Only the officers knew," Vallet replied.

"You're an officer?" Alastor stared at him. He wasn't wearing a coat or hat. "Sir," he added.

"Does it matter now?" Vallet said. "Shall I be captain of our little craft, for as long as it lasts? Be easy, Nevelon." They fell silent for a time, then Vallet spoke. "Tell me about Port Bellship. Did you grow up there?"

Alastor nodded. "My family has a sugar plantation."

"Really? And you chose to join the Navy rather than stay home and drink rum?"

"I thought I might see something of the world. Serve my emperor. Later, perhaps become a merchant sailor." He glanced at the Expiry. He was certain now.

The current was taking them toward it.

Vallet noticed. "Yes," he said, acknowledging the obvious. He didn't sound afraid, or even worried. Just tired. "This is as close as I've ever been."

"They say it cuts the world in half."

"It runs from farthest north to farthest south, that much we know to be true," Vallet said, "but whether or not the other half of the world lies beyond it, who can say?" He nodded toward the gray wall of mist that stretched as far as they could see in either direction. "No one who has ever crossed into that has ever come back. It might well be the edge of the world. It might be a wall between us and Hell."

"I fear we shall find out," Alastor said, although he also felt too exhausted to properly dread their fate.

Vallet glanced toward the Drehhu ships.

Two were moving in their direction.

"We know what the alternative is," Vallet said. "If the Drehhu do not kill us, they will enslave us."

Up ahead, from the direction of the Expiry, Alastor heard a single unholy shriek, followed quickly by another, then more, until there was a chorus of them.

"That doesn't sound promising."

The wall of mist loomed over them, filling their vision so that it was impossible to tell how distant it was, or how near. Not far off were four naviors on another makeshift raft. They vanished into it, and he expected to hear them scream, but there was no sound. A moment later he thought he heard something, but it might have been his imagination. The sky grew darker, and the approaching Drehhu ships became shadows in the distance.

They heard more shrieks of despair, and then other sounds— deep, stuttering clicks and weird, glissando wails, rising and falling in pitch from a high keening to tones so low he felt more than heard them. And a faint shushing, like an inconstant wind but also like distant whispering in an unknown language.

As full night came on, he thought he saw faint, shifting colors in the darkness.

"When will it happen?" Alastor asked.

"Perhaps we are already within," Vallet replied.

"It does not feel different." But even as he said it, he began to experience a prickling on his flesh, and his heart beat faster. It felt as something was shining on the side of him—the one that seemed to be facing the Expiry. A light his eyes could not perceive.

There was another strange noise: a grinding, churning sort of sound.

"Damn!" Vallet suddenly shouted. "Behind us."

Alastor turned. He saw lights and the outline of a ship. A Drehhu ship. The awful noise was coming from it. A lantern of some sort turned toward them, and the beam fell on their makeshift raft. The enemy ship began to turn, then came directly toward them.

In that light, Alastor could see the Expiry, no more than ten yards away.

"We could swim," he said. "Deny them their prize."

"A slave can escape," Vallet said. "He can escape and return to his home and drink rum in the evenings." He nodded at the wall of mist. "From that, there is no return."

Alastor nodded. He could see figures moving on the ship now. Not human. Bigger, with broader shoulders. They had four limbs like men, but those were long and spindly, and they made him think more of spiders than of people.

"A slave can escape," Alastor agreed.

BOOK ONE

THE

COST OF

SUGAR

CHAPTER ONE

AMMOLITE

1009 E.N.

THE FIRST time Ammolite looked in a mirror, she was sixteen.

She vomited.

Ammolite was a slave. She did not remember her mother selling her, but Veulkh assured her that it had happened.

"A silver bar and a necklace of glass gems," he informed her. "That was your price."

Of course, that was after he began talking to her.

Her earliest memories were of wandering the opalescent, faintly glowing halls of his manse, of standing alone on stone balconies, traveling her gaze over the snow-covered peaks that surely held up the sky. Down the almost sheer rock face into which the manse was built, to the mysterious green valley far below. She left bits of food on the balcony for the birds, and over time some would take their treats from her fingers. She fancied they were her friends and gave them names.

A woman came each day to feed her, read to her, and later teach her to read, but Ammolite never knew her name. No sentiment developed between them. The woman did her job, and hardly spoke a word to her that was not written in a book. Once Ammolite could read passably, the woman showed her the library, and thereafter did not come again.

A new woman brought her meals and did not speak at all. None of the other servants talked to her, either, and she came to realize that some of them were not even capable of speech.

She read and she stared from the balconies, moving through her world almost like a ghost, and though she knew she had a master—and that his name was Veulkh—she never saw him.

Until, one day, she did.

MOUNTED ON a wall in her room was a calendar, a round mechanical thing of brass and crystal that counted off the days of her life. Once she came to understand it, she knew on a given day that she was—for instance—six years and seventy-five days of age. She did not often consult it, for each day was like any other, and the number of them hardly seemed to matter.

But one morning the calendar, clicking along as usual, suddenly belled a single, beautiful tone. She was awake already, and she stared at the device in astonishment. This was something different, something that had never happened before. It filled her with an unexpected sense of hope and anticipation.

She was exactly sixteen years old.

Before she could rise and dress, a small, hunched woman she had never seen before entered the room, bearing a gown of black silk.

"You will wear this," the woman said.

The gown had unfamiliar fastenings but the woman helped her put it on. Up until then, Ammolite's clothing had been simple shifts she pulled on over her head, so she did not know much about clothes, but the dress seemed far too big for her. It piled on the floor and tried to slip from her shoulders. She felt lost in it.

Then the woman led her through the manor into halls she had never seen, to a room with a table large enough to accommodate twice a dozen people but which was set with only two places. At one of these places sat Veulkh.

She was a little surprised at how young he looked. She knew he was a sorcerer, and from her reading she knew that it took many years to become a master of those arts. From some of the things she had overheard the servants say, she thought he must be very old indeed, but his dark hair and beard lacked any hint of silver, and his face was handsome and young.

And yet she still did not like to look upon it. There was something there that bothered her.

The woman led her to her seat. Like the dress, it seemed too large.

"Ammolite," he said, absently. She wasn't sure he was speaking to her at first, but then he faced her directly. Though his features were composed, almost serene, his eyes were peculiar, as if he was looking beyond or perhaps *into* her.

The woman brought each of them a glass of something red.

"I named you that," Veulkh said, sipping at the red liquid. "Ammolite." Unsure what to do, she took her glass and tasted its contents. It was strange and harsh, like fruit juice but with something a little spoiled in it.

When she did not say anything, he crooked a finger at her.

"You may speak," he said.

"I did not know you named me," she said.

"You had another name, before I purchased you," he said. "I don't remember what it was." He smiled. "It hardly matters, does it?"

"I suppose not, Master," she replied.

He took another drink of the red stuff.

"This is called wine," he told her. "Vin in the language of Ophion. Nawash, in Modjal. It has other names. It is made from grapes."

"Is it made by magic?" she asked.

"Yes," he said. "A kind of alchemy is involved."

She took another tentative swallow. It still didn't taste good.

"I mentioned Ophion and Modjal," he said. "Do you know what I was referring to?"

"Ophion is an empire," she said. "Its capital is named Ophion Magne. It is said that a god by that name died and was buried there. They have an emperor and a council of savants. They are famous for textiles—"

"And Modjal?"

"Another empire, southeast of Ophion. Also with a capital of the same name, also said to be the resting place of an ancient god. Their emperor is known as the Qho—"

"Very good," he said. "You've been reading the books I provided you."

"Yes, Master."

He nodded approvingly.

"Do you understand, Ammolite, what it is to be a slave?"

"It means that you own me," she replied.

"That is correct," Veulkh said. "Like this wine, and the glass it is poured in. If I wish to hurl it against the wall and shatter it, that is entirely my decision. The glass and the wine have no say in the matter."

"I understand, Master."

He drained the rest of his drink in a single gulp and then cocked his arm back to dash it against the wall—but then he smiled and settled the glass back on the table. The woman came to refill it from a crystal pitcher.

"Have you ever wondered why you are here?"

She had, but she did not say so. She shook her head and drank a little more of the wine.

"You are here," he said, "as any slave is, because there are one or more tasks I require of you."

"I understand, Master," she said, "but I do not know what they are."

"Finish your wine, and I will show you," he said.

He watched in silence as she drank. It became easier as she went along. A sort of warmth crept over her, and her nervousness began to fade.

There is magic in this, she thought.

She wished he would talk more. She liked being spoken to.

"I've read about Velesa, as well," she attempted. "That is where we are, isn't it?"

"Who told you that?" he asked, a bit sharply.

"No one," she said, "but your books are mostly in the language of Velesa, and your servants speak it—and that nation is known for high mountains."

"You're quite certain none of my servants mentioned it?"

"I'm certain, Master."

"Well, you are mistaken," he said. "That is not where we are." He settled back, but a little frown remained on his face. He gestured for her to finish the wine. When she was done, he signaled to the woman, who left the room. Then he stood.

"Come, Ammolite," he said.

She followed him, feeling a bit sluggish and clumsy. Her head was a little whirly. He led her through a door and into a room furnished mostly in red, and sat her upon a large bed. Then he knelt before her and took her hands. It was such a shock her first instinct was to pull away—hardly anyone had ever touched her, and she never touched anyone. She didn't like it. His fingers felt warm, even hot, but they were gentle, and so she tried to breathe slowly, to bear it until it was over.

He placed her palms on his temples.

"Close your eyes," he said. "Look. See her."

She didn't know what he meant, but she closed her eyes. At first she saw nothing other than darkness, the backs of her eyelids, but gradually something appeared, a mist, a light.

The light became a face, a woman's face. She had dark eyes and pale skin, and her hair was as black as smoke. She trembled; it felt like a thousand insects were crawling upon her skin—and under it.

"There," he said. "Open your eyes."

She did so and found herself staring into his face.

"Orra," he murmured. His eyes had changed. They seemed more alive, full of some barely contained emotion. As she stared, he began to weep.

"You must say you love me," he said.

"I-I, l-love you," she stammered, suddenly more afraid than ever. Then he pushed his lips onto hers. She felt a rush of claustrophobia, as if she couldn't move her limbs, and tried to shove him away. Her body felt… bigger. Different. Not hers, somehow.

"You must say I please you," he said. "You must."

He was touching her now, touching her everywhere. His fingers were still gentle, but she wanted to scream, to get away.

"I have waited so long, Orra," he whispered into her ear. "You've been gone so long, but I kept you, kept you…" He put his lips on her again, rougher this time, and on her neck and chest. He pressed her back on the bed as he pushed up her dress.

WHEN IT was over, she still did not know what had happened, but she was sore and sick. She cried, but he kept speaking to her, telling her to say she loved him and how pleased she was. It was almost as if he was begging, and so she did, through the sobs.

"You don't understand, do you?"

"No."

"Go there." He pointed. "Turn the mirror around."

She did so, happy to be out of the bed, away from him. He had pointed at a wooden frame, mounted on a swivel. She had read about mirrors, had caught faint glimpses of herself in water basins and the polished marble in some of the halls, but had never seen one. She turned the frame.

Ammolite had milky hair, and a small, narrow face. She thought her eyes were pale blue or maybe even white, but what she saw in the mirror was the woman with the black hair. The dress was not loose on her; she filled it with all the curves of the grown women who had attended her. When Ammolite moved her hand, the dark-tressed woman in the glass did the same.

And then she vomited.

Over on the bed, Veulkh laughed at her.

When she was done, trembling, she looked back up at the

mirror, and the woman was gone, replaced by a sixteen-year-old girl in a dress far too large for her.

I want to die, she thought.

It would not be the last time.

SHE DIDN'T know the word for what had happened to her, and there was no one to tell her. The books in the library contained information on a wide variety of subjects, but nothing concerning what that thing was and why he put it in her.

As the calendar in her room ticked by her days and her birthdays—seventeen, eighteen, nineteen, twenty—she came to endure it. She became better and better at saying the things he wanted her to say, in the tone of voice he wanted. She learned to make it go more quickly.

In time, he stopped instructing her entirely, but instead gazed at her as if she were the only thing in the world that mattered. He told her again and again how he loved her, but she did not really know what that meant. She finally found a book that described the forms of "love." One of them—eros—seemed to involve the things he did to her body with his. Another sort of love—pragma—seemed to explain the way he behaved after he was done with that.

It was in those moments that he spoke to her of things he and Orra had shared, long ago, the countries they had visited, places he would take her again. She realized that, in Veulkh's mind, she had become two entirely different people—Ammolite and Orra. Sometimes she feared the same separation was happening in her own mind.

As Ammolite she could not bear his touch. It was easier to pretend she was Orra when he took her to the bed.

Except for one thing.

Orra—whoever and whenever she was—must have loved him as he loved her. Ammolite had only the mistiest notion of what love might be, but she knew she did not love Veulkh. She was, in fact, not even fond of him, as the books described it, no matter how embarrassingly sincere his pledges of devotion to her were.

There was another change, as well, and she took full advantage of it. Each night she was Orra and slept in his chambers, but by day—as Ammolite—she could go where she wished within the seemingly endless manse.

Besides the bedroom and dining room, Veulkh's suite contained a kitchen with a balcony and a view of the mountains. Adjoining it was a steam room and bath tiled in turquoise and polished red coral depicting dolphins and sea serpents. What interested her most, however, was the spiral stair that led upward. Treading it, she discovered Veulkh's library, which made for much more interesting reading than her own.

There were tomes on alchemy and thaumaturgy, venoms and vitriol, the humors of the universe and the human body, the atomies that dwell in living blood. Many of the books concerned weather and the nature of it, and of the world, its mountains and rivers and seas. Then there were the volumes written in scripts she could not read, but whose illustrations suggested they might be books of spells.

The first time Veulkh discovered her in the library, she thought she might be punished, but he hardly seemed to notice her. As she had once felt like a ghost, she had now *become* a ghost to him, for when she was Ammolite he hardly seemed to notice her at all.

One day, not long after her twentieth birthday, she decided to see how invisible she truly was, to discover if she could find the exit from the manse and simply walk away.

But if there was a way out, she never found it.

So she continued her self-education. She tried to prise out the meanings of the cryptic symbols in the spellbooks. She searched for some explanation of how Veulkh changed her into Orra, but found nothing except that transformation was one of the most difficult and dangerous of magicks.

IT TOOK her two years to find the book, the thing for which she had been looking without knowing exactly what she was seeking. By that time, she had taught herself a pair of the obscure languages in which many of the texts were written. It was a treatise on synapses, the locations where the powers of the world crossed or converged. The most powerful were natural, but they could also be created.

Soon after her first night with him, Veulkh took her to see his conjury, where he did his most powerful magics. She was certain it was one such synapse.

From the book she learned of another sort of synapsis, one each sorcerer fashioned for themselves. It was sometimes referred to as a "heart" or "core," and was something like a key used to unlock the other powers of the world, an intermediary between will and practice.

That heart was also a vulnerability, for once it had been made, the sorcerer could not survive without it.

If she could find Veulkh's heart…

She hardly dared think it at first. The book didn't describe what such a thing would look like, but a few weeks after reading the book, she began to search. Carefully.

Veulkh's conjury was above the library, a vast space carved deep into the living stone of the mountain, but with one face open to the wind. The floor was concave, and so smooth that she nearly slipped the first time she set foot upon it. Besides the stairway entrance there were two additional portals—one quite large, the other of a size with those throughout the manse. Both were always locked.

Sometimes she watched him work. It was never the same twice. At times he surrounded himself with dark fumes and sang in a guttural language. On other occasions, he drank potions, traced symbols on the floor, or sketched them in the air with a burning wand. Sometimes he made no preparation other than to walk to the center of the room and stand silently.

Whatever his behavior, the hair pricked up on the nape of her neck and she felt strange tastes in the back of her throat. Light and color became weird, and faint noises sounded within her skull. It frightened her, but she was also strangely drawn to it.

She also began to see what it did to him, how each time afterward he was both more and less than he had been before. Sometimes he lay in a daze, neither truly awake nor asleep, twitching at things she did not see. When this happened, however, Kos, the captain of his ravens, was always near, along with four or five other guards. The ravens dressed in red, umber, and black-checked doublets and were armed with sword and dagger.

They were not slaves. He paid them in gold.

At times the stairwell door was locked. On many of the occasions when he was rendered weak, she could not see what he did. On those days, the very stone of the mountain shook, as if thunder had been loosed inside of it. At first it had alarmed her, but eventually she learned to accept it as a natural way of things.

"Why do you do it?" she asked him one night, when she wore Orra's face. She had drunk more wine than usual and felt talkative.

"Because I can," he replied. For a moment, she wasn't sure he knew what she was asking, but then he rolled on his side and looked her in the eyes. "Princes beg for my services," he said. "Emperors fling gold at my feet, and yet I am beholden to no one."

"What of the Cryptarchia?" she asked.

An expression of impatience began to inform his features. "What do you know of the Cryptarchia?" he asked.

"That it's something like a guild," she replied. "A sorcerous guild."

"That clucking bunch of hens." He sighed. "I condescend to follow their rubrics when it suits me, but I long ago rose above them. I am my own. The cryptarchs—politicians, librarians, and their strigas-sniffing bitches. It can hardly be named sorcery, what they practice. There are very few of my kind, Orra. I am one of the last."

"But there are others?"

"A few," he replied. "None so powerful as me. And now we shall speak no more of this."

She knew his moods, and so pressed no further. For several months things went on as they always had.

Then the calendar struck her twenty-first birthday.

CHAPTER TWO

CHRYSANTHE

COSTE DE SUCRE, MESEMBRIA

1014 E.N.

CHRYSANTHE KNEW Lucien was going to kiss her.

A zephyr soughed through the sugar cane fields that rolled to the right and down from the hilltop path, stirring the curls of her golden hair. A flamboyance of flamingos rose through a saffron haze, drawing their silhouettes across the cinnamon and indigo clouds mounded on the horizon. Pale green sprites flitted in the jagged fronds of the palm forest bordering the left side of the trail. The hem of her periwinkle gown brushed softly against the grass.

It seemed as if all the world was in a state of pleasant agitation.

And then they stopped walking.

Lucien was taller, so he had to bend. It gave her time to turn her face, so his lips landed on her cheek. He paused for a moment, his brown eyes peering uncertainly, and then abruptly straightened.

"I'm sorry," he said. "I suppose I wasn't thinking."

"I suspect you were doing a great deal of thinking."

She smiled, to soften it.

He folded his arms.

"It's just, the time we've spent together—when you asked me to escort you…"

"But I didn't, Lucien," she said. "You asked to accompany me. By the gate, as I was leaving."

A little furrow appeared on his forehead, and she thought again how handsome he was—pretty, almost, with his high cheekbones and aquiline nose. Although he was only twenty-five years of age, the line of his cinnamon hair was already receding from his brow, yet it lent him some needed gravity. As always, he was dressed fashionably—today in a canary shirt, a cravat of fawn ribbon, and a redingote of the same color. He held in his hands a small-brimmed bicorn hat.

"Yes," he said. "I suppose that's true—but really, how could I allow a lady to go solitary into the countryside?"

"You are gallant," she said, "and I am happy to have your company. Only… behave."

Lucien smiled: nervously, she thought. He was an entirely affable character, intelligent and well-read. She enjoyed their conversations. Of good birth, he was lately from distant, fabulous Ophion, an investor in her father's enterprises on an extended stay to learn how the sugar business was run. Quite different from the local characters who called on her.

A breath of fresh air, at least at first. And her mother adored him, with her eye always turned toward noble connections to lift the family from its mercantile roots.

Chrysanthe turned from the large path onto a smaller one that wound off through the palms.

"It is getting late," Lucien said. "The sun is nearly gone under. Perhaps we should turn back."

"Only a little further," she said. "It's been a long time since I've come this way. There's an old chapel just ahead. It's quite beautiful, especially at dusk."

"A proper chapel, you mean, or some old native collection of rocks?"

"Well, you can judge it for yourself."

They walked a few more paces.

"This seems like a dreadful idea," he said as they moved further from the fields and into the thickening forest. "We might become lost. Or some wild animal—"

"You have your sword, don't you?" she said. "You can defend me if need be, can you not?"

"Well, yes."

"And as for becoming lost—look, this is a well-worn trail. More so than I remember it, really. Last I came here it was quite overgrown."

"Still. I will have to answer to your mother if I keep you out after dark."

"A spring dampens the path here," she warned. "Take care, the ground is slippery." She took her own advice, stepping carefully through the slick white clay. The chapel rose ahead, caught in a low beam of westering light that sifted through the trees. She found a pleasant view and stopped to admire it, leaning against the husky bole of a palm.

Even in its age and disrepair she thought the chapel was beautiful. Built of white stone, its every surface was figured with serpents, flowers, dancing figures, and symbols of air and night.

"Lovely, isn't it?" she said. "In their day, the Tamanja built magnificent things. Before the Drehhu destroyed their civilization."

"There's not so much to them now," Lucien said. "Passable

laborers, but of little use in any higher capacity. They are lucky to have our protection."

"Yes," she said. "Our protection."

"I admit, though, that it's a fetching sight," Lucien said. "May I now escort you home?"

"You know," Chrysanthe said, "there is a ghost here. If you stand just in this place, sometimes she makes herself known." She took a few steps toward the chapel and then stopped. Took a deep, slow breath as Lucien joined her. "You feel that?" she whispered. "Like water running across your face?"

"I—yes!" Lucien said. "That is quite amazing."

Chrysanthe smiled. She had been only eight when she discovered the ghost.

"Close your eyes," she said, shutting hers. For a moment, there was nothing but darkness, but then a face formed, a girl's face with broad cheekbones and green eyes.

Mah simki? Simi Sasani, a voice murmured.

"Oh!" Lucien said. Chrysanthe opened her eyes and saw that he had jumped back a yard.

"Were you startled?" she asked. "I did warn you."

"It's just… your voice sounded so strange. Not like you at all."

"Oh, did I speak?" Chrysanthe asked.

"Yes, in some strange language."

"That was *her*," she said. "The ghost. The language is an antique form of Tamanja. She asked my name and said hers was Lotus."

"I did not hear a ghost speak, only you."

She nodded. "I am sensitive to ghosts," she replied. "I always have been, like my grandmother was. Parfait Hazhasa at the basilica says it's not common, but not unheard of either."

"I see." Lucien nodded. "How terribly interesting. Now may I renew my offer to walk you home?" He still seemed agitated.

"That's agreeable," she said, and watched the relief spread on his face.

"Wait a moment," she said. "Do you hear something?"

"Another ghost?" he asked.

"No. In the chapel."

"No," he replied. "Nothing."

"Let's have a look."

"Chrysanthe!" he said sharply. "If someone is there, they might well be thieves or vagabonds."

"Well, if so, they have no right to take up residence on my father's estates," she said. "You have your sword. We shall investigate."

"You are far too rash," he complained.

But he followed as she crept toward the chapel. The building's base was oval, some forty feet in length, with an entrance on the east side. Before they had reached the opening, a man stepped out. He was a rough-looking fellow, dressed in worn cotton shirt and pants. His lips were bisected by a scar that resembled a white caterpillar when he closed his mouth. He had a short, heavy sword thrust in his belt.

He glared at the two of them.

"What is this?" he demanded.

"What are you doing in there?" she demanded. "I am Chrysanthe Nevelon. These are Nevelon holdings. Step aside, please." Beside her, Lucien drew his sword.

"Do as she says."

Reluctantly, the man moved away from the door. Chrysanthe approached the chapel and looked within. The fearful, wide-eyed gazes of some fifteen children looked back at her. They were dirty, clad in rags, and bound together by chains.

"Danesele!" one of them cried.

"Yes, Eram," she said. "We shall have this all fixed, very soon."

She turned back to Lucien, who now stood with the other man, facing her.

"Chrysanthe…" he began. His sword did not quite threaten her, but aimed at some point between her feet and his.

"I do not like coincidences, Lucien," she told him. "True happenstance is vanishing rare. The children began disappearing soon after you arrived. I inquired about and discovered that you had made some odd purchases—chains, for instance—and I once noticed a bluish-black stain on your kerchief. It looked like ahzha, which is often used by slavers to pacify their victims.

"At times," she continued, "you had on your coat a scent of burnt dung, which is what the villagers use for fuel. *What business would you have in the villages?* I wondered. In time, my only question became where you were keeping your prey until you could move them to the trade, and then I noticed the white clay on your boots. This is the only place I know of where that particular color of soil is present.

"And you." She nodded at the other man. "I recognize you. You work for my father. How could you betray him so?"

Lucien looked terrified, his features working.

"Chrysanthe," he said. "This all can be explained—"

"Yes," she said. "The explanation is that you're selling into slavery children under my father's protection."

"They are little better than slaves as it is," he said, starting to look angry.

"That is not true," she said. "They are paid wages, and they may not be purchased or sold."

"Accidents happen," the other man suddenly said. "There is a place, not far from here. Many crocodiles. She went out alone, she never comes back…"

Lucien pursed his lips and broke eye contact. He looked like a trapped civet.

"Lucien," Chrysanthe said. "There are two reasons I did not let you kiss me. The first, I think you now know. The second reason is that if my brothers saw you taking such liberties with me, they might kill you."

"Your brothers?" he said. "They were not there."

"Oh, Lucien," she said. "Of course they were."

Lucien paled and turned as her eldest brother Tycho emerged from the trees. At twenty-four he was six years her senior, as brown-skinned as their father. Like her, his hair fell in curls to his shoulders, although in his case the locks were almost ebony. He wore a hunting jacket and broad-brimmed straw hat that stood in marked contrast to Lucien's finery.

"Another of your games played out, sister?"

Upon his arrival, Lucien's partner in crime suddenly bolted toward the jungle deeps, only to be arrested at sword-point by Gabrien, the next eldest, his cropped red-gold hair like a mirror of the drowning sun. He had their mother's thin, fine nose, which along with his coloring—and certain behaviors—had earned him the nickname Li Goupil, or "the Fox." Theron—the youngest at fifteen—came close behind, a bow and six arrows couched casually in one hand. Theron and Chrysanthe shared the same heart-shaped face, deep brown complexion, and blonde hair. Despite the age difference, people often thought them twins.

Lucien spun and sprang toward her, his expression fervid. She had almost been expecting something like that and had quietly slipped a bodkin into her hand, but her shoes were still slippery from the mud and she slid on the ancient limestone of the chapel. She dropped her knife and, before she could find her balance, Lucien grabbed her.

"Listen," he cried. "I mean none of you any harm. I only intended to earn a bit of profit."

"You took a walk off that road," Tycho said, "when you put hands on my sister." He laid his hand on the grip of his saber.

"Stepping into a big crack," Theron confirmed, laying an arrow on his bowstring.

"Maybe we should visit those oh-so-convenient crocodiles," Gabrien suggested.

"No, *listen*," Lucien pleaded, desperately. His sword was at her throat; she could feel the edge nicking her. "You three back off. I only want to reach the emperor's consul and assure my survival from you... barbarians."

"All of this sweet talk," Gabrien said. "You're right, Santh, quite a romantic fellow."

"Lucien," Chrysanthe said. "Listen to me quite carefully. The penalty for kidnapping children is something your family will be able to pay off, in time, but if you hurt me—Lord forbid that you should kill me—there will be no court for you. You will be hacked to pieces, and your head put on a spike so the vultures can peck it to the bone."

He seemed to sag, but the sword did not waver.

"They will kill me anyway," he said. He was weeping.

"I will ask them not to."

He tightened his grip. "Why should...?" he began, but then a hand appeared in front of her face, coming from behind. It grabbed the blade at her throat and pushed it away. Lucien yelped and let her go. She stumbled back against the chapel as someone slammed Lucien to the ground, following him down.

No, not someone. Two men, in the sable-and-aubergine uniforms of the Emperor's Navy. Lucien tried to fight back to his feet, but one of the men dealt him a terrific blow to the chin. The other fellow picked himself up and stood aside, throwing her a concerned look with his wide blue eyes.

"Crespin!" she shouted. "Oh, Crespin!"

Her brother's companion, a lanky fellow with unruly brown hair spilling from beneath a seaman's cap, kicked Lucien in the ribs.

"Miserable excuse for a dog!" he shouted. "Shit from a bastard hyena…"

"Renost!" she cautioned. "Do not kill him."

Renost kicked the man again. "I'm not your brother," he said. "I'm not bound by your request."

"We need him, Renost," she insisted. "To find the other children."

Renost stood there, panting heavily for a moment, his black eyes blazing. Then he nodded.

"But for the grace of her," he told the moaning Lucien, then he spit on him. Crespin had reached her by then, and she threw her arms around him.

"We were bringing you a little surprise when Theron reported that you had wandered off with this fellow," Tycho said, nodding at Lucien. "I suppose it's a bit more of a surprise now."

"It is," she said. "Of course it is. A wonderful surprise. Crespin, I thought you had another year at sea before we would see you again. And you, Renost…"

She suddenly realized Renost was bleeding heavily from one hand. It must have been he who had grabbed Lucien's sword.

"That?" he grunted, noticing her attention. "Just a nick." Then his eyes went wide, and he fumbled to remove his hat. "Danesele," he said.

"Travel has made you more presentable, Renost," she said, "but formal address is unnecessary. Despite your protests, you are as much a brother to me as these others." It was then she noticed a third fellow in the emperor's colors, a nice-looking young man with straw-colored hair watching everything with what she took to be surprised amusement.

"Sir," she said, nodding.

"Oh, sister," Crespin said. "I am remiss. This is our companion, the most excellent seigneur Hector de la Forest, our ship's surgeon. He came ashore with us at our urging, so he might see for himself that our country is not so savage as he has heard."

"I am most pleased to meet you," Forest said, making a little bow. "And to you, Crespin, I must apologize for my former opinion. Not a jot of savagery to be seen here. But perhaps our friend Renost could use a bit of aid?"

Renost shrugged. Blood continued to pour from his hand.

"Really," Chrysanthe said. "Let's wrap that up." She ran her gaze over the whimpering, supine form of Lucien, and his accomplice, who—despite his sun-darkened face—seemed as pale as a cotton boll.

"Unchain these children," she told him.

"Yes, lady," he said.

"Theron," Tycho said, "fetch the horses." He turned to Chrysanthe. "We'll see to them," he said. "Crespin and Renost will escort you back home." She checked an objection—she wanted to see the children returned, but who knew how long Crespin would be in port.

"Thank you, Tycho," she said. "And you two," she added to Theron and Gabrien. "Where would I be without you?"

"Crocodile food, I reckon," Gabrien said.

NIGHT FELL softly, stirred by warm winds fragrant with the perfumes of orchids and water lilies. Beyond the terrace, fireflies danced above the swollen waters of the Laham River as bright Hesperus set into the trees and lesser stars brightened. A night bird trilled, accompanied by the strains of a harp. Chrysanthe glanced over at Forest, who was gazing out over the river.

"I'm sorry for your rude introduction to our country, seigneur de la Forest."

"Eye-opening to be sure," he said, "but I've spent some time in company with your brother, so these events are perhaps not so surprising." He swept his glass around. "And this is all so lovely," he said. "You are all so gracious to invite me to your home."

"Where do you call home, seigneur?"

"Please, call me Hector," he replied. "My home is a little-known place, I'm afraid. Poluulos."

"The island in the Mesogeios Sea?" she said. "Known for its excellent timber?"

"You astonish me," Forest said. He looked over at Crespin. "Your sister astonishes me."

"Oh, yes," Crespin said. "We are all quite astonished."

Forest looked back to her and nodded. "Yes, that is indeed the place. In fact, its timber was once so excellent that, at present, not a single tree remains on that little rock."

"That, I was not aware of," Chrysanthe said.

Hector spread his hands. "Well," he said, "the timber is gone, but we still have young boys in plenty to grow up and go into the emperor's service, and so here I am, in this very excellent company. Tell me, Danesele, is your life always so exciting as it was today?"

"Yes," Renost answered. "Because she makes it so."

"Exactly," Crespin said. "You realize, Chrysanthe, that eventually one these escapades of yours will end... badly."

"It did end badly, for Lucien," Tycho pointed out, taking his seat. He had traded his hunting attire for a zawb, the loose linen robe favored by the native Tamanja. The younger boys were still cleaning up.

"I mean for her," Crespin said. "And she knows it."

"I cannot stand idly by while my father is robbed or his reputation compromised," she protested.

"Tycho is in charge when Father is away," Crespin replied. "He is fully capable of seeing after the business. It's not like when were children, pretending to be agents of the empire—"

"Remember that secret language you two used to scribble in?" Renost said.

"It wasn't a language," Chrysanthe said. "It was a cypher." She shot a mock frown at her brother. "Did you come all and across the sea just to lecture me, dear brother?"

Crespin spread his hands. "The lecture is done," he said. "I only urge you to exercise some sense."

"Like you, I suppose?" she said. "Renost, Hector, tell me truthfully. Has my brother stayed clear of trouble during his time in the Navy?"

Renost grinned. "Well, that all depends on what you mean by trouble."

"Renost!" Crespin said.

"Is it trouble, for instance, to offend the Veil of Codaey by offering his daughter inappropriate gifts?"

"Flowers!" Crespin protested.

"Red jonquines, to be particular," Renost said. "They have a very specific symbolism in Codaey. Shall I explain?"

"No need," Chrysanthe said hastily, glancing at her younger sister Phoebe, whom she found gazing at Renost with adoring eyes. When the girl noticed Chrysanthe watching her, she quickly returned her regard back to her harp strings.

"I was innocent of their meaning," Crespin alleged.

"Was it trouble to climb upon the roof of the holy sepulcher of Phejen?" Renost went on. "Trouble only for the city watch, who pursued him throughout the town for the better part of the night."

"Us," Crespin amended, waving a finger between them. "Pursued *us*."

Renost raised his wine. "Well," he allowed, "It was an excellent view." The two men clinked their glasses together.

"I see," Chrysanthe said. "So I'm to be advised against a little housecleaning, while you two leave every port in shambles?"

Crespin frowned. "Is this true?" he asked Renost. "Every port?"

"No," Hector said. "The two of you left Isle Saint in good order. Hardly touched."

"There," Crespin said. "You overstate the case, sister."

"*Trop*, enough!" Chrysanthe said. "No more of your mishaps, but tell me this—what happy chance brings you home to us early?"

Crespin's squared features settled into more serious lines. "The same turn of fate that will bring Father back home tomorrow, or the next."

The harp stopped abruptly.

"Father returns?" Phoebe gasped.

"He does," Crespin replied.

"We shall all be together, then!" Phoebe said joyfully. At fifteen, her capacity for mercurial elation—and misery—seemed boundless.

"For a time," Crespin said.

Chrysanthe felt a sudden worry creep into her ear and down to her throat.

"What is it, Crespin?"

"War," he replied. "We are going to war."

Silence fell for a moment. Chrysanthe was considering what to say when the door burst open behind her.

"Chrysanthe!" her mother bellowed. "What have you done?"

CHAPTER THREE

HOUND

THE VALLEY OF ELMEKIJE

1014 E.N.

AS HE watched the baron's horsemen gallop down below, Hound was suddenly sorry he'd done such a good job in laying the false trail. They had fallen for it and were going the wrong way—the chase was over before it had begun. The idiots were only yards away, but they would never see him, hidden as he was in the leafy stand of hog-laurels.

That can be fixed, he thought.

With a wild shout, he bounded down the hill and flung himself at the rearmost horseman. With the back of his tomahawk, he rang the fellow's helmet like a bell. Before the rider had toppled from his saddle and slammed heavily to earth, Hound was already hurtling up the hill on the other side of the path.

"He's there!" one of the men shouted.

Belatedly a few arrows hissed through the oaks, none very close to him. He whooped mockingly as he once again vanished from their sight, then chuckled at the litany of curses that followed.

Running along the ridge top for a few paces, he descended into the next valley in long leaps that sent him skidding on leaf mold. It felt almost as if he was flying. The curses were still there, and the crashing of horses and armored men through the undergrowth.

Hound was not so encumbered—he wore nothing but a loincloth and a belt that supported his small ax and a bag of smooth stones.

He vaulted over the stream at the base of the valley, ran a few more steps, and then stopped in front of a wall of thorny briars. Putting his ax back in his belt, he took one of the pebbles from his bag and appraised it before uncoiling the sling from his wrist. Then he fitted the stone into the elk-hide pocket.

The men came down the hill now. One of them, named Detel—a burly fellow with red hair—spotted him.

"Shoot!" Detel bellowed. A few more arrows came his way, this time with better aim, and Hound stepped behind a sweetgum.

"You little piece of govno," Detel shouted. "Today is the end of you."

"Well, everyone has their day," Hound yelled back. He stuck his head out from behind the trunk. "But tell me—what are you fellows so mad about?" He ducked back as a feathered shaft thunked into the tree.

"Trespass in my lord's forest," the man responded. "Every kind of petty thievery. Vandalism. Witchery. Chicken stealing—"

"I think you covered chickens under petty thievery," Hound shot back. "Yes?"

"Get him!" Detel roared.

Hound took the time to pick out the best of the archers. Whirling his sling, he stepped from behind the tree. The man wore a helmet with a nose guard, so Hound sent the missile into his unprotected throat. Then he flung himself into the briars, dropping down on hands and knees to scuttle along the slightly less congested forest floor.

He emerged from the thorns at the edge of a cliff which dropped about twice the height of his body down to a beaver pond. He jumped and hit the deepest part. Surfacing, he swam to shore. From there, he turned east and began to work his way back behind his pursuers, reckoning there might be some fun yet to be had with them.

He checked the sky, saw a raven circling, and smiled.

Climbing a huge magnolia, he perched in the upper branches and watched the first of the baron's knights hack his way through the briars, lose his balance, and topple into the beaver pond. Another man emerged: Hound gauged the distance. They were just at the edge of his range, so chances were another stone would only alert them to his location. Which might be fun—starting the chase up again—but probably wouldn't be. Better he return to Grandmother to tell her what he had seen.

He was starting down the almost ladder-like arrangement of limbs when he heard a twig snap. Looking down, he found himself facing the point of an arrow on a drawn bow. Wielding the bow was a lean man with surprisingly blue eyes and not much hair. He stood in a copse of fern trees nearly as tall as he was. A pack rested on the ground not far from his feet.

"Easy, there," the man said in Velesan, but with an accent that sounded as if he was from someplace east. "They'll pay me more for you alive than dead."

"Course they would—that goes without saying."

"So drop your chopper down, the sling and the stones."

"Let me think on that," Hound said.

"I can hit a bird on the wing," the man informed him. "I can put this shaft through an arm, and the next through your other."

He didn't sound like he was bragging.

45

"Hold off," Hound said, dropping his weapons to the fern-covered floor. The man kicked them away from the tree, never relinquishing his aim.

"Now come on down," he said.

"They hired you in from someplace, didn't they?" Hound said as he descended. "Kind of flattering. You're smart, too. Let them provide a distraction while, all along, you were tracking me."

"That's about right."

"You know they'll kill me," Hound said. "And for what? A bit of fun?"

"That's not for me to sort out," the man said. "I'm just doing what I'm paid for."

Hound settled his feet on the ground and faced the man.

"Toruti," Hound said.

"What?"

"A word in Kansa," Hound said. "It means 'attack'."

"Don't test—"

A massive red-brown shape bounded from the undergrowth and slammed the man to the ground. The bow whined and the arrow sighed off through the ferns.

"Wasn't talking to you," Hound said. "Talking to Rose." The man wasn't likely listening; the huge dog had him pinned with her forepaws on his shoulders and was yanking his head back and forth by way of his ear. Hound fetched his weapons, then picked up the man's bow and cut the string with his ax.

"Alright Rose," he said. "Let's not end him."

Rose looked up at him, a severed ear in her teeth. She kept the man pinned while Hound searched his pack. In it he found chains which had no doubt been meant for him.

The man started to scream for help.

"I can always have her take your throat out," Hound said.

The man stopped shouting and settled for groaning.

"My ear," he moaned.

"Give him his ear back, Rose," Hound said.

The dog dropped her bloody prize on the man's face. Then Hound chained him and hefted up the pack, reckoning there might be other things worth having. He heard a flutter of wings as Soot settled on his shoulder.

"There you are," he said to the raven. He nodded at the bound man. "You could have let me know about him." He turned and began to set off.

"You can't leave me here," the man said.

"Yeah," Hound said. "Yeah, I can, but look—those other fellows will be here in a rabbit's piss. You'll be fine."

"It's true what they told me," the man said. "I thought they were simple."

"What did they tell you?"

"That you're a witch, and consort with demons."

Hound blinked. "You mean Soot and Rose?" He pointed first at the raven, and then the dog.

"Demons."

"Yep," Hound said, "and you can spread that around, if you want." Then he left, quickly. The baron's men were stupid, but not deaf.

HE COULD always feel it when he entered Grandmother's forest, never mind which direction he came in from. There was just something different about the air, the light, the way everything seemed to lean slightly inward. Here was his cradle, his hearth, the center of his world.

Here he was safe.

It was the only home he remembered, but it was not where he was born—Grandmother found him as a baby, alone in the woods. She taught him to speak Kansa, to forage and hunt. As he grew older, he wandered the forests and grasslands of the valley, and later the hills and mountains around it. He found the village of Berze on the river Vlone and watched how other people lived. Eventually he was befriended by some of the bolder children in the village, and from them he learned Velesan, the language of the south.

For a time he traded in Berze, bringing pelts, mushrooms, honey, and such to exchange for iron tools, sweets, bread, and wine. During that time, he lived half in the world of men—until he took up with Leste, a girl also fancied by the son of the baron whose castle overshadowed the town. Then he was suddenly accused of all sorts of things—witchcraft, theft, hunting illegally in the baron's forest. Only the last of these was true, but it didn't matter. There had always been those who were suspicious of him, especially the elders. So, he was forbidden to approach the village.

Hound decided that if he was going to be accused of such things, he might as well do them, and began amusing himself at the baron's expense. When that grew boring and the wanderlust struck him, he would travel deep into the mountains and the villagers would begin to think he was dead or gone forever.

When he became weary of being alone, he returned to pilfer and vandalize, drive cattle into the woods, and play tricks on the baron's huntsmen and messengers—always to return to the safety of Grandmother's forest.

He followed along a little stream and soon reached her cave. It didn't seem like much from the outside—just an opening in a moss-covered hillside not much larger than the door of a house—but the roots of the cave went deep. *Very* deep, maybe to the bottom of the world. He had explored it a bit when he was younger, but preferred his adventures under the sky.

Grandmother was there, as always. Dressed in a homespun shift and shawl, she hunched near the fire he'd started that morning. Her hair was black today, with no sign of the gray from the day before, and her eyes were green rather than brown. She was never the same from one dawn to the next, Grandmother. Sometimes she didn't even look like a person. She once told him that for many years she hadn't worn any appearance at all, but had made the effort after he came along.

"Springling," she said. "How long have you been gone this time?"

"Only a part of a day," he said.

"It's hard to tell," she said. "A year, a day, the same to me."

"I know, Grandmother."

"But not for you," she said, fixing him with her emerald gaze. "How many winters have you seen?"

"Seventeen or eighteen," he replied. It was a conversation they had had before, fairly often. It was more or less her way of saying hello. He began unloading the pack, which he found contained some bread, a small skin of wine, a purse with ten silver Velesan korls, and a whetstone.

"Eighteen," grandmother said. "It must be eighteen. That's a long time for me to be awake." She smiled. "But I have enjoyed you, Springling."

"I love you too, Grandmother," he said, and he glanced up. "I saw strangers at the baron's castle this morning. I think they've been there for a few days. Two of the servants were talking, and one said they were from Ophion Magne, but no one was supposed to know that. She also said the baron was afraid of them." He returned his attention to the pack.

Grandmother nodded but didn't say anything.

"Where is Ophion?" he asked. "Is it far?"

"I don't know," she said. "The sound of the name is familiar. Someone I knew once, I think." Something about the way she said it arrested him. He looked away from the pack and back to her.

"Is something wrong?" he asked.

"You'll be gone soon."

"I go all the time," he said. "I always come back."

"No," she said. "Gone."

"You mean dead?" he asked. "What do you mean?"

She shook her head. "You will be gone by tomorrow."

CHAPTER FOUR

THE EMPEROR'S CALL

"HELLO, DEAR mother," Crespin said, standing. Renost also hastily rose to his feet, followed by Hector.

"Crespin?" she gasped. "Crespin?" She looked around accusingly. "Why did no one tell me my son has returned?" she demanded. "Why was this kept from me? We should have had a feast, a celebration."

"It was at my request, Mother." Crespin took a few steps, took their mother in his arms, and kissed her cheek. "I didn't want any fuss, most certainly not a party. And I wanted to surprise you."

"Well, you certainly have done that," she muttered. "Look at me."

Chrysanthe couldn't quite suppress an exasperated sigh. Iole Nevelon looked beautiful. She always did, and treated it as a duty to be so—although it was not difficult, given her natural gifts. The years had dulled the luster of her gilded tresses, but only a little, and her pale features were fine and regular. She was never seen uncoifed or in disarray, and yet here she was acting as if she were wearing a bloodstained swine-slaughtering apron rather than a gown of silk brocade.

Mother shifted her accusing gaze back to Chrysanthe.

"I haven't forgotten about you," she said. "And you boys. Lucien de Delphin is of noble blood, and you beat him half to death. Any prospects you ever had, Chrysanthe—"

"You must think low of me to believe I would consider such a man," Chrysanthe said.

"All men are animals," Ione said, "and they all can be tamed. The business you claim he was engaged in was unfortunate, but far from unforgivable."

"He put a sword to our sister's throat," Theron said, stepping into the room. "He's lucky to be alive."

"We'll see who is lucky when his complaint reaches the court," Ione replied. Then she waved the subject off with the back of her hand. "Enough of that. Introduce me to this young man."

Crespin did so, as Hector bowed. The two exchanged a few pleasantries before his mother returned her attention to him.

"What brings you home, Crespin?"

"War!" Phoebe blurted. "And Father returns as well."

"Alastor?" she said. "What war? Who attacks us?"

"It is we who are attacking, Mother," Crespin said. "The emperor has called us up: not just the Navy, but parts of the mercantile fleets, as well." He was silent for a moment; to Chrysanthe's immense surprise, her mother did not interject anything, but granted him the pause.

"We're to attack Basilisk," he finally said. "We will throw down the Basilisk Throne and have an end to the whole matter."

"Sacre merde," Gabrien swore.

"Gabrien," Ione snapped, but there was a bit of a quiver in her voice.

"Why?" Chrysanthe asked. "It's been years…"

"Four hundred and some quibbling," a new voice interrupted. Chrysanthe bounded to her feet in delight.

"Father!" she shouted.

Alastor Nevelon was trim, angular, and composed. He rarely moved unless with a particular purpose. His black hair was shot with gray, but his blue-green eyes shone like the shallows of the sea. A faint smile traced his lips.

"Husband!" Ione said. "You as well?" She glared at Crespin. "How cruel of you not to tell me!"

"I was coming around to it," Crespin said, "but I didn't know when he would arrive—I thought no earlier than tomorrow, to be honest. You had fair wind, Father."

"Passing," the older man replied. "I have a superior ship and an excellent crew to—"

He was interrupted by Phoebe hurling herself at him, and then the rest crowded around. Crespin, Chrysanthe noticed, hung back until last. The relationship between father and son had been uneasy for some time, and when Crespin entered the Imperial Navy rather than joining Father in the sugar trade, there had been some unpleasant words on both sides.

"Is it really war, Papa?" Phoebe asked as Alastor took a glass of wine from Tycho and settled onto a chair.

He nodded. "Four hundred years we've been fighting the Drehhu. When the first fleets found this place, those creatures had already conquered most of the world. I need not remind anyone of their depredations, the horrors our forefathers discovered when they liberated the slaves. The horrors I…"

He stopped, frowned and took a sip of his wine. A profound silence followed his unfinished statement, and they all knew why.

Alastor Nevelon, her father, had been captured at the battle of the Expiry and had been enslaved by the Drehhu for three years before making his escape and returning to the land of his birth. It was not something he usually mentioned.

Finally, he cleared his throat and continued.

"For all these centuries we've pushed them back, inch by bloody inch, until only Basilisk remains."

"Only?" Tycho said skeptically. "They may no longer possess an empire, but they still have more than enough of their demon ships and weapons to defend their city. The last fleet that tested them was crushed."

"That was then," Alastor said.

"How are things different?" Chrysanthe asked.

"In three ways," her father said. "The first is that they are weaker. Their fortresses at Escepel and Triey are out of their hands. The second is that the Cryptarchia has agreed to supply each of our ships with a strixe, even for those who cannot pay the guild tax. Finally, Ophion does not venture this alone. Fleets from Velesa and Modjal will join us."

"Also," Renost added, "the last time Basilisk was attempted, Crespin, Hector, and I were not involved." He smiled and held up his wineglass, but Chrysanthe noticed that Crespin was fighting a frown. He was so like Father at times, trying to shelter behind an emotionless mask—but he wasn't nearly so successful at it.

"It sounds *glorious*," Phoebe said.

"You won't think so if Father or Crespin or Renost here comes back on his shield," Chrysanthe said. "Why? Why *now*?"

Alastor took another drink of his wine.

"It is not for us to debate," he said. "The emperor has called for us, and we shall go."

"The emperor didn't call me," Crespin said. "I was already in his service."

"So you were," Alastor replied, and Chrysanthe saw there was something there, something new and raw between them. But her father did not acknowledge it further. "Tycho," he said instead. "Tell me how things are coming along. The new fields, back along the river?"

"Some ticks to work out," Tycho said. "Nothing serious or interesting. You might ask Chrysanthe about her latest adventure, however."

As her father turned toward her, his face stern, she felt her cheeks reddening.

"Adventure?" he said. "I thought we had discussed these 'adventures'."

Chrysanthe reached for her wineglass.

"Not so much discussed," she replied, "as negotiated—and negotiations need have no end, but can eternally…" She trailed off as his head tilted a little.

She knew the look.

"Well," she said, after a drink and a deep breath. "You should know. It was about Lucien, you see…"

THE NEXT morning, Chrysanthe found Phoebe in the parlor, lying on a rug with a large book spread open before her. She bent over her sister's shoulder to have a look. The pages were turned to a depiction of a waterway hedged on either side by massive cliffs. At the base of each cliff stood gigantic metal statues, manlike but not men. Their arms and legs were both a bit too long, their shoulders far too broad.

"Anvvod," Phoebe said, "and the Colossus Gate."

While at first glance some thought Chrysanthe and Theron were twins, Phoebe actually *was* Theron's twin. But they did not look alike. Her brown hair had hints of copper in it, and her face was close to round.

Chrysanthe tapped the image of one of the metal statues.

"The colossi aren't there anymore," she said. "They were destroyed a hundred years ago."

"I know," Phoebe said. "Heron l'Archier defeated them."

"I think the two hundred ships he had with him might have helped him a little," she said dryly. "Contrary to what your books say, it is rare for an admiral to leave his command and attack the foe single-handedly."

Phoebe frowned. "In *Li Romanz de Heron*…"

"That is fiction," Chrysanthe said. "You must learn to distinguish between fiction and history."

"History is dull."

"The actual Battle of the Colossus Gate was anything but dull," Chrysanthe said. "Hundreds of ships were destroyed. Thousands died, and when it was over, Basilisk still stood."

"But the colossi were demolished," Phoebe insisted. "Father and Crespin will not have to face them, at least." When her sister clung to a concept, she stubbornly refused to loosen her grip, even a little. Chrysanthe continued.

"No, but they will need to confront weapons that fling fire and iron, black sorcery and diabolic ships—and after that, the walls of the fortress itself."

"The Drehhu are an evil which must be defeated," Phoebe insisted. "I'm proud that Father and Crespin and… Renost… are going to battle against them."

Chrysanthe sighed, rose, and pulled another book from the shelves. She lay down on the floor next to Phoebe and opened it to the map in the center.

"The Drehhu Empire," she said. "Four centuries ago. It comprised most of the world, as you can see."

"I know that."

"Here, here, and here," she went on, "in what is now outermost Ophion, Velesa, and Modjal. The ends of the world, and the only lands that were free of the Drehhu Empire."

"And the Christ of Ophion made a miracle," Phoebe said, "and sent the fleets."

"It may have been Christ Ophion," Chrysanthe allowed. "Some older texts suggest it was a conjuring by the elder Cryptarchia, but yes, the fleets arrived, mariniers from elsewhere. With the people of the ends of the world, they pushed against the margins of the Drehhu Empire. In time, they won more territory. The Accord was reached, and Ophion, Modjal, and Velesa foreswore any aggression toward one another. Where they took land from the Drehhu, they made colonies. They divided the world up amongst themselves, all overseen by the Cryptarchia, which owes no allegiance to any single government but wields power in all of them.

"Our own province of Mesembria was liberated no more than a hundred years ago," she continued, "and was judged to become part of Ophion. Our ancestor, Orion Nevelon, was granted a charter by the Emperor Alexandros I for his service in that liberation, and so here we are."

"Why are you telling me all this?" Phoebe asked, a little petulantly. "I know it already."

Chrysanthe flipped forward in the book, to another map.

"Now we have three empires," she said. "Ophion, Modjal, and Velesa. Each with colonies spread around the world, and each of these empires has slavery, just as the Drehhu do."

"We don't own slaves," Phoebe said.

"Because Father, having been enslaved, abhors that institution. He formed the Mesembrian Mercantile Alliance, which follows the belief that free workers who have an interest in their business work harder and better at their trades. Yet Ophion does not forbid slavery, nor do either of the other two empires. We *could* own slaves, if we were so inclined."

"Are you trying to suggest that we're as bad as the Drehhu?" Phoebe asked, a hostile note in her voice.

"Not as bad," Chrysanthe replied, "but maybe not so much better." She traced her hands across the map. "Sugar, rum, and cotton move from Mesembria north and east to ports in mother Ophion, and then east to through the inland seas to Velesa and back south to Savor in the Modjal empire. Timber and furs ship down the through the Mer de Typhon from Velesa. Spices, precious stones, silk—these things come to us from the port of Savor. But most of what is traded there does not come from Modjal. It comes from further east, from Eosian lands, and the only way to go there by ship is through here."

She tapped the east side of the map, which was mostly void of detail. It showed a long peninsula arcing from Modjal to the south and east, where it almost joined with the larger mass of Timur. All along the narrow strip of land volcanoes were depicted, belching smoke and flame.

"The Salamandra," she said.

"I know all of this," Phoebe said. "To reach Basilisk one must brave burning mountains and treacherous reefs, and—"

"My point is," Chrysanthe interrupted, "that Basilisk and its fleet guards the only place a ship might pass through, and so the easternmost lands are denied us, at least by sea. We must rely on the Drehhu, and thus we must pay their tariffs."

Phoebe peered at the map more closely.

"Why not sail further south and pass around Timor?"

"That is precisely what the fleet tried, when Father sailed with it," Chrysanthe said. "They hoped to come at Basilisk from the east, where they would not be expected, but it is an exceptionally long trip, much further than if one could pass through the strait in the Salamandra. And there is this." She tapped the edge of the map.

"Oh," Phoebe said. "The Expiry."

"Yes. To go that way requires an awfully close approach to the Expiry."

"And nothing that crosses into the Expiry ever comes back out."

"That is true," Chrysanthe said. "More than half of the ships in that ill-fated fleet passed into it and were never seen again. All of the survivors of the battle were enslaved, including Father." She shuddered inwardly, knowing how the experience had affected her father, the strongest man she had ever known.

"And yet you still insist the Drehhu are not evil?"

"That's not the point," Chrysanthe replied. "I'm saying this war isn't happening just because the Drehhu are evil. It's happening because trade is the lifeblood of our civilization, and Basilisk restricts it. For us, here in Mesembria, you might say the war is about the cost of sugar."

"Very cynically put," a voice said from the door.

Phoebe looked back over her shoulder and her cheeks darkened.

"Renost!" she said, embarrassed, climbing to her feet, patting at her dress so as not to show her legs. Chrysanthe rolled up to her knees and stood. "You should have knocked," Phoebe said. "You've caught us all disheveled."

"The door was open," Renost said. "And what's this sudden

modesty? I remember you hanging upside down from tree branches, not so long ago."

"I was a girl then!" Phoebe protested. "I am a woman now, if you hadn't noticed."

"And a most beautiful young woman," Renost agreed.

Phoebe blushed again. "You ought not to say things like that, Renost," she said. "It isn't proper." She squirmed a bit. "Although it would not be out of line if you were to… with mother's permission of course… coffee—" Phoebe suddenly covered her face with her hands. Then, with a little sob, she fled from the room.

"What in the world is wrong with her?" Renost asked.

"I think you are not so innocent that you do not know," Chrysanthe said.

His head dropped a little. "I think you overestimate my instincts in that area."

"Hmm," she replied, a bit doubtfully. "How is your hand?"

"Nothing serious," he said.

"I wish you had not injured yourself on account of my poor judgment," she told him.

"I couldn't have done otherwise," he said. Then he stood there, fidgeting for a moment. It was strange, and utterly uncharacteristic of him. As if she made him nervous, which was impossible, of course. They had grown up together.

"Do you remember the time," he finally said, "when we pretended you, Crespin, and I were Tritos, Akhos, and Parthenia? And we captured the Great Bull back from Ilion?"

She smiled at the memory. "As I recall, the Great Bull was portrayed by Dionysus, my pet pig."

"*Right*," he said, too quickly. "You remember, and afterward—"

Chrysanthe heard wind chimes in the courtyard and smelled ginger cake baking in the cookhouse. The sunlight coming through the window grew brighter as a cloud passed. In the corner of the room, at the ceiling, a cottage spider was taking down a web.

"Stop," she said softly. "I remember. The pretend wedding. Renost—"

"It was not pretend for me," he said softly. "Nor is it now."

"I know," she said, "but Renost, we were children. Such affection is encouraged in the young. In adults, it is not—and Crespin has determined to be an adult."

"You've known this all along?" he said.

"Of course."

"And does *he* know?"

"If he does, he will not admit it to himself," she said. "He loves you."

"But not in that way."

"Even if he did, it would not matter," she said. "He will do what it expected of him. He will take a wife and father children."

"You seem in no rush to marry."

"Indeed," she said. "I am not. Perhaps I *will* not."

"It is expected of you," he said.

"Of course," she replied, "but I am not my brother, Renost. Why do you bring this up now?"

"I thought you could advise me," he said. "I feel I should confess to him."

"Because you're going to war? You've been in battle before."

"I fear this shall be different."

"I hope it shall not be," she replied. "But if you truly ask my counsel—do not do this. The outcome will not be to your liking, and it may damage your friendship."

He nodded. "That is what I feared you would say."

———

"WHAT'S THE matter with you, Renost?" Crespin asked, accepting the rum bottle from his sullen friend and taking a long drink before passing it along to Hector.

The three men sat on a broken crate in the factory district, between the massive yellow brick warehouses and the docks. They weren't alone in doing so. Barilors—weather-beaten, gnarled old men—clustered on barrels, boxes, and small heaps of brick. They sat drinking rum from ceramic pitchers, talking, playing eshecs and generally laying about. Most were pensioners from the Navy or merchant fleets. As boys, Crespin and Renost had come here to listen to them tell tall tales of their lives at sea. They had taken to calling each other mon vieil—"my old man"—in imitation of the barilors.

After a year in strange ports it felt… comfortable.

"It's nothing," Renost said. "An ill humor. It will pass."

"I hope so," Crespin said, taking the rum back from Hector. "There's nothing worse than a morose drunk."

"Very well said," Renost replied. "I shall brighten up, then." He nodded toward their ship, the *Pelerin,* a sturdy, six-masted vessel with portals for sweeps. "All too soon we'll be at sea again."

"Yes," Crespin said, "but not on that ship. Not me, at least."

"What do you mean?" Renost said. "You're third officer."

"I was," he replied. "Now I'm on the *Leucothea.*"

"Your father's ship?" Renost said. "It's not even a naval vessel."

"It is now. They've made my father an admiral for this little adventure, and he wants me on his ship. No one seems to care what I want."

"What *do* you want?"

"I want to stay with the *Pelerin* and my crewmates," Crespin said.

"I want to fight with the Navy, not deliver supplies."

"The mercantile fleets are outfitted to fight, as I understand it," Hector said. "They have quilaines, and each has a strixe on board."

"Yes, should we encounter danger on the voyage, we can put up a fight. Should every last ship of the Navy be lost, perhaps we will exchange fire with the Drehhu. And these strixes—they are so new, unproven. How much help will they be, really?"

"The Cryptarchia has employed them for years," Hector said.

"And how many wars have *they* fought?" Crespin asked.

Hector shrugged. "Leave that aside. A fleet fights on its belly as much as anything else. Relieved of carrying so much food and extra munitions, the Navy can pack its ships with more fighters. The mercantile fleet is key to our victory. Should it not arrive, the Navy will find itself starved and without shot for their quilaines."

"That's all true, I'm certain," Crespin said, "but it's not where I want to be."

"Perhaps the emperor gives no never-mind where you want to be," Renost said.

"It's not the emperor made this decision," Crespin said. "It was my father… and why this peevish tone? Are you glad we are to be separated?"

Renost frowned, then shook his head. "No," he murmured. "I had assumed we would sail together. But—"

"Well, about that," Crespin interrupted. "If you want to come with me, it can be arranged."

Renost blinked, and then slowly a smile lifted his face. "Of course, mon vieil." He slapped Crespin on the back and his mood seemed to improve.

"I'm relieved," Crespin said. "I was starting to worry I would have to die alone. He glanced apologetically at Hector. "I could put in a word with my father for you, as well."

"There's no need," Hector said. "Your father was short a surgeon. On the *Pelerin* I was lieutenant, but on the *Leucothea* I shall be chief."

"A promotion," Renost said. "Well done. No wonder you had such pretty words about the mercantile fleet."

"Yes," Hector said. "And so we shall all die together, Crespin."

"Yes,'" Renost said. "No thanks to our damn surgeon."

CHAPTER FIVE

GRANDMOTHER

WHEN HOUND woke the next morning, Grandmother was stirring the ashes of the fire, holding a stick in her long, slender fingers. Her hair was rust and gold, like autumn leaves. Her eyes were as dark as coals and her lips curiously red.

"They're here," she said. "They're waiting for you."

"Who?" he asked, rubbing his eyes.

"You'll have to ask them," she said. "They've been very respectful, brought the proper gifts. They know the old ways." It was often hard to work out what Grandmother was talking about, and today she seemed more oblique than usual. He reckoned she might be referring to the people from Ophion.

Her fingers lifted, and he saw she had scratched a pattern there. He also saw that her fingers were stained with blood just past her knuckles.

"My valley," she said. "The mountains around, you see?"

He nodded. "I've seen maps before, in the village."

She traced her finger through a series of ridges and flatlands, until finally she passed beyond where he had been in his travels.

"Here," she said. "A mountain with three peaks stepping down, tallest, middle, lowest."

"What about it?"

She sighed. "I have loved you," she said. "It has been so long. I nearly remember who I am, but now you must go. They have paid the price."

"You sold me?" he said.

"No. I only grant them the chance to speak to you, here, where you are still safe. You can choose to refuse them and remain with me."

"Well, then I shall," he said.

"No," she replied. "You will go with them."

"But if I have the choice—"

She placed her hand on his shoulder.

"Talk to them," she said.

SOOT FOUND them first, cawing and circling in the dark morning sky, but moments later Hound heard the racket of their horses and voices pitched low. They were in the hollow just inside Grandmother's forest. It was the second time he had ever known someone other than himself to cross the boundary. The first had been a single man, four years ago.

He had not survived.

Hound circled around so he could see them from the hill above, Rose shadowing him a few yards away. There were twenty of them and more than twice as many horses. Three of them wore armor of a kind he had never seen before—it was made of metal sheet and covered their limbs as well as their chests. None of them had their helmets on, however; not at the moment. Against his sling they would be as vulnerable as naked children.

The three were armed with long spears and swords. Most of the other men were clothed in quilted leathers, and they had crossbows as well as swords. They had with them one woman, dressed much as the men except that her black quilted hauberk dropped below her knees like a dress. Beneath that she wore dark red leggings. She and one man stood a little apart from the rest. This man wore plain traveling clothes and a leather cap.

Hound considered what to do. Grandmother seemed to think these people had come for him, but why? She had been unclear about what she meant about him being "gone." He loved her, but also knew that she was used to things dying.

Would she send him to his death?

He didn't know, but she'd said he still would be safe here. To his knowledge, she had never actually lied to him.

"Down there," he shouted. "What is it you want?"

It was almost comical how all their heads turned his way at once. The plain-clad man stepped forward a few paces.

"Are you sent by Elmekije?" he asked. He spoke Velesan, but with an accent Hound did not recognize.

"I don't know anyone of that name," he replied. "Do you mean Grandmother?"

The man looked puzzled.

"You're the witch-boy the villagers talk of?" the woman asked. "The Hound?"

"It's just Hound," he said.

"Then it's you we're searching for," the man said.

"And why is that?" he asked. "Yesterday a stranger tried to snare me. Today more strangers arrive asking after me."

"The baron thought he could capture you and sell you to us," the man said. "We were not privy to the attempt until it was over. He has been… disciplined."

Hound's ears perked a bit at that. Who were these people who could "discipline" the baron?

"What do you want of me?"

"Doesn't it have to take your commands?" one of the men in armor said to the woman. "You summoned it, after all."

"No," she replied. "That isn't how it works. He must choose to go with us."

Go where? Hound almost said it aloud, but then he remembered Grandmother's map.

"You need a guide," he said. "To lead you to a certain peak in the Vereshalm Mountains."

"That is correct," the man in the cap said.

"And why should I do that?" Hound shot back.

"You will be paid," he said. "In coin, or whatever else we have to offer."

"I don't have much use for coin," he said. "Why do you want to go there?"

Before anyone could reply, the woman motioned for them to be silent. "I'm coming up to you," she said. "Don't be alarmed."

"Selene—" the man began.

"It will be fine, Martin."

Warily Hound watched her approach. He had never seen anyone like her. Her skin was so brown it was nearly black, and yet there was still something washed-out about her. Her face had a drawn and weary look. Pretty, though. Her eyes were almost black, but with golden flecks. Her hair, likewise, was mostly black, with a few strands of pale yellow.

She stopped a short distance away from him. He glanced at Rose, but the big dog seemed unconcerned.

"My name is Selene," she said. "Your name is really Hound?"

"Yes."

"Who named you?"

"I named myself, as a matter of fact."

She shrugged.

"Hound, I can't tell you why we're going there, but it is important, and we need you. And I promise you—it will not be dull."

He felt a sort of tug inside. In the back of his mind, he had always planned to venture further into those mountains, and it had been a long time since he had had been in the company of anyone besides Grandmother.

"Not dull, eh?" he said. "You mean dangerous."

"From what I've heard of you, that's no matter," she said, "I thought it would be insulting to say it to you."

He grinned a little.

"Will I get to see you naked?"

"No," she said without blinking.

"There's no bargaining on that point?"

"None."

He studied her strange eyes. He could go along for a while. If it got boring, he could always leave. Grandmother often said things that could be true in one way, and not in others. He could come back if he wanted, but maybe where they were going, he wouldn't *want* to come back. Maybe he *would* die.

It had to happen sometime.

"I won't ride one of those things," he said, gesturing at the horses. "I go on my own feet and at my own pace, and if this is some sort of trick, I'll kill all of you."

Her eyes widened slightly.

"We're not here to harm you or capture you," she said. "I swear to you. We *need* you."

"Another girl told me that once. She was lying."

Selene frowned. "I'm not a girl," she said. "And I'm not lying. You may not come back from this trip, but it won't be because we betrayed you. We all might die, for that matter. Without you—"

He held up his hand.

"You can stop now."

He turned and ran back to Grandmother's cave, but for the first time he could remember, she wasn't waiting to greet him. He entered, and she wasn't there.

"Grandmother?" he asked, then called, but she didn't answer. He had an odd clutching in his throat, and his eyes felt damp. A warm wind blew from the cave and seemed to wrap around him for a long moment. Then it, too, was gone.

Rose let out a strange, mournful wail.

Hound glanced once more around the only home he had ever known. Then, with a little shrug, he set about gathering a few things, placing them in the pack he had taken from the manhunter. When he went searching for warmer clothes, he found not the tatty buckskins he had worn on his last trip into the mountains, but a new shirt and long pants of supple elk-hide, embroidered with dark green serpentine coils.

"Thank you, Grandmother," he said as he placed the clothes into the pack. "And goodbye." Then he trotted back to where Selene and the men were preparing to leave, discouraged looks on their faces.

Selene's face brightened when he returned.

Seeing that was worth a day of his time, at least.

CHAPTER SIX

THE GATES
OF CHANCE

ACCOMPANIED BY an escort—a guardsman named Chaur—Chrysanthe knocked lightly on the door of her father's office. He looked up from his papers and gestured for her to come in, waving for the escort to remain outside.

"Close the door behind you," he said.

She felt a flush of apprehension. Father had listened to her explanation of the business with Lucien, pretty much without comment. She had a feeling that the commentary was about to begin, but when she had settled onto the chair he indicated and she really had a chance to study his face, it wasn't what she expected. It didn't carry a stern or angry expression, but rather one of tenderness… and perhaps sorrow. It was almost shocking.

What could make his guard slip so?

"What's the matter, Papa?" she asked.

His mask snapped back into place, and he shook his head from side to side.

"Perceptive as always," he sighed.

"Is it about Lucien?"

"Yes, and no," he said. "Mind you, the man is a cur, and he got what he deserved. But it was unwise for you to be involved. You should have let Tycho handle it."

"I… I know," she said.

His left eyebrow lifted slightly.

"That must have been hard for you to say."

She nodded. "What trouble have I brought upon us?"

"It makes my decision so much harder," he said. She waited for him to explain, and after a moment of staring at nothing, he did.

"If I could choose one of my children—or anyone, for that matter—to tend to my affairs while I am away, I would choose you." He paused. "You must never tell Tycho this. He is a good man, and quite able to run the business, but you see things as others do not. You are headstrong, yet that can be trained into a useful quality."

"I don't understand," she said. "Is Tycho accompanying you to war?"

"No, he will remain here to see after things."

"Then why—"

"I am only expressing my regard for your intelligence," he said, a little brusquely, then he appeared to compose himself again. She sat back, thoroughly puzzled.

"Here is the matter," he continued. "In some few days, a ship will arrive from the capital. I shall by then already be at sea. The ship will remain here only long enough to take on a passenger, and that passenger will be one of my children."

He paused to let her absorb that.

"As a hostage," she murmured, feeling suddenly almost light-headed with understanding. "Of course."

He nodded. "The emperor does not make a man an admiral and put him in charge of a hundred ships without some assurance of that man's loyalty, now and in the future. So I must surrender one of my own to live in Ophion Magne until this business is concluded. Ordinarily I would send Theron, as he could benefit from an education in the capital. He would also stand less risk of running afoul of Lucien's family."

"You're letting them have me," she said.

"I am," he replied. "Because I need you there."

"I don't understand."

"This war," he replied. "There is something suspicious about the whole thing, something I can feel but the shape of which I cannot see. Only someone in the heart of it all has a chance to parse it out, and Theron… his qualities do not suit him for that task."

"You want me to be your spy?"

"In essence."

"In fact," she amended.

"Yes," he admitted. "In fact. You will not be imprisoned, or anything of the kind. It will be arranged for you to stay with one of your cousins—but it will not be without peril. Ophion is not like any place you have ever known. It is a nest of vipers, and if you step the wrong way, you will be bitten."

In that instant, the discussion seemed unreal—as was the fact that her father was willing to sacrifice her. For a moment her mind caught only on that, but then she recalled his expression when she first entered the room. She remembered that he and Crespin were going off to fight in a war from which they might not return. How could she not do her part?

"I am a Nevelon," she told. "I will do this."

"I never doubted that you would," he replied, but his tone had nothing of victory in it.

"My brothers will be trouble," she said, pushing on. "If you aren't here to curb them, they might—"

"Get themselves arrested or killed," he finished. "Yes, I know, and for that reason they must not be informed of this until you are gone. No one must."

She nodded.

"Supposing I discover something," she said. "How am I to communicate it to you?"

"That has also been arranged," he replied. He produced a silver box from his desk drawer and placed it in the on table. It was no longer than her index finger, half as wide, and had a hinged lid with a small clasp to keep it closed. "The means of communication are contained here," he said. "I shall explain to you how to use it, and you must keep this concealed. Tell no one of it—except one man. His name is Bonaventure, and you must contrive to meet him however you can."

She nodded.

"Good," her father said. He tapped the box.

"Now, as to this…"

CRESPIN SPENT several days exploring the ruts of his life. He visited old lovers and friends. With his brothers, he hunted spotted antelope in the deep forest, then drank with Renost until the first light of morning at The Lighthouse Tavern, and had a breakfast of sour wine and fried tripe at The Crocodile.

He road horseback with Chrysanthe alongside the lazy meander of the Laham river, and they picnicked beneath the fever trees on their accustomed bank with its view of Lake Hazham, where gigantic hippopotami stirred the water and ruby swans winged overhead. Again, he complained about being forced to sail on the *Leucothea*.

Chrysanthe, for her part, seemed to be in a peculiar mood. The lips of her small mouth were slightly puckered, a sign that she was working on a puzzle of some sort.

"Do you miss all of this when you're away?" she asked him.

He shrugged. "Sometimes, yes, of course. Being home is like putting on worn-in shoes, but for me everything here seems smaller now. There is so much more out there to see, Santh."

"Do you worry," she said softly, "that you will never return? I cannot imagine that. Never seeing Mother again, or Fiyala at her cook fire. Or the lake on so perfect a day."

He realized, then, what the matter was.

"I've no intention of dying, sister," he said. "This war will be over in no time. I'll be back."

She smiled an enigmatic little smile.

"Your odds of survival are better with Father," she told him. "You know that."

"That may be," he allowed, "but I'm no longer a child. I should be allowed to make my own decisions."

"It comforts me that you will be together."

"Well," he said, shaking his head, "then I suppose it's not a total disaster."

DESPITE HIS protestations, his mother did manage a party on the eve of his departure, and he enjoyed it more than he thought he would. He remembered Chrysanthe's words and took time to study each of his brothers and sisters, their familiar faces, the sound of their voices and laughter, at once distinct and similar.

He wondered if this was the last time they would all be together.

They were there the next morning at the docks, he in his new uniform of mustard and brown, with Renost and Father as they boarded the *Leucothea*. As the vessel set sail, he stood at the rail and watched them dwindle until they were eclipsed by a bend in the river, and once more he put home behind him and turned his face toward whatever came next. The gates of chance had been thrown open, and he could but pass through them.

CHRYSANTHE WATCHED long after the *Leucothea* was gone from sight. As the rest prepared to depart for the house—everyone but Gabrien—her mother urged her to return before the rain. Then they left.

Gabrien sat with her silently for a while, listening with her to the cries of the gulls and the chatter on ships making ready to join their flagship out at sea.

"They'll be back," her brother finally said.

"Of course they will," she replied.

"I asked Father to allow me to go with him," Gabrien said, frowning. "He refused."

"As well he should," she replied. "Mother will—*we* will need you here. Suppose pirates arrive, or reavers from some barbarian shore? In times of war, when our ships are away, such things may happen. The emperor does not need one more man. The House Nevelon does."

"Li Goupil!" a feminine voice called from behind them. She recognized it. "A word with you?"

"And Marie Enart needs you," she said, suppressing a smile.

A little grin touched his face. "I suppose I do have important work to do here." But he continued to look out to sea, without acknowledging the girl at all.

"Goupil!" the girl repeated.

"Then why are you ignoring her?" Chrysanthe asked, after a moment.

"Girls are not attracted to men who come to them," he replied. "Only to the ones they must go to."

"I see," she replied. "So little I know."

He looked at her seriously.

"Your armor has so far turned away every arrow Eros has aimed at you," Gabrien told her, "but when one finally finds the chink in it, you will be hopeless. I, on the other hand, prefer to toughen myself by taking every dart he shoots."

"If that is another way of saying you are fickle and I am particular," she said, "then I agree."

"You'll see," he said.

"I leave you to your prey," she said, standing.

"I should walk you home."

"There's no need."

"But it will drive Marie mad," he replied. He glanced back to where the young woman had fallen silent but was still watching them.

Chrysanthe felt curiously light as she started home through the streets of Port Bellship, Gabrien walking silently next to her. Gray clouds were building on the horizon for the afternoon rains but here the sun still shone, so the yellow tile roofs of the merchants' houses gleamed like gold. The rose-colored bricks with which they were built appeared almost sanguine, and their iron-fretted balconies were mostly full of the well-off, drinking wine and taking in the atmosphere.

They passed through the Place of the Basilica and she stopped for a moment, gazing at the highest spire, wondering if perhaps she should stop and pray once more to the Christ of Tamanja before leaving. The Christ of Ophion was a stranger to her, and she knew few of his mysteries.

She chose not to, so they continued on through the smaller houses of the outskirts. What these structures lacked in size they made up in color, their walls stuccoed sage, indigo, turmeric, ecru, or lilac. Beyond them were the palmetto-thatched roofs of the men's compounds, whose habitants mostly labored in the cane fields and returned to their distant villages on holy days.

Their house, Chastel de Nevelon, stood on a hill just outside of town. Close to a hundred years old, it had a central courtyard surrounded by three stories of large, high-ceilinged rooms and ample windows to let the air flow. It was built from the pale ginger brick made upriver in Tawinquar, with a portico of red marble arches on the front and sides. The house was raised around a central courtyard in the Tamanja style, which her great-grandfather correctly believed was better suited to the climate then those that followed the colonial plan. The roof had a high pitch to keep the long rains at bay. A fortified wall ten feet tall surrounded it, which had proven useful in times past, although not for several decades.

Gabrien saw her to the gate, then began sauntering back toward town, doubtless to take advantage of the anxiety he had engendered in Marie. Chrysanthe thought again of the ship that would be coming for her, and wondered what to pack, *how* to pack to live in

Ophion Magne. Her mother would know how to prepare, but since all of this was to be a secret, Chrysanthe couldn't ask her.

The smell of smoke and spice found her and she abruptly, *powerfully*, wanted to see Fiyala, the family cook. She followed the scents through the gardens to the side of the house where the kitchen stood, a sturdy brick building detached from the main structure. The door was open and Fiyala inside, cutting onions into a pot while her granddaughter Pirah plucked a large duck. Chrysanthe smelled garlic, ginger, cloves, black pepper, coriander, and the onions as they joined the other spices in the pot.

Fiyala looked up and a smile split her wrinkled face. Her curly hair—once a dark auburn—was now mostly gray, the unruly mass of it barely bound by a headscarf.

"Danesele Chrysanthe," she said. "I hope you're having a perfect day."

"I wish you wouldn't call me that," Chrysanthe said. "It makes me feel old. Besides, we're not nobility."

"If the Enart and de Sarade girls can style themselves 'danesele,' I don't see why you can't."

"The Enarts and de Sarades put on airs," Chrysanthe said. The fact was, since her grandmother's time, the meaning of the word "danesele" had begun to slip in stature, to be applied to any unmarried women from a family of means. Still, she balked at it.

"I'd rather you call me what you used to."

"*Quayquay*?" the old woman said, smiling.

"That's for babies," Pirah said.

"Hush, you," Fiyala told the girl.

"I used to sit out here when I was little," Chrysanthe told Pirah. "Just like you. I used to pluck ducks, too."

"Not just like me," Pirah said. "You didn't *have* to do it." Suddenly Chrysanthe felt something shift, like a wind changing, and a blush burned her cheeks.

"Didn't I tell you to hush?" Fiyala snapped. "You tell the lady you're sorry. After that, keep that mouth closed." She turned back to Chrysanthe. "She doesn't know what she's saying."

"No, that's not true," Chrysanthe said. "She does. I just—" To her shame, she realized she was crying. It was all finding her at once. Fiyala dropped her knife and took Chrysanthe tightly in her arms. She smelled of homemade rosewater and smoke.

"Quayquay," she murmured. "Baby, what's wrong? Are you having a bad day? What can I do for you?"

You can let me sit in here like I was a little girl once more, and listen to your stories, and I can help you cook. I can feel like I belong here again, one last time.

That's what she wanted to say.

But Pirah was right. She had only ever pretended to belong in the cookhouse, and it was less the words of the little girl that hurt her, and more Fiyala's reaction. As if—after serving three generations of Nevelons—she still feared being dismissed because her granddaughter said the wrong thing. She was almost the same as family. Chrysanthe had always felt that way.

Yet she was wrong, wasn't she? What would happen to Fiyala when the woman was too old to cook? Would she have a pension? Chrysanthe remembered Lucien's comment about her father's employees being little better than slaves. At the time it had seemed self-serving.

Now…

"It's nothing," she told Fiyala. "It's not your fault. I'm sorry. I must go."

I must go.

CHAPTER SEVEN

IN THE
PITCH POT

It is easy to find one's way to the Coste de Sucre,
Its verdant, sun-dappled shores,
Colorful ports, music, laughter
Sweet-flowing rum.
Far harder it is to leave.

THE POEM was nearly a hundred years old, but familiar to everyone. In school, Crespin had been forced to memorize the whole thing, but he only remembered bits. This part he always recalled when leaving home, because it had a double meaning.

Visitors to the Coste de Sucre—such as the poet who penned those words—found it a pleasant place, especially if they were from cooler climes. They often did not wish to leave, and indeed, many of them did not depart. Crespin—at least on his first trip away—found leaving difficult as well, for many reasons.

The passage had another, more literal meaning. The coast lay in the Pitch Pot, the great stretch of the sea where winds were often rare and always unpredictable. It was possible to spend days or weeks trying to leave the Pitch Pot.

They had been out of port for two days, now, and still he could see the distant outline of Mesembria across a too-calm sea. Behind the land the pale coral sky was deepening toward orange.

He walked the length of the *Leucothea* several times, greeting the crew on duty. Many of them answered with only minimal courtesy, and he didn't really blame them. If the son of an admiral was suddenly promoted to first officer on a ship where he had been serving for years, he wouldn't be happy about it either. There were soldiers on board, too—heavily armored xelons and light infantry supplied by the emperor—but they weren't Navy, and relations between naviors and the army units they carried had always been a bit prickly. They kept to themselves and did not fraternize either with the mariniers or the officers, which included Crespin.

Understandable as was the attitude of the mariniers, it made his job harder, a fact his father must surely know, and it made his duty hours quiet. This at least gave him the opportunity to learn the ship.

The *Leucothea* wasn't designed for war—she had been built for speed and distance, to carry loads of sugar and rum to faraway Modjal, take on a cargo of spices and silk to sell in the teeming ports around Mesogeios and the Mer de Typhon, and return to Mesembria with holds full of expensive goods like fine tableware and brocade cloth for wealthy planters. She was incredibly maneuverable for a ship her size, and could sail circles around any pirate vessel she was likely to meet. Long and narrow, from a distance she appeared to be mostly sail.

For weaponry she had only four smallish quilaines, engines powered by tightly twisted silk that fired large bolts or stones. His old ship, the *Pelerin*, boasted sixteen of them, and heavy flatboards to protect them, but the *Leucothea* had something the *Pelerin* did not— enormous holds. Instead of being loaded with spice and silk they were packed with provisions, shot for quilaines, arrows, pitch, timber, rum, rope, and a hundred other things to replenish the fleet of war.

Most of the other ships in the mercantile fleet were similar to the *Leucothea*, though there were a few heavier vessels that sacrificed maneuverability for cargo space. Almost none of them had oars, as warships did, but his father's fleet was tasked primarily with supplying the fighting ships, secondarily with fighting. His father had some theories about how they might be employed in battle, however, and had apparently sold the emperor that wet cargo.

Lacking oars, the merchant ships were helpless without wind. Not so the Drehhu ships, which were motivated by demons and had no care whether the wind blew or not.

He approached the stern for the third time and saw a woman there, leaning against the flatboards. She wore a plain gown of light blue linen. He could not see her face.

"Danesele," he said, trying to announce his presence without startling her. She turned slowly from her view of the sea to glance at him over her shoulder. Her features were fair, her hair straw-colored, her eyes gray. He found her face pleasant—maybe pretty—but not quite beautiful.

"Good morning," she said, turning back to the sea.

He stepped to the rail and looked sidelong at her.

"We haven't been introduced," he said. "I'm Crespin."

"I know who you are," she told him. He thought he detected

something in the way she said it, as if she already found him distasteful in some way.

"I see," he said. "I haven't the same advantage."

"Calliope," she informed him with an accent he couldn't place.

"I thought I had met everyone on ship."

"I like the sunrise," she said. "And the night, but I don't like the sun." She looked frankly at him. "You haven't been up early enough to meet me," she said. "Until now."

"Well, I'm glad I had the midnight watch, this time," he said.

"No," she said.

"No, what?"

"I have been on this ship for a year and twenty days," she replied. "It has a crew of eighty-five, including the soldiers we took on in Ophion Magne. Of that number, seven are women, including me. I have become very good at saying 'no.' Even if it is to the admiral's son."

"I only meant to be friendly," he said. "Nothing more." But he felt a little put upon. Who was she to talk to him so? She didn't know him.

"I didn't ask to be on this boat," he continued into the silence. "I was in the Imperial Navy. I had shipmates. Now, thanks to my father's whimsy, I'm here, the very place I've spent my life trying to escape." With dismay he heard the words rush out of him, and was instantly sorry he had said them.

"He's doing you a favor," she said.

"How is this a favor? Everyone on this ship resents me. Including you, it seems."

"It must be so hard for you," she said. For an instant, he thought she was sympathizing with him. Then, from her expression, he recognized mockery. "The sun is up," she said, nodding at the disc just appearing on the horizon, and without another word she straightened and walked away.

He stared after her a moment, fuming, thinking of things he should have said.

HECTOR FOUND him a bit later, still nursing his anger.

"What's the matter?" Hector asked.

"I've met the most awful woman," he replied.

"Calliope?" Hector said, and he grinned. "Yes, I had a go at her the other day. She settles accounts very quickly."

Crespin remembered what she had said about being a woman aboard a ship full of men and sighed.

"It's for the best, you know," Hector said. "Dangerous, that, you know?"

"What do you mean? Who is she, anyway?"

"Oh, you *didn't* know?" Hector said. "She's a strixe."

Crespin stared at him for a moment.

"Of course she is." He groaned. "I guess I was expecting…" He trailed off.

"Old and ugly?" Hector finished.

"Yes. Not that she's all that pretty—"

Hector cut him off with a laugh.

"Give us a few months at sea," he said, "and we'll come back to that remark." His hair ruffled in a sudden gust. "Hell take me, is that some wind at last?"

———

TINY REDBEARD monkeys scampered through the spreading limbs of the gigantic old fig trees that arched above the stone path through the old jade garden where Chrysanthe walked with Penelope au Leu. Penelope was lovely, with long, graceful limbs and small lips that could turn up into a most impish sort of smile. Chrysanthe had known her almost since birth; as when they were children, they strolled hand in hand. But something had changed between them. Penelope's bearing was not as light as it once had been, and that smile appeared only occasionally.

She seemed nervous.

"I'm glad you called on me," Penelope said. "It's been an age."

"The better part of a year," Chrysanthe acknowledged. "I never intended to stay away so long."

"I know," Penelope said, "and yet it's the same walk going either way between our houses. We've both been busy, haven't we? We're not children anymore."

Chrysanthe nodded.

"I was so astonished to hear of Lucien's misdeeds," Penelope ventured.

Chrysanthe shrugged. "It is a shame. He would never have been the one for me, but he might have saved himself a beating."

"To think of those poor children."

"It was Lucien's opinion that, since they were already all but enslaved, it would be no matter to them if they actually became so."

"It's an absurd opinion," Penelope said.

"Perhaps it is a matter of perspective," Chrysanthe replied.

"It is a matter of fact," Penelope insisted. "The child of a slave can be stripped from its parents and sold like a bolt of cloth. That is not true of our laborers."

"Yes, at least that is true," she said. "At least."

"You are troubled," Penelope said. "About more than some excuse Lucien made for himself."

"You know me well."

"Very well," Penelope said softly, squeezing her hand. She sighed. "This war. I wish it were not so."

"I wish the same," Chrysanthe said, "but nothing will stop it now, I think."

"I would rather go with the men, if I could," Penelope said. "It would be better than waiting here, not knowing if they are dead or alive. If they will ever return."

"Your brother is going, then?"

"Yes," Penelope said. "And... my fiancé."

For a heartbeat, Chrysanthe was sure she had misheard, and for another she believed Penelope was joking, but then she realized neither was true.

"You are affianced?" Chrysanthe said. "I did not know of it."

"It has only just now happened."

"And the lucky man?"

"Florent Laval," she said.

"Florent?"

"I know that tone," Penelope said. "You do not approve."

"No, it's not that, I... Didn't you once say he was the dullest man you knew?"

"Yes, well he still is," Penelope said. "But he is kind. And safe."

Safe. The word pushed itself between them, and she felt Penelope's fingers loosen, trying to disengage from hers.

Chrysanthe tightened her own grip.

"Can I not wish something more than that for you?"

Penelope's gaze wandered off, but when it came back it settled directly on Chrysanthe's.

"No, my dearest friend," she said. "I am afraid you cannot." For a moment, Chrysanthe could not find her breath. When she did, she gave Penelope's hand a squeeze.

"Then I must wish you all the happiness you can find in your situation."

FOUR DAYS later, while reading in the courtyard, she heard the clatter of a carriage. Setting the book on the bench, Chrysanthe went to peer out of the window, although she knew from her shoes up who it was. So, she wasn't surprised to find the emperor's uniform on the coachmen. Patting her dress, she felt through it to the undergarments below, and the little box concealed in the pocket there. On ship, who knew who might handle her things? She had determined to always keep it with her, safe and secret.

"You're packed, I take it?" a voice behind her said.

"Mother?" She turned and found her there. "You knew?"

"Of course I knew," she said. "Who else could arrange for you to be escorted to the ship when your brothers are all conveniently away?"

"They're going to be furious."

"They will," her mother allowed, "but I will deal with them." She studied Chrysanthe closely.

"I wish I could have wished them farewell," Chrysanthe said. "I have written each a letter, if you could deliver them for me. They are on my bed."

"That was thoughtful," Mother said. "Of course I will."

"Thank you."

An uneasy pause followed, broken by her mother. "I've packed some extra things for you," she said. "Clothing more appropriate for the court, for instance. Some fragrance—"

"You know I don't bother with such things," Chrysanthe said.

Her mother's face flushed red.

"You *will* bother, Chrysanthe Nevelon," she snapped. "You will behave as a lady in every respect, from the instant you meet those men outside until the very moment you return to this house. Do you understand me?"

It was too much for Chrysanthe.

"Mother, I am going as hostage for this family, not skylarking in search of the especially important husband you so desperately wish on me," she said. "I know you think of little more than appearance and connections and how a table should be set, but that is not me. I will not be returning to you a married woman."

"Chrysanthe Nevelon," her mother said, her eyes flashing, "my only prayer is that you return to me at all. Which—if you do not play the part assigned to you—is not likely to happen." Chrysanthe realized with a shock that tears were trickling from her mother's eyes. With her own throat closing, she stepped forward and took her mother in her arms.

"I'm sorry, Mama," she said. "I didn't mean… I'm scared."

For a long moment, her mother said nothing, but just held her, held her as she hadn't since Chrysanthe was a little girl.

"You should be," he mother finally said. "I want you scared."

She released her then and wiped at her daughter's eyes.

"You must listen to me, Chrysanthe. You will meet people in Ophion Magne who seem pleasant and agreeable, and who are fondly considering the best way to ruin you. There are others that might become your protectors. Telling the difference between the two will be very difficult. You must therefore hand no one a knife that can be plunged into your back. Your appearance and behavior must be above reproach."

"I understand."

"You think you do," her mother said, "but there are things that will strike against, things over which you have no control. We are part of the Empire, but Ophion Magne is not Mesembria. Everything about you, from your accent to the color of your skin, will mark you in their eyes as provincial at best and an illiterate bumpkin at worst. You must show them that they are wrong. The things I've taught you—those things you deem so useless—those are the armor and sword you *will* need."

She closed her eyes for an instant, then opened them again.

"You must understand what is at stake. What you risk. It is not just yourself and your own prospects. It is not merely our connections as a family. It is *all* of this. Everything you see."

Her mother pulled back for a moment, as Chrysanthe struggled to understand. The older woman exaggerated, often—most of the time, maybe—but to Chrysanthe this did not seem to be one of those occasions. There was a desperate earnestness about her that seemed completely genuine.

And then it came to her.

"Are you talking about the *charter*?"

"That is precisely what I am talking about," her mother said. "There is nothing in the Empire that the throne does not, in principle, own."

"But it was given us more than a hundred years ago," Chrysanthe. "This has been our land, our home, for generations."

"And if the emperor deems us unworthy, it can be passed to

someone else tomorrow," she said. "There are many eager to have it, of that you can be sure. In fact, Lucien has already demanded the charter in payment for the beating he suffered at the hands of your brothers."

"Surely he cannot seriously believe—"

"Now?" her mother said. "No. There is no better name in the Empire than Nevelon. His petition failed to move forward, but if our name were ever to become tarnished—even if only a little—that could change. Lucien may petition again when he reaches the court, or any of a dozen others. If your father fails to return from Basilisk, there is little doubt someone will try to wrest the inheritance from Tycho. If that occurs, we must be found without fault."

For a moment Chrysanthe felt heavy, too heavy to breathe, to move, to do anything. Why hadn't her father told her this?

Because he thought she already knew. That she understood the weight he was placing on her shoulders. And she should have. She most *certainly* should have. Chrysanthe knew their family history, but she had taken for granted that things would continue as they had, no matter what.

She raised her gaze until it met her mother's.

"That will not happen, Mama," she said.

For a long moment neither of them said anything. Then her mother nodded.

"Very well," the elder woman replied. "I've gotten flustered. I must look a sight." She took Chrysanthe's hands in hers and gave her a feeble grin. "But since you brought up the subject of husband, who knows? You might indeed see a chance at a good match. Proper comportment will not hurt you there."

Chrysanthe squeezed her mother's hands.

"I love you, too, Mama," she said.

CHAPTER EIGHT

WITH THE WINDS

THE WIND was fickle, but they managed to leave the Pitch Pot, sailing into the more predictable south malfé winds. These blew near constantly from the southeast, which posed its own problem. Southeast was the direction they needed to go. The ocean current was helpful, but only slightly so, as it flowed toward the southwest.

This was an old problem, however, and had been solved a century or so before. Sailing southwest with the current, they moved away from their destination. Eventually this would bring them to the southern Argestae, where that wind and the current would carry them back east, around Cape Haparis and on toward their destination. The shorter route would have been to follow the coast due south, but that would mean sailing directly into the wind and against the current. That would be far, far slower.

Crespin had a hard time shaking Calliope's mockery, and after a time he knew why. He arose before dawn, and found her in the same spot.

"You were right," he said.

"I usually am," she replied. "About what?"

"The proudest day of my life was when I told my father I was joining the Navy. I felt like a man, in control of my destiny. Being on this ship, under his command—it made me feel like a boy again. As if it had all been taken from me. I've been moaning about my fate rather than doing something about it. I'm sorry I subjected you to it."

"This isn't much better," she said, but then she smiled slightly. "A little better, yes. What is it about me that makes you think I care to hear your problems?"

That left him speechless for a moment, and he realized that it was very likely he would never say anything that she thought worth hearing. Then it occurred to him that it was because he was always talking about himself.

"You won't hear any more of about my worries."

"I'll take that as a promise," she replied. She closed her eyes. "The moon is about to rise," she murmured. He felt as if he should leave, then, but something held him there.

"What is it like? he asked. "To do what you do?"

"It is beautiful," she said, "and miserable. And necessary."

THE MOMENT arrived when Crespin heard one too many remarks made under the breath. The peppercorn that sank the ship was uttered by a thin marinier named Grefin.

Grefin always had a lot to say, usually in the form of a joke or a complaint, or both. This time it was something to the effect that even a monkey could be an officer if his father owned the ship, and he said it loudly enough that too many people heard it. Crespin was watching the ship's wake when it happened. He closed his eyes for an instant, opened them, and turned.

A small gang of them were watching him.

If these men had been imperial naviors, a comment like that would have resulted in a flogging—and technically, he *could* have Grefin flogged. But these men were not naviors: they were mariniers, civilian sailors, and he knew flogging one of them wouldn't help his situation at all.

So, when he turned around, he didn't single out Grefin, but instead pointed a finger at Alkaios. Unlike Grefin, Alkaios didn't say much and generally minded his business. In fact, he was often the butt of Grefin's jokes. He was also the biggest man on the ship. His chest was massive, and his arms might have been twisted from the sinews of an elephant.

"What did you just say?" Crespin demanded of him.

Alkaios looked confused.

"What? Nothing, sir."

"First you call me a monkey, and now you're lying about it? What sort of man are you?"

"I'm not lying, sir," Alkaios replied.

Grefin, meanwhile, started to grin.

"Well," Crespin said, "I say you are." Then he spat at him.

"It wasn't me, sir," the man insisted. His features were beginning to cloud with anger.

"Well, who was it then? Who are you going to accuse?"

The big man glared at Grefin but didn't answer.

"Sir," another man, Remi, said. "This isn't the Navy, sir."

"Oh," Crespin responded, "You don't say? Believe me, I'm very well aware that this isn't the Navy. If it were the Navy, all of you jackasses would have long ago been thrown overboard for the sharks. But this is what I have in front of me, such as it is." He jerked his head toward Alkaios. "*Someone* said it, and I say it was you. Now are you a fighter, or should I start reading you poetry and go on about your eyes?"

That was finally enough—Alkaios charged forward.

Crespin slipped aside and punched him in the ear. It felt like hitting a stone wall. The big man roared and swung at him; Crespin ducked and jabbed at his chin before dancing back out of range, but this time he wasn't quite fast enough. Alkaios clipped him in the arm. It didn't hurt much, but Crespin stumbled as if it had. Emboldened, the marinier charged again. Crespin dropped to the side and swept his leg around, tripping his huge opponent, sending him into the deck with an audible thud. He watched the sailor climb back to his feet and start forward again, a little more cautiously.

Crespin stepped in and jabbed. Alkaios ignored him and punched him in the face. It felt like being hit with a sledgehammer, and the next thing he knew he was on the deck, pushing himself up with his arms, blood pouring from his nose. Alkaios grabbed him in a bear hug and began squeezing the air out of him. Crespin boxed him in the ears and felt the grip release.

When he had his feet on the deck again, he punched Alkaios just below his sternum, then again in the armpit. The big man gasped and sagged as the wind left his lungs. Crespin dizzily watched him crumple to the deck.

"Does anyone else want to call me a monkey?" he asked, wiping his bleeding nose.

"What's this?"

Crespin looked up to see his father emerging from the officer's quarters.

"Nothing, sir," Crespin said, reaching to help Alkaios to his feet. "We tripped."

The admiral regarded him for a moment.

"I expect you'll watch your feet from now on," he said. "All of you."

"Admiral."

Everyone turned at the feminine voice. Calliope was there, standing in the shadow of the hatch, her eyes squinted.

"What is it, miss?" his father said.

"I've heard from the strixe on the *Balaine*," she replied. "A squall is approaching from the southeast."

Now that they were in open sea, the fleet had spread itself into a rough column with the *Leucothea* in front. The *Balaine* was farthest to the rear and would naturally apprehend the storm first. Staring southeast, Crespin still couldn't see any foul weather, but he did make out the flashing pattern of light from the lucnograph of the next ship back, reporting the same thing Calliope had.

Crespin wiped his bloody nose. This much forewarning was good. It gave them plenty of time to make ready to run before the gale. He thought his father would give the order instantly, but instead, the admiral paused.

"Admiral?" he asked.

His father turned to Calliope.

"Every ship east of the *Salaminia* is to heave to, drop their sails, and raise their gale-sheets. Beat into the wind. Every ship westward, full sail and bear off south."

Crespin blinked. That was insane.

"Lieutenant Captain," his father said to Crespin, "take those orders to the lucnograph operator and send them down the column."

"But sir—"

"See that the quilaines and everything else of any weight are stowed in the hold," the admiral said. He leaned nearer, and his voice dropped to a whisper. "And do not beat any more of my men."

CHAPTER NINE

THE UPLANDS

THE FIRST day was easy going, as they followed the valley southeast. Deep forest gave way to patches of trees and tall grass prairie. Hound kept one eye on Soot, high against the blue sky. When the raven saw something dangerous, he usually did a little aerial dance as an alert.

The riders spoke to one another in a language Hound did not know, although by the end of the day, he had picked up a few words: "merde," for instance, he was fairly sure meant "shit." Martin and Selene were clearly in charge, and the three men in the suits of armor didn't seem all that happy about it. The other men addressed the men in armor as "chevalier" and were pretty obviously subordinate to them, with each chevalier commanding five men.

They camped in the open. Hound found a good tree to sleep in, and the next morning they continued on.

The sun was about halfway up the sky when Soot did his dance. It was mostly unnecessary. Hound had already spotted the circling vultures, and noted that none of them ever descended. No one else in the party seemed to notice anything until they were near enough to smell the carrion. Then an argument started between Martin and one of the chevaliers. After a moment, the chevalier broke off and turned to Hound.

"What do you make of that?" he asked Hound in rough Velesan.

"Something dead over there."

"Maybe lions have killed something?"

"Maybe," Hound allowed.

The chevalier nodded, turned his horse that way, and urged it to a gallop. His men followed.

"Ariston!" Martin bellowed after him.

"If you need those men," Hound said, "you'd best go with them." Then he ran after the horsemen. Martin swore in his own language and followed, as did the rest.

They found the chevalier in a stand of trees, staring at a motley collection of savaged, half-eaten animals. One of them was a three-horned deer, but most had been rendered unrecognizable. Where bones were visible, he could see that they had been broken through. A cloud of black flies hovered over the mess, and the smell of rot was almost overpowering.

Hound bounded up into the upper branches of a magnolia to watch the fun.

Ariston noticed.

"What does this?" he demanded.

"Hell-pig," Hound said.

"What's a hell-pig?" the man demanded.

Hound pointed just into the trees.

"That," he replied. What had appeared to be dapples of sunlight through leaves was suddenly in furious motion.

"Merde!" the chevalier yelped as the boar came crashing into the clearing to defend its grizzly cache. It was a big one, too—at the shoulder it was half again the height of a tall man. Before anyone could react with more than profanity, it had seized one of the horses by the neck and used its massive jaws to crush the life from it. The man astride the poor beast yelped as he hurtled to the ground.

To his credit, Ariston shook off his shock, hefted his lance, and charged the monster. He struck it in the mass of muscle just behind its skull. It shrieked and jerked its head back, shattering the wooden shaft, then charged at his tormentor. The chevalier wheeled his horse tightly, drawing his sword as he did so. The snapping of crossbows filled the air, but the hell-pig didn't seem to notice the quarrels that hit it. It nipped at the rump of Ariston's horse, which jumped violently to avoid injury, tossing the chevalier through the air to land with a tremendous clank amongst the rotting corpses.

The boar gave an ear-shattering squeal as another of the horsemen plunged his spear into it—this time in the side, just behind its foreleg. The weapon sank deep, and the beast stumbled from the impact of horse, rider, and spear.

It recovered and charged its new attacker, but then suddenly drove toward Selene. Before she could move, Martin was standing in front of her, feet braced wide. His hand darted out almost too fast to see, striking the boar in the side of the head as he spun away, so the beast only brushed by him rather than ramming into him. The hell-pig staggered sideways, and Hound noticed that where the beast's eye had been, there was now only a bloody hole.

With another shriek, it collapsed. It tried to rise once more, but the warriors were all around it, hacking and stabbing it with their weapons.

Martin glanced up at him in the tree, a small frown on his face. His right hand was bloody past his wrist.

He killed it with his hand, Hound thought. That's something I've never seen before. Maybe this trip would be more interesting than he thought.

THAT NIGHT they camped in the hills east of the valley. Once the fire was started and everything arranged, Martin came and found him in his tree.

"You knew what it was," the man accused. "Long before we got there."

"Yes," Hound replied. "Anything else—Ariston's lion, for instance—the vultures would have at least had a try at all that meat." He cocked his head. "What does he want with a lion, anyway?"

"Chevaliers," Martin sighed. "They like trophies. He's been talking about lions since we set off."

"Hell-pigs eat lions," Hound said. "They eat pretty much everything."

"I'm aware of that *now*," Martin said. "Why didn't you warn us?"

Hound smiled. "I wanted to see what you would do, and I wasn't disappointed. That thing you did with your hand. Now I see why you don't carry weapons. Is it some sort of magic?"

"What the untutored call magic is nothing more than bending the world to one's will," Martin said.

"I'm not sure that's an answer."

"We lost a horse," Martin said. "It could just as easily have been a man. Next time, warn us."

———

THEY PRESSED further into the mountains. Hound steered them around lions and panthers without Ariston ever knowing they were there. They avoided two Kansa hunting parties. The odds were remote that the tribesmen would attack so well-armed a group, but you could never tell with the Kansa.

Three days of traveling found them winding up and down passes in the lower Vereshalm Mountains. The grasslands disappeared, replaced by lush, open forest. It was cooler there, so Hound donned Grandmother's gift of elk-hide clothing.

The expedition had plenty of food loaded on the extra horses, but it wasn't much to Hound's taste, so he hunted small game as they went along, and the mountains grew around them. He also talked with Selene, who told him of her home in Ophion, describing towns so large he wondered if she was lying just to see if he would believe it. He learned more of her language as they went along.

After two weeks they passed the limits of his earlier travels, but he remembered Grandmother's directions well enough, and reckoned another two or three days would have them in view of the peak for which they were looking. One afternoon, as the others set up camp, Hound scrambled up a steep slope and climbed the broken stone spine that led to the bald summit. It wasn't particularly high, but the view was spectacular. The mountains cut at the sky in all directions, lowest in the west, where the sun was lighting fire to the horizon.

He closed his eyes and felt the wind on him, the vastness around, the sky itself entering his lungs and leaving them. When he opened them, he looked back the way they had come, finding the landmarks that would lead him home. Above, Soot turned lazily in the air, unconcerned.

Just as he was about to go back down, a motion caught his eye. He tightened his gaze, trying to understand what he was seeing. When he did, he descended to the camp and found Martin and Selene.

"Someone is following you," he told them. "On horses. Probably twice your number. It's hard to tell from this far."

Martin frowned. "You're certain they're following us?"

"I'm pretty sure. What else would they be doing up here? We've been making our own trail, not following one, and they are following it."

"Who could it be?" Selene asked. "What does it mean?"

"It means," Martin said grimly, "that we've been betrayed." He tapped his finger against the log he was sitting on. "But if they're following us, they don't have a guide. They can't find the place unless we do."

"We can go no further, then," Selene said.

"No," Martin agreed. "We have to fight them here, or nearby. At least we shall have the advantage of surprise."

"They're almost a day behind," Hound said. "It's why Soot didn't warn us about them." He stood and cracked his neck. "See you in the morning." Then he walked toward the tree where he had placed his things.

When it grew dark enough, he gathered his few belongings, woke Rose from her drowse, and started back toward home.

CHAPTER TEN

THE EXPIRY

ALL TOO soon, Crespin could see the storm, a black wall off their babord side. He watched it, still wondering what his father was thinking, still fuming at his last words. The admiral had to know the position in which he had put Crespin, and he had to understand that at some point Crespin would have to do something about it to be effective as an officer. But instead of support he received remonstration. It was beyond belief.

The wind began to pick up, and he turned his mind to unraveling his father's logic—another thing he felt he shouldn't have to do. A second officer should be informed of the captain's plans. That had certainly been the case on the *Pelerin*.

There were two ways to deal with a storm and the waves it brought. Both involved the length of the ship being perpendicular to those waves. They could head into them, as the admiral had ordered the trailing ships to do, or go with them, which was generally the safer approach.

Instead, they had been placed broadside to the approaching squall, and the first big wave would easily capsize them. It might make sense if land or shallows or a reef lay near them, but they were in open ocean.

Unless…

Crespin had been so preoccupied that he hadn't checked their position in days, so he went below to the chartroom and looked at the maps his father had spread out, locating their position—and the blood-red line that ran down the edge of the map.

The Expiry.

The line no one had ever crossed and returned. Crespin fancied himself good at reckoning, but that belief fell into shambles. He had reckoned they were still many leagues from that deadly border, but they were hardly more than seven. If they ran ahead of the storm, they would be swept headlong into the barrier.

The Expiry line ran from north to south, but was slanted relative to their course. If they went due north, they would quickly come closer to it. By running south, they would gain distance. In the end, they would still have to turn into the storm, and it would blow them toward the Expiry. His father was trying to widen the distance before they were forced to do that.

Congratulations, Crespin old fellow, he thought harshly. *You've just proven to your father that you're an idiot.* He went back up on deck and stared glumly to the east, at the dark clouds gathering there. He barely noticed Renost as he stepped up and leaned against the rail.

"Why Alkaios?" his friend asked. "You know very well Grefin said it."

"Grefin is too small," Crespin replied. "I wouldn't have made a point."

"But now Alkaios—"

"Will get a double ration of rum for a week or two, and maybe he will see to it that Grefin holds his opinion from now on."

"If we survive that long, you mean," Renost said, making the sign against evil at the storm.

"The admiral knows what he's doing," Crespin replied.

"We're not supposed to have storms this far south," Renost pressed. "Not this time of year. Doesn't feel right."

"Just a storm," Crespin insisted.

Renost's eyes shifted to regard something behind him. Crespin followed his gaze and saw Calliope approaching. She wasn't looking at them, or at the storm, but rather west, off their estribord side, where the sun was declining. She seemed more wan than usual—and a little unsteady on her feet.

"There," she said in an odd, dreamy voice.

For a moment, Crespin did not understand what she meant, but then he saw it. Although still an hour or two short of reaching the horizon, the sun had begun to flatten on the bottom. The sea itself did not seem to extend far enough, but rather vanished into an indistinct grayness.

"The Expiry," Calliope said. "I've never been close enough to see it." She turned, and he was startled to see that her eyes were flecked with yellow. They didn't seem quite focused.

"Nor have I," Crespin said, trying not to stare. "Nor ever wanted to."

There was much conjecture concerning the Expiry. Some thought that, because the currents flowed so strongly toward it, the edge of the world lay beyond. Others believed massive serpents lurked in the mist, ready to rend any ship that entered. Still others speculated it was a wall erected by God to separate the world from paradise. In truth, no one knew what it was, only that no one had found the end of it. It traced an immense circle around the world, and no ship that entered had ever returned.

"You may be getting a closer look," Renost told her, eyes cutting to the storm. The blurred line extended south and west, where it vanished into a normal horizon. Looking north, it went off to the east, effectively behind them. South it curved off to the west, exactly as shown on the map.

He looked back at the storm and gauged the distance, doing so with a sinking feeling. It didn't look to him like they would make it far enough.

"Danesele," his father's voice said from behind him. "You should get below."

"Admiral," Calliope said. She raised a flask to her mouth and took a drink. Crespin smelled rum.

"Renost," the admiral said, "Would you escort the young lady below?"

"Yes sir," Renost replied. He offered his arm, but Calliope ignored it until she stumbled a little—then she caught onto it for the next few steps.

Then he was alone with his father.

"Do you have some reason to question my orders in front of the men?" the admiral asked, mildly.

"No, sir," he said.

"You didn't know how close we were to the Expiry, did you?"

"No, sir. I've been stupid, sir."

"No. That would be forgivable. What you *have* been is inattentive to your duties. You think yourself a navior, and as such above the running of a mere merchant ship."

Crespin really hated it when his father was right, and he hated admitting it even more.

"Why did you do this to me?" he snapped. "I *am* a good sailor, or at least the Navy thought so. I should be where I belong, on the *Pelerin*."

"But you are not," the admiral said. "You are here. I need you to be a man, Crespin, and an officer. I need you to be the man I know you *can* be. There are far worse things ahead than this storm."

Crespin searched for an angry reply, but instead he just nodded.

"Good," his father said. "Go about your business. Make certain we are prepared to turn."

"Yes, sir."

THE *LEUCOTHEA* had twenty sails of various sorts, and they were currently fully rigged so the ship could make the best speed possible. When the storm reached them, they would have to take them all down, and quickly. He found the crewmen responsible for the job and explained exactly what was to be done when his father gave the order.

All the while the squall raced toward them, lightning flashing in its depths as if demons were at war.

Time seemed to drag. He felt that the order was overdue, and it made him nervous. On the *Pelerin*, he would have known when to drop sail, but the *Pelerin* had far fewer sails to take down than the *Leucothea*. He did not have a feel for her yet.

The water began to chop, hard. The wind picked up. Crespin watched his father, standing next to the helmsman, Blacon.

"Heave to," his father finally said.

"*Heave to!*" Crespin repeated, with all the volume his lungs could muster. He tried not to fidget as the ship turned reluctantly to confront the oncoming waves. He glanced behind. In the distance, the Expiry was just visible. His father nodded at him.

"*Drop the sails!*" Crespin hollered, the wind in his face. The words were hardly out of his mouth before the great sheets released from their booms and began collapsing to the deck. Given more time, he would have ordered them furled, but in this situation that would have taken much too long.

"*Hoist the gale-sheets!*" he commanded.

The wind was really on them now, and the waves lifting and dropping the bow. He watched the dance of the men in the rigging, replacing the white cloud of full sail with four small triangular ones. They were made of heavier stuff and dyed a dark blue to attract the Virgin's intercession. At full sail, the wind might flip the ship over, or snap masts. With no sail at all, they couldn't keep from turning broadside. The gale-sheets would allow them to use the storm against itself.

He felt an unexpected swell of pride. These men knew what they were doing—and they did it *fast*. He began to understand that it was not false modesty when his father credited them with the success of his voyages. Military they weren't, but they were disciplined when it came to the work.

Then the storm was on them.

The *Leucothea* climbed a wave so tall it pointed her bowsprit halfway up the sky. She hung on the top and Crespin, to his horror, felt her begin to yaw and then roll to babord, tilting the deck horizontally, as well. Over the roar and the waves, he heard a shriek as someone fell from above. Whoever it was struck the deck and slid, fetching against the flatboards, and then—as the ship crested the wave and fell down the other side—went hurling toward the bow as it slapped into the trough and sent a huge spray of water onto the deck.

Crespin didn't stop to think about what he did next.

Letting go his hold on the mast, he stumbled across the heaving deck. The next wave was building in front of them, already lifting their prow again, and he saw through the rain and spray the figure of the man, grasping the railing from the other side, his body already hanging over the sea. Crespin scrambled to him, reached under his arms and heaved as they tilted again toward the storm-dark heavens.

Lightning snaked into the dark water, and the hail came mixed with the rain, drumming on the ship, tearing at flesh. He got the man on ship, but then another wave surged across the deck, and he felt himself lifted. As he lost hold of the man, he knew he was being swept overboard himself.

Then someone gripped his arm so tightly he cried out in pain. For a moment it felt as if the sea would win anyway, but then he was dragged back on deck. Blinking the spume out of his eyes, he saw it was Alkaios who had saved him.

He nodded his thanks, then made his way unsteadily back to the helm.

The steersman was tacking into the wind, but they were still being swept back. The Expiry was no longer visible, but he knew it was there. He felt it like a knife at his back, gripped the rail, trying to force his gaze farther. Then he heard someone yelling, and suddenly a massive shadow appeared through the squall.

"Ah, sacre merde," he choked back.

It was another ship—which one he could not say, because she was capsized and rolling with the waves, straight toward them. He stood there, for an instant, frozen.

"Hard a babord!" he heard his father shout.

It seemed impossible. There was no time...

The *Leucothea* began her turn away from the capsized vessel. She didn't finish it. The collision threw him from his feet, and he crashed against something, hard. A huge wave slapped at their side, and mariniers rained from the rigging. The deck tilted as the ship tried to roll, and in that instant, he thought they were done.

Then they were somehow pointed back into the wind.

He made his way across the pitching deck to his father.

THE STORM broke soon after, and stars appeared. The collision had been a mere glance. Their hull was intact, and the wind had dropped to a sigh. He ordered the sails back up, which took some time, and continued trying to tack to the southeast, against the current.

When the sun came up, the Expiry filled the western sky, and in the early morning light he watched one of their ships—the Gorgon, missing her mainmast—drift through it and vanish. A few moments later, the wind brought a distant chorus of screams.

"That was nearly us," Renost said.

"It still could be," Crespin replied.

Renost nodded, then he pointed with his eyes. Crespin glanced behind him and saw his father standing at the flatboards, staring after the vanished ship, his expression unreadable.

CHAPTER ELEVEN

STRANGE DOGS

HOUND PASSED unnoticed within a stone's cast of the second group and was on his way back to Grandmother's cave when curiosity overcame him. He doubled back and found a perch from which to observe whoever was following Selene and Martin.

They were babbling in the same language as Martin's group, and were armed and armored in much the same way. There were many more of them, though—fifty-two by his count—and one of them he recognized. The manhunter, with a bandage where his ear had been. He was probably doing the tracking for them.

There were no women in this group, only hard-looking men. They also had what looked like dogs with them, but they weren't like any dogs he had ever seen. They were long-legged and sharp-eared, gray with black stripes. They hadn't noticed him, however, so their sense of smell and hearing must not be that keen. Maybe they were more for fighting than tracking. He counted ten of those, and each seemed to be paired with one of the men.

Even attacking from ambush, Selene and the rest were probably going to be slaughtered. That was easy to see, and it was too bad. He liked Selene. It would be interesting to see how Martin would fight against crossbow bolts and swords.

But not *that* interesting. He continued northwest.

For a while, but then something new occurred to him, something that might be fun. So once again he turned himself southeast.

HE KILLED the first one as they were fording a river, a chevalier who didn't have his helmet on. The others watched the man sway in the saddle and drop into the water. They became agitated, but it wasn't until the blood started downstream that they realized they were under attack, and by then he had hit two more. Then they began to scurry for cover. They didn't even know from which direction he was picking them off.

Now they were forty-nine. Grinning, he loped off.

It got a little harder after that, because they all made sure they had their helmets on, but before sundown he managed to kill four more, shatter two wrists, and half-blind one fellow. It slightly worried him, though, that he no longer saw the manhunter among them. Hound had planned to kill him first, but then it occurred to him that it might spoil the game. The question was, was the fellow having another go at him, or had he abandoned his new employers?

He glanced over at Rose.

"Stay close," he whispered. "Watch my back."

THE MOON hadn't yet risen when Rose growled, low in her throat. Hound knew the sound—someone or something was near, something she didn't like. He slowly uncurled from his place in the notch of a tree, stood, and slipped his tomahawk from his belt, straining his senses against the dark.

After a moment, he heard slow, soft padding on the leaves— something on four legs. Then many somethings. He thought he could make out the shape of the nearest. It was hard to tell, because it was no longer moving. None of them were.

It had to be the dogs, but they weren't acting like dogs—at least not most dogs. If they were hunting him, why hadn't they attacked? He guessed they probably had him surrounded, and if they were like Rose, they could see as well at night as in the day— if not better.

But *he* couldn't, not without the moon, and maybe not with it, under these trees. He couldn't run. He couldn't use his sling. Rose might be able to kill a few of them, and he might get lucky and get one or two—but ten was too many.

If he waited until light, he would be facing more than dogs.

Hound had underestimated these people—badly.

He stood there, remembering the terrain. To his back the land rose, not too sharply. He was facing the camp, which was also on high ground beyond a marshy vale. The dogs had probably come straight through that, but men in armor likely would have a bit more trouble. They might have to go around. His best chance lay uphill, and then hopefully over it and down to the river.

Well then, he thought, and he settled back down to rest.

The moon came up, a quarter empty, and that enabled him to see them, sitting on their haunches, waiting. He could make out the ground and rough contours of the landscape. So, too, could the men he heard moving unsubtly through the forest.

"Ready, Rose? he murmured.

He faced uphill, picked out the three dogs he could see waiting in that direction, and slung a stone at each of them. He couldn't see well enough to know what part of them he hit, but all of them began an earsplitting yapping that sounded very little like any dog he had ever heard.

Jumping down, he ran, tomahawk in hand. A dark shape leapt at him, and he dodged as he struck its head with the weapon.

Rose turned to face those behind him.

"Stay with me, Rose," he shouted. Then he had no more breath for talking; it all went for his legs. Rose did as he said, however, and ran beside him.

The tree trunks were visible enough for him to dodge them, but limbs whipped his face and chest. The dogs easily kept pace, just on his heels and flanking him on either side, and he realized with dismay that they were driving him like a deer, turning him back toward the approaching men. What's more, their yaps had begun to sound less random and more like some sort of speech. What were these things? He thought he knew everything that lived in the forest.

Pivoting abruptly to his left, he threw his ax. It buried in the head of a dog and the animal dropped. Hound raced past the corpse, bent, and yanked it loose without missing a stride, then redoubled his efforts, trying to keep ahead of the dog on his flank. Rose got the idea and shifted to his left, snarling and snapping at the beast.

He was on a downslope now, and knew the river couldn't be far, but he didn't see it until he came to the bluff. Knowing he didn't have a choice, he leapt as far as he could, hoping he didn't hit a rock or

GREG KEYES

snag. As his feet left the ground, something hit him in the leg—*hard*—and spun him half around. He had a glimpse of the manhunter, his face a mask of fury, already setting another arrow to his string.

Then Hound hit the water, and agony clenched his body. He struck downstream, trying to stay underwater.

THE NEXT thing he knew, Rose was tugging at his shirt, dragging him up on a muddy bank. His sinuses burned and he spat water from his mouth, shaking his head to try and clear it. He yanked at the arrow in his leg, but it wouldn't come free, and the pain was so great he nearly passed out again.

Rose jerked at him once more, urgently, and Hound became aware of shouting from upriver. Torches flickered in the trees, flames bending as their bearers raced to find him.

Forcing himself up he began to run again, although now it was more like a fast limp.

BY THE time the sun rose, he was nearing the pass beyond which he had left Selene and her party, but didn't think he would ever reach it. Crossing the river had given him the lead, but he didn't have much strength left in him. His leg throbbed and his lungs felt scorched.

Hound made it to the mouth of the pass, and decided he was done. They could only come at him from one direction now, so he took shelter behind a fallen boulder and unwound his sling. Then he waited for them to arrive. Rose stayed with him, wary and stiff-legged. He noticed Soot, high overhead. The raven would have a good view of this.

Hearing something downslope, he sent a stone whipping in that direction and was rewarded by a yelp of pain. Then half-a-dozen bolts struck his shelter. When he peered back out, they had moved close enough to be visible, but his next hastily slung missile didn't hit any of them.

He took another shot, and then he saw the manhunter sprinting toward him. His stone missed, and he ducked back to cover and took his tomahawk in hand.

"Here we go, Rose," he said.

But then a peculiar thing happened. The manhunter came into view, shaft drawn. He seemed to be surrounded by a yellowish cloud, and he looked puzzled. Then he turned and began firing his arrows at the men below, all in rapid succession. He had sped four darts before his former allies began to return fire. He shot and moved, and for a timeless moment, it seemed as if he would dodge every bolt let fly at him—but finally one found its way to his chest, and then another his neck. As he collapsed, he nocked another arrow and loosed it.

Then the golden cloud that surrounded him lifted and began drifting away. Hound saw that it originated from farther up in the pass, where he could not see.

Below, he heard someone scream. When he peered out again, one of the warriors had just beheaded the man next to him, and was now hacking at another.

"Strixe!" someone shouted.

Then all Hell seemed to break loose. Crossbow bolts suddenly came winging down from the cliffs above, along with assorted small boulders.

Martin, he realized.

Since they weren't paying attention to him anymore, Hound renewed his own attacks. The remaining warriors broke and tried to escape downhill—where they ran straight into Ariston, the other chevaliers, and Martin. When it was over, there were no survivors—neither dog nor human—among their pursuers.

Martin found Hound lying behind the stone.

"Good job," he said. "You led them right into the trap."

"Yes," Hound agreed. "That I did."

"It was stupid of you to take them on by yourself," he heard Selene say. He glanced up, ready to quip, but her appearance shocked him into silence. Her eyes were only half focused—and they had turned bright yellow. Ichor drooled from her nostrils, also yellow, and she shimmered a bit as if seen across a grassland on a very hot day. She twitched, and seemed barely in control of her limbs.

Her face was the most startling—it looked as if she had been dead for a day or so.

"It was stupid of you to try to walk," Martin said to her, taking hold as her knees began to buckle. Her head bobbled a little, and she tried to smile. It came off as weirdly silly, like a little girl's.

"Wanted to see him," she said. "Our hero."

Hound realized that they didn't know he had abandoned them to their fate. They thought his intention had been to help them all along.

"That's me," he said.

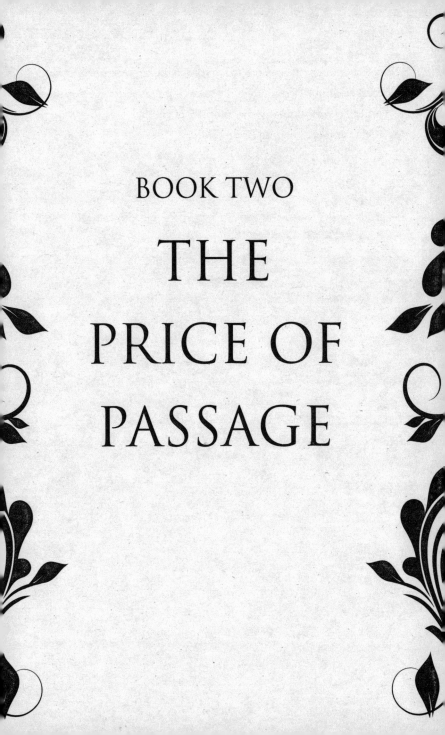

BOOK TWO

THE

PRICE OF

PASSAGE

CHAPTER ONE

THE RED CITY

FOR FIVE tense days they inched away from the Expiry, until finally the fleet came to fair winds. Their sails full, the currents finally with them, they flew toward the rising sun. Rounding the aptly named Cape of Winds, they met a storm far greater than their first, but without the Expiry to worry about, they weathered it more easily.

When they reached the island of Banaraq, there was an opportunity to assess. They had lost only four ships, but most of the fleet had sustained damage. Many of the ships—the *Leucothea* included—had managed to repair at sea, but some fifteen vessels were without the necessary resources and likely would not survive the trip across the Kohadal Ocean, much less the battle on the other side. If another storm came, matters would be worse. Mostly they needed timber and pitch, and perhaps a bit of provisioning.

Crespin spent much of his time above decks, watching the shoreline as they sailed up the west coast of the large island, studying the unfamiliar shapes of the trees. Now and then he saw small villages of thatched huts and the sails of small vessels. Most of the island was said to be inhabited by wild cannibals constantly making war on one another—and anyone who had the misfortune to wreck on their shores. Their charts showed only one harbor of the size they needed and with a town to supply them. Zamir, the Red City. Crespin had heard of the place; in times past, it had served as the home port for several bands of pirates.

They arrived at the outskirts of the harbor in early morning. Crespin, Renost, and the admiral watched Zamir emerge in dawn's light.

"It really is the color of blood," Renost said. "I've heard it said that each stone represents a murder."

"The stone comes from the mountains in the north," the admiral said. "It's that color when they quarry it."

"If I may say so, sir," Renost said, "that's a much less interesting story."

"The least interesting explanation is usually the truth," the admiral replied. "Although caution is required here. Modjal put a governor over these pirates a decade ago, but there are rumors of ships hereabouts vanishing even now."

Crespin counted the boats in the harbor.

"I don't think they're a match for us, sir."

"If we must fight, no, but we don't want a fight. We want commerce. We'll send one ship in with an envoy to negotiate."

"Why not send them a lucnograph, sir?"

"We will, but only to announce that an envoy is on the way. The more trivial a place is, the more important they want to be made to feel. They're probably already concerned that we're here. Things will go more smoothly if we treat with them face-to-face."

"Which ship should I take, sir?" Crespin asked.

The admiral glanced sideways at him. "Your diplomatic skills are untested."

"Given my rank and position in the fleet, I am the natural candidate," Crespin insisted.

"I'm aware of that," the admiral said. "I didn't say you weren't going." He paused a moment. "Anyway, it should be a pure formality. Take the *Panther* and pick a command crew."

"I THINK there's some mistake, sir," Alkaios told Crespin as he boarded the *Panther,* just behind Renost and Hector.

Crespin shook his head. "There's no mistake," he said. "I went hard on you, and you still saved my life. I need a man I can trust."

"Begging pardon, sir, but how do you know I wasn't just saving you for myself?"

"That hadn't occurred to me," Crespin replied. "Is it the case?"

"Naw," the big man said. "I figured out why you did it. But Christ, sir, how did you learn to fight like that?"

"That's Navy training," Crespin replied.

"I wouldn't mind learning a bit of that."

"I wouldn't mind training you," Crespin replied, "but right now, this is in front of us." He nodded at the city.

"Pirates all," Alkaios muttered. "But I'm with you, sir."

The *Panther* had lost her captain to the storm when the main stays snapped, and the toppling mast knocked him overboard. Now she was Crespin's first command, for however brief a time. She was smaller and shallower in draft than the *Leucothea.* The captain aside, most of her complement had survived, including their strixe.

As they entered the inner harbor a galley approached them, its oars dipping rhythmically into the waves. When it was near enough, Crespin had the *Panther* heave to, putting them still in the water. The other vessel continued to approach until their bows were nearly touching.

The captain of the Zamiran craft was dressed in a blue and green sarong. His leopard-skin jacket was cinched by a sash bearing marks on it that suggested he was from the governor's staff. He seemed to be waiting for something. Crespin guessed he was supposed to speak first.

"I am Captain Crespin Nevelon of the navy of his Imperial Majesty Ambrosios III. Who might I have the honor of addressing?"

"I am Karadi the Sword-Breaker, dhenqay to the Veil of Zamir. For what reason do you bring a fleet of war to our country?" He had an accent thick enough that Crespin couldn't tell if he was outraged or worried.

"We are not a fleet of war," Crespin lied. "We're a merchant fleet. We need certain supplies essential to affect repairs. We're here to trade."

"A merchant fleet," Karadi said, dubiously scanning the lengthy line of ships. "I suppose, then, you have a means of payment?"

"Of course," Crespin replied.

"That must be negotiated with the veil, in his palace," Karadi said. "Until then, no other ship may enter the harbor."

"That is acceptable," Crespin said.

THE GOVERNOR'S "palace" was a fortress on a hill overlooking the harbor, built of the same red rock as everything else that wasn't a wattle-and-daub hut—which, on closer inspection, was much of the city. It wasn't obvious from a distance because those humbler buildings had been painted red in imitation of the stone structures.

No great amount of thought seemed to have gone into the design of the fortress itself. The central keep was essentially a cube, surrounded by a second wall that seemed older—probably the defenses of the pirates who had first settled here. Inside it was a tangle of narrow corridors laid out in no particular fashion. It reminded him of the meandering trails small animals tunneled into the thornbushes of his home country.

What had once probably been a central courtyard had been mostly filled with rickety-looking structures of wood and stone several stories high. Walkways connected—and probably supported—the upper reaches.

The veil greeted them in a room which was doubtless meant to impress, both because of its size and because it was adorned with stuffed lions, daggercats, spotted bears, and one sad-looking elephant.

The veil himself sat on a lacquered sea-turtle of prodigious size. A small man with a black beard and mustache, he was kitted out in a robe of peacock feathers. A golden circlet with a single large emerald adorned his brow. A small army of courtiers in similarly garish clothing accompanied Crespin and his men into the hall.

Crespin and Renost bowed to the veil and presented him with a small urn containing a minor fortune in saffron.

"A token of our esteem," he said.

The veil nodded and made a small motion with his hand. Music began—some sort of zither, drums, a fiddle, and a flute. A young woman suddenly took Crespin's arm and tugged on it, and he saw that everyone was beginning to dance. Renost and Hector, too, had partners, although Alkaios was just watching, looking a bit unsettled. Despite the strangeness of the instrumentation Crespin recognized the tune as that of a country carole furet, which began as a circle holding hands and then became more complicated as women dashed across, snatched new partners, and took their places back in the circle.

After a few moments, Crespin began to enjoy himself. A young woman with ebon curls and green eyes took him from his original partner; a trim beauty with some silver in her hair grabbed him next. The dance never paused, one tune following immediately upon another.

When he took a break, he found a moon-faced woman with a hundred oiled braids pushing a flagon into his hand. The drink burned like rum and smelled something like a banana. Another young woman came by and offered him dark red and bright green fruit, and then he was pulled back into the dance.

For a time it went like that—back to the dance, more drink, platters of fried fish, squid, fruit, banana fritters, rice cakes, meatballs spiced with cumin, coriander, garlic, and cardamom. It had been a long time since he'd eaten anything besides ship's fare. Loosened by drink, he almost forgot what he was there for, until Karadi came and escorted him to stand before the veil.

"I hope my humble attempt at hospitality is acceptable," the veil said.

"More than acceptable," Crespin said. "I find it all delightful."

"I am pleased," the veil said. "So, let us talk."

"Very well, sir. You've been informed of our problem?"

"I have, and I should very much like to welcome you. My men can help you with repairs if you wish. Let your sailors spend their pay in our taverns—but not too many at a time, you understand. It will benefit us all."

"That's very kind of your Grace. I will inform the admiral immediately."

"I will have my consent sent to him by lucnograph," the veil said. "You and your companions may continue to enjoy our hospitality."

Crespin had tried not to become drunk, and had very nearly succeeded. Suddenly he felt a bit wary. On the other hand, what could the veil do? Kill him or make him hostage, maybe—but why? In either case his father was likely to sail in and reduce Zamir to a smoldering mess. Such was the Imperial standard when its officers were abused, as was widely known.

The first woman was grabbing at him again, trying to pull him back to the dance.

He had been at sea for a while…

HER NAME was Saja. She was brown and lithe and funny and knew a few tricks that were new to him. They lay together on a quilted bed in a small rooftop garden. The wind was salty and warm, and the stars above glistened like diamonds.

"That was nice," he said, tracing his finger along her inner thigh.

"I thought so, too."

"Can we sleep up here?"

"No," she said. "We have things to do."

"I'm tired," he admitted, "but I'm willing to go again."

She laughed softly. "No, not that. Come along, get dressed."

"Where are we going?"

"Away from here," she said. "I want to show you something." She stood, a pleasing outline against the stars, and reached for a bundle he hadn't seen before. She began dressing, but not in the sarong and chemise of which he had so recently relieved her.

Instead she donned pants, shirt, and leather vest. Puzzled, he started hunting for his own clothes.

"He isn't the veil, you see," Saja said, when he was done. "Come along. Let's find your friends."

"I've no idea where they are."

"They were provided quarters," she replied. "An associate of mine was to lead them there."

RENOST AND Alkaios were curled together on a mat, sound asleep. Crespin prodded them both with his toe.

"Rise up, fellows," he said.

Renost opened one eye. "This is an unkind prank," he replied. "I've only just closed my eyes. It can't be morning."

"It isn't," Crespin said, "but we have business." He nodded at Saja.

"Your belle de la nuit? What of her?"

"Just come along. You, too, Alkaios," he told the big man, who was now also awake. They found Hector in the next room, with the green-eyed woman from the dance. He was already awake and rose without disturbing his companion.

"We must be quiet now," Saja whispered. She led them through narrow corridors out of the fortress. At the edge of the town, she uncovered a cache of sabers and repeating crossbows.

"Captain," Renost said. "A word?"

Crespin nodded at Saja and walked off a little way with his friend.

"Who is this woman," Renost asked, "and just what are we doing with her?"

"She assures me that there is something of importance for me to see," Crespin replied, "and that the veil is not who he says he is.

Something is amiss, here, and I intend to find out what."

"Oh, she *assures* you?" Renost snapped. "And you trust her with our lives... why?"

"We outnumber her, Renost."

"As far as you know, which is not so far as I can throw Alkaios."

"When did you become so cautious, Renost?"

"I know you," Renost said. "Your mind never fully functions when a woman is involved. Are you in love with this one, too? I shouldn't be surprised. It's been the best part of two hours since you met."

"Stay here if you want," Crespin said. "I'm going with her."

"Uhhh," Renost growled.

They armed themselves while Saja lit torches. Then they set off through the dark jungle. It was easily as deep as the woodlands back home, but for the most part the plants were utterly alien to him. The torchlight winked back at them from hundreds of luminous eyes, but whatever bore those glowing orbs rustled and vanished as they drew near.

"It's all right to talk now," Saja said after a time.

"If he's not the veil, then who is he?" Crespin asked.

"His name is Kol," she said. "He was on the veil's staff. They quarreled over something, and he stabbed the veil to death. He disposed of the body and then gave it out that the veil was recalled to Modjal, leaving him in charge."

"How do you know all of this?"

"The veil watches Zamir—but someone must watch the veil."

"You're a spy, then, from Modjal."

"Yes—or I was. This will probably uncover me."

Crespin suddenly felt less than complimented. Her seduction of him had been purely business.

"You understand we can't get involved in local affairs," he said. "We can try to get word to Modjal for you, but that aside—"

"I did not expect you would take my word," Saja said. "Kol knows that eventually he will be called to account. So he has made plans. You need to see."

Crespin could hear the ocean now, breaking against rocks. The trail led uphill, and after perhaps another half an hour they emerged onto a cliff overlooking a natural harbor. Dawn was beginning, and in the early light he saw vessels anchored there, as well as a tent city on the beach. For a moment, he thought it was part of the fleet.

Then he saw that the ships were unfamiliar, and not the long-lined mercantile vessels of his father's command. Rather, he saw galleys, coques, frigates, beles de guerres.

A fleet of war.

Among the ships of sail and timber, six craft lay apart. These were without sail, formed of eldritch line, made more of metal than wood.

Drehhu ships.

CHAPTER TWO

LA MONTAIGNE DEL SORCIER

IT WAS a few days before Selene was steady enough to travel again, which was fine with Hound: after Martin took the arrow out of his leg and burnt the wound with the red-hot tip of a knife, he didn't feel a lot like walking.

He did walk, though, once they set off again. Limping, still refusing to put himself up on one of the big clumsy beasts, although it was offered—often. Rose stayed closer to him than usual, as if she thought she might carry him if need be. The chevaliers and their men were in good spirits, having slaughtered a party nearly twice their size without losing a man. The horse lost to the hell-pig was replaced, and several more acquired in the bargain.

They gave a good bit of the credit to Hound.

Selene was more attentive to him, as well, which he liked. She still seemed a little shaky, but her natural color had returned, and the strange gold of her eyes retreated to little specks.

"Who were those people?" he asked when they stopped for a rest at the edge of a highland meadow, where a small crash of hornless rhinoceroses grazed. "Why did they want to kill you?"

She brushed her gold-shot hair back and looked thoughtful.

"We—Martin and I, the rest—we're trying to do something special. Something very important, but things are complicated. There are some people who would try to stop us if they knew what we were up to. We thought they didn't know. Apparently, we were wrong. Now I'm worried more will come after us."

"I don't think so," Hound said. "They were following your trail. They didn't know where you were going."

"I hope you're right," she said, and she smiled. "It was a lucky day for us when you decided to help us. Luckier than we could have ever known."

He wondered how she would feel if she knew what he had intended.

"How did you do it?" he asked. "That thing you did?"

"I'm a strix," she said, as if that was all the explanation needed.

"I heard someone use that word," he told her. "Scream it, actually. I don't know what it means."

"I guess you wouldn't," she said. "Not all the way out here." She was silent for a moment. "You see, I can get into things," she said finally. "Inside of them. Change them."

"Like the manhunter," he said. "The man with the bow. You got into him and made him kill his own companions."

"It was easy with him—he didn't like them much. He was only with them because he wanted revenge on you."

"How do you do it? Can I learn?"

"No." She shook her head. "Or at least probably not. Only a

few—very few—males are able. Most are not. As to how I do it, that, I'm afraid, is my secret."

"You can enter any living thing?"

"And many things that are not alive."

"But it hurts you when you do it?"

She gave him a wan smile and patted his shoulder.

"That is enough on this topic."

FIVE DAYS later, scouting ahead, Hound saw the mountain with three peaks. By the end of the next day they reached a valley that led up to it. Before they began their descent into the valley, however, Hound noticed an upright stone. Although it was covered in lichen, he saw some sort of symbols that were carved on it.

Martin approached the stone cautiously, and when he touched it he quickly drew his hand back as if he feared it was hot. When nothing happened, he brushed back the moss, then muttered a few words in a language Hound had never heard before.

"Quel?" one of the chevaliers said.

"La Montaigne del Sorcier," Martin replied.

"What does that mean?" Hound asked.

"It means we're in the right place," Selene told him.

Hound nodded. He had noticed another scratching in the rock, this one more recent—a simple picture of a man with a little oval for a body, a circle for a head, lines for arms and fingers. He had only one very long leg, which—as it extended—looked more like a tail. He had seen the symbol before, on a stone much like this one, at the boundary of Grandmother's forest. The Kansa left it as a warning not to enter uninvited.

"A dangerous place," Hound said.

She nodded grimly.

THE VALLEY was pleasant enough, full of game and with no sign whatsoever of human presence. Even in the comparative wilderness they had crossed, they had occasionally found hunting trails. None of them led to the mountain, though, and in the valley there were none at all.

When they reached the foot of the mountain, it was midafternoon. The sky was clear, but in the distance, Hound heard what sounded like a crack of thunder, and the ground beneath him quivered, as if something truly huge was moving beneath the surface. Martin flinched visibly and began peering along the slopes above. All the men put their hands to weapons. It took several long moments of silence before they relaxed again, to a degree, and began setting up camp. Everyone seemed uneasy; aside from the familiar motions of gathering wood and grooming the horses, Hound sensed a great deal of uncertainty, as if even Martin did not know what would happen now.

He rested for a while, then limped up a little higher so he could have a better view of the valley. He hadn't gone all that far when he glimpsed movement through the trees.

Crouching behind a pine, he watched as three men on horseback emerged from behind a slope. They approached Selene and her party. They were dressed in chainmail and breastplates, and wore conical helmets decorated with plumes of raven feathers. Each possessed a lance and a sword, but none of them had anything in hand.

He took a stone and placed it in his sling.

Martin and Selene walked out to meet the horsemen. Hound could hear them talking, but couldn't make out what they were saying. After a few moments, Martin said something to the chevaliers, and their men started packing up again. Moments later, they mounted up and began to follow the newcomers.

Hound dithered for a moment, but his curiosity got the better of him and he started down the slope to rejoin them. Just as he came into the open, he saw Selene's face, turned back toward him. She shook her head *no* and motioned for him to stay back.

He squatted back down, wondering what exactly was happening. There had been talk of payment, and although he had scoffed at it, he had imagined he would be offered something when his part was done—if nothing else, a goodbye. The more he thought about it, the more he remembered Selene's gesture and the expression on her face, the more he became convinced that she didn't want the new arrivals to know about him. Just in case...

Just in case what?

He waited a few more moments and began tracking them.

Their trail led around the skirt of the mountain, and when night came, they didn't stop. He didn't either, relying on Rose's keen sense of smell to find the way. The air was cool and damp, and frogmouths exchanged high-pitched chuckles in the branches above. A gloom-owl whooped, quite near, and Soot scratched nervously on his shoulder. The villagers, he remembered, thought gloom-owls foretold of particularly bad luck, usually sickness or death.

Around midnight there was an earsplitting stroke of thunder, but no flash of lightning, and the sky was clear. The earth shook again. Hound remembered the earlier, distant sound. Rose growled deep in her throat.

He picked up his pace.

They didn't have far to go. The moon was risen and nearly full, so he could see that the tracks entered a bowl-shaped depression in the living stone of the fell. But no tracks came out of it.

Selene and the rest were simply gone.

He knelt to study the depression more carefully. It was curiously regular, and there was nothing in it at all, not even a leaf. He picked up a fallen branch and tossed it in. It bounced and rattled to a stop. He reached to touch the surface and found it smooth, as if it had been polished.

"What is this, Rose?" he wondered, quietly. He stood and paced around it—then stopped when he came to a low-hanging tree branch that ended a few paces from the outside of the circle. It had been cut off, and the exposed wood was as smooth as the stone, but it hadn't crossed into the circle.

He turned his gaze upward and began to understand. Branches there had been severed, as well. He realized that whatever had made the dimple in the earth had been in the shape of a large ball, and everything that had been in it was gone—stone, branches, Selene.

But gone where?

Did it really matter? Or was it time to return home?

No. If he didn't find out what happened here, he knew it would drive him crazy. He found a tree in which to take his rest.

THE NEXT morning, he sent Soot out to look for Selene and Martin—or anyone else in or around the mountain—while he and Rose foraged for breakfast. He was surprised when the raven returned just after midday, clicking and whistling that he had found something. Hound waited while Soot picked at what was left of the deer carcass, and then they set off.

Following the bird, back the way they had come the night before, he passed the aborted campsite and continued onward, climbing a long ridge that curled up one flank of the highest peak. It was hard going with his wounded leg, and he had to stop frequently. Eventually he was stopped completely by a sheer rock face that soared upward twice as high as his best sling-cast. Soot flew on, soaring higher and higher, drawing Hound's gaze up the vertical stone. There, the bird—a speck so tiny he wouldn't have noticed him if he hadn't been watching the whole while—settled onto something.

At first, Hound thought it was just a cleft in the rock, but then he saw that the shape was regular. Arched, in fact. Now that his eye had picked it out, he made out another the same size and shape—and then several more.

Someone had carved windows into the mountain.

What was behind the windows?

He sat down to ponder the matter.

CHAPTER THREE

FIRST
ENGAGEMENT

THE DREHHU ships were stranger than Crespin had imagined. They were shaped like boats, with pointed bows and flat sterns, but were proportionally broader than the ships Crespin knew. Round holes pierced the above-water hull, six or seven to a side. Behind these, he knew, were weapons.

Each had no sails, no mast, just one long enclosed cabin. The top of the cabin was flat, creating a sort of upper deck. Toward the back of the ships, some type of machinery protruded from the deck—pipes or metal coils, he couldn't be sure.

"Why are they here?" he said. "I can understand why the false veil would invite them here, but what advantage is there for the Drehhu in this remote place?"

"The Drehhu know the three empires plan to attack them," Saja replied.

For a moment Crespin felt trapped. Who was Saja, really? A spy from Modjal, or an ally of the Drehhu trying to gain information from him? Perhaps Renost was right.

"What are you talking about?"

She rolled her eyes. "You don't really think such a massive undertaking would go unnoticed, did you?"

Actually, Crespin had, but he'd been naïve. The Drehhu possessed enormous wealth, and certainly would use some fraction of it to maintain sources inside of the three empires. With the thousands of persons involved in the planning, there was surely plenty of free talk. He himself had spread the news in Bellship. He hadn't been instructed not to, or ever imagined Drehhu spies in his hometown.

"They're building ships," Renost said. He pointed beyond the tents. There, indeed, were more of the uncanny vessels in various stages of construction. Many were nearly finished. They couldn't build ships without forges, timber cutters, metal, steady supplies of food, and who knew what went into their engines and weapons. Zamir must be supplying most of that, along with the bulk of the fleet laid out before him.

This was a major undertaking.

"The ships from Ophion Magne must tack this way to reach the eastward winds," Crespin reasoned, "and they will pass through the Pitch Pot, just as we did. If they are becalmed, they will make easy targets for the Drehhu ships, which have no need of wind.

"How long have they been here?" he asked Saja.

"Four months. As you can see, they've been using their time well."

Crespin walked his gaze over the strange vessels and their occupants. Most were human; the Drehhu as a race were few, but rich in slaves which made up the majority of both their workforce and their military. Yet the handful of masters he saw were easy to spot, because they weren't shaped exactly like men. They were half again the size of the largest human. Their shoulders were extremely broad, legs and arms too long and almost the same length. Sometimes they went on all fours, at which time there was something spider-like about them.

None of them were close enough for him to make out their features.

"Merde," Renost said. "Let's get back to the admiral."

"They're making ready," Renost said. He waved his hands not at the Drehhu ships, but at the mass of more conventional vessels. Indeed, the crews were preparing to sail.

"We have time," Saja told him, pointing east, where the arms of the bay extended. "It will take time for them to leave the harbor. To attack your fleet, they then must go around the headland. Traveling in the light, we can return to Zamir in less than an hour."

AS THEY raced back through the forest, Crespin desperately hoped they *did* have enough time. The Mesembrian fleet would probably be in the harbor now, anchored, sails furled. Plump quail with no legs.

Fortunately, they weren't as far from the city as he thought. The darkness and the pace it entailed had made it seem more. Soon Zamir was visible ahead of them. He was just beginning to count his fortunes when an arrow grazed his arm, cutting a neat, bloody score through his shirt.

Renost yelped. They all took cover behind trees.

A party of perhaps fifteen men was waiting in ambush. Someone was cursing at one of the men for loosing too early.

Crespin unslung his crossbow, as did the others. Despite its overly ornate design, it was put together like the typical repeating weapon the Navy issued. His left hand supported the length of the bow, a stock rested it against his shoulder, and his right hand worked the trigger. Along the bottom of the weapon was a metal slide. When he pulled it toward him, it drew back the bowstring and dropped a quarrel into place. It could be shot seven times before needing to be reloaded.

He glanced over at Renost, who flashed him a devil's grin. Then his friend leapt from cover and ran toward their attackers, weaving left and right.

"Shoot at me?" Renost shouted. "I'll knob your widows tonight!"

"Merde," Crespin muttered. He found one of the bowmen tracking Renost with the tip of his arrow, and sent a bolt at him. The fellow jerked back as it struck his chest, and now Crespin leapt up, too, trying to spot his next target. He found his intended victim just in time to watch him crumple, courtesy of either Saja or maybe Hector. Alkaios was charging, just behind Renost. Crespin eyed another bowman, released another quarrel, and pierced him through the thigh.

Renost stopped his charge, stood straight, took aim, and shot. Then he dropped the crossbow and unsheathed his saber.

Crespin aimed at the next man he saw, discharged, and ran after them. By the time he reached the enemy, only one bowman remained, trying desperately to find a target in Renost, who was dancing with three swordsmen, his curved blade flicking and whirling seemingly in all directions at once. Crespin brought his bow up, but a quarrel from Saja appeared in his target's belly.

The soldier bent over and stumbled away from the fight.

Dropping the crossbow, Crespin drew his sword and charged toward Alkaios, who had four enemies converging on him with naked blades. The marinier turned in circles, waiting for one of them to come at him. One did, just as Crespin arrived, and another yelled a warning.

Two men broke off from Alkaios to favor him.

Crespin had no intention of letting them flank him. He feinted at the one in front, then cut savagely at the man coming around on his left. Startled, the man managed to lift his weapon to parry the head-cut—but that, too, was a feint. With a turn of his wrist Crespin instead pulled his blade through the crook of his enemy's arm. The forearm dropped limp, hanging by a thread of tissue.

Crespin almost fell as he scrambled back from the other fellow. He tried desperately to get his sword up to meet the wild attack, but knew in his gut he didn't have time.

Then the man staggered. He reached up to his neck and found the bolt that had impaled it. He tried to pull it out, making a weird gargling that was probably an attempt at a scream. Crespin ran him through.

There was a sudden gasp behind him, and he turned to see another man staring at him, mouth agape, a wicked curved blade poised over his head. Crespin swung his blade around, but the fellow crumpled, revealing Hector behind him, withdrawing his own sword from the assassin's back. Crespin felt a ghost walk along his spine toward the grave. If Hector hadn't been there…

"My thanks."

"A little of nothing," Hector replied, wiping his blade. "This one was skulking in the underbrush, like a viper."

"It's a good thing I had my mongoose with me, then," Crespin said.

The battle seemed to be over. Alkaios was cut in two places on his arms. One of his attackers was on the ground, his face smashed in, probably by the guard of the big man's weapon. The other looked as if he'd had his neck broken. Renost was leaning against a tree, panting.

"That's it?" he asked.

Saja stepped from the forest. "There's one more," she said. "I shot him, but I don't think he's dead."

Before Crespin could say anything, she trotted off into the trees, and returned a few moments later.

"That's all," she said.

"Do you smell smoke?" Renost asked.

A GRAY-BLACK haze lay on the harbor.

Christ of Ophion, they've fired our ships during the night, Crespin thought.

Then he realized the ships weren't burning—Zamir was. The fleet of Ophion was no longer at the edge of the harbor, but massed within striking distance of the city—and was in fact bombarding it with burning missiles launched from quilaines.

Down at the docks, a land battle raged. The *Panther* was still there, and two other ships. A troop of xelons had landed and were pushing inland against a mass of Zamirans.

"That looks like the fight we ought to be in," Renost said.

Crespin glanced at Alkaios. His arms had been bandaged with cloth from his shirt.

"I'm fine, sir," he grunted.

"Good man," Crespin said. "Spread out behind the left flank and take cover behind whatever isn't burning. Then start shooting from behind them. Yell a lot. Make it seem as if there are more of us than there are." He waited until they all had positions, then let out a war-whoop and shot into the press.

For a moment the enemy line held, but as the men in it realized they were being assaulted from the rear, they began to panic, to flee or try to locate their new attackers. That gave the xelons a chance to roll up that flank and envelope the pirates, who also seemed poorly trained. Within moments, the Zamirans were in full rout. The way to the *Panther* was clear.

Crespin and his companions continued to the docks. D'Arza, the captain from the *Sea Eagle* met him there.

"There's an enemy fleet," Crespin informed him. "Just up the coast, on its way here. They have Drehhu vessels with them."

D'Arza's eyes widened. Then he turned to his lieutenant.

"Alert the admiral by lucnograph," he said. He turned back to Crespin. "How long do you think we have?"

Crespin turned to Saja.

"The most of a day," she said. "Depending on the wind."

The lieutenant sprinted off toward the lucnograph.

"What's happening here?" Crespin asked.

A grim smile settled over D'Arza's face. "They sent rowboats out after the moon was down," he said. "Tried to fire our ships with pitch, but your father had the strixes on low watch and they were found out—although they did manage to torch the *Melisande*. We had to retaliate, of course." He looked a bit uncomfortable. "It was assumed that you were slain or imprisoned, so…"

"No, I understand," Crespin said. "I know imperial policy, I can assure you."

A moment later the lieutenant returned.

"We're to break off here and go to meet the Zamiran flotilla." He turned to Crespin. "Captain," he said, "you are to remain in the command of the *Panther* and get her underway as soon as possible. Relay to the admiral whatever information you may have regarding the size of the enemy force."

"Very well," Crespin said. He turned to Saja. "Thank you," he said. "What will you do now? If Kol knows you betrayed him, you will be in grave danger. You can come with us, but it may be no safer."

She stepped up and kissed him.

"I'll manage," she said. "I have things to do here yet."

ANXIOUS TO get underway, Crespin paced the deck of the *Panther*, urging the crew to speed and even lending his own hand to the rigging. The *Leucothea* and a few of the ships farther out were already under sail. The winds were fair, but it was assured that the *Panther* would be in the rear of the fleet.

Crespin called for the ship's strixe and began assembling his men. Like most of the other merchant ships in the fleet, the *Panther* had been supplied with soldiers from the Imperial Army, and there were two sorts—the xelons and the infantry. Xelons were armored head-to-toe and bore steel-plated shields the size and shape of doors. They were armed with long, stout spears and short swords in case a spear was broken or carried off in the body of an enemy. They were most often employed as the first wave of a landing on hostile soil, but had their uses shipboard as well.

The infantrymen were hardly armored at all. Most were equipped with bow and cutlass, and many took up positions in the rigging to better use the former. The xelons arranged themselves on the bow, locking their shields together, as the infantrymen strung their bows.

The lack of military experience in the crews of the merchant ships began to show. The captains of the ships were as capable as any military commander when it came to managing their own craft, but merchant ships generally traveled alone, and getting into formation wasn't something with which most of them had a lot of experience—especially the formation his father had in mind, which was like nothing Crespin had ever seen. Rather than coming together in a line to face the enemy like a moving wall, the admiral had them organized into four columns. The *Panther* was at the back of the column that had the *Leucothea* at the front.

They had not quite cleared the harbor when the enemy ships appeared. The largest had already established a long line, with the six Drehhu vessels spaced evenly among them, two of them making up the ends.

"I wonder how this will go," Renost murmured as he and Hector stepped up alongside their friend.

"However it goes," Hector said, "I suspect I will have work to do."

"Do you have everything you need?" Crespin asked.

"The surgery is not as well-supplied as the one on the *Leucothea*," Hector said, "but I will make do."

IN CONTRAST to the tales of glory spread by the romances, the naval manuals made it clear that no Drehhu fleet had ever been defeated unless confronted by at least four times its number. The wars with the ancient enemy had been won, not by strategy or heroics, but by massive sacrifice of life. Humans lived for fewer years and bred faster than the Drehhu. Over the centuries, that had proven to be an advantage, but in individual encounters, it was bad to be a man in a fight against the Drehhu.

Now they had the strix, upon which some pinned much hope. Crespin had his doubts, but at least most of the ships they faced were of the ordinary sort. He observed the Zamiran line, which was fast becoming an arc.

"They'll encircle us," Crespin muttered. "This is mad."

Flame and smoke billowed suddenly from the holes in the Drehhu ships. An instant after the flare, a rolling *boom* sounded flat and hard across the waves, surprisingly loud. Two of the ships at the heads of the columns—the *Sovereign* and the *Bastard*—suddenly burst into flames. Or rather, their sails did. None of the Mesembrian ships returned fire. They were still too far out of range.

The *Leucothea* survived the first volley intact and swept toward the easternmost ship in the Drehhu arc. The enemy ship gouted more smoke from its side. A few seconds later, Crespin heard the sound. Observing the *Leucothea* almost through her stern, he couldn't see what damage she might have suffered. Whatever the case, she kept going, right into the next volley.

Fire was everywhere now, and at least three of their ships seemed to be taking on water. They were about to be routed by a flotilla a fraction of their size.

And then the Drehhu ship nearest the *Leucothea* exploded, her rear deck buckling suddenly upward, flame and smoke boiling up in a ball, tongues of fire lapping from the weapon ports. Booms swung on the *Leucothea* as she changed course and approached the next enemy ship. She met with another thundering volley, and then that Drehhu vessel also exploded. With that his father's ship gracefully steered away from the enemy line, listing slightly in the water, several of her sheets in flames.

For a moment, Crespin watched, dumbfounded.

"What did that?" Renost yelped, echoing Crespin's astonishment.

"The strixe," Crespin said. "Calliope."

"Seinte Merde," Renost said.

Meantime, they had come into range of less arcane weapons. Like flocks of darkling sparrows, arrows flew up from both fleets, passing through one another on their deadly flights, and then the larger missiles from quilaines, some leaving fuming black trails from the burning pitch that clung to them.

This, at least, was warfare Crespin understood, but he began to see that his father's strategy was effective here as well. He had been entirely dubious of this plan when they discussed it. Now it was just another thing he had been wrong about.

The heavily armed Zamiran ships presented broadside, to better use their own quilaines. The Mesembrian ships had far fewer such weapons, but what they did have were concentrated on their prows. Entering the fight nose-first, they offered far less target.

The remaining Drehhu ships, unbound by wind, swiftly came around their flank, doing unbelievable damage as they came, setting sails aflame and shattering hulls. Two ships ahead of Crespin bore off to intercept the easternmost, and Crespin ordered his helmsman to do the same.

Finally, the *Panther*'s strixe arrived on deck.

Crespin had met her briefly upon taking command. She looked about thirty, with perpetually sunken yellow eyes and lank brown hair strewn with dull golden threads. He couldn't remember where she was from, but her name was Elpis.

When she appeared, the *Panther* was the third ship in their column away from the enemy, but soon they were the second, as the *Kraken* succumbed to the Drehhu weapons. Her mainmast splintered and sheet blazing, she steered away, taking on water. The *Nerrea*, next ship in line, hammered the Drehhu vessels with blazing quilaine bolts, but the metal skin of the strange ships turned them away as easily as a stout shield deflected arrows. The patches of flames they left sputtered impotently out. The enemy seemed impervious to any weapon.

The strixe, Crespin grimly realized, would be their only hope.

"Are you ready?" he asked her.

"Ready, sir," Elpis said. She had the same distant, dreamy quality that Calliope had possessed the day of the storm, and appeared even more unsteady on her feet. Her eyes seemed unable to fix on any one thing.

"You'll know when we're close enough?"

She nodded. "It's different for all of us," she said. "All the little maidens, so the same, so different. Rainbows with all the wrong colors. Different from day to day, or night to tide."

She may have noticed the confusion on his face.

"I will know," she said. "I made sure."

Something dribbled from her left nostril. He might have assumed it to be blood, but it was the color of saffron. Elpis began humming a changeable, antic tune, now and then blurting words that didn't make any sense.

Another volley from the Drehhu, this one aimed at the Nerrea. Crespin felt as much as heard the impact, and saw one of the Nerrea's sails catch fire, but an instant later, several of the Drehhu weapons exploded in their mounts. The arcane vessel kept coming, however, and its remaining weapons fired again, thundering into the Nerrea.

Mortally wounded, the Mesembrian vessel limped off to the south, taking on water.

The Panther was alone on the eastern flank.

A glance around revealed that the middle was broken, and the Mesembrian fleet was encircling the Zamirans from there and from both ends. Fully two-thirds of the enemy ships were gone; Crespin wasn't certain what the Mesembrian losses were.

At first, he thought the Drehhu ship was turning to run, but that was wishful thinking. It was instead churning directly toward them, aiming to ram.

"Steady!" Crespin told the steersman.

The enemy had two weapon-holes on her bow, and smoke jetted from them. Something smashed into the line of xelons at the forward rail; Crespin watched in astonished horror as one of the men spun half-around and just—fell apart.

The dead warrior's companions closed the gap as two infantrymen dragged the parts of his body clear of the line.

"There's my work," Hector said, and then ran to see who was wounded and who was dead.

Crespin forced himself to look away and instead turn to Elpis. Her eyes were closed, and she seemed to have half-turned around a corner that wasn't there. He could not see all of her, but could not explain *why* or what it was he couldn't see. A yellow mist oozed from her lips and from beneath her eyelids, even from the pores of her flesh.

As the Drehhu ship gathered speed, the yellow cloud reached toward it.

"Now," she sighed.

"Bear off," Crespin shouted. "One-quarter to estribord."

The weapons fired again, one striking the *Panther* below her bowsprit and the other tearing through a yard.

Elpis' song turned to more of a groan. Her body contorted, her head twisted back grotesquely.

The diabolical ship came on. A Drehhu stood on the bow, and Crespin could see his face—broader than human, almost square. His expression might have been one of contempt as he raised some sort of weapon and pointed it at them. It looked something like a blowgun, but the Drehhu didn't put it to his mouth.

Whatever it was, it exploded, sending the Drehhu staggering back, screaming in a surprisingly shrill voice, given his size. He didn't scream for long, however, because the entire ship went up in a fireball, just as the others had.

The strixe lifted so that only her toes were on the deck, and her hair drifted as though she was underwater.

Another, she whispered—or he thought she did. Her lips had not moved, but the word was there, in his head. Suppressing a shudder, he ordered the *Panther* turned toward the remaining Drehhu vessel. It was farther away but bearing toward them—or perhaps past them to the open sea. The yellow mist reached out, and flame and steam plumed from their attacker.

Elpis settled back onto the deck. Golden tears poured from the corners of her eyes. She opened her mouth as if to speak but vomited instead, a yellow torrent.

She looked up at him.

"Oh," she said.

And then folded down into the pool of gold.

CHAPTER FOUR

VISITORS

"ORRA," VEULKH said, as he lay back on his pillow and stroked her side. "Do you remember Hala?"

"The enchantress of Nightbrimm," Ammolite replied. "We visited her once, a long time ago."

"Yes," he said. "I've lately learned she is dead."

"Oh," she said. "I'm sorry."

He tilted his head. "She was always a bit careless," he replied. "She liked attention too much, for one thing. Liked to be seen."

"What happened to her?"

"There's no telling," he said. "I didn't ask them." He groaned and then sat up, swinging his legs off the bed. "That reminds me," he said. "I have work to do."

"Please do not leave me, my love," she murmured.

He smiled, and then something changed in his eyes.

"Are you mocking me?" he asked, softly.

She reached for his hand and took it in her own.

"Never," she promised.

His face softened and he stood up, reaching for a robe.

"I will be late," he said. "You need not wait for me."

As Ammolite watched him leave the room, a warm shiver ran through her as her appearance changed. She rose quickly and went to the wash basin, scrubbing her body, trying to get the smell of him off her. Then she put on a black silk robe and left his room. There was no place she hated more, and every second she spent away from it was dear to her.

She had long ago figured out that the wine had something to do with her transformation—it was offered to her every night. Even a little was enough, but she found things easier if she drank a lot. Sometimes, like tonight, she felt the need for perhaps a little more afterward. Sometimes, if she drank enough, the next day she didn't remember the previous night at all.

Going to the table she poured herself a glass, gulped it down, and then poured another. She picked a little meat from her uneaten meal and wrapped it in a table linen. Then she went to her balcony.

Veulkh had come to her early tonight, and there was still light outside. She watched the sunset, trying to focus on the play of color in the sky, on the breeze against her face and the faint evergreen scent of the thuja clinging to crevices in the cliff.

She heard a flutter of wings and saw with delight that her friend the raven was back. He had appeared a few days earlier, and she had taken to feeding him scraps from the kitchen. She took the meat from the linen and held it out to him. He cocked his head, croaked, then made a little clicking sound.

"You still don't trust me." She sighed, and placed the food on the balustrade. The raven waited for her to move away, then picked at the meat.

Ammolite leaned out a little, looking down, wondering how long it would take to fall all the way to the valley floor. She supposed she could discover that by dropping something and counting, but realized she didn't really want to know. She did try to imagine the fall, the wind pushing on her, lifting her like a bird, like her friend the raven, to fly far and far away.

It might be her only escape. Her dream of finding Veulkh's secret, mortal heart—of killing him—seemed just that. A dream. Years of searching and reading hadn't offered her any new clues. She had begun to doubt the heart existed at all. Veulkh was hundreds, maybe thousands of years old. Maybe he was truly immortal, and she had no hope of ending him. But *she* was mortal enough.

She could escape into limbo.

There was a slight sound behind her and she turned, expecting to find one of the servants there.

He was young, maybe younger than her, with a wild head of chestnut hair barely restrained in a ponytail. He was dressed in embroidered skins, and had a little ax shoved into his belt. His eyes were almond-shaped and the orbs nearly black. She had never seen him before.

The raven fluttered over and settled on his shoulder.

"I hope you aren't going to scream," he said.

Ammolite realized two things at once. She was pretty drunk, and this boy did not belong here. Like the raven, he was from outside.

"Why should I scream?"

"Maybe I frighten you," he said. "I don't know."

A thought formed rather suddenly. She knew Veulkh had safeguards against any unwelcome person entering his manse. How had this boy come here? Was he armed with some potent magic, perhaps by a rival sorcerer?

"Are you—are you here to kill Veulkh?" she asked.

"I don't know anyone by that name," he said, "and as for killing, I have no particular plans one way or the other. It depends on the situation."

"What have you come for, then?"

He pursed his lips for a moment.

"My name is Hound," he said.

Then he just looked at her expectantly. He obviously wanted her to say something, but she couldn't figure out just what. Why had he told her his name instead of answering her question?

"And your name is…?"

"Oh," she said, feeling stupid. "I'm…"

For a horrible moment, the only name she could think of was Orra. Veulkh hadn't called her anything else in years, and no one else ever spoke to her. Then she remembered.

"Ammolite," she said. "I'm Ammolite."

"I like that name," he said. "Are you from this place, Ammolite?"

The sound of her name chimed like a golden bell. It made her gasp.

"What's the matter?"

"Just—no one's ever asked for my name before. It's been a long time since anyone's even said it."

He grinned. "Ammolite," he said.

She felt dizzy and dropped her gaze from his dark eyes.

"I wasn't born here," she said, "but I don't remember anyplace else."

"Your parents live here?"

"I never knew my parents—although Veulkh says my mother sold me to him."

"Sold you?"

"Of course. I'm a slave."

He looked a little confused for a moment, and then his eyes widened.

"Oh," he said, and then he paused. "I didn't know my mother or father either," he finally said. "We have that in common."

"I guess so," she said, wondering why it mattered enough to say.

"This Veulkh fellow then—he's your master?"

"Yes," she replied.

"And there are other people here?"

"Yes. Other slaves, and the ravens—"

"Ravens?"

"Oh!" She smiled. "Men, not birds. His guards. It's just what he calls them."

"I see," he replied.

"How did you get here, Hound?" she asked.

"I climbed," he said.

"No," she said. "That doesn't seem possible."

"It took a long time," he said.

She looked back down the cliff face, wondering if he could be telling the truth. He had arrived somehow.

"Why?" she asked.

"I'm looking for some people," he said. "A woman named Selene, a man named Martin, other men in armor, with swords."

"I don't know those names," she said, "but then, I don't know everyone's name." In truth, she hardly knew anyone's name, but was embarrassed to tell him that much.

"These people would be new, only arrived a few days ago."

"No," she said. "I've seen no one new, but I suppose I could look, if you wanted."

"I would like that very much," he said, and he smiled. "You know, I've never met anyone like you before."

"What do you mean?"

"I just haven't," he said. "Do you know where you're from?"

"No," she said. "Veulkh said he bought me in a place called Basilisk, but he also said I wasn't from there." Her eyes shifted to the raven. "Is he your bird?"

"Soot? He's nobody's bird, but he helps me out. In return, he eats well." He glanced at the linen in her hand. "Although it looks like he has a new friend."

"I believed so," she replied. "I guess he was just waiting on you to climb."

"I don't suppose you have any more food, do you?" he asked. "I haven't eaten much lately."

Ammolite studied him for a moment. She knew she shouldn't be talking to him. If Veulkh found out, there was no guessing what he would do. But she wanted to talk to him more. Much more.

"Stay here," she said. "If you see or hear anyone who isn't me, you should hide."

SHE WAS afraid he would be gone when she returned, but he was still there. Between mouthfuls, he told her something about his journeys and the world outside. She listened with fascination to his unfamiliar voice. The way he looked at her, she knew that eventually he would tire of talking, take off her clothes, and lie on her as Veulkh did, but she hoped to keep him chatting for a while before that happened. So she asked him every question that came into her head, and something began to take shape in her—the outline of a possibility.

If Hound knew a way up, he would know a way down, and he could show her. And then…

She didn't know what. Something better.

Ammolite didn't say any of that to Hound, because in the darker corners of her mind a worry also took form—that Hound might be some conjuration of Veulkh's, sent to test her loyalty. Or he might be Veulkh himself, in disguise, having some sort of fun at her expense.

Hound finally yawned, and did stop talking, and she braced herself for what was to come.

"I'll find a place to sleep and meet you back here tomorrow," Hound said. "Send something with Soot when you want to meet me." Then he left.

She stood there awhile, alone and confused.

THE NEXT morning she woke with a headache, but was relieved to discover she was alone in the bed. Veulkh had not returned. She went down and bathed, then dressed and—feeling a little better—set off in search of Hound's friends. She did not think she would find them. Veulkh did not have visitors, at least not to her knowledge.

It was true that many sought his services; he had told her so, but the requests—and the payment—came through his ravens. Yet there was much she did not know, and Veulkh's manse was immense, sprawling through the living rock of the mountain, and any number of visitors could be hidden in it. He told her that once it had been like a small city, with hundreds of slaves and servants, but that was now many years in the past. She believed that the number of people in his service had declined, even in her lifetime.

She remembered his comment about Hala's death, then. If he had just received word of it, someone must have brought the news. It could have been one of the ravens, of course, but something about the way he said it—he had referred to the bearers of the news vaguely as "them." He was usually much more specific. "*Kos told me…*"

Passing through the old halls where no one went anymore, she moved through a courtyard lit by a tiny shaft high, high above. A tangle of wild vines reached vainly for the distant opening. Their roots had cracked the baroquely patterned tile of the floor. When she was little, she had come here to watch the bats fly out in the evening. She went further, passing through galleries of paintings palled in dust, statues of bronze and marble, collections of glass in many forms.

The next hall was empty, a cavernous space where her footfalls composed a music of echoes. About then, she began to realize how pointless her search was.

Veulkh did not trust anyone. He believed there were many people who wanted to murder him, and guarded himself well. If he had visitors, they would not be in the abandoned, forgotten regions of the house. He would keep them near, under his control, probably someplace where only he could come and go. The sort of place she would never find by looking for it.

And then she knew where to go.

She returned to his rooms and found him in the conjury. He wasn't doing anything that she could see, other than staring off into the distance. She went back downstairs and put on a dress: a new one of fine brocade, dark green, with seven buttons on each sleeve and fifty down the front. She drank a glass of wine and went to him.

When he saw her he began to frown, but then she felt Orra slip into her, fill her out, and he smiled.

"What is it, my love?" he asked.

"I've missed you," she said. "You did not come back to bed last night."

"No," he said. "I suppose I didn't."

"Is something wrong? Is there anything I can do?"

He shook his head.

She stepped nearer.

"I like you in your conjury," she said. "In your power."

"I am powerful wherever I go," he said.

"But here you *are* your power," she replied. "From here you strike fear in the hearts of kings. From here you command the winds."

She laid a hand on his cheek.

"If you're trying to distract me," he said, "you're doing well." He took her hand and began to lead her back to the stair.

"No," she whispered in his ear. "Here. In your conjury. Let it be here."

His eyes took on a fierce light and he drew her to him, more roughly than usual.

The stone was hard on her back, at times so much so that she had to twist cries of pain into counterfeit moans of pleasure. But it was over much more quickly than usual, and then he was gasping on top of her, an unfamiliar look in his eyes.

"Orra," he moaned. "If only…" He trailed off, his gaze distant for a moment, but then focusing on her with terrible intensity. "I can't do without you," he said.

It seemed as if, in that instant, he was no longer talking to Orra, but to *her*, and in the gap of her next breath Ammolite felt a longing she couldn't name or even recognize.

"You never will have to," she said, trying to sound confident, like Orra. "I will always be yours."

He shuddered, then, and lifted himself off her, rising to pace a few steps with his back to her. To Ammolite, it felt like the moment had come—and that it would quickly pass if she did not act.

"Is this about Hala?" she asked. "Did they bring other bad news?"

"They came to employ me," he muttered.

And there it was. Her chest tightened, wondering what he would do when he realized what he had just given away, how she would explain to him that she knew he had visitors.

Now was not the time to falter.

"You are what you are," she said. "Emperors cast gold at your feet. Let them beg you for what they want. Let them grovel before you. I should like to see that."

He studied her for a moment.

"Do you think I am afraid of them?" he asked. "Is that what you think?"

"I do not," she replied.

"Dress yourself," he said. He watched her as she did so, before putting his own robe back on. Then he took her hand and led her across the conjury to the larger door that was always locked. He placed his hand on it and she saw all the muscles of his arm tighten. It seemed as though he was striving against the solid stone. His features blurred and she felt a tingle across her bare flesh. His breathing became convulsive and the veins on his head stood out.

Then the door opened with a slight click and swung wide.

Beyond was an equally wide hall. He led her past chambers stacked with bags of grain, salt, spices, preserved meat, cloth—all the necessities and luxuries of life. It had never occurred to her to wonder where her meals and clothes came from, and she realized she still did not know. These things were merely stored here; from where and how they had arrived was still a mystery.

Further on were more storehouses, filled with swords, spears, arrows, armor, and many things she did not recognize at all. Now and then, passages turned from the hallway they followed, but Veulkh ignored them, taking her straight toward another large door. Stone statues stood either side of this last section, each unique, each turned to watch anyone who approached. In all, there were four of them. One was decidedly male, his naked body patterned in scales. His arms became serpents, and horns curved from his forehead. Across from him was a woman with stars for eyes and the fangs of an asp. The next, male, seemed to be formed of flame and smoke, and the final statue, another female, rose from a plume of water. Wings grew from her forehead.

This door opened easily. Beyond it lay a large hall, with a long, elaborately patterned carpet leading to an armchair carved from some sort of dark green stone and incised with sigils and symbols she had seen in his books. Kos and four other ravens were in the room.

He continued to the throne, to a tapestry behind it that depicted the eight winds as feathered dragons. He lifted the edge, revealing a little door through which they passed into a chamber just large enough for someone to stand in.

"Remain here," he said. "Make no sound."

She stood still, and he closed the door.

It was dark inside, so she quickly found a spyhole by the light it let in. Pressing her eye to it, she saw Veulkh speaking to Kos. The raven then left, and Veulkh seated himself on his throne. From her vantage point, all she could see of him was his left arm.

After a time, Kos returned with a new man, escorted by two more ravens. The man was naked, the first person she had ever seen unclothed other than Veulkh and herself in the mirror. He was put together pretty much the same way Veulkh was, but he was somewhat thicker in every dimension, and heavily scarred, especially on the arms and legs. There was a sort of dimple in his chin. He held his head up, and there was no fear in his eyes.

"Lord Veulkh—" the man began.

"Kneel," Veulkh snapped.

The man cocked his head, shrugged, and took a knee.

"Both knees," Veulkh said.

The man did as he was told.

"Tell me why you are here," Veulkh demanded.

"As I explained yesterday, we have need of your—"

"Why are you *here*," Veulkh interrupted. "In my home? There are ways of contacting me, a procedure to petition my favor, but you came to my *home*. Why?"

"Because," the man said, "we could not trust that procedure. Not now. Not with something this important."

"I decide what is important," Veulkh said. "Not the Cryptarchia. Me."

"The archmystai believed this was the only way to contact you without drawing attention," the man said. "The enemies of the Cryptarchia are your enemies, as well."

"If they weren't before, they are now," Veulkh replied. "How did you find me?"

"I don't know how they found you," the man replied "but they did, which means others can. That would be very bad for you, I think."

"Are you threatening me?"

"Lord Veulkh, how can I threaten you? I am in your power. I put myself and my comrades at your mercy because I believed you to be a man of principle, a man who repays his debts and honors his obligations. Do this thing, and the Cryptarchia will never burden you with another task. We will erase any knowledge of your whereabouts."

On the surface, the man's tone sounded deferential, but Ammolite realized that Veulkh was right—he *was* being threatened. This man had come here to prove that Veulkh was vulnerable, and to suggest that, if all did not go well, that vulnerability would be exploited.

Veulkh didn't speak for a moment.

"What is this thing?" he finally asked.

"Do any of your servants speak the logos?"

"Of course not," Veulkh replied.

The man then began to talk in a language she had never heard before, although after a moment she began to think it was one she had learned to read. Still, she could not follow him. He spoke for several minutes without interruption, then fell silent.

For what seemed an eternity, nothing happened at all. Then Veulkh rose from his chair, and without a word left the chamber. The ravens took the man, and a few moments later one came for her and escorted her back to her rooms.

CHAPTER FIVE

THE PRIZE

CRESPIN KNELT by Elpis but detected no pulse in her wrists or breath from her mouth.

"Captain!" Renost shouted.

Crespin looked up at the call. Across the waves, the Drehhu ship continued to bear down on them. It was wounded, but not destroyed.

Before he could an issue an order, the Drehhu weapons spoke in the tongue of dragons. Wood splintered as the *Panther*'s mainmast was struck and the sail took flame. The enemy began to draw up broadside, so near they had no chance of missing with their next shot. The *Panther* still had some sail, but Crespin quickly saw it would be impossible to turn enough to avoid what was sure to be a crippling attack.

Yet the wind, at least, was behind them.

"Go straight at them," he shouted, "and ready grapnels. Tie us to that ship!"

As the two ships came together, the *Panther*'s crew prepared. The xelons locked their heavy shields against one another as archers lined up behind them.

"They should have finished us from a distance," Crespin told his men. "Let's make them regret that."

"Hoi!" Alkaios shouted. The men echoed him.

"Archers, whenever you're ready."

At his word, a cloud of fletched missiles arced toward the enemy craft. At nearly the same moment the Drehhu weapons sounded again, this time smashing into the hull. Something about the feel of it, the hollow drum of the deck beneath his feet told him that the *Panther* had sustained a mortal wound. The Drehhu thought so, too, and began to turn away.

"Grapnels," Crespin commanded.

Their quilaines sang and projected a pair of great metal hooks over the space between the ships, dragging chain behind them. Both cleared the enemy flatboards, and the mariniers quickly tightened the chains as the grapnels took hold. They began to crank the two ships together.

Drehhu slaves and a handful of their masters were lined up along their rail, many armed with the long pipes which began spitting and snapping, sending arcane shot into the xelons. For the most part, however, their heavy shields seemed effective against the invisible missiles. Crespin's archers answered, and many of the unarmored slaves collapsed.

Then the vessels came together.

For a moment the two sides stared at each other, as if not quite realizing how changed the situation was. Then the Drehhu began to work furiously at their weapons, perhaps making them ready to use again.

"For the emperor!" Crespin shouted, drawing his saber.

The xelons rose as one.

The *Panther* sat a bit higher in the water than the Drehhu ship, and that was very much to their advantage. The lancers slammed down and into the Drehhu line, their long spears churning underhand as Crespin urged on the charge. There came another volley of lesser explosions and something hot creased his thigh, but he ignored it, cutting over the heads of the xelons, who now knelt to form a wall.

The Drehhu and their slaves seemed to abandon their arcane weapons and began fighting with massive, ugly-looking hangers. They smashed a hole in the shield line, but Crespin and Alkaios were there to fill the gap until the lancers could regroup.

They pushed forward, inch by bloody inch. The Drehhu force was outnumbered, but they fought like the devils they were rumored to be. Whenever his men moved past a hatch, Crespin sent some below to prevent the enemy from popping up behind them. Fire and smoke had done much of that work for him, as it turned out, but judging from the sounds of fighting, enough remained below to keep them busy.

The deck had begun to tilt early in the fight, and was inclining even more as the foundering *Panther* began dragging the Drehhu ship down with her.

Crespin took Renost aside.

"Where is Hector?" he asked.

"Below, trying to get the wounded back on deck."

"Good," he said. "Send a detail to help him. Then take some of the archers and detach the grapnels. Make sure everyone that can comes across first. This is our ship now, or we have none. The *Panther* is done."

———

THE DREHHU did not surrender, which Crespin knew was typical of their kind. The last of them died by suicide, slitting his own throat when he saw that Crespin's men had a chance to overpower him. A few of the slaves survived and gave up their arms. Crespin had them bound and taken below.

Whatever diabolic engines powered the vessel, they had been destroyed, so they were adrift. The current was dragging them away from Banaraq, along with the remains of the *Panther*.

The battle looked to be over—what remained of the Zamiran fleet soon vanished over the eastern horizon, and not much later the sun went under in the west. Before the light was gone, however, he made out the silhouette of a ship that seemed to be beating against the wind toward them.

"Find something to burn," he said. "We'll light a beacon."

The Drehhu ship was not as strange inside as it was without. It was, after all, a ship, and ships needed to be of a certain shape. The crew needed food and sleeping accommodations. This discovery was something of a relief; for so long he'd thought of the Drehhu as otherworldly monsters who sustained themselves with dark arts. Now he knew firsthand that they were not only mortal, but in some ways ordinary. Their hammocks were bigger, but otherwise just like his own.

Not everything was familiar, however. Much of the aft space was taken up with sheer deviltry—contraptions of metal pipes and cogs and shapes for which he had no words. One large cylinder looked like something had burst out from inside it—perhaps the demon that had motivated the ship.

They got the beacon going and assembled on the deck as Crespin made a tally of the dead and the living. The *Panther*'s crew had originally been forty, including the military personnel and the strixe.

Thirteen remained standing, and Hector was doing what he could for another five. And they were still far from Basilisk, from the real war.

How many more men and women would die under his command?

The approaching ship turned out to be the *Prokyon*. Her captain—a balding, cheerful fellow named La Joulier—welcomed them aboard, and told his men to take whatever provisions they could from the Drehhu ship and scuttle her.

"Why not tow it in?" Crespin asked. "There may be something of use on board other than food."

The ship's strixe—a slight young woman with close-cropped black hair—had been standing by silently. Now she shook her head.

"There is nothing there you *may* use," she said. "Your contract with the Cryptarchia forbids it."

"But wood is wood, metal is metal," he argued. "We've many ships to repair—"

"Not with that," the strixe replied. "It must go to the abyss."

Crespin relented, but it still seemed a waste—and it nagged at him. If the restriction had come from the emperor, that would be one thing. But that the emperor himself had to bow to the Cryptarchia seemed wrong. Of course, the rulers of Velesa and Modjal were equally compelled.

Crespin wondered exactly whose war he was fighting.

HIS FATHER watched Crespin board the *Leucothea* with no more than a slight nod of his head. Then he turned to speak to his other officers as Crespin waited. After a few moments, the admiral waved him over.

"Let's take some coffee," his father said.

When Crespin was a boy, he had preferred coffee with cream

and molasses, but cream did not keep aboard a ship, and he had learned to enjoy it in the marinier's fashion—cold, laced with rum, orange juice, cloves, and cinnamon. Between sips he laid out his adventures in and around Zamir, albeit omitting some details—such as the nature of his initial encounter with Saja.

"You were fortunate," his father said. "What if the woman had been an agent of the Drehhu? You would now be captive."

"But she wasn't, sir," he said. "If she had wanted to capture me…" He trailed off, awkwardly.

"I see," his father said. "Even worse. You were fortunate."

"I'll agree to that."

His father frowned at him for a moment, then shrugged.

"Still. Things would have gone worse for us if the pirates and their Drehhu allies had come upon us unawares. The warning you brought was timely."

Crespin was almost taken aback. The rebuke he had expected—but that last almost sounded like praise, and for a moment he couldn't think how to respond.

"Your strategy worked," he finally said. "The use you put the strixe to."

"Did it?" his father grunted. "We lost seventeen ships and many more are damaged, by a force only a fraction of our size. They gave far more than we took, and that only because they didn't know about our strixes. One of the Drehhu ships escaped, and there is very little chance they will be intercepted before returning to Basilisk. Even that assumes they have no way—as we do—of communicating over distance. Our capabilities may already be known to their warlocks. In either case, they now have some idea of our range. Not an entirely accurate idea, fortunately, so we might surprise them one more time."

"What do you mean?"

"The strixes have differing abilities," he said. "Some can act across greater distances than others. The ships carrying those with the greatest reach I deliberately put in the rear—with the exception of my own."

Crespin absorbed that with a certain amount of shock.

"You sacrificed the vanguard," he said.

His father's face didn't change. "This is war, Crespin. We do what we must. Most of our advantage—if it could even be called that—is now gone. If they know our full range when we reach Basilisk, we will lose seven ships for every one of theirs. Maybe more."

"But—"

"I tell you this only because it is possible that something will happen to me. A few other key officers will be briefed. No one else is to know. Do you understand?"

"Yes, sir."

"Very well." He dismissed the subject with the back of his hand, then changed tack. "We are more in need of repairs now than when we arrived, and it must be done quickly."

"The Drehhu shipyard—" Crespin began.

"Yes, I thought of that," the admiral said. "The Cryptarchia has made it clear we are not to go near it. We must secure Zamir."

"More fighting," Crespin said.

"Maybe not," his father replied. "When word of our victory reached the city, the veil—or false veil, I suppose—seems to have fled. So far as I can tell, no one is in charge, and they aren't inclined to fight anymore; not when they can make coin from us. But we must establish some sort of order here." He leaned back. "See if you can find this woman, this agent of Modjal. Perhaps she can be of help in appointing some sort of council."

———

THEY DOCKED a few hours later. Crespin went ashore with Renost and a contingent of xelons to look for Saja. His inquiries came to naught, and he began to worry that she had been captured or slain by Kol's men.

His father was right about the Zamirans—they seemed to have lost interest in fighting. Repairs began quickly on some of the ships, including the *Leucothea*. The next morning, Crespin rose before dawn. As he'd hoped, he found Calliope watching the light gather in the east.

"Good morning," she said at his approach. The light was still quite faint, but it looked as if—like Elpis—a few strands of her hair were now gold in color. Not nearly so many, and maybe it was just a trick of the morning light.

"I hope you are well," he said.

"Passably so," she said, but she looked very tired, and her words were a little slurred. Even from a few feet away, he smelled rum.

"Does it hurt?" he asked. He remembered Elpis, hanging in the air, somehow only half there.

She didn't answer for a long time.

"I heard about Elpis, on the *Panther*," she said.

"Yes," he said. "I was there when she died." He swallowed. "I want to know what happened. What killed her?"

Calliope smiled, but there seemed to be little sincerity in her expression.

"Did she scream or cry out? Did she seem to be in pain?"

He thought about it.

"No," he said.

She looked him directly in the eyes, and he saw flecks of gold in hers. He felt as if he was seeing her for the first time, with all artifice stripped away.

"It doesn't hurt," she said, very softly. "It… no, it doesn't hurt, but when it stops…" Tears ran down her face, and she was trembling. Without any thought, he reached out and took her in his arms. She seemed to melt against him, and she felt tiny.

"It's alright," he said, not knowing what he meant. He turned her face toward his, wiped her tears. The rum on her breath was like perfume, and he kissed her.

For just a moment, she responded, but then she pushed him away.

"No," she said. Then she hurried from the deck.

THE WEATHER was fair that evening, so when Crespin went off watch he slung his hammock above deck, in the corner by the stern. The men gave him his space. He was tired beyond measure, but sleep eluded him. The battle stayed with him, as did the memory of Elpis, the strange little sound she'd made when she died.

His stupidity with Calliope.

He drank a fair amount of rum, but it only seemed to make matters worse.

A few of the stars stopped shining, and he realized someone had come up without him knowing it and was standing over him.

"I heard you were looking for me."

He recognized the voice.

"Saja," he said.

"Indeed," she said. "Your friend Hector told me where to find you."

"It could have waited for morning."

"Perhaps so," she said, "but what I have in mind would be fine right now." She bent down and found his lips. That first kiss went on for a while, and he discovered that—despite all his angst—he could yet find a little enthusiasm. Then a thought occurred.

"This isn't necessary," he said.

"No," she said, "but if you shut up and make a little room, it could be fun."

IT WAS, and afterward he slept. He woke the next day tangled with Saja in the hammock, his blanket drawn over them. A little embarrassed, he glanced around to see if anyone was observing.

Calliope stood a few yards away, next to the rail, gazing out over the water, her face presented in profile. He was wondering what he would say, when she slowly turned her back to him and walked away.

CHAPTER SIX

THE BARGAIN

ABOVE THE balcony, Hound found a ledge large enough for sleep. He woke as the sky began to gray, then heard noise.

Slipping down, he hung onto the outside of the balustrade so he could see into the room without easily being seen himself. There was only a narrow view of the chamber, but after a moment, Ammolite passed through it. She was naked, which immediately doubled his interest in whatever she was doing. He eased around for a better view, in time to see her step down into a pool of water, where she began to bathe.

Wondering whether he could trust her, he decided that, even if he could, he should observe her for a time. When she finished her bath and left the room, he quietly entered the manse and crept into the bathing room. From there, through a cracked door, he had a view of a corridor that branched in three directions. As he waited, trying to guess which way she had gone, she reappeared—dressed, much to his chagrin—crossing from the opening on the left and vanishing into the one on the right. He gave her plenty of time, then started after her, trailing her scent of soap and rose petals through the meandering halls of the place.

As they moved farther from the windows, he expected it to grow darker, but then he noticed that the walls themselves were luminescent—in some places faintly so and in others quite radiant. The colors were those of a dark rainbow, a slick of oil on a blackwater oxbow.

Several times he had to hide, to avoid the other inhabitants of the house, and for a while he lost track of Ammolite. The closest he came to being caught was when she inexplicably doubled back and returned to her apartments, changed her clothing, and set out again. Continuing to shadow her, he witnessed something strange, even by his standards.

Ammolite changed her shape.

She joined a man he assumed was Veulkh in what must have been the sorcerer's lair. He took off her clothes and coupled with her the way animals did when in rut. When it was over, they dressed again. The man led her to a large door and—after what seemed a moment or two of strain—opened it. The two of them went through and vanished from sight.

The door remained open.

He waited a bit, pondering what he had just seen. Was Ammolite like Grandmother, able to take any shape she pleased? Or had the sorcerer transformed her with a spell? She hadn't changed until she approached him.

Eventually Hound started across the chamber. He had only taken a few steps when he felt a prickling on his skin. Glancing around, he saw that the floor was concave, like the depression at the foot of the mountain. So was the ceiling, for that matter: again, as if a huge ball of something had once been there and then vanished, leaving a hollow. It seemed to him that there must be some sort of connection.

The lair was open to the sky at one end. Hound envisioned Selene and the rest entering some sort of spherical carriage—like the soap bubbles the village children played with, but much larger—and then drifting up to settle here.

Approaching the door he peeked through, saw no one, and started down the corridor. After a time he heard footfalls and ducked into a side room. When he peered out, he saw two men dressed like those who had led away Selene and the others. With them was Martin, who was naked. They moved past and through the door at the end of the hall.

Rather than following, he decided to look for Selene, going back down the corridor the way they had come. Soon he encountered a locked door.

Stymied, he retraced his steps to the central hall. It was still empty, so he started toward where the men had taken Martin. As he did so, the door at the end of the hall began to open. He sprinted into a nearby corridor and padded down it as far as he dared. There weren't any rooms into which he could duck, so he lay flat on the floor, next to one wall.

The sorcerer walked past in the other hall, followed a few moments later by Martin and the two men. He continued to lie silently for a while longer, which turned out to be fortunate, because a bit later Ammolite also passed by, escorted by one of the armed men.

After what seemed like a safe amount of time, he got back up and returned the way he had come. Cautiously he went down the hall from which Martin had been led. This time the door was open.

Hound took out his sling and put a stone in it before going through into a round room from which three other passages diverged. Down one he heard footsteps and men talking, so he went down another, turning a corner and stopping to wait.

Presently he heard the door close, followed by a grating sound.

That's probably not good.

He went back carefully, in case one of the men had stayed behind, but there was no trace of either. As he had expected, the way out was locked again, so he proceeded down the middle way—the corridor from which they had come.

This passage opened into a large, well-lit chamber. Unlike the rest of the manse, where the light came from the walls, here it came from far above, and seemed to be real sunlight, diffusing down through holes in the ceiling. Moss carpeted the floor, and tall, thin trees with lacy leaves stretched toward the light.

Around the room horizontal slabs of stone rose as high as his waist, each spaced an arm's breadth apart. Many were empty, but others had occupants—human-shaped figures cocooned in the green tendrils of feathery vines that grew from the floor. One of the bodies wasn't completely covered; he moved closer.

It was Martin. His eyes were closed, and even as Hound watched, the vines moved to gently wrap about him.

He felt something brush his ankle and jerked his leg away when he saw that it was one of the plants. His foot felt suddenly numb, and a profound lethargy settled over him. He managed to stumble back another few feet until he was on stone, out of reach of the groping strands. By that time, the numbness and the desire to sleep had begun to subside.

The sorcerer was keeping Selene and Martin—along with the

chevaliers and their men—imprisoned and asleep. Hound couldn't free them without being snared himself, yet the guards had somehow both removed and returned Martin without being affected.

Scanning the chamber, he didn't find anything to explain how the guards had done it. Whatever made it possible, they must have taken it with them. He pondered his next move—he could wait, and kill the next one who came in. Then if he woke the prisoners, they might be able to fight their way out, although it didn't look as though their armor and weapons were wrapped up with them.

Martin had been naked.

So was Selene, probably…

Hound still didn't know what was going on, and he didn't want to get caught in here. He needed to discover another way out.

It didn't take long for him to find it. One of the trees had grown all the way to the ceiling, thrusting branches through the holes. There were vines around the base of it, but they didn't seem to like the trees and did not climb them. Of course, the trees might prove dangerous in some other way, here in the wizard's garden, but it was a chance he was willing to take.

Gauging the distance, he backed up as far as he could—and ran.

The vines were too slow. He danced between them and, when they grew too thick, launched himself at the tree. He hit the trunk, which was about the diameter of his thigh. To his dismay it bent with his weight, bowing dangerously. If it snapped, or the top came loose above…

Slowly it rebounded to an upright position.

There was the soft touch of a tendril on his ankle, and he climbed as quickly as he could. The limbs of the tree had worked themselves through what he now saw were holes drilled in the very stone. Worse, they weren't holes exactly, but shafts about twice as long as he was tall.

And really, really narrow.

Balanced in the tree, he stripped off his pants and shirt, bundled them up with his ax and sling, and bound them with his belt. He tied the other end of the belt around his ankles. To pass through, he would have to contort his shoulders and raise his arms straight over his head, first pushing from the nearest limb, then wiggling and pulling with arms. His lungs didn't have room to fully inflate, so his breath came quick and shallow, and he began to worry that the shaft was narrowing at the top.

Then he began to sweat, slickening the smooth stone. It made it easier to wriggle up, but he didn't dare rest for fear of sliding back down. All of his muscles had to remain tense and braced.

He didn't know how long it was before his fingers found the edge of the hole; it seemed like years. That wasn't the end of it, however— there was no way to use his arms until his elbows were out.

Hound emerged onto a dome of natural stone, high above the valley. The sun was nearing the western rim of the world, which meant he had spent much of the day traveling a little more than twice his own length. And why? What was he doing this for?

For Selene? Because he wanted her to think well of him? What did he care about that? Why shouldn't he just be on his way, do whatever came to mind, *when* it came to mind? What reward did he expect?

He sighed, then whistled, and clicked a few times. After a moment, he repeated the call. A bit later Soot arrived. He had a scrap of paper in his beak.

Hound took it, stared at it for a moment, and then cast it away.

"I CAN'T read," Hound said.

Ammolite jumped at the sound of his voice, then whirled so she could see him.

"Oh," she said. "I didn't know." She smiled a little. "I think I saw one of your friends."

He listened without comment as she described Martin, and his conversation with the sorcerer. He didn't think she was lying, but she might be leaving something out.

"Did Veulkh tell you what Martin wanted?" he asked.

She shook her head. "Something he doesn't want to do. He's in his conjury." She frowned a little when she said it and couldn't quite meet his gaze. He wanted to ask her about how she changed, and why, but he didn't yet want to give away that he had followed her.

"Do you know anything about how he keeps his prisoners?"

"No," she said. "If he had prisoners before I never knew it. Why do you think your friends are prisoners?"

"The way you describe how they brought him in. Naked, with guards."

"Veulkh is cautious," she said. "He has enemies, and clothes can hide weapons."

Martin's hands *were* his weapons. Why hadn't he used them? Hound realized he didn't know much about sorcerers, or understand what drove them to do the things they did.

"Your friend didn't act as though he was worried," Ammolite added. "In fact, he seemed rather confident."

"Yes, that's Martin."

She didn't reply to that, but just stood looking at him.

Her eyes were pale, almost white. He remembered his brief glimpse of her body, and then the much longer sight of the woman she turned into. He started to wonder what would happen if her kissed her. Her face seemed like the only thing in the world.

He started to take a step.

She beat him to it. Her lips touched his, lightly at first, then with hunger. He pulled her close and felt the heat of her body. Her kisses moved to his ear, the crook of his neck. Leste had never kissed him like that. She had been as clumsy as he. Ammolite was not clumsy. She was driving him mad, and he liked it very much.

Just as he thought he could endure no more, she drew back.

"I must check on Veulkh," she said. "Make sure he is still in the conjury. Then we might be able to slip into one of my secret places."

He nodded, panting, his legs feeling weak. Then she was gone.

HOUND WAS on the balcony, watching the last of the sunset, just starting to wonder where she was, when he felt something behind him. He turned, quickly.

Veulkh was standing there.

Hound started to leap for the handholds above, but his feet never left the ground. It felt as if they had become stone, part of the balcony itself. He unwrapped his sling and quickly took out a pebble, but he suddenly couldn't inhale. Rather, his chest was rising and falling, but no breath went in, and he felt as if his entire body had been stung. Black spots danced before his eyes.

Then nothing.

HE WOKE naked, in the conjury, flat on his back and unable to move. Veulkh paced into his field of vision.

"You entered my house uninvited," the sorcerer said. He didn't sound angry. "Why?"

Would the sorcerer know if he lied? What had the girl told him? And what could he say? That he had spent three days climbing a mountain… for the fun of it?

"I was looking for some friends of mine."

"Describe these friends."

Hound did so, and Veulkh continued to question him—about Martin, Selene, the chevaliers, their journey to the mountain.

"Why weren't you with them when my men escorted them here?"

"My job was to bring them to the mountain," he said. "No further."

"And yet you came further. At considerable effort."

"I heard a sound like thunder. Their tracks led into a place and vanished. I became curious."

Veulkh nodded. "How is she?" he asked.

"I don't know who you mean."

"Elmekije," he said. "How is she? Did she have a message for me?"

Hound felt a little jolt run through him. That was the name Martin had called Grandmother.

"Yes," he lied. "She said not to harm me or my companions."

"No, then," Veulkh said. "No message—but I suppose you *are* the message, aren't you?" He leaned near. "You were on my balcony," he said. "Did you see anyone other than me?"

"No." Maybe Ammolite had betrayed him, but if she hadn't, he didn't want to make trouble for her.

Veulkh continued to stare at him, searching. Then a look came over him. It appeared to be relief. So the sorcerer couldn't *always* spot a lie.

Veulkh looked to one of his guards.

"Fetch me Martin and Selene," he commanded. "See they are bathed and dressed. This one, too. We shall have dinner in the hall."

HOUND WASN'T sure what most of the food was, and he didn't care. There was some sort of meat in a sweet sauce, and what might have been fish ground to a paste and fried. A soup that smelled of leeks and garlic but tasted like fire. The people in Berze did odd things to food, but this went way beyond that. It was as if whoever cooked it didn't want it to be recognized as food at all.

Still, it was filling and sometimes interesting and the wine was making him feel a lot better about everything.

Aside from the servant bringing the food, the dining hall was occupied by only the sorcerer, Martin, Selene, and Hound. He wondered where Ammolite was.

Selene had seemed genuinely happy to see him, but other than greetings, no one said much until after the meal was finished. When all the food was cleared, a servant brought a bottle of something pale green in color and poured each of them some in a small clear cup. Hound sniffed it. It smelled like pine needles.

"What you ask of me," Veulkh said, staring at his cup, "is considerable."

"We are aware of that," Selene said.

"It is not the particular task, although I understand why you sought me out. In this dissipated era, I am probably the only one left who can accomplish it. What concerns me is that I must travel, which I do not like to do."

"We will, of course, accompany you to ensure your safety," Martin said.

"My ravens will accompany me," Veulkh said. "What I have seen of you and your men does not recommend you as bodyguards."

"With respect, Lord Veulkh," Selene said, "We willingly acquiesced to your men. We made no attempt to protect ourselves. Then you deprived us of our wits the instant we arrived. This says nothing about our ability to defend you." She paused. "We are charged with defending you, sir."

"I know what you are," Veulkh told her. "Your abilities are useless against me."

"I've made no effort to hide what I am," she replied, "and my abilities are at your service."

"Hand the sun a torch, so he can see his way," Veulkh scoffed.

Selene smiled and shrugged.

"What changed your mind?" Martin said. "You seemed set against this."

"The matter is complicated," Veulkh said. "At the heart of it, a thing must be done which is beyond even my abilities. I was set against it, but then a boy climbed my mountain and into my window, and that objection was erased. Did you know?"

"Honestly," Martin said. "I have no idea what you're talking about."

Hound didn't either, unless there was a mountain that had to be climbed. Unexpectedly, all their gazes settled on him.

"You mean you need Hound to do this," Selene said.

"Yes," Veulkh replied.

"What if I don't want to go?" Hound said.

"Hound," Selene said. "It's important."

"Not to me."

"And yet you mounted a cliff after we left, to find out where we were."

"I'd still like to see you naked."

She pursed her lips, perhaps as if considering his request this time.

"If you don't go," the sorcerer said, "the deed cannot be done. The Cryptarchia will assume I am merely being difficult, yes?"

"Yes," Martin said.

"In which case, I will effectively be at war with them. My interests will return to my own security, and I will do everything I can to make certain no one else ever reaches this place."

Why does Veulkh have to say everything in the most complicated way possible? Hound wondered. He was like his food. Who needs a sweet sauce to make meat taste good?

"You mean you'll kill us," Hound said.

"Not necessarily," the sorcerer replied. "I mean you won't leave."

Hound thought of the sleeping vines. That didn't seem a lot better than death.

"Then I'll come," Hound said, "But they come, too." He gestured to Martin and Selene. "And I need Rose."

Veulkh looked puzzled.

"His dog," Martin said. "A very useful beast."

Veulkh sat there with a frown on his face, but finally nodded. "Very well," he said. "That will be acceptable. The extra swords might prove useful where we'll be going, and it will be advantageous to have emissaries who have no prior connection to me."

He reached for his glass and raised it.

"O orkos Cryptarchias," he said.

"O orkos," Martin and Selene repeated.

Then they drank. Hound followed their example. It did taste a little like pine needles, mixed with fire.

CHAPTER SEVEN

OPHION MAGNE

QUINTENT D'OTHRES did not look like a viper. He was strong in the jaw, had a nice arc of a nose and high cheekbones. Indeed, his face might have been the model for a marble statue. When he directed his brown-eyed gaze toward Chrysanthe, an amiable smile appeared. He was an inch taller than her.

Possibly the handsomest man she had ever seen.

She therefore trusted him not at all.

THE SEA voyage was the longest she had ever experienced, taking forty-three days from the time she boarded until the moment she set foot on the enormous quay of Ophion Magne. They had three times put into port—first at Chaharam, a sprawling city of towers and domes all built of the same sand-colored stone. The people, however, wore robes so bright and colorful that at a distance they resembled parrots, kingfishers, or rainbow spites. And that was the only way she got to see them, as she was not allowed to leave the ship.

Their second landfall was in the city of Drome, in the Isles des Seismoi. The city was nothing special, but as they approached the islands it appeared as if the horizon was aflame, with clouds of black smoke billowing high into the air. She was reminded of her father and brother, headed toward a much larger range of volcanoes—the Salamandra—and of the danger they were in.

Their penultimate stop was the Isle of Ship, just past the Gates of Atlas, where the ecru buildings seemed to climb upon one another, looking something like a gigantic termite mound. From then on, they sailed near the coast, past the Mesogian cities that looked like terracotta, and thence into the Sea of Ophion, the Cor de la Monde, and its graceful pastel towns with fairy-tale spires.

And finally, the Island of Ophion and the fabled city of a hundred towers.

Intellectually she knew how big Ophion Magne would be. She'd had little to do but read on the voyage, and had packed as many books as possible—most of them concerning the history of Ophion and the wars of the Reclamation. To actually see it, however, sprawled out before her in the mist was simply stunning.

They came to dock in a port which itself held more people than she had ever seen in one place, with perhaps a hundred ships in mooring, a virtual forest of masts crowded up to an immense plaza paved in cobblestone. Gigantic warehouses of lemon brick with sharply sloping roofs of coffee-colored slate stood across the space, blocking her view of the city itself. Everywhere she saw merchants dressed in wildly patterned short-sleeved jackets that gathered at the hips and then flared as they dropped just below the knee.

These merchants were directing workers—probably slaves— who wore rather drab beige, brown, or gray shirts and knee-length trousers. Here and there were men of uncertain rank garbed in Modjal fashion or in the wools and velvets common to Velesa. And there were women—some looked no older than thirteen—dressed in an appalling fashion, wearing clothes meant to reveal more than they covered. She thought she knew why they were there, and it made her feel a little ill.

The docks—like any she had known—were rank with the scent of rotting fish and tar. There were no soldiers, no naviors, no ships flying military flags. Those were all at sea.

"Danesele Nevelon?" a man asked. "But you must be. The rumors of your beauty hardly do you justice. I am Quintent d'Othres, at your service. I hope we are to be friends."

She looked for a barb in that. Did he imply a rumor was that she was ugly, or that talk of her beauty was overblown? Try as she might, however, she couldn't find anything deceptive in his bearing. Perhaps he was simply being pleasant.

Yet her mother's infectious paranoia persisted.

"I am Chrysanthe Nevelon," she said.

He was dressed as if for riding, with green breeches stuffed into tall boots and a rather plain brown coat that reached to his knees, split in back and on the sides.

"I am very glad to meet you, Danesele. I'm sent to accompany you to Roselant."

Chrysanthe took a little step back. "It was understood that I was to stay at Vaudin, with my cousins."

Quintent produced a piece of paper from a coat pocket and handed it to her. It was fastened with the emperor's seal and written in a flowery hand. The language was dense, but it essentially stated that the master of Roselant wished the honor of hosting her during her stay, and that the emperor had granted it to him.

"I don't know these people," she said. "Roselant."

"Well, I'm one of them," he said. "The master of Roselant is my uncle."

She continued to stare at the document. Her father had not planned on this, of that she was certain. What did it mean?

Despite her concerns, there was nothing she could do, was there? There was no one to whom she could appeal, not with the emperor's seal on the letter. There was no choice but to go with this man, and keep her wits about her. Perhaps she could find a way to visit Vaudin and discover what had happened.

"Very well, sir," she said.

He waved his hand, and some men she had not noticed before came, lifted her luggage, and conducted it to a four-horse carriage on the plaza. Five additional horses, tacked up for riding, stood nearby, along with two men dressed much like Quintent.

"In what part of the city is Roselant?" she asked.

"It's not in the city," Quintent replied. "You can be thankful for that. Roselant is in the countryside, a bit more than a day's ride from here." He smiled. "In fact, we'll go out the Westgate, and you'll not be in the city for any length of time at all."

"But I've come all this way," she protested. There would be no chance of seeing her cousins, Chrysanthe realized, and learning what might be going on. "For more than a month I've been looking forward to seeing Ophion Magne."

"Surely you saw it as you arrived," he replied. "The view from the outer harbor is very good."

She smiled. "I believe you expressed some hope that we might be friends."

"Aha," he said. "I see. Well, if that's how it is—we're in no great hurry. If you wish to see the city, I would be happy to give you a tour by carriage."

THEY TOOK a street that led between a pair of warehouses and soon passed through a massive gate embellished with ram-headed serpents and winged bulls.

Then they were in the city proper, on the widest street she had ever seen—although it still wasn't roomy enough for the quantity of people who used it. Buildings three and four stories tall rose at its verges. Ahead—through the haze that filled the streets—she could just make out the golden dome of a basilica.

The carriage was almost like a boat, trying to make its way upstream in a river. The crowds parted before them, but grudgingly. And what a stream! Men and women in their finest, others in rags, children with brown-smudged clothes and cheeks...

At once, it hit her.

The smell. She very nearly retched.

Foremost was the reek of feces. Horse, dog, and almost certainly human. Sticking her head out the window and looking down, she saw the wheels of the carriage furrowing through what she had first assumed to be mud. But that was not the sum of the assault upon her senses. There was the simple stink of rot, of maggoty meat—and she recognized now that what she had presumed was fog was the acrid smoke from thousands of chimneys.

"There is nothing quite so refreshing as a ride through the

city," Quintent said.

Chrysanthe wiped her watering eyes. "How can people live like this?" she gasped.

"If you spend enough time here, you become used to it, I'm told. I've never thought to test that theory myself."

"I don't understand," she said. "Even before the Drehhu conquered this place, Ophion Magne had sewers, aqueducts, all sorts of conveniences."

"That was a long time ago," he told her. "In the last two decades the population here has nearly doubled as people move in from the colonies and the countryside, seeking work. You will hardly ever see a slave in the city, because it's cheaper to hire one of these poor fellows."

"Well, I understand now what you were trying to save me from," she said, "but I'm glad to see it anyway."

He looked skeptical.

"Is there any destination you have in mind?" he asked.

"I should like to see Li Jardil del'Empire." she said, "and the palace, of course. And—"

"Bearing in mind," Quintent said, "that at some point we must begin our journey to Roselant."

"Of course we must," she said. "But must we go today?"

"I've made no arrangement for lodging."

"Vaudin," she said. "My cousins will welcome us, I'm sure—and if I am to stay so far out in the country, I should at least pay them a call."

He thought that over for a moment.

"We will pay them a call," he said. "It seems only fair, as you were expecting to stay with them."

"Thank you," she said. "Very much."

"Are we friends now?" he asked.

"We are on the path to friendship."

VAUDIN WAS a tidy house of two stories in the center of a walled garden. It wasn't as grand as her father's house, but it was charming, with its peaked roof and crow-stepped gables. A servant met them at the door, and soon a woman of about forty years in a brocade housecoat arrived to greet them. Chrysanthe recognized her.

"Cousin Daphne," she said.

The woman stared at her blankly.

"Don't you remember me?" Chrysanthe asked. "From your visit to Bellship?"

The woman's eyebrows went up and a smile broadened her face.

"Santh? Little Santh? Look at you." She stepped forward and gave Chrysanthe a hug. When she stepped back, she looked confused. "They told us you were to stay at Roselant."

"So I am," Chrysanthe replied, "but Mr. d'Othres was kind enough to bring me by for a visit." Daphne's gaze darted past her to where Quintent stood. Again, she looked startled.

"Dam d'Othres," she said, making a little curtsy. "My apologies, I should have known. Please come in, the both of you, if our house is not too humble."

Chrysanthe studied Quintent in a new light. While it had become fashionable to refer to an unmarried woman as "danesele" whether noble or not, the same was not true of "dam" and "dame," which could only refer to those of gentle birth.

"Your house is quite splendid," he replied. "I would be glad of your company."

Daphne led them to a sitting room with several small couches, a harp, and various portraits, one of which she recognized as a painting of the great-grandfather she and Daphne shared. A few moments after they were seated, a young woman around Chrysanthe's age arrived with a tray containing a pot of coffee, some cups, and cookies of some sort. She served them, curtsied, and left.

"I hope it is to your liking," Daphne said.

To Chrysanthe's taste the coffee seemed stale, with a bit too much cream in it to compensate. It was also served hot, whereas she was used to having it chilled in the springhouse—or on rare occasions, over ice. The cookies were good, though: spiced with ginger, clove, and white pepper.

"It's wonderful," she said. "It's been more than a month since I've had a decent cup, and no cream at all."

"Very pleasing," Quintent said.

"Well, you must tell me everything," Daphne said. "Your mother? She is well?"

Trying not to let her impatience rise to the surface, Chrysanthe began to describe the happenings at home, endeavoring to think of some clever way to turn the conversation to her ends. With Quintent there, however, listening to everything, she couldn't see how that was possible.

She broke off as a man entered the room. He had a shock of hair gone completely white and a pleasantly wrinkled face to match.

"Well, there she is," he said, "and grown into a fine lady. Give your old cousin a hug, Chrysanthe." He held out his arms. She rose and went to him.

"So good to see you, cousin Leon," she said, as the old man folded her in his arms, perhaps a bit more tightly than she would have liked.

"*Later*," he whispered in her ear, so low that she almost wasn't sure he had said it. Leon turned and bowed to Quintent. "Dam d'Othres," he said. "What a pleasure, and what a happy surprise that you've brought Chrysanthe to visit us. When news reached of us of the change in plans, we were afraid we would not see her."

"Of course, you can visit her at Roselant," Quintent said. "In fact, you must."

"That is very kind of you, sir," Leon Nevelon replied. "I might take you up on that, and of course, I pray you will lodge with us tonight."

"I shouldn't want to impose," Quintent said. "I have horses and some men with me."

"All welcome," Leon said. "Far from an imposition, it would be a blessing."

"Please?" Chrysanthe said. "You allowed that we are in no great hurry."

Quintent looked a little unsure, but he finally nodded.

"How can I refuse such hospitality?"

BY DINNERTIME, the rest of the household had arrived, a crowd of fifteen. One was Daphne's brother, a young man with a wife and two children, one not yet walking. Daphne herself had been widowed, but not before bearing five children of her own, two of which had their own families to make up the balance. Leon's wife was long dead.

They were all extremely impressed with Quintent and— probably by extension—with Chrysanthe. He in his turn was polite and deferential, although she was certain that everyone else present—herself included—was well below his station.

The meal, like the coffee, was a little bland. It came in courses—a terrine of pheasant livers followed by boiled beef in a sauce that could have used more ginger and pepper and any amount of cardamom. The green sauce for the fish was a little better, garlicky and sharp on the tongue. Fried sweetbreads next, then a salad of chicories and—finally—a soft, pungent cheese with what looked like brambleberries, except that they were red, pink, and pale yellow in color rather than purple. It was served with a sweet wine that tasted of honey.

The wine, in general, was excellent, and cast a sort of rosy glow over the evening. It felt as if it had been a year, rather than a month and a half, since she had sat on the terrace with her family. This wasn't the same experience, but it was social, and it felt good.

Later, in her quarters, she felt less enchanted. Through the window in her room, Ophion Magne was black, the most complete absence of light she had ever experienced. Even the stars were invisible. There was no breath of wind, no trilling of nightbirds, no soft wheezing of hippos in the river.

Instead she heard snatches of conversations, the clack of hooves, dogs howling, a distant scream that quivered in her mind long after the sound was gone. It was as if she was in the pit of Hell, surrounded by damned souls.

She tried to distract herself by writing a few words about the day, but that went quickly as she had used almost all her paper on the voyage. As always, she penned in the cypher that she and Crespin had developed as children. It was a habit out of which she had never grown when writing for herself.

The paper filled, she set it aside to dry.

Staring at the candle by the bed, she wondered if she would have the courage to put it out, when someone rapped softly on her door.

She drew on her dressing gown and cracked it open.

It was the young woman who had earlier brought the coffee. Her hair was still bound up in a black scarf, and she still wore her black-and-gray livery—but all looked disheveled, as if hastily thrown on. She carried a candle.

"You're to come with me, please, Danesele."

"To where?"

"Someone wants to talk to you."

Someone. The girl was a servant. If it was Leon sending for her, why didn't she just name him, or call him "master"? But what if it wasn't her cousin? What if it was Quintent? He had acquiesced too easily to her wishes. What if he thought he was due a reward of some sort?

"Who wants to see me?" she asked.

"I really cannot say."

It had to be Leon, and she could not miss this chance. If the other—she knew very well how to refuse an unwanted advance.

But then she realized something.

Her brothers were not here. Would her cousins defend her against a lord of Ophion?

Chrysanthe looked herself over, making certain the gown was properly fastened, then took a shawl from beside the bed and pulled it around her shoulders. Thus armored, she followed the girl, who led her through the darkened halls until they reached a door on the eastern wing. Her pulse quickened because they were still on the second floor, which seemed to be mostly sleeping quarters. Perhaps there was parlor hidden away here, or a small library.

There was not. The door opened onto a bedroom. Half sprawled on the bed, propped up by a pile of pillows, was a man she had never seen before.

CHAPTER EIGHT

SYNAPSES

VEULKH'S EYES seemed to stare beyond the world. His body appeared to fade, become somehow less real. The very atmosphere crawled on Hound's skin like termites, and for a moment he felt something familiar, like a remembered smell or taste but neither of those. Something sensed deeper, in his nerve and marrow. It reminded him of Grandmother but was at the same time quite alien.

Then the air clapped, and Hound felt himself turned inside out. His ears popped painfully and rang like bells as he fell to his knees in a whirl of green and brown. Trying not to vomit, he closed his eyes and felt smooth stone beneath his hands.

By the time his head stopped spinning, he knew where he was—the depression in the forest where Selene and the others had vanished.

Where he had now appeared.

He certainly hadn't drifted down in a bubble. Had he flown

down? Been hurled like a javelin? But he didn't remember falling. He was there, then he was here.

That was a good trick.

It also explained how Veulkh got his supplies without roads or stairs. Perhaps there was another place like this—maybe very far from his mountain. He would send his ravens for supplies, then bring them back, leaving no trail to follow, no clue to his location.

Hound climbed to his feet and began to look for Rose.

Veulkh said they were going on a journey. How far would they be traveling? Maybe very far. Perhaps to a place so distant he wouldn't be able to find his way back. This could be his last chance to leave.

He knew he wouldn't.

He was too curious and Ammolite… he wanted to kiss her again, and for longer. He wondered if she had betrayed him, stunned him with her lips and then informed Veulkh where to find him. Even if she had—even if Ammolite was not his friend—he didn't like the thought of Selene being dead or sleeping her life to its end in the vines.

It took a few hours, but Rose found him, and together they returned to the place. The dog growled and her neck stiffened, but she followed him in.

AMMOLITE WAS staring at the empty bed when she heard a rumble from the corner of the room. She gasped and stepped back as she saw some sort of monster was there, curled up with Hound.

"Ammolite?" Hound whispered, sitting up.

"What is that?" she asked.

"This is Rose," he said. "My friend."

"That's where Veulkh sent you," she guessed. "To get him."

"Her," Hound corrected, "but yes—and she won't hurt you. She is only dangerous to my enemies."

Was he accusing her of something? Did he think she had betrayed him?

"I'm sorry," she said. "There was nothing I could do. He walked in on me and told me to stay in his room. I thought you would hide."

"I should have," he said, grinning a little sheepishly. "I was too distracted."

"It's daylight," she said. "He's terribly busy. Do you want me to distract you again?"

He was still watching her warily, hesitating. She felt her breath quicken. She wanted him to like her, like her enough to help her escape, so she had kissed him—and he had liked it, she could tell. For her it was... strange. She had only kissed one pair of lips, known one body. She was curious about Hound.

"Well?" she murmured.

He stood up and nodded.

"Not here," she said. "Just in case. I know a good place."

As she led him out, Rose stood up to follow them.

"I would rather she didn't come along," Ammolite said.

He nodded and said something in a language she didn't know. The beast settled back to the floor.

IT WENT very quickly with Hound, and she had to fight not to laugh at his enthusiasm and genuine, joyful surprise.

"I like the look of you," Hound told her, after, as they lay together on the bed in her childhood room. For years she had been the only one who came here. The entire hall was abandoned now.

Ammolite looked down and realized that Hound was talking about her—her face, her body, not Orra's. This had never happened with Veulkh, of course. In fact, a part of her had wondered if her real body could even do what they had just done. But it had all felt the same—the only differences were due to Hound being a different person.

And that he was looking at *her*. She felt suddenly shy, and pulled at a sheet to cover herself.

"Why would you do that?" he asked.

"It's… I'm not used to it," she said. "It makes me feel strange to be looked at."

"But we just—"

"I know," she said. "I can't explain it."

"All right, then," he said. "Should I cover myself, too?"

"No," she said. "That's not necessary."

Hound nodded. She thought about it for a moment.

"I do this with Veulkh," she said, "but he uses his sorcery to make me look like—someone else. Someone he was in love with. I think she may be dead now."

Hound got a funny expression on his face.

"I followed you," he said, after a moment. "I saw you in his lair—his conjury."

"Oh." She felt the wind suck out of her for a moment. He had watched. He had seen Orra.

For the first time in years, she began to weep.

"Do you dislike it?" Hound asked. "Being her?" He wiped gently at her tears with his fingers.

"Yes." She shrugged. "And I don't like him. I've thought of throwing myself from the balcony. I was considering that when I met you, and then I started to think…" She trailed off.

"That I would take you from here?"

"Yes."

He was silent for a moment. "Is that why you kissed me? Is that why we——"

"I thought so," she said. "Now I don't know. Veulkh says we're going on a long journey. He says I must remain Orra for the entire time. He won't say why."

"But I've seen you," Hound said. He grinned. "All of you."

"He must never know that," she said. "Never. Or we are both in terrible danger."

Hound was silent for a long moment, and she suddenly realized how much peril she was in. She didn't know Hound at all, did she? And he had struck some sort of bargain with Veulkh. She was completely in Hound's power now.

"I can't put you on my back and climb down the mountain," he finally said. "We'll have to go with them, pretend we don't know each other until I see a good chance. Do you understand?"

She nodded, feeling suddenly lighter.

Was it possible? Would he do it?

Could he?

"How does he move things?" Hound asked. "Like he did me?"

"What do you mean?"

She listened as he explained, and realized that her years of reading Veulkh's books hadn't been in vain.

"Did you know," she said, "that all of the waters of the world are connected, deep beneath the earth? There are no seas or rivers or oceans, but just one ocean. If you lived beneath the water like a fish, you could travel anywhere that water goes."

"I didn't know that, but it makes sense."

"All of the air is connected, too," she went on. "The sky, the wind, the breath in your lungs. Birds travel on the air. And then there is the earth, which has its own currents—some cold and slow, some quick and extremely hot. I've read some of his books on these subjects, but I don't understand it as he does. Only that there are special places—even places that can be made—where the hidden trails in air and earth or water intersect.

"They are called 'synapses.' Some are great, others small. His conjury is one of the great ones—he built his mansion around it. The one at the foot of the mountain is probably lesser. He may have even put it there in case he had to send someone down. There are magicks used to travel those secret ways."

He didn't entirely understand, and decided to change the topic.

"Do you know where we're going, or why?"

"No," she said. "Can't you ask your friends?"

He shook his head. "They won't tell me, but we're leaving tomorrow." He reached for her sheet. "It may be a long time before I get to see you like this again," he said.

She glanced down and was a bit startled at what she saw.

"Really?" she said. "Already?"

His smile broadened.

CHAPTER NINE

LI BAUD

"AH," THE man said. "There you are."

He took a long drink of wine directly from a bottle and set it on the stand next to the bed. He looked up and down the length of her, and when his gaze met hers, he grinned. She felt a sort of jolt go through her and knew she was blushing. His desire was so frank, so unapologetic, she found it difficult to breathe.

He was not a particularly good-looking man. Perhaps twenty years her senior, and it looked as if he had spent most of that time eating and drinking to excess. The silk robe he had draped himself in made no attempt to hide his paunch. His fading auburn hair was unkempt.

Without making any effort to straighten his posture, he turned on his side and patted the bed next to him. For an incredible moment, she thought he was gesturing for her to sit there. But then the servant girl continued over to him and took that place, reclining languidly against his chest. He stroked her hair.

"Please," he said. "Have a seat." He gestured to the end of the bed. Face still burning, she struggled to keep her composure.

"I must insist on knowing who you are, and what you want with me," she said.

"Prudent," he said. "Circumspect. If my name will comfort you, by all means have it. I am Anaxagoras Bonaventure. But I am better known, in many circles, as Li Baud."

For a moment, astonishment closed her mouth.

This was Bonaventure?

"The Lewd"? The man her father instructed her to seek out?

"I have not been in those circles, sir," she said. "Nor am I acquainted with such language."

"Then why are you blushing?" he asked, wagging a finger at her. "And 'those circles'? You are entering them now." He picked up the wine bottle. "A drink?" he asked.

"No, thank you."

He shrugged and handed it to the girl, who took a long draught before returning it to Bonaventure.

"You are here," he said, "to spy for your father."

"I am here," she said, "because the emperor requires it."

"That's also true," Bonaventure said, "but it's not the particular truth that concerns us. Have a seat."

Chrysanthe was feeling dizzy enough anyway, so she did so, trying to stay as far from the old lecher as possible.

"Your father told you none of the particulars, I'm sure," he went on. "To do so would have been unwise, even had he known them all, which he did not."

"How is it you are in my cousin's house?" she demanded. "Fondling his servant?"

He rolled his eyes. "Luce, whose servant are you?"

"Only yours, mon Baud," Luce replied. She shot Chrysanthe a devilish little grin.

"As to the other," Bonaventure continued, "I am a guest of your cousin. When I heard that you were here, against expectations, I took the opportunity to have this conversation a little ahead of schedule, as it were. I had originally planned to somehow meet you at Roselant."

"My father meant for me to stay here."

"Yes," Bonaventure replied, "but the game has changed. And so you know, it was my suggestion that you stay at Roselant."

She tried to keep her face expressionless.

"Why?" she asked.

He took another drink from the bottle.

"Did you know there was a riot in the city, four nights ago?"

"No," she said. "No one mentioned it."

"It wasn't the first, either," he said. "There have been smaller mobs that attacked warehouses and such, but these came against the palace. Many were killed, which only makes matters worse. The entire city is a cauldron, on the verge of boiling over. And someone is behind it."

"I saw the conditions people live in here," she said. "Why isn't that explanation enough? When people are hungry and dirty, they can easily be driven to violence."

"Of course," he replied, "but there is ample evidence that someone is directing the mob's inchoate anger toward the emperor. There have been pamphlets and other propaganda. In general, they blame the emperor's new adventure against the Drehhu for worsening conditions here in the capital."

"Is this true?"

"No," he replied. "The starving would be starving with or without this war. It's more a matter of the emperor seeming out of touch with his people, preferring foreign adventures to working out some form of relief for the people of the city. Which is, in fact, true. The emperor, simply put, is an idiot."

Chrysanthe was so shocked that anyone would say such a thing, she had no response. Rather than stammer, she kept quiet.

"He is, however," Bonaventure went on, "*my* idiot, and things will get no better—for anyone—if the Elanthoi come into power." There at last was a name she knew. Several emperors had sprung from that family, and they were powerful still.

"You believe the Elanthoi are behind this?"

"They are *certainly* behind it," he said. "They've coveted the throne since they lost it a century ago. But I cannot prove it. You might be able to." He stopped and looked at her expectantly.

Everything about the man offended her. She felt tainted just by his presence. It seemed impossible that this could be a person her father trusted, or would even speak to—and even more outrageous that she had not been warned of his nature. For all she knew, Bonaventure was the enemy, and he was bending her toward the destruction of herself and the Nevelon family.

If this man was even who he claimed to be.

Yet if what he said was true, her father would want her to do everything she could to preserve the emperor. Although it was the emperor's war her father had sent her to learn about.

"Were the Elanthoi in favor of the war?"

"Yes," he said. "On the surface, at least, but that's not where the real push came from. That came from the Cryptarchia. How else could the three empires be coaxed into acting in concert?"

"Does the Cryptarchia favor the Elanthoi?" she asked. "I thought they were above politics."

He stared at her for an instant with an expression of purest surprise. Then he let out a great belly-laugh. She felt her face redden yet again.

He gasped and wiped a tear from his eye.

"The Cryptarchia… above politics?" he finally said. "Only in the sense that they squat upon the very top of politics. They are entirely political creatures, owing allegiance only to themselves, and never to any particular empire. Which has the effect of irritating emperors. Ours, in particular, has had his share of disagreements with the cryptarchs. So yes, they may well be backing the Elanthoi, if only to have a more compliant emperor."

"What do you imagine I can accomplish at Roselant?" she asked. "As you can see, I am entirely ignorant of these matters."

"Perhaps, but you have your father's confidence, and so mine. Roselant petitioned the emperor for the right to host you. I suggested that he allow them to do so, because I believe there are allies of the Elanthoi and the Cryptarchia among them. The Elanthoi are a grasping, venal lot, are always hoping to advance themselves through whatever means they can. Roselant may be the very heart of this matter—and you will be there."

"My father told me not to trust anyone."

"Excellent advice," Bonaventure replied. "Trust prevents one from seeing clearly. You need to see clearly."

"And then report what I see to you, whom I do not trust?"

He shrugged. "When the time comes, you will probably work out what to do. Or not. Don't imagine that I'm placing all my faith in you. I have other instruments."

It was as if she was in a daze—so stunned by the absolute impropriety of this man, this room, this situation. It all seemed unreal. Now, as she watched Bonaventure reach around to stroke Luce's breast, it was all too much.

"I must leave," she said. "I'm going."

"You know enough for now," Bonaventure said. "I will be in touch."

"Luce," she said. "Would you escort me back to my room?"

"I believe, Danesele, you can escort yourself," the girl said. Then she tilted her head back so Bonaventure could kiss her.

Chrysanthe turned in a rush and fled.

CHAPTER TEN

THE PALAIS

SHE HOPED to wake and find it all a dream, but Chrysanthe was never able to go to sleep, and lay restless in her bed. Finally she rose with the light and bathed using the sponge and basin of clean water that had been provided. She did this more quickly than usual, fearful that Bonaventure somehow could see her, violate her body with his greedy eyes.

Should she tell Leon what sort of monster he had let into his home? That Luce was Bonaventure's spy in his house?

Did Leon already know?

If so, then she was surely lost, and no one she knew would be what they seemed. Perhaps not even her father.

Breakfast was casual, and the family joined it as they woke. She dreaded seeing Bonaventure come down the stairs, wondered how she would be able to behave around him—but he never appeared. Luce did, looking as proper and groomed and acting as respectful as when Chrysanthe had first met her. Nothing in her manner suggested that she had done anything but sleep the night before, alone, quietly, in her own bed.

Leon and Daphne made small talk, but neither made any mention of the so-called "Li Baud."

She did not raise the subject.

Quintent joined them, and she found that she was desperately glad to see him. He was the one person in the house that she could be fairly certain had no direct connection to Bonaventure. After all, it had been her idea to pay her cousins a visit, and he had resisted it. Of course, if what she had been told was true, Quintent might well be part of a conspiracy to usurp the emperor. At the moment, however, that seemed more forgivable than having any part of the situation she had been put into the night before.

Quintent made polite conversation for an appropriate period, and then announced—as if with great reluctance—that it was time they were on their way.

This time, Chrysanthe made no objection.

From the carriage she watched the city pass with a different eye, noticing the sullen clusters of men gathered in front of taverns, grumbling in hushed voices, the hostile glances she and her escort received, the gaunt frames of those without enough to eat. Where before she had believed indifference made the crowd part too slowly from their path, she now began to suspect a form of passive resistance.

"Where are we going?" she asked.

"You said you wanted to see the palace," Quintent said. "We have the time."

"Yes," she replied, pleasantly surprised. "Thank you."

As she watched the famous Spiral Keep rise above the rooftops, her heart lifted a bit, but when they entered the broad Place del Palais, she saw a crowd gathered there—men and some women in rough clothing. A smaller group of soldiers with pikes, swords, and crossbows had placed themselves between the mob and the palace. At the moment, nothing was happening except a considerable amount of shouting.

Abruptly, someone slammed into the carriage door, reaching in, grasping at her. She glimpsed an expression of contempt and anger, a mouth only half-filled with teeth, and a bristle of black hair. He was shouting something, but stopped suddenly as one of Quintent's men struck him with a truncheon. He dropped from sight and she sat there, her heart trying to pound through the bone of her breast.

"I…" she managed, and no more.

"I'm so sorry," Quintent said as the carriage came to a stop. "I should have ridden ahead to make certain it was safe."

She nodded, catching her breath.

"This is perhaps not the best time for sightseeing," Quintent went on.

"Are we expected?" she asked.

"I scheduled a brief audience with the emperor," he said, "but excuses may be made."

She gazed about. Driven back by the guards, the crowd seemed to be dispersing, and the plaza was gaining a semblance of order. She thought about her mother's words, and the charter that granted her father his lands and livelihood. Did one make excuses when one had an engagement with the emperor? Could doing so cost her and her family everything?

It seemed very likely.

She was upset, yes, but she was not a child.

"No," she said. "I am quite well. We shall keep our appointment."

"If that is your wish," Quintent replied. He nodded to the coachman and the vehicle returned to motion.

THE PLACE del Palais was cleared, and coaches queued up at the front gate, but theirs did not join the line. Instead, Quintent directed his driver to take them around the side of the palace, where they soon crowded into a lively area that contained the largest stables she had ever seen and small, thickly piled apartments that she assumed must be servant's quarters.

It was like a small village to itself, complete with vendors hawking barrows of shellfish, breads, cheese, and fruit. Why they were approaching by this route was a mystery to her, but Chrysanthe decided to hold her questions so as to not reveal how completely out of her depth she was.

Their driver passed his carriage and horses off to stable hands. Then Quintent escorted her to a battered wooden door that opened into a large, low, smokey room. The scale was so great it took her a moment to recognize that they were in a kitchen, that the smoke came from several coal-fired hearths, and steam from enormous cauldrons. A few of the servants glanced at them through the corners of their eyes, but quickly returned to their work.

From there they proceeded into a maze of corridors that eventually brought them to a room lit through large ceiling windows. A dozen young men and woman scurried around broad tables spread with fabulous fabrics of all sorts, shelves filled with bolts of material, manakins draped in half-finished attire. A man of middle years who seemed to be presiding over the barely ordered chaos looked up as they entered.

"Quintent," he said. "How nice of you to come by." He ran his glance quickly over Chrysanthe.

"Maistre Anthién, I have the great pleasure of presenting Chrysanthe Nevelon."

"Diex vos sait, Danesele," Anthién said. "How are the provinces?"

Chrysanthe felt her face warm and tried not to glance down at her outfit.

"Is it so obvious?" she asked.

"Maistre, play nice," Quintent said.

"Do not mistake me," Anthién responded. "I admire the fashion of—it's Mesembria, isn't it? The Coste de Sucre, perhaps?"

Chrysanthe nodded.

"The freedom of the silhouette, the unbridled use of color, the timeless quality—I only wish I were so free. Instead I must hew to the absurdist details of a vapid, joyless sequence of whims. And so I apologize in advance."

"For what, Maistre?" Chrysanthe asked.

"I can only imagine that Quintent brought you here for me to dress you." He tilted his head, then waved a girl over. "Get her particulars," he said, then he turned back. "I assume it must be today?"

"By the early hours of the afternoon," Quintent said.

"Of course. There is no time to make anything from nothing, but I believe I have something that may be fitted to her by that hour. You may return by the first of the clock."

"If you would come with me, Danesele," the girl said. She was fair and freckled, and likely not more than nine. She led Chrysanthe into a small room with a couch, a table with a candle, and a small shelf of books. "You'll need to remove what you're wearing, please," the girl said.

"May I know your name?"

"It's Nicole, Danesele."

"Thank you, Nicole," she said. "May I retain my undergarments?"

"Yes," Nicole said.

Chrysanthe took off her dress and waited as the girl used a tape measure to assess her various proportions.

"How did you make your skin such a deep brown?" the girl asked her. "I should love skin like that. Is it some sort of pigment?"

"I have this from my father," Chrysanthe replied, "who is in fact of an even deeper shade. My mother is almost as fair as you."

"You were born like this?"

"I was."

"Oh," the girl said. She sounded disappointed. After a moment, she finished up her task and scurried off.

It was at least three hours until noon. Chrysanthe went to the shelf and looked through the books. Most were novels of courtly or pastoral love, and did not interest her. There was a single autobiographical account of the Marquis de Priv. She was only a few pages into it before she realized it, too was a work of fiction; the "Marquis" was born a woman but had sworn to her father to live life as a man, with all of the complications that entailed, most of which were meant to be funny. It was entertaining enough, so she continued to read of the young "man" and his misadventures and was pretty deep in when the door opened and another young woman entered.

"Oh," Chrysanthe said, keenly aware that she was in her undergarments, while the newcomer was clothed in a vivid purple gown with more buttons on its bodice than Chrysanthe had ever seen in one place. A stiff collar entirely enveloped her neck and throat. It looked uncomfortable.

"I'm sorry," she said. "They told me to wait here."

"Yes, so I heard," the young woman said. "Would you make room on the couch please? I should like to sit."

"Of course," Chrysanthe said, unfolding her legs and scooting over. The young woman sat. She looked to be sixteen or seventeen, at most.

"You're actually reading that?" she said, as she sat down.

"It's the least objectionable book present," Chrysanthe replied.

"May I see it?"

Chrysanthe handed it over.

"Oh," she said. "It is one of these."

"One of what?"

"A romance. A costume romance."

"I'm familiar with many sorts of romance," Chrysanthe said, "but this I have never heard of."

"Well, you see, in each story there is some reason given that this girl must dress as a man and live as a man. In time she will discover that she has the tastes of a man—you see? And fall in love with another woman. Or it could as easily be about a man who must dress as a woman. The results are just as predictable."

"This is an entire genre?"

"It is, and a naughty one." She cocked her head. "You're a provincial, yes? This must not be at all shocking to you."

"What do you mean?"

"Is it not true? That girls lie with girls and boys with boys?" She smiled. "Oh, and I am Emeline."

For a moment Chrysanthe just blinked, trying to gather her composure.

"In childhood," she said at last, "we are taught to tend our affections toward those of our same sex. It is not unusual."

"To prevent pregnancy, you mean," Emeline said.

Chrysanthe frowned. "Affection and... what you imply are not necessarily the same thing," she said.

"I notice that you hedge," Emeline said.

"I do not," Chrysanthe said, "but I admit that I am uncomfortable with the topic."

"Do you find *me* attractive?"

"I become more uncomfortable."

"It's just as well," Emeline said. "I am betrothed, but just so you know—what might be entertaining in a lewd book, or acceptable in some far-flung province is here, in Ophion Magne—in reality— fantastical and simply dangerous."

"I will believe you," Chrysanthe said, eager to be done with the whole subject. "Are you also here for a fitting?"

Emeline smiled. "No. I took a fancy to meet you, that is all."

"How could you even know of me?"

"The hostage from Mesembria? The daughter of Admiral Nevelon? How could I not?"

"Really?"

"Really." She rose. "And now, unfortunately, I must flee, or else there will be gossip that you ravaged me. As a woman affianced, I can't have such talk. Another day. I'm sure we will meet again."

With that, Emeline was gone, leaving Chrysanthe feeling—more than ever—as if she was foundering in deep and unknown waters.

BY THE bell-clock outside, it was a bit over two hours later that several young women showed up with a gown for her final fitting.

By that time, she had read enough of the romance to know that Emeline was completely correct in her assumptions. The "Marquis" had "abducted" the willing daughter of the Comte de Telier, and after a number of humorous false starts based on assumptions about identity, the two were firmly—and carnally—connected.

As the dress was sewn onto her, Chrysanthe wondered if she might not have done better to pretend to have been a Nevelon son, rather than daughter. It was a ridiculous thought—anything could work out in the fantastic world of a romance, but reality was not as forgiving. A hundred factors conspired against bringing off such a ruse.

Still. She might have had a chance, had she boarded the ship as a man, come to this new place as a man. But even if such a thing could be done, it was too late now. And besides, everyone in Ophion Magne seemed to know who she was and entirely too much about her, anyway.

If there had ever been any doubt as to her feminine nature, the dress removed it. It was quite tight, although not uncomfortably so, and clung to her from her neck to just below her hips in an unseemly way, with no bustle or ribbon in the back to conceal the shape of her. From there to her ankles, it fell quite straight. A sort of loose sarong was wrapped and belted at the largest extent of her hips. The fabric was more colorful than she had come to expect; the dress itself was saffron, the belt patterned in rust and brown, the strange overskirt a gauzy orange. The girls wound a small, loose turban of red silk around her hair and placed a feather plume through it.

When all was done, Maistre Anthién returned to survey his handiwork. He made a few small adjustments here and there.

"The cloth is brighter than I expected," Chrysanthe said.

"Well, you are from Mesembria, and will be expected to appear exotic," Anthién replied.

"No one from Mesembria dresses like this," she said. "My own clothes are more representative."

"Child," he sighed, "don't tax me. This will do, I assure you."

They found Quintent waiting outside in the larger room.

"You've been here this whole time?" she asked.

"No," he replied. "I had the opportunity to conduct some business, did so, and have only just returned. Are you prepared for your audience with the emperor?"

She glanced down at her outfit.

"Yes?" she replied.

"Yes," Quintent repeated. He delivered a little bow toward Anthién. "Maistre, my thanks. You have never failed me."

"Illusion is my trade," the older man replied. "I take pride in it."

QUINTENT WALKED close to her, with only a fingerbreadth separating them. He never pulled ahead of her, and yet she could always tell when he was about to turn down one of the many side corridors, because he took the slightest of pauses and turned his eyes in the direction they should go. To the casual observer, she thought, it would appear as if they both knew the route by heart. She could not be sure, but it felt like a kindness. If she seemed uncertain, or if he actually took her arm to guide her, it would appear less than seemly.

After a half-dozen turns, they came to a much grander corridor, and soon entered the largest room she had ever seen. The floor was of variegated stone tiles polished to a high sheen; the ceiling rose into a high dome bejeweled so as to resemble a night sky and the constellations. After a moment's regard, she realized that it didn't represent any real sky.

She stopped to be certain.

Quintent waited patiently.

"That is the Harp," she said, nodding toward one of the constellations. "It is seen only in the most southern skies. And yet there is the Chariot, which belongs to the north. These constellations could never be seen together."

"Indeed," Quintent said. "Those are the heavens that look down upon the Empire of Ophion, wherever its constituent parts might lie."

She drew her gaze down from the ceiling to the tapestries on the wall and the two tall chairs on a raised dais at the far end of the room.

"It's the Sale de li Trone," she murmured.

"Yes," he replied.

"My audience with the emperor is here?"

"Of course not. He despises this place and uses it only for occasions of high state. Nevertheless, I thought you would like to see it."

CHAPTER ELEVEN

THE EMPEROR

THE EMPEROR looked something like his portraits. He had the curved nose and green eyes, anyway, and his chin was properly square, almost as if an anvil had been pushed into his skull. But his hair was thinner and more receding, and in general he was more… puffy, than in his likenesses.

He affected a mustache so thin it might have been drawn on, and his eyebrows were the same. He wore a long white chemise with a colorfully floral dressing gown of silk thrown over it, and reclined comfortably on a couchelette, an oval-shaped bed with a raised back and sides. She was unpleasantly reminded of Bonaventure on the bed at her cousin's house.

If the emperor was in disarray, the others in his chamber were not. She counted twelve in all, a mixture of men and women and one young boy, all impeccably dressed in muted colors. None of the gowns in the room looked remotely like the one she wore.

Everyone was standing, except the boy, who sat on a small stool. A small gold and brown hound lay nestled against the emperor's chest.

The emperor's eyes drifted up from the hound as a footman introduced Quintent, then Chrysanthe. She smiled broadly.

"Who do you see, Minister Bossu?" he asked.

Chrysanthe held her smile, waiting to see which of the assembled guests was the minister. But none of them spoke. Her chest tightened; their gazes felt as if they pricked her skin.

"Yes," the emperor said. "Yes, I believe that is who she is. Didn't you hear her announced?"

At that point, Chrysanthe realized the emperor was talking to his dog.

What is this? she wondered.

"Don't understand, you say?" the emperor continued. "No indeed, how could I forget? You don't know a single damned word, do you, Minister Bossu?"

Everyone suddenly laughed. The emperor glanced around at the courtiers, nodding his head.

"Every time, eh?" He chucked the dog under the chin. "Oh, Bossu," he said, then he looked up at Chrysanthe. "But he is correct, is he not? You are the Nevelon hostage, aren't you?"

Chrysanthe found it difficult to breathe. This was the *emperor*. How was she supposed to respond? She remembered her mother's warnings. If she said the wrong thing here, and earned the emperor's disdain, what would happen? Would her family be ruined? Given the way the courtiers were studying her, it seemed possible.

"Minister Bossu is quite astute," Chrysanthe finally said. She expected a laugh at that, but the room was dead silent. She began to feel a hint of panic.

"Well, you needn't flatter him," the emperor said. "I've just established that he can't understand a thing he hears."

Again the room was full of forced gaiety.

"Yes, Imperial Majesty," she said. "Silly of me."

The emperor blinked and cocked his head. His eyes widened.

"By the stars," the emperor said. "Your voice is quite lovely. The accent is musical. I can all but imagine myself on a grand barge on the River Nihar, drawn along by a team of galumphing water-horses. Just your voice takes me there, you know. And your dress, your complexion—such a lovely infusion of color in our drab world." He sat up a little. "Indulge my fantasy. If I were on such a barge in your colony, what wonders might I behold?"

Chrysanthe tried to take a deeper breath without seeming to, though the dress was so tight that her every movement had to be obvious. Was this a test of some sort? The River Nihar was indeed on her home continent, but many hundreds of leagues from Port Bellship. It would have taken far longer to reach than her trip to Ophion Magne. She had never been there.

By water-horses she took him to mean hippopotamuses. As bad ideas went, that was top rate. Yet clearly the emperor was expecting something of her, and she doubted it was for her to correct his geography. He had asked her for a fantasy, hadn't he? Then she would indulge that, and hope for the best.

"Well," she said. "The river itself is overarched with the spreading branches of fever trees, all feathery leaves and flowers like creamy spheres. Birds of many colors dart about. Look, there is a rainbow spite, and now a viridian parrot more green than any leaf. A purple ambulatory hornbill the size of a child runs through the undergrowth on long, scaly legs. Honey-catchers no larger than bumblebees dart amongst the great trumpet-shaped flowers in the shallows, where also wade giant flamingos and an alabaster ibis, believed by the Tamanja to be the incarnation of a god."

A breath…

"There's a monkey, with a head as red as a rose, who swings on arms longer than the rest of its body. A golden denger with the body of a squirrel and the face of a fox cocks its head to regard you, and those rough-looking logs on the banks suddenly plunge into the murky water, swimming in the direction of our barge. They are crocodiles, with gaping jaws and teeth like razors. And beyond, in the forest, white stone smothered in moss and vines, the ruins of an ancient race, a metropolis now swallowed by jungle…"

"Stop there," the emperor said. "Olivier, come here."

A young man near the back of the room emerged from the crowd, nearly stumbling as he did so.

"Imperial Majesty," he said.

"Did you hear that? In a few words, with no instruments, she has bested your last effort. Make me a divertissement in two acts—no, make it three. Nevelon here can advise you as to the instrumentation. You may consult with her when we are done."

"Of course, Imperial Majesty," the young man said.

The emperor nodded. Then he tilted his head toward the dog.

"Yes," he said. "Why, I shall ask her," he said. Then he looked back at Chrysanthe. "Minister Bossu wishes to know how our most civic cause is taken in Mesembria. Our holy crusade against the Drehhu."

"We are all in support of it," she said.

The emperor frowned and held up a finger.

"Are there—let us imagine a for instance—gangs of malcontents protesting this most pressing imperial undertaking?"

"No, Imperial Majesty, nothing of that sort."

"Do they print pamphlets full of deceitful lies regarding our cause?"

"I should know if there were, Majesty, and there are not."

"I see," he said, his face bunching briefly into angry lines, but then smoothing. He looked down at Minster Bossu. "Our colonies send us their children as proof of their good faith. Of their fidelity. And yet here, in so called 'civilized' lands, we are beset by ungrateful and ungracious dissembling and whinging of a most treacherous nature."

"It is only a few malcontents," a man with a large, red-veined nose ventured. "The people are with you."

"I am their emperor," he replied. "How is it even a question, this matter of loyalty?"

"They will understand when the battle is finished," the man said.

"Bossu says the same thing," the emperor replied, "and yet he is a dog, is he not?"

"He... is, Majesty."

"Then tell him so, Rhidon."

"Minister Bossu," Rhidon said. "You are, indeed, but a dog."

"Rhidon," the emperor said. "Get ahold of yourself. Have we not this very day and hour established he cannot understand a damned word you say?"

Silence.

Then there was laughter.

"Oh, Rhidon," the emperor said. "Is it any wonder I prefer Bossu's counsel over yours?" The laughter escalated. The emperor winked at her. Then he nodded, and everyone fell silent as he returned his attentions to the dog.

Chrysanthe continued to stand, wondering what to do, then Quintent bowed. She followed his lead, and afterward the chamberlain led them out. When they reached the hall, Chrysanthe stumbled.

Quintent quickly took her arm.

"I'm fine," she said.

"You forgot to breathe, I think."

"That was terrifying," she whispered. "How could a friend allow me to enter *that* so unprepared?"

"I cannot recall you allowing that we are friends," Quintent said.

"I suppose the fault is mine then," she replied. She felt a surge of irritation, but reminded herself that she should expect nothing. Quintent appeared kind, most of the time. It was just such a person her mother had warned her against.

She let the silence hang, rather than appear stupid. After a moment, he shrugged.

"You did very well," he said. "Any attempt to prepare you might have muddled your own good instincts. Besides, one never knows how the emperor will interpret anything."

"Yet you say I did well."

He shrugged. "I think *he* liked you, at least."

She looked up. "Which is to say?"

"That everyone else in the room likely despises you."

"Oh," she said. "Well, I suppose it's just as well we won't be staying in the city."

"That will work out to your advantage, I think," he said. Then he looked past her. "Oh, yes," he said. "You had best speak to this one."

She turned and saw Olivier.

"Danesele," he said. "If I may steal a moment of our time—"

"Drums," she said, "and the lyre. And reeded flutes. Wooden and brass chimes."

"Danesele—"

"We must be on our way," Quintent said.

"I can write you a longer note," Chrysanthe said.

"Very kind," Olivier said. "I am the emperor's chanteor. If you address it in that fashion, it will find me."

"I will do so," she said.

"Please be quick," Olivier said. Then he bowed and, head down, returned to the emperor's room.

As Quintent guided her back to the carriage, Chrysanthe's spirits began to flag. She tried to turn her thoughts from the audience, but that brought her back to the earlier scene—the riot, the man clawing at her carriage. Her mother had tried to warn her about this place, but it was all much worse than she had imagined. And she had only just arrived.

By the time they were in the carriage, she was on the verge of tears. It was embarrassing, and annoying. She did not want Quintent to see her in this light, and yet she had no choice. They were shut in together for who knew how long.

Why did she feel so weak? She had known worse. When Lucien held his sword to her throat, no tears had threatened—but then it had only been her life threatened, not the welfare of everyone she held dear.

She quietly began to weep.

Quintent politely looked away, pretending not to notice. She did not stop crying until they passed the city walls and were into the country.

ONCE THEY were clear of the city, things quickly became more pleasant. Forest groves and long, dark green hedges broke up rolling fields of grass and clover where sheep, cows, and horses grazed. Neat little half-timbered farmhouses looked almost as if they had grown up from the earth. She saw a manor on a high hill, and a little village with one steeple below. She wondered if it was Roselant, but the coachman did not turn at the crossroads.

Darkness fell, and a pale crescent moon seemed to follow them along the horizon. A night bird sang a slippery trill, sounding almost like a windgobble from back home, the difference being a slight one of pitch and duration. The cool air carried the perfumes of flowers and grass, with no trace of the city's stench.

Rocked by the motion of the carriage, she fell asleep.

Chrysanthe woke in the gray of morning, her head resting on something soft. She started when she realized it was Quintent's shoulder. He in turn was slumped against his side of the carriage. Mortified, she gently lifted her head, hoping he wouldn't wake, that he hadn't been awake when she shifted in her sleep. Surely she had leaned against her own door as Hypnos drew her into dream.

A mist lay softly on the fields, but thinned as the sun rose. It was nearly gone when they entered a town, a quaint little place with a single basilica of white stone that looked as if it could easily be three or four hundred years old. The houses were mostly of the same stone, although some were half-timbered, like the farmhouses. Children waved at her as they passed through, and she waved back. Tradesmen glanced up from their work and some said a word or two to the horsemen accompanying the carriage. She was struck by how uniformly pale-skinned the people were, and how relatively drab their clothing, as if the only colors they recognized were those found in clouds, ash, and lampblack.

There was a small sound and she turned. Quintent was awake, rubbing his eyes with the back of his hand.

"Good morning," he said, and he glanced outside. "Ah. We're nearly there." He turned to her. "Did you sleep well?"

"Very well," she said, alert for any signal that he was aware he had been her pillow for a time.

"I'm glad," he replied. "I personally find it difficult to sleep in the city."

"I had the same experience."

"You shall sleep well at Roselant, I think," he said.

THE GROUNDS of Roselant began where the town ended. The road led through open woodland, then formal gardens laid out in geometric patterns and liberally ornamented with statues of ancient gods and heroes. It was nearly a mile before they reached the chastel itself.

The mansion was enormous, dwarfing her father's house. Built in a semicircle, the middle of which stood five stories high while the wings had only three, it had more windows than she had ever seen. Overall, it looked like a pleasant place to be imprisoned.

"Did you grow up here?" she asked Quintent.

"I did not," he replied. "I grew up in my father's house in Othres, but I did spend many fond days here as a boy."

"You said you were related."

He nodded. "The master of this house is Nicolas d'Othres. His father was my great-grandfather, Gui, so he is my grand-uncle, and I am some sort of cousin to most who dwell here."

"After you deliver me, will you remain?"

"Of course," he said. "At least for a time. How else will our friendship deepen?"

She smiled. "It is said friendship develops most profoundly at a distance, and through mutual and thoughtful correspondence. But I will be happy to have a familiar face."

"Three days and I'm already familiar? How soon before I'm last week's fish?"

"That," she said, "is entirely up to you."

BY THE time they reached the house, the family and staff had been alerted and turned out to greet her. Nicolas d'Othres was a spindle of a man long in years, with an uncertain look in his eyes. His wife, Ysabel, was much younger—in her fifties, Chrysanthe guessed. She had an air about her that suggested everything she saw and heard was translated into numbers.

Then there was a cloud of their children, grandchildren, and great-grandchildren. She did her best to pin names to her perceptions. Margot—tall, young, face like a grape leaf, amber hair, polite but reserved. Tristan, wonder-eyed, streak of gray in chestnut, limping. Nicolas the younger, about her age, copper-tressed, wouldn't meet her eye, but she caught him glancing a little lower…

She marked twenty-three in all. None seemed, on the surface, to be the sort to overthrow an emperor. Plesance—the daughter of Tristan, granddaughter of Nicolas—seemed to dislike her immediately, but Chrysanthe thought it might have something to do with the way the young woman looked at Quintent. As Chrysanthe worked it out, Plesance was his third cousin, which wasn't unheard of for a match, especially if noble blood was involved.

The crowd swept Quintent away, and soon she too was escorted to her room, a pleasant third-story apartment with a view of the gardens.

A servant-girl of perhaps fifteen named Orenge helped her unpack and hung her things in the wardrobe. Chrysanthe tried to resist the suspicion that this girl, too, might be an instrument of Bonaventure's and, like Luce, had known his disgusting attentions—but that was unfortunately not possible. Or perhaps it was fortunate. Three people had told her now that suspicion was one of her only weapons.

The girl finished her tasks and left, and Chrysanthe was finally alone again. She did not know how long that would last—everyone, including Plesance, had insisted on showing her some part of the house or grounds as soon as possible.

Her window faced west. She opened it to the evening air and watched Helios cast long shadows in the gardens as he descended slowly into the distant trees. It wasn't home, but it was at least quiet.

She thought back through her meeting with the family, searching through the conversations, their mannerisms, their expressions, wondering what her time here would be like. Were they all plotting to ruin her, as her mother had predicted?

Someone knocked softly on the door. She answered and found Orenge, who offered her a letter and a small curtsey. She took the former, puzzled by the d'Othres seal, and carefully opened it.

Danesele, it began.

It has lately been explained to me that friendship is best cultivated through mutual and thoughtful correspondence. To that end, I pen this letter. It occurs to me that you have until now had a less than happy impression of our country. I should now like to make a few points in its favor. The first being that you are now in it…

She began to laugh, for the first time in quite some time. When she was done, she read it again.

If Quintent was a viper, he was certainly trying to hide the fact. So were all the d'Othres, for that matter. The only truly unpleasant person she had met thus far was Bonaventure, and according to her father, he was the one she was supposed to trust.

Maybe Quintent *did* hide a secret, disagreeable face. Certainly, Lucien had, although she had suspected him early on of wrongdoing. And she had discovered and proven his malfeasance not by shunning him, but by encouraging him.

She would do the same with Quintent. If he was not honest, she would discover it. If he was—well, that would be a nice surprise. He was not, ultimately, to her taste, but flirtation, practiced properly, was not harmful, and could be enjoyed for its own sake.

"It is the thing you want to believe that you must be most skeptical of," her father often said. *"There is no trickster more persuasive than your own unguarded mind."*

She opened up her traveling chest and withdrew the little drakewood box in which she kept her pen and ink, thinking to begin an answer to Quintent while the failing light allowed. To her chagrin, she remembered she had used to the last of her paper the night before.

She went to the powder table, a smallish desk with a top that lifted, revealing a mirror on the reverse side and numerous compartments and drawers beneath. She propped up the mirror with its foot and was a little startled by her own face: at how dark it appeared after being in the company of so many very pale people. Her hair was in a bit of disarray, as well, which normally wouldn't bother her much. Now it fed into her worries about what sort of impression she had made on the household.

What was done was done, though.

Rummaging around in the desk, hoping to find some paper there, she realized that in moments it would be too dark to write. She would have to find a candle, as well. The table had powders and perfumes in plenty, but paper eluded her.

A sudden light startled her, a shimmer of silver like starlight on the glass, and in that light the hollows and contours of a face took shape, as if reflected in a pool on a moonlit night. It had a narrow, long chin and high cheekbones, and the small lips were slightly parted. A ghost? Chrysanthe was so startled that she leapt up, her knees striking the desk and sending it toppling over. She spun around, heart pounding in her chest, searching wildly behind her.

If this was a ghost, it was nothing like the one near the shrine back home. It left behind a fear, a horror, a longing that she had never experienced before.

Orenge stood in the doorway, holding a flickering taper. She looked shocked and dismayed.

"I'm so sorry, Danesele," she said. "I was only bringing you some light. The door was open. I didn't mean to startle you."

Chrysanthe's heart was still pounding. Perhaps there had been no ghost. The candle, an old mirror, doubtless with many flaws. Perhaps it had only been the girl's reflection she had seen. Yet Orenge had a nearly round face and a wide mouth…

And Chrysanthe was certain she had closed the door.

"It's fine," she said. "It was no fault of yours."

"Let me help you with the powder table," the girl said.

"I can manage." Chrysanthe took the taper from Orenge. "Thank you for the candle." The girl bobbed and left. Chrysanthe closed the door behind her and placed the candle in a little holder on the table by the bed. The she turned her attention to the overturned vanity.

It wasn't that heavy, and to her relief the glass hadn't shattered. She was starting to close it when she noticed in the flickering yellow light that one of the compartments seemed deeper than before. She fetched the candle and looked closer. What she'd thought was the bottom of it had slid over a bit, revealing a narrow space beneath. In it was what appeared to be paper.

She pushed the false bottom further and found that it was, in fact, a book of some sort. It had no title. She picked it up and opened it to the middle. It was handwritten and seemed to be a journal or diary, but penned in a language she did not know, at least at first glance. Most of the letters were familiar, but in some words, numbers appeared, and characters from the alphabet of Modjal.

It struck her then that it wasn't a strange language. Like her own invented writing, it was a cypher of some sort.

Remembering the face in the mirror, the lightless hollows of its eyes, she shivered.

CHAPTER TWELVE

SULAR BULAN

AGAIN HOUND found himself on all fours, his brains trying to spin out of his head. It was worse this time, far worse, and it took longer to recover, but even before he could see clearly, he knew he was in a very different place. The startled birdcalls were outlandish, the air stank of rotting vegetation and salt, and was so humid that he wondered at first if he was drowning. It was so hot sweat was already beading on his skin.

A man screamed, and continued screaming. Hound heard someone trying to soothe the fellow as the shrieks became groans, then labored panting, and finally silence.

"Some don't survive this sort of passage," Veulkh said to Martin. "I told you that."

The depression in the earth was like the two Hound had already seen, but it was surrounded by the crumbling remains of buildings. Walls of gray-white stone still stood, in some places higher than he was tall. Beyond, the ground itself had been flagged with the same stone, although enormous trees had forced themselves up through the pavement, naked trunks reaching improbably high, only at their tops spreading branches and leaves that sequestered most of the sunlight. Mounds of rubble overgrown with ferns and moss sprawled all around them.

Hound felt a sort of low buzzing, deep in his ear.

"Where are we?" Martin asked.

"Can't you see?" Veulkh said. The sorcerer appeared tired and unsteady. "You are amid Sular Bulan."

Martin looked to Selene, who just shrugged.

"Very well," Martin said. "But where is Sular Bulan? Are we in Haparis? Kaman?"

"You've no need to know that," Veulkh said, "so long as I know where we are."

The buzzing got worse, and there was a tickling along his spine.

"We shouldn't be here," Hound said. "There's something here. Something bad."

Veulkh nodded approvingly. "Yes, you can feel Him, can't you? Can you tell in which direction?"

"All around us," Hound murmured.

"But there must be one direction where He seems more—or less."

Hound knelt, put his palms to the earth, and closed his eyes.

For an instant, he felt nothing more than the buzzing already in his ear. Then something beneath the skin of the earth moved, something gigantic. It shifted only a fraction, but images played against the back of his eyelids. Oily black coils tightening and loosening.

"We should leave," Hound said. "Right now. This place belongs to… something."

"Him," Veulkh had said.

"Which way?" Veulkh asked.

Hound groped, trying to find the answer. Rose found it first and began trotting off, the hair stiff on her neck and tail between her legs.

"That way," he said.

Hound wandered around uneasily as the chevaliers and ravens mounted and made ready, securing the packs that had been loosened when they arrived. He glanced at Ammolite, in her form as Orra, but she would not meet his gaze.

After what seemed like far too long, they started off, hooves clattering on the white pavement. They passed statues with features weathered beyond recognition or covered in moss, round depressions rimmed with stone and thick with scum, twisting spires of granite. The place seemed to go on forever.

"It's hard to believe a town was ever this big," he told Selene.

"You should see Ophion Magne," she said. "Or Savor. There are cities this large and larger in the world, alive and teeming with people."

"I don't know that I would like that," he said. "Too many people."

She smiled down at him. "You saved us again, I think," she said. "Veulkh would not have come without you."

"Perhaps you will reconsider my request," he replied. After lying with Ammolite, he more than ever wanted to see how similar—and how different—Selene might be. How she would feel against him.

She didn't say anything for a moment.

"Do you know anything of love?" she asked.

For a moment, he thought she meant the physical act, and felt a sudden glimmer of hope. Then he understood from her tone and expression she was being more serious, so he considered what she had said.

"I thought I was in love once," he replied. "It felt like I had swallowed something that hurt, but I had to keep it down. It ached worse when I was away from her and not much at all when I was with her."

"That sounds like love," she said. "What happened?"

"There was a man I thought was my friend. He wasn't. We both knew her since we were children, but he was from town, and I wasn't. He was the son of the baron, and I wasn't. So, when he found us together, he began to say things. Telling people things, things that should have been secret. So now he has her, in his castle. And I'm still out here."

"What did *she* want?" Selene asked.

The droning in his skull was getting louder, and Hound didn't really want to talk about this. It wasn't a memory he treasured, but Selene seemed to honestly want to know.

"I went to his castle once," he said. "When he wasn't there, and I crept into her room. I told her I would take her away, and we could be together. She told me she loved me, and then she told me she couldn't live that way—without her family, without the town. She told me no. So I left."

"I'm sorry," Selene said. "First loves are often difficult."

"And the rest are easier?"

She smiled, thinly. "I don't know."

The droning in his skull continued to grow louder and began to sound almost like speech in a language he did not understand. The forest felt like a noose, tightening around them, and the earth as if it was sliding under his feet, pulling him back the way they had come.

A moment later they found themselves staring at the place where they had first arrived.

"We're going in circles," Martin said.

"Hound, you lead us," Veulkh commanded. "No more chatting."

In his gut, Hound felt as if somehow it was too late. He remembered the man who had once somehow entered Grandmother's forest against her wishes. He had wandered aimlessly until he died of hunger. This place was like that, but here Hound was a stranger. He belonged no more than any of the rest.

If He—the thing in the ground—was awake, fully awake, they would suffer the same fate as grandmother's intruder.

But He wasn't awake. Not yet.

Hound whistled, and a moment later the raven settled on his shoulder.

"See us out of this, Soot," he told the bird.

Soot grakked and then flew off. Once again, they set off through the abandoned city. The raven vanished through the canopy, reappearing now and then to lead them on.

"Why here?" Martin asked. "Why in such a place?"

"There was another, a safer synapsis," Veulkh said. "We might still be able to go there, but if we do so, it will take half a year or more to reach our destination."

"That's too long," Martin said. "We have a bit more than a month, at best."

"Yes—now you understand my reluctance."

They came to a wall the horses could not pass, and began to follow along it, searching for a way through. Hound could feel Him in his feet now, as if He were grasping through the earth, trying to catch his ankles.

Two horses stumbled at once.

Hound raced ahead. Everything seemed to tilt, grow steeper, as if he was trying to climb out of a hole, even though the land was almost perfectly flat. He heard cries of terror behind him but refused to turn— if there was something there, he knew it was better not to see it.

"Don't look!" Martin screamed, echoing his thought. "For God's sake, don't look!"

Soot came flying low, chattering with agitation, darting ahead, hopping on the ground, then taking flight again. Hound saw a break in the wall, but his legs felt spent, and it took everything in him to push through the last several steps, until the barrier was behind him.

Immediately his feet felt freer, and he bolted like a wild animal. He didn't stop to rest until he could barely feel Him. Only then did he look to behind to see who was still following.

Veulkh was there, and Ammolite. Martin and a wild-eyed Selene.

Martin did a head count. The chevalier Nicanor was missing, along with two ravens.

There was no talk of going back to look for them.

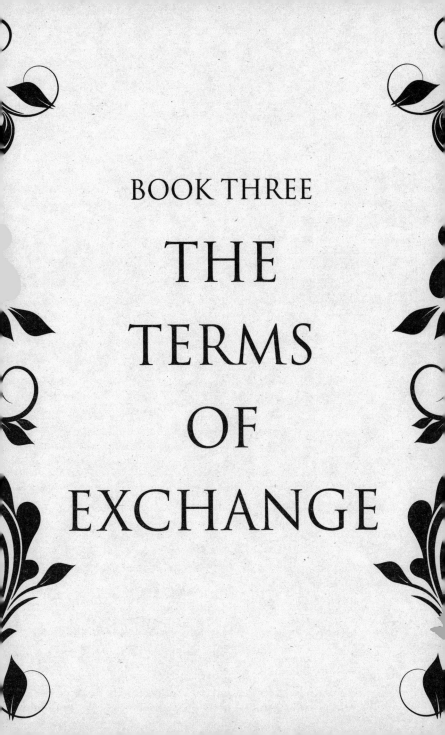

BOOK THREE

THE

TERMS

OF

EXCHANGE

CHAPTER ONE

LACRIME

ORENGE BROUGHT Chrysanthe a breakfast of coffee and sweet rolls. It was something of a surprise; at home breakfast was usually an affair for the table, before the sun was up, and involved not only the family but often many of the plantation's foremen and laborers, depending upon the season. The plans of the day were made at the table. It was the most important and usually the heaviest meal.

Here, breakfast seemed like an afterthought.

Unsure as to what she should do after eating, she put on an amber gown, then turned her attention to the book she'd found the night before. The hand was delicate but not overly embellished. It seemed feminine, but that could not be a given. The entries were each titled with what she presumed to be the date, because they were written in a series of "words" that were similar except for a character or two.

After puzzling at if for a while, she realized that each started with either one or two numerals in the Modjal fashion. At first she thought they might be months or days, but the sequence didn't make sense. One entry began with 6, and so did the next several, but then came a series beginning with 9, followed by 7/2 and then 8/2. Still, something seemed naggingly familiar about the pattern—8/2 was succeeded by 8/3, then 7/1, 8/1, 4/1, 5, 3, 4/2, 4/3, and then back to 6, followed again by 9, 7/2. The series was repeating itself.

When she counted them all there were twelve variations. So— it probably was the months. Once she decided that, things went more quickly—7/1 was Jenvier, which had seven letters. The /1 distinguished it from Octobre, which also had seven letters, so 4/1 was Marz, 4/2 June and 4/3 Juil, and so on, each month denoted by the letters in its name and its position in the year. The day names were a bit harder, because they seemed to be spelled out as in "thirty-one," which was written in the author's disguised alphabet. Still, if she managed to figure any of them out, it would take her a long way toward solving for the rest.

Likely it was nothing of interest—she herself kept a cyphered journal, but little of it was actually worth keeping secret.

At least, not until now.

The face in the mirror still haunted her. Ghosts were real—limbo, after all, was crowded, and in some places the veil between worlds was weak—but in her experience, they were rare, and the odds of stumbling upon one her first night in a new place seemed quite low. If she had seen one, then, she suspected it was by design. Or perhaps it had just been a trick of light and her own fraught perception.

Her concentration was broken a little later when someone knocked at her door. She opened it to discover Margot and Plesance standing there.

"Oh," she said. "Good morning."

"And to you," Margot said. Plesance looked her up and down, wide-eyed.

"You aren't dressed," Plesance said.

Chrysanthe considered the amber gown.

"I believe I am," she said.

"Not for walking," Plesance said.

Chrysanthe noticed then that both women wore dresses of olive green, with sleeves that came to their elbows. Their hems were an inch or two higher than looked right to Chrysanthe, revealing their laced brown boots. Her own hem touched the floor, and she wore silk slippers.

"I suppose not," Chrysanthe said. "I hadn't realized we would be walking."

"But I told you yesterday," Plesance said.

Margot put a hand on her cousin's shoulder. "She had a great number of words placed in her ears yesterday."

"It's true," Chrysanthe said. "I took your invitation to be a general one, the actual appointment to be settled upon later. I am very sorry."

Plesance lifted her chin. "That's fine," she said, her lips pinched a bit. "Do you have anything to wear?"

"I'm sure I can find something."

"We'll wait," Plesance said.

As she moved to disrobe, the two stepped in and closed the door. Chrysanthe paused. Were they going to watch her?

She decided it didn't matter. If they were trying to embarrass her, she wouldn't let on that they had succeeded. She found one of the dresses her mother had packed with similar sleeves and hem, and a pair of calf-high boots to go beneath.

Her mother had foreseen this. Of course.

"Well, that's better," Plesance said. "Especially if we were going to walk last year—or better yet, the year before."

"Plesance," Margot said, "Don't be disagreeable. She is our guest."

"She's our prisoner."

"Plesance!"

"Well, it's true," Plesance said. "You can keep the cock in a covered cage, but you will still hear it crow."

Margot sighed and placed her hand on Chrysanthe's arm.

"I'm so sorry," she said. "You've no idea what it's like being around her all the time."

Plesance smiled. "Well, she's going to learn," she said. "We're going to be best friends, I think, Miss Nevelon."

"That seems certain," Chrysanthe answered.

THEY WALKED through the gardens of Roselant and onward to open fields and pleasant, rolling hills buttered yellow by blooming lion's teeth. Plesance chattered constantly, regaling her with colorful character assassinations of at least half of the household. Now and then Margot urged her to moderation, but her efforts seemed half-hearted.

They were accompanied by two serving girls of about fourteen, who bore heavy packs. The group arrived at the top of a hill, and Chrysanthe was pleasantly surprised to behold the sea below them.

"This is a good spot," Margot said. "Beneath that apple tree."

The serving girls went to the tree and began laying out a large blanket, then the makings of a picnic.

"It's a lovely view," Chrysanthe said.

"It is," Plesance said. "There are no baboons or savages or crocodiles in it, as you may be used to, but it is nice enough."

Chrysanthe put on a false smile, and watched as the girls laid out the meal, parts of which she did not recognize.

"My room is quite nice," she said, as the three of them settled on the blanket. "I hope no one was troubled to move from it."

"Oh, it was empty," Plesance said. "For some months now." Her grin became more wicked. "That is a scandal all of its own."

"Plesance," Margot sighed.

"Well, she asked," Plesance said. "Why should I hold back from telling?"

Margot's only answer was a little shrug.

"Try this," Plesance said, indicating a sort of grayish loaf. She cut a bit with a small knife; it quivered visibly before she spread it on a slice of bread. Chrysanthe accepted the proffering and took a little bite. Gelatinous and cold, it tasted like fish.

"Aspilic of eel," Plesance said.

"Interesting," Chrysanthe replied, wondering why on earth someone would concoct something with such an utter lack of seasoning.

"Her name was Sandrine d'Ospios," Plesance said. "The woman who last inhabited that little chamber pot you're staying in. A spinster of some twenty-four years, or so we thought. She was originally employed as a nurse for the swarm of little brats you've already had the misfortune to meet."

Plesance took a small goblet of amber fluid from one of the servant girls as the other handed one to Chrysanthe. The wine in it had a sweet, flowery taste.

Plesance made a face. "This is from our own grapes," she said, looking sharply at the girl. "Didn't I ask for the Vin Clere?"

"There was none to be found, Danesele," the girl said.

"Well, that's vexing."

"I think it's quite good," Chrysanthe said.

Plesance raised an eyebrow.

"They make much wine, in the tropics?" she asked.

"No," Chrysanthe replied. "Grapes do not grow well there. What wine we have is imported."

"Hence your opinion," Plesance said. She took a sip and made a face. "But it will do." She crinkled her brow. "Whatever do you drink? Besides whatever 'wine' you import?"

"Well," Chrysanthe said, trying to stay pleasant, "There is rum, of course, usually mixed with the juice of various fruits, and there is injirab, made from ginger."

"Oh dear," Plesance said. "How exotic." She brushed at her nose as if a fly were there, although Chrysanthe did not see anything.

"Now then," Plesance went on, "this thing with Sandrine d'Ospios. She had something of an affinity for numbers, it seems, and she began to help grandmother with the household accounting. That brought her into contact with Ferrand Severin, our grand boursier. Her interest in numbers multiplied, you might say." She laughed. "Multiplied, you see?"

"I understood the joke," Chrysanthe said. "You mean to say the boursier and d'Ospios had an affair?"

"That is all rumor," Margot cautioned. "Neither of them ever admitted to it."

"No, of course not," Plesance said, "but Severin, you understand, was never known to smile, and yet in those days he did, and even was heard once to tell a joke. And then, suddenly, our dear Miss d'Ospios was gone, wasn't she? Now Severin broods in his counting-house, speaking to no one, dourer than ever he was before she came."

"He sounds like a lonely soul," Chrysanthe said. "Perhaps theirs was an innocent friendship."

"As a goose might be a dog but for its feathers," Plesance said. "But that hardly matters, you know. Once such a rumor is begun, it might as well be true. One is already stained by the accusation, and ruin is inevitable." She smiled, perhaps to make certain her implication was understood.

Chrysanthe understood, of course. Plesance was making it plain how precarious Chrysanthe's own position was, how easily her reputation could be ruined if Plesance took the notion to assault it. Back home, her character was well known, and it would take more than a rumor or wayward word to tarnish it. Here, however, such was not the case. If her mother was right—and about such things she was rarely wrong—even what seemed like a silly thing could ruin them all. Father and Crespin might return from war to find themselves without land or home.

"Where did she go, this Miss d'Ospios?" Chrysanthe asked.

"I hardly know," Plesance replied. "She left, that's all, without speaking a word to anyone. I doubt she will find decent employment now. Likely she has become a prostitute or some such."

"And Severin?"

"Well, he's not dispensable," Plesance said. "As I said, all he does is keep the ledgers and sulk. I suppose he feels some regret—he has become regular in attending the basilica. Every evening, in fact."

Chrysanthe took another sip of the wine. Could the journal have belonged to Sandrine d'Ospios? If so, why would she have left it?

Now, more than ever, she was determined to decipher it. And to learn more about Severin, the boursier.

NOT ONLY did the aspilic lack flavor, so did the entire picnic. Dinner at her cousin's house had been somewhat bland, but some spice had been used. These dishes hardly knew the touch of salt. She sought for a way to ask politely about it, but hadn't settled on the proper question before Margot asked her if the food was very different in Mesembria.

"Yes," she answered. "At home, good deal of spice is used."

"But of course it is," Plesance remarked. "Spices come from that part of the world, don't they? They must be very cheap indeed. Very common. Even in Ophion City, I'm told, the price of pepper and cloves has become quite low over the past several years, and yet some still delude themselves that throwing handfuls of raw cardamom and cinnamon into a dish proclaims their wealth and standing. They are nothing more than little bits of wood."

Chrysanthe was starting to become fatigued with Plesance's little digs at her provincial origins.

"There's more to it than that," she said. "Spices not only enhance taste, they also help to balance the humors. That jellied eel, for instance—it is of a very cold, wet humor. Without counterpoising it with something of a hot nature—like pepper—there is a risk to health. Pneumonia for instance."

"Every child knows that," Plesance said. "Can you actually be unaware of lacrime?"

Chrysanthe rolled the word around in her head. It meant "tear drop", but that was surely not what Plesance intended by the term.

"Apparently," she replied.

Plesance reached into the single small pocket on the side of her waist and pulled forth a little vial. She handed it over.

"A single drop," she said. "On your tongue."

Chrysanthe took the vial and regarded it for a moment. If Plesance planned to poison her, she could have put it in her food or drink. So she unstopped the tiny bottle and found it had a small golden dropper, with a clear bead of liquid clinging to it. She shook it onto her tongue.

For a moment, it only felt cold, like a shard of ice, but in the next heartbeat it seemed to burst into flame. She gasped, and her lungs and sinuses filled with heat. After the first shock, it didn't hurt. The warmth radiated out from her center and her skin began to feel as if it was throwing off sparks, and everything she saw seemed bathed in rosy light.

Plesance was laughing, but it was a distant sound. Unbidden, Chrysanthe had a sudden memory of the warm damp surprise of her first kiss, and then—in a rush—she was suddenly imagining Margot taking her by the arms, pulling her toward her lips.

"*Oh,*" she breathed, closing her eyes. The sensations began to fade, but it was several minutes before she felt composed enough to speak. In the meanwhile, Plesance and Margot each took a drop.

"You see?" Plesance said.

"No," Chrysanthe said, trying not to stare. "I mean, what was that?"

"Lacrime," Plesance repeated in a slightly dreamy voice.

"They say each drop is the distillation of some ten pounds of spice," Margot said. "In this case, cinnamon."

"But I don't taste anything, least of all cinnamon."

"That's the beauty of it," Plesance said, "and now you needn't worry about that eel causing you distemper. Its cold nature is *quite* counter-balanced."

"If anything, over-balanced," Chrysanthe said. She still felt flushed and short of breath, and could not push thoughts of kissing from her brain. It was well known that cinnamon could arouse, if too much was consumed. She had felt its effects before, but nothing remotely like this.

———

MORE THAN an hour later, as they returned to Roselant, they came across Quintent riding through a meadow. Her limbs were still warm from the lacrime, and Chrysanthe felt a big, stupid smile spread on her face. With horror she tried to banish it in favor of a neutral expression.

Why was he here?

Had he been looking for her?

"I thought as much," she heard Plesance mutter, sotto voce. She was looking at Chrysanthe as she said it, as if reading her mind. Was it that obvious? The young woman raised her voice as Quintent drew nearer.

"Good afternoon, cousin," she said. "We're so glad to see you. It's a happy coincidence to cross your path."

"No coincidence," Quintent said. "Rather I was sent for you. It seems you've been monopolizing our guest. Your grandmother would like to have coffee with her on the next clock-strike."

"Have we been out too long?" Plesance said innocently. "Is it three already?"

"Very nearly," Quintent said. "You know she will not take kindly to being left waiting."

"Silly me," Plesance said. "It went straight out of my head. We hardly have time to keep the appointment, do we?"

Chrysanthe very much doubted that the time had escaped her. It was more likely that Plesance was trying to sabotage her first one-on-one meeting with the lady of Roselant.

"You'd best ride with me," Quintent said. "So you won't be too late."

"I…" She knew she was blushing.

"Is something the matter?"

"No," she said. "I would prefer to meet her on time."

Moments later, they were galloping toward Roselant. Her arms were clenched around his waist. Now she was imagining kissing *him*, of all things, which was—not usual. She had to remind herself that he was not to her taste. Nevertheless, she desperately tried to distract herself by envisioning warts and spoiled meat and books with unhappy endings.

Chrysanthe would think more than twice the next time she accepted anything from Plesance, of that she was certain.

"Thank you for the letter," she heard herself blurt out. "I found it very amusing. It was kind of you."

"Shouldn't this be reserved for the letter you're writing me?" he asked.

"Yes, of course."

"Is everything well?" he asked. "Your accommodations are acceptable?"

"Yes," she replied. "Although, according to Plesance, it's little more than a chamber pot. Its last inhabitant was a nurse of some sort."

"You must mean Miss d'Ospios. I met her once. Very polite and well-spoken. Her father was an officer in the army, on the staff of an ambassador. As I recall, she spent many of her early years at his post with him in Modjal." He half-turned to glance back at her. "I don't doubt that Plesance recounted the circumstances of her departure."

"She did," Chrysanthe said. "She seems to relish those sorts of things."

Suddenly her mind was in her room, with the journal. What if the language encoded there was Modjali? That would make an enormous difference, and she had a working knowledge of the tongue.

"I wonder…" she mused aloud.

"What was that?"

"The journal," she said. "Perhaps—" Then she stopped, her ears burning. What was she doing? Had her sense gone entirely missing? "I mean, *my* journal," she said. "I must remember to update it this evening."

"I should think so," he said. "A lunch with those two should be worthy of more than one remark."

Roselant appeared through the trees, and soon they came up to the house itself, a full five minutes before the clock-strike. Quintent dismounted first and then helped her down.

"Thank you," she said.

"You're very welcome," he said. "Perhaps next time we ride we shall each have a horse." He smiled. "Or perhaps not."

To her relief, Chrysanthe felt fully in control of herself once again.

"One evening soon, I should very much like to pay a call at the basilica," she said. "If you have the time and inclination, I would be pleased if you would ride with me there."

"Of course."

"And two horses, please."

YSABEL D'OTHRES settled back into what might diplomatically be called a somewhat overlarge armchair and more candidly described as a small throne. It was entirely upholstered in quilted pearl samite embroidered in slightly darker thread. She wore a coffee-colored gown, and Chrysanthe thought she resembled a clam in a shell far too large for her.

"How did you find the countryside?" the older woman asked.

"Quite beautiful," Chrysanthe said.

"Very different from what you're used to, I imagine."

"Yes, Ma Dame," she said.

"I visited Mesembria once, with my uncle. Your own province of Laham, in fact. My uncle had business with your grandfather. That was before you were born, of course, but your parents were quite kind to me, and afterwards I felt like I had experienced something of an adventure. So now I'm in a position to return the favor. I'm so happy to do so."

"Thank you, Ma Dame," she said. "I am very pleased to be here."

Ysabel nodded. "I know you understand the particular circumstances of your lodging with us," she said, "but I want you to understand that those circumstances are purely formal. We must pray that this war is soon at an end, and we can all return to our proper business. So long as you are here, though, I want you to think of yourself only as an honored guest under our protection. I could never face your father if some misfortune were to befall you—and so none shall."

"Thank you, Ma Dame, that's reassuring," she said.

She smiled. "Knowing your mother, I imagine she would receive it as a kindness if I were to take a few steps toward finding you a match."

Chrysanthe smiled back. "You do indeed know my mother well," she said, "but there is no need for matchmaking."

"Why? Do you flatter yourself that a match is already likely?" Ysabel didn't exactly sound angry, but she seemed a bit colder.

"No," Chrysanthe replied, "I only mean to say that I'm not presently seeking a husband."

"I see," Ysabel said. "Well, that may be, but if I don't at least put up an appearance of trying, your mother will never forgive me."

"Well, I'm always agreeable to making new friends."

"Surely you had suitors back home," the lady persisted.

"A few," she replied, thinking of Lucien. It must have shown on her face.

"I see," Ysabel said. "Well, we shall do better here. I believe I will hold a small country dance for your benefit. You are a handsome girl, to be sure, albeit a little… exotic." She inclined her head to the side. "What do you suppose your father is worth?" she said. "It could influence my choice of guests."

Chrysanthe blinked. "I'm not certain I should discuss such things."

"Should not, or cannot?"

That stung her a little.

"I help my father in the bookkeeping," she said, "So I'm aware of the particulars of his dealings, but I don't feel comfortable discussing such things without his express leave."

"You know how to keep account?" Ysabel said. "Few young women have that skill." Her voice hadn't changed, but everything else suddenly seemed to have. The light in the room shone differently. Chrysanthe noticed a dog barking, far, far away.

"My father expects all of his children to be useful," she said, trying not to show her chagrin. She had been off-balance since arriving in Ophion. The unexpected change of sponsors, the effortless charm of Quintent, the obscene Bonaventure, the riot, the bizarre meeting with the emperor, the face in the mirror, and a day of overstimulation and implied threats had buried her reason beneath emotion.

That had to end. Her acumen was her only defense.

"A sensible man," Ysabel said. "An educated daughter is always useful." For a moment, her expression hardened. Then she smiled, and her blue eyes became merry. "You've had a long day," she said. "And I have no intention of making it longer. Take some leisure before dinner."

"Thank you, Ma Dame."

———

CHRYSANTHE WAS impatient to return to her rooms, so of course on the way there she met half of the women in the chastel, all eager to speak to her regarding some male friend of theirs. Apparently, Dame Ysabel was not the only person with a mind to get her engaged. Remaining polite, she tried to keep a smile glued on, but all the while she was turning over in her head the matter of the journal.

Whatever was going on here—whatever it was that Bonaventure thought she might uncover—she now believed it was directly related to the vanished Miss d'Ospios. Had she and the boursier been having an affair? Perhaps, and perhaps not. That wasn't the pertinent issue. What mattered was that she knew how to do numbers. D'Ospios must have discovered something in the accounting that the family wished to remain secret.

But what? Had they been purchasing arms to use against the emperor? She didn't even know what businesses the master of Roselant was involved in, and she certainly couldn't ask. Ysabel was no fool—if she hadn't known before that Chrysanthe was spying for her father, she did now.

Chrysanthe had to see the boursier's books.

How in heaven's name was she supposed to do that?

The instant she opened the door to her room, she knew something was wrong. Everything was in disorder, and her first thought was that Orenge had been called away in the middle of cleaning. But her wardrobe had been emptied and her dresses all were piled on the floor, which made no sense. Had Plesance come in to do some sort of mischief?

The curtain moved, and someone stepped from behind it. He was wearing a long brown coat, a broad-brimmed hat, and a mask covering his face but for the eyes. He raised his hand toward her, and she saw he held a long, wicked-looking dagger.

CHAPTER TWO

STRANGE TONGUES

"I STILL feel Him," Hound told Veulkh, as the thoroughly rattled expedition started pulling itself together.

"That was predictable," the sorcerer replied. "The more He wakes, the farther His reach. I hoped He would subside once we were free of the city. Still, when we are out of the valley we should be quit of Him, at least in the most direct sense." He looked around. "There once was a road that ran to the southeast. See if you can find it."

Like the city, the road had been paved and was not difficult to find. Before long it wound up a slope so steep that it slowed the travelers to a crawl, but they still managed to reach the top of the ridge in time to make camp before sundown.

Veulkh's ravens set up a black tent that seemed far larger than necessary. Once it was ready, Veulkh and Ammolite went into it, and Hound found that he kept looking at it, wondering what was going on inside. He decided his time would be better spent exploring their surroundings.

The highlands were more to Hound's liking than the valley. They were cool and misty, and the trees weren't nearly as big or tall. There were plants he recognized, or nearly recognized. Laurels and oaks, for instance, and a remarkable variety of pitcher plants.

But they wouldn't be in the highlands long. He crested the ridge and beheld a series of hills that broke into what seemed like an endless sea of treetops. Here and there, the bends of a river were visible, copper coils in the fading light.

He thought he was too uneasy to sleep, but he curled up with Rose on a rock outcrop. Near sunup the dog nuzzled him awake. She was agitated, sniffing the air.

"Let's see what it is," Hound whispered.

The dog led him back into camp. Three men were on watch near a small fire. One of them was Martin. The rest were asleep on bedrolls—the ravens on one side of camp, the chevaliers and their men on the other. Rose approached the chevaliers.

At first, Hound didn't know what he was seeing. There was a man's boots and legs and part of his belly, but then it looked as if he had pulled some sort of bag or bladder over his head—a pretty bag, with curly patterns of yellow, green and black.

Then he saw that the bag had eyes, and it was attached to a long tail as big around as a poplar trunk—but coiled. Shuddering a little, he realized he had seen this before, except that it had been a mouse instead of a man, and a snake of sensible size. This snake was much bigger than sensible. As he watched, its muscles contracted, drawing the dead man a little farther into its gullet.

He went to fetch Martin.

———

"WHY DIDN'T he scream? Martin asked. The men from both sides of the camp gathered around now, staring in disbelief.

"That's Alont," someone said.

"*Was* Alont," the chevalier Ariston corrected. "Now he's snake merde."

"He didn't scream because he didn't have the wind to," Hound said. "It caught him in its coils when he was asleep, and after that he never got another breath."

"We should kill it," one of the ravens said. That brought a general chorus of assent.

"No," Veulkh said, stepping out of the tent. Ammolite, in her other shape, stood just behind him. "The man is already dead, and killing snakes brings evil luck. Especially this snake. Especially here. If we're lucky, He may be satisfied with this and go back to sleep."

Hound still felt Him, especially when he faced northeast, but he didn't see any sense in saying so. The sooner they got going, the better.

LONG AFTER the effects of their transit had subsided in Hound and the others—days after escaping the whatever-it-was in the old city—Ammolite still felt dizzy. Only from time to time, however, and she wondered if it was because she had remained Orra for so long, or if it had more to do with the space all around her, the lack of a walls and a ceiling.

She had sometimes felt a similar vertigo on her balcony, but there the manse was still at her back. Here, things seemed to go on forever. Even the earth wasn't solid—or flat and even. Except for the conjury, the floors in the manse were level and polished. Here there were bumps, slopes, ledges, logs, and stones.

Despite the expanse around her, she felt more captive than ever. At night, in Veulkh's tent, things continued as always. The first time she was afraid he would somehow discover what she had done with Hound, but he didn't, and on reflection she realized that Orra had never lain with Hound, only Ammolite.

Now she was always Orra—she could never escape into Ammolite to be unnoticed and alone. Even when she needed to relieve herself, either Veulkh or Kos was there. She was never more than ten feet from one or the other of them, and when anyone attempted to speak to her, they met with rebuke.

At first riding on horseback had been painful, but it got better over time. In that first wild flight she had ridden with Veulkh, clinging to his waist, but later he insisted that she learn to ride by herself. Hound, she noticed, never mounted a horse, but trotted alongside, usually talking to the woman named Selene.

Ammolite did not like Selene, and often wondered if she and Hound coupled at night, while she was with Veulkh. If they did not, Hound certainly seemed to want to. Selene did not appear to be a slave, so it was possible that she did not couple with anyone, the thought of which made Ammolite dislike the woman even more.

She also wondered if Hound might be forgetting his promise to help her escape. To be fair, thus far the only chance they might have had to run away was in the confusion of that first day.

The jungle seemed endless and was full of nasty things, the worst of which seemed to come out at night. Besides the snake that had crushed the life out of the chevalier, on the third night something bit one of the ravens while he was sleeping. His arm turned black, and she thought he would die. In the end Veulkh supervised cutting off the limb and cauterizing the wound. Though still weak, he seemed to be getting better.

Ten days after leaving the ruins of Sular Bulan, while they were crossing a stream, someone shot one of the chevaliers with an arrow. His armor turned it, and he wasn't hurt, but everyone grew more cautious. Ammolite reflected that if the arrow had hit her, it probably would have killed her. Veulkh thought the same thing. He called over Hound, who glanced at her briefly. She felt her face warm and hoped her master didn't notice.

"Lady Orra," Hound said. "I hope you are well."

"Don't concern yourself with her health," Veulkh snapped. "That is my charge." She wondered what Hound was seeing in his mind's eye—Ammolite in costume, or had Orra seduced him, as well?

"Who is shooting at us?" Veulkh demanded.

"I don't know their names," Hound told him, grinning, and she was impressed with his impertinence.

"That's not what I meant."

"There are only about six or eight of them, I think. We're probably in their hunting territory. Or they might be a war party, looking to earn trophies. The Kansa do that, especially in winter, when there isn't much else to do."

"They're like you," Martin said. He and Selene approached. "They'll keep harassing us, but we'll never see them."

"Maybe," Hound replied.

"Could you go out, lessen their number?" Martin asked. "It might be enough to make them leave us alone."

"This is their country," Hound said, "not mine. I don't know this forest, these trees, giant snakes, spiders the size of squirrels. I would be more at their mercy than they at mine."

"That makes sense," Martin said. "Suggestion withdrawn."

Hound glanced at Selene.

"No," he said. "I'll see what I can do." And with that he bounded off through the trees, his dog and raven with him.

Did Selene have a little look of triumph on her face? Or was it something else?

The expedition continued without Hound. Since arriving in the hot, sticky lowlands, many of the fighting men had taken to leaving off their helmets, but she noticed they all had them on again.

Hound rejoined them as they were encamping. He was carrying a spear.

"Killed two," he said. "The rest went off southwest." He tossed something bloody to Martin, who caught it. Ammolite thought it might be human ears, pierced and tied on a thong.

"They're kind of short, about my height," he said. "Not wearing much but pretty feathers and tattoos. They've got spears like this, and clubs, as well. One of them had a sword. They're pretty smart. I got lucky."

"Do you think they will return?"

Hound shrugged. "I don't know."

FIVE DAYS passed without incident. The terrain grew flatter, and much of it was festering black water swamp, which they were forced to skirt for fear they might sink into it. There, too, were the gigantic lizard-like monsters that lurked in the waters, which Veulkh and Martin called crocodiles. Black flies and mosquitoes ate constantly at her. Veulkh took to adding pepper and cinnamon to their wine, to prevent the wet humors from making them ill.

On the next day, Hound suddenly stopped and stiffened.

"They're back," he said, "and there are a lot more of them."

The ravens dismounted and quickly led their horses to stand in a circle around Veulkh and Ammolite. At first, she wondered why they brought the horses, but then she understood that the animals would act as shields, if necessary.

The chevaliers remained mounted, but they, too, ranged themselves in a ring, ready for attack from any direction. She still didn't see anything. Aside from the snorting of the horses, the jungle was utterly silent.

Then horns began blowing, and there was motion through the trees—in every direction. A moment later, seven men strode fearlessly out of the jungle.

As Hound had reported, they weren't wearing much. Their bodies were lean and muscular and liberally decorated with coil and zig-zag tattoos. The obvious leader wore an elaborate headdress of purple, green, and red feathers. Unlike the others, he didn't carry a spear in his hand, but he wore a sword in an ornately beaded sheath slung on his back.

"Na reh su," the man said. She wasn't sure if it was a question or a demand.

Martin stepped forward.

"I don't understand you," he said in Velesan. When he got no response, he changed to the language she heard him speaking with the chevaliers, and then to another. On his fourth try, the leader perked up, and began speaking, haltingly.

"His name is Tang," Martin translated. "He's a sort of sub-chief of the Ngachok people. He wants to know who we are and what we are doing in his territory. He says we are known to have come from the place of Rong Lah, which is forbidden. He asks if we are *rajn*."

"What?" Selene said.

Martin said something else. The chief struggled for a moment.

"Dzunu," he finally said.

"Dzunu," Martin repeated. "I think he means demons."

"Ask him if he has ever heard of Sular Bulan," Veulkh said.

Martin asked, and despite his dark skin, the man seemed to blanch. Then he started speaking again, rapidly. Martin listened intently, then translated.

"He says that—some other tribe—calls it that, or something similar. His people do not speak that name for fear of waking Him. So they call him Rong Lah."

Veulkh stepped forward.

"Sulavulan?"

The man took a step back and made some sort of sign in the air. The others edged away, as well.

"Isu kuas?" Veulkh said.

"Ao," the man replied.

Veulkh then began speaking a language no one had yet spoken. The chief listened, wide-eyed at first, but looking increasingly more skeptical. He said something that angered Veulkh, who suddenly clenched his fists. The veins stood out on his head and the shadows of the trees began to deepen.

Then the earth beneath her feet jumped. Ammolite shrieked, and she wasn't the only one. The forest rang with cries of terror, human and otherwise.

The earth stilled. The sunlight came back.

The chief still stood there, trying to look proud, but his eyes darted about as if searching for something terrible.

"Isu *Vajah?*" Veulkh asked.

"Vajah," the man answered. Then he backed out of the clearing. The forest rustled as the warriors all around them departed, no longer making any effort at stealth.

"What was all that about?" Martin asked.

"I told him that we are demons come out of Sular Bulan, and if they bother us, we will strike the men down with a plague and eat their children alive."

"HE WAS speaking Drehhu," Martin said, once Veulkh was out of earshot.

"Who?" Selene asked. "Veulkh?"

"No," Martin replied. "I've no idea what that was. Tang, the chief—the language I found we had in common was Drehhu."

"What's that?" Hound asked.

"You've never heard of the Drehhu?" Selene said.

"No," he replied. "At least not by that name."

"They used to rule most of the world," she said.

"And now they don't?"

"No. When they first began their conquests, they had demonic weapons that made them invincible. Their ships moved without wind or current."

"Why didn't their enemies build such ships and such weapons?"

"There are two reasons for that," Martin said. "The first is because it was difficult. The Drehhu guarded their secrets, and would destroy their weapons rather than let them fall into enemy hands. If they suspected anyone of learning—or teaching—their magicks, assassins would end them. But the more important reason is that those things were, *are*, evil."

Hound drew his tomahawk from his belt.

"How can a weapon be evil?" he asked. "It only does what the one holding it wants."

"The Drehhu weapons are different," Selene said. "They taint those who use them. The Drehhu became monsters, long ago, because the power they used corrupted them. If our ancestors had taken up their arms, we would have ended the same."

"How do you know this?"

"That is the business of the Cryptarchia," she said. "To know. To learn what is acceptable and what is not. From time to time, some tried to use the Drehhu magicks, usually with good intentions, sometimes not. They were always stopped, just as the Drehhu were."

"Then they no longer exist, these Drehhu?"

"Some remain," Martin said. "They were driven back to the distant lands from which they came. For almost a century, the three empires have been at peace with them. Or at least, not at war."

"What does it mean that Tang speaks their language?"

"Once, everyone did," Martin said. "Or almost everyone. It was the language every slave had to know. For that reason it was despised, so when territories were liberated, they usually reverted to their native tongues or those of their liberators. Quite likely Tang's ancestors were escaped slaves, so he remembers the tongue."

"He speaks it poorly, though," Hound said. "It's not his own language."

"Correct," Martin said. "Which means he has some use for it, but not much."

"The Kansa have a trade language they use to speak to other peoples," Hound said.

"What I think this means," Martin said, "is that we're near the Drehhu homeland. Near enough for their language to be worth learning for purposes of trade and negotiation. We might even be within what remains of their kingdom."

Hound remembered that Martin had asked Veulkh where they were, and the sorcerer had refused to tell him.

"Do you think Veulkh would betray us?" Selene asked. "To the Drehhu?"

"He understood," Hound said. "When you were talking to the chief, he knew what you were saying. Then he was able to communicate with the Ngachok."

"He's old," Selene said. "Very old, and all of his past is not clear. The Cryptarchia may have chosen poorly."

"There was no choice," Martin said. "He is the only one. Maybe he is walking us into a Drehhu trap. We still must go. We'll just go with our eyes open."

CHAPTER THREE

THE BASILICA

CHRYSANTHE BACKED toward the door, but the man was faster, overtaking her in three quick steps. She turned to run, but he caught her, his hand cupping her mouth, muffling her scream. She felt the dagger prick against her neck.

"Quiet," the man whispered through his mask. "Quiet or I shall silence you permanently."

Chrysanthe felt her pulse in her entire body. *He has not killed me yet*, she thought. She nodded.

"Good girl," the man said. "I'm going to move my hand from your mouth, and you tell me where it is. If you do anything else, and especially if you scream, I will cut your throat and be long gone back out of the window before anyone comes to find what you're going on about. Nod if that's understood."

She nodded. Slowly, he pulled his hand away.

"Where is it?" he repeated.

At the moment, Chrysanthe caught another movement from the corner of her eye; someone stepping from behind the wardrobe. The man saw it, too, but by then whoever-it-was had made it all the way to the door and opened it.

"Whoever you are," Margot said in a soft voice. "You had better go. Or else *I* shall scream. And… and maybe you will murder me, too, but it will be all the harder for you to escape. Our men *will* find you. So let Chrysanthe go."

For a moment, the man did not move. The knife remained where it was. Then she felt the tip move off her skin.

"Until later," the man whispered. Then he was gone. She didn't turn, but after a few heartbeats Margot rushed past her. Chrysanthe heard the window slam closed and the latches click into place.

Her knees began to wobble a bit. Margot reappeared at her side.

"Merciful Virgin, are you hurt?" she asked. "Did he do you harm?"

"Not to my body," Chrysanthe said. She glanced back at the closed window, around at the wreck of her room. "I want to leave here," she said.

"Of course," Margot said. "We must tell someone. We must—"

"No," Chrysanthe said. "I need to think."

Margot nodded. She stepped outside and looked up and down the halls.

"Come with me, then," she said.

She took Chrysanthe's hand, but did not lead her into the hall. Instead she moved to the wardrobe, and then behind it. She pressed on the wall and a section of it eased open, revealing a passage behind.

"What is this?" Chrysanthe asked. "What's through there?"

"It goes along the outer wall," Margot replied, "to another room." She smiled uncertainly. "I grew up here, you know. We had great fun with these little doors. There are quite a few of them."

Still dazed, she allowed Margot to lead her through the narrow passage until they reached another of the secret doors, although it was plainly visible from inside. Margot pressed it open and there was, indeed, a modest sitting room with a couch, several chairs, a table, a small harp and a shelf with a few books. To their right was an ordinary door. The room had a single window, closed and latched and very narrow, too small for a person to enter.

"Will this do?" Margot asked. She paused. "We could continue on, to some place more public."

"Where does that door go?"

"A hall parallel to the one from which your room opens. I think we are safe from intruders here."

"Do you?" Chrysanthe asked, studying her companion. The young woman had changed outfits since their picnic. She now wore clothing more suited for the indoors, a pale rose gown and matching slippers.

"Is something wrong?" Margot asked.

"Everything is wrong," Chrysanthe replied. "Someone just threatened my life."

"I was there," Margot reminded her.

"Yes," Chrysanthe said. "You were. That requires some explanation."

Margot's thin eyebrows rose. "I wasn't with him, if that's what you mean," she said. "I wasn't party to… whatever that was." She looked hurt.

Chrysanthe found her breathing was finally beginning to even out. "I'm sorry if I offended you," she said, "but the coincidence—that you and my attacker should both be in my room, at the same time—"

Margot reddened and looked down at the floor. "I came to see you," she said. "I wanted to apologize. For Plesance, and for not warning you about the lacrime. I came this way, through the hidden passages, but before I went into the room I heard him crashing around. I was terrified, and so just stood there, not knowing what to do. Then I heard you come in, and I thought—well, I had to do something."

Chrysanthe studied Margot's face. Her expression seemed earnest enough.

"That was brave of you," she said. "You probably saved my life."

"What did he want? Why did he search your room?"

"I don't know," Chrysanthe said, although she had a very good idea. "But—thank you."

Margot nodded. She clasped her hands together. For a few long breaths, it was silent in the room.

"I am not brave," Margot finally told her. "I acted without thinking. I did not—I did not want harm to come to you. I thought if I went for help, it would arrive too late."

"That sounds like thinking," Chrysanthe said. "Quick thinking." She smiled and tilted her head. "You could have been hurt yourself. But tell me—why did you enter my room secretly, rather than simply coming in by the front?"

Margot closed her eyes for a moment, then opened them again.

"I was afraid someone might see me," she said. "I was afraid there would be talk."

"Talk of what?"

Margot stepped closer.

"I saw the way you looked at me," she said softly. "By the sea. I cannot be mistaken—or I thought I could not. I came to be sure."

Chrysanthe opened her mouth, but she found she had nothing to say. Margot took it for something else and reached for her.

"Margot," she said, "please." Chrysanthe caught her hands and stepped back.

The young woman stopped. Her eyes widened.

"*Was* I wrong?" she said. "I have heard about the colonies. About the things that happen there."

"It seems everyone has," Chrysanthe said. "Everyone but me."

"So it wasn't true, what I thought I saw."

Chrysanthe sighed. "No," she said. "I mean yes. You were not entirely wrong. In my attractions, I have always been drawn to my own sex, and I admit that I like your demeanor."

"You find me attractive?"

"You are lovely," Chrysanthe said. "The lacrime... inflamed me, and I have no experience with controlling such sudden and strong emotions."

"I have," Margot said, "but my reaction was the same. I wanted you to kiss me, to hold me..."

Margot started forward again, and again Chrysanthe stepped back.

"Yes," she said, "I consent that we may have a mutual attraction, but it isn't going to happen."

"Why? We are here, alone—no one will know."

"I would know. We are hardly acquainted with each other, and I am not nearly as frivolous as all of you seem to imagine. Besides, however secret we were here, eventually someone would learn of it. And what would happen then?"

"I don't want to think about that right now."

"But I *must* think about it, you see," Chrysanthe replied. "Whatever you may believe about colonials—whatever you think of me, by extension—I am not wanton. I do not tryst in secret. Even if I did so with a man, it would be a fatal blow to my reputation.

Here, in Ophion Magne, with a woman?" She shook her head.

"It happens," Margot said. "There are books written about it."

"Those silly costume romances? Which of us shall dress as a man? We are both already known as women."

Margot nodded and stepped back.

"Yes," she said. "You're right, of course. If we were found out…"

"And someone *would* find out."

"I've always considered myself sensible," Margot said. "I'm sorry to say I haven't been so today. It's good that you were sensible enough for the both of us. I guess I can take comfort in knowing you will tell no one of my embarrassing behavior."

"Be assured," Chrysanthe said.

Margot smiled briefly. She lifted her hand to indicate the door.

"Well," she said. "I guess—"

"A moment," Chrysanthe said. "The man. Do you have any idea who he might have been?"

"None at all," she said.

"Very well," Chrysanthe said.

Margot nodded and started for the door.

"Margot?" Chrysanthe said.

"Yes?"

"I *am* flattered."

"I see," Margot said. "May I tell the guardsman of this now?"

Chrysanthe considered that for a long moment.

"No," she finally said. "Please tell no one."

"I must. What if that horrible fellow returns? You must be moved, to another room, one without a window."

Chrysanthe shook her head. "Moving me won't help," she said. "Please be discreet."

"I can have a guard stationed nearer your room. I know one that will not ask questions or make an issue of it."

"If you please," Chrysanthe said. "But no more than that."

Margot nodded and left.

WHEN MARGOT was gone, Chrysanthe returned to her room.

She sat on the bed, then looked around at the mess. She glanced at the window, through which the man had exited. Margot had assumed he'd come in that way, too, but Chrysanthe remembered that the window had been closed and latched. It was far more likely that the man had entered through the door, or even through the same secret entrance Margot had employed. What she'd told Margot was true, however; moving her would make her no more secure, nor would alerting the house to her plight.

As a precaution, she pushed the wardrobe in front of the secret door. But there was little more that she could do. The man had been more interested in finding something than murdering her, although she had no doubt he would have slit her throat once he'd found it.

But what had he been looking for?

She felt the inner pocket of her dress, the little box her father had given her. It was still there, still safe. Had that been what the thief was after? But something else occurred to her. She reached under the bed, where she had hidden the journal.

It was gone. How could anyone have known she'd even found it?

Then she remembered. Addled by lacrime, on horseback with Quintent, she had said something.

Quintent had a brown coat and hat.

She didn't want to believe it.

Really didn't want to believe it.

But even if she did, if she allowed that Quintent had put on a mask, invaded her room, searched her things for the journal, and threatened her at knifepoint, there was still something that didn't make sense.

Whatever he had been looking for, he hadn't found it.

And yet the journal was gone.

She went through the motions of the rest of her day. She both hoped and dreaded seeing Quintent, but he did not appear, even for dinner. Exhausted in every way, she returned to her room, hoping to find some rest. In the morning, perhaps her mind would work better.

If she woke at all.

AFTER A time, Chrysanthe gave up on sleep. Even though she was in a strange room in an unfamiliar house, she had managed to believe that she was safe in her bed. That illusion was no longer available to her. Someone had managed to enter without raising any sort of alarm, and they could probably do so again.

Who could move about the mansion unnoticed? An inhabitant could. A house servant could, but someone from, say, the stables would be noticed.

Quintent could.

He was of noble birth. No one would question him. As far as she knew, Ysabel herself might have sent the man. She couldn't trust anyone here. And the journal was gone.

Without the journal, what did she have? Her investigations were at end, weren't they?

CHAPTER FOUR

THE MAN IN THE BROWN COAT

WHEN MORNING finally came, she felt braver, and she knew the answer to her own question. Without the journal, there was still the boursier. By the time Orenge came with breakfast, she had the room straightened as if it had never been searched.

The girl brought more than breakfast; she also brought a note from Quintent.

> *My most amiable Chrysanthe,*
>
> *It is with deepest regret that I must postpone escorting you to the basilica in the near future. I have been called away on some rather tedious but necessary business for what will likely be several days. It is my loss that I shall be deprived of your company, but I must also look to the inconvenience this is to you.*

I have instructed my man Jean to conduct you to worship or anywhere else if the mood strikes you. He is uncomplicated but loyal, and knows the town well. I think you will find him a comfortable guide.

There was a bit more of Quintent trying to be poetical, but she was left with a dry and bitter taste in her mouth. That he had suddenly been called away seemed altogether too coincidental. Surely there were many men with brown coats, but this seemed a bit much.

She had believed she was being wise to trust him until he gave her reason not to, but she only now began to understand how much she had become invested in believing that Quintent was her friend. She remembered her father's advice about an unguarded mind and felt ashamed. Chrysanthe had believed her skepticism was enough to protect her. She had been wrong.

Maybe Quintent was innocent. Maybe he was not. Either way, she could not let it prevent her doing what she had promised her father.

"Orenge," she said, when the girl came to collect the breakfast plates. "This man of Dam d'Othres, by the name of Jean. Do you know him?"

"I do indeed," the girl said.

"Please send word to him that I require an escort to the basilica, would you?"

THE CONSTRUCTION of the basilica mirrored the architecture of the known universe, each detail meant to remind the worshipper of ultimate truth. The stone floor represented the world on which they walked—in this case, quite literally, for the continents were inlaid there, red marble for land and white for the sea. A raised bench of black stone bounded the circular floor and depicted the Expiry, the horizontal limit of the material world.

The basilica told the tale of a finite universe, the primeval victory of substance over spirit.

Only in the raised ceiling could one glimpse infinity, where gold and silver stars on an azure vault signified the limitless heavens, the bright realm of immortality denied to humanity by the Lords of Evil who now ruled it. The world was a prison, the sky the window to the ultimate and unlimited liberty that lay beyond.

Every soul that had ever died on Earth was lost in limbo, a star yearning to rejoin the heavens from which it had been exiled by birth, kept vital only by the prayers and offerings of the living, until such time as the Virgin and her children—the Christs of Ophion, of Modjal, of Velesa, Tamanja, and all the other High Exiles—were prepared for the final battle to regain lost paradise. In the meantime, the devout could only preserve the spirits of their dead and prepare themselves to be worthy when the Reconquest arrived, when the Lords of Evil were finally deposed, and the material world shattered like an egg so the spirits trapped within could finally be free.

Until then, Earth was both haven and dungeon for those who dwelt upon it.

"Pretty, eh?" her companion said as they entered.

Jean was exactly as Quintent described him. He was also young, just a little older than she. He seemed to know almost everyone they met, and she soon gathered that he was a true native. She took to asking him who people were when they saw or encountered them, although in most cases she did not care. Once in the basilica, however, the practice served her well, for when she asked about a man of somewhat more than middle years, with a bent nose, clad in gray frock and hose, he answered without hesitation or suspicion that it was Severin.

The object of her quest.

Severin was in the second circle of the nave, reserved for credents, reciting to one of the parfaits.

"You needn't follow me further, unless you wish," she told Jean.

"I'm to keep an eye on you."

"I'm sure I'll be safe in the basilica," she said. "But if you wish to accompany me to the second circle, I shall be happy of your company."

"Oh, Danesele," he said. "I've not the learning for that. I'm a simple, just come in to light candles for my bele-mere and such."

"Well," Chrysanthe said. "I shan't be long."

"As you say, dan'sel."

Moving to the small altar next to the one where Severin whispered to a young parfait, she took her position on her knees. Chrysanthe's own intercessor, a woman of advanced years whose bright green eyes shown from a deeply wrinkled field, nodded as she approached.

"To what mystery do you speak?" the old woman asked.

"The mystery of Ourania," Chrysanthe replied.

"Go on, daughter," the parfait said.

It had been a long time since Chrysanthe had spoken a mystery, but from her twelfth to her fourteenth year she had studied and recited every day in the basilica of Bellship. It all came back to her, with very little hesitation. She was less than half done when Severin finished, the parfait handed him a key, and he went on his way.

When she was done reciting, the old woman nodded approvingly.

"You speak the logos beautifully," she said.

"Thank you, mother," she said.

The second circle was walled away from the first, and within were numerous small chapels. Some were created for groups, others for individuals, and some were even furnished with lock and key. She asked for a key like the one that had been given to the boursier, and paid the small tithe required for the privilege. Then she entered the curving hall.

Severin was in the first chapel, a community space. Chrysanthe went there, as well, lighting candles for her mother's father and both of her father's parents, all deceased, as well as for Hesh, a friend of hers who had contracted storm fever and died very young. Looking from the corner of her eye, she saw Severin notice her and nod, but did not return the regard. When he rose, she contrived to bump into him.

"I'm so sorry," he said, seeming flustered.

Up close, he was not exactly handsome, but neither was he determinedly unattractive. His eyes caught her; they were dark, his gaze turned mostly inward, so when his attention turned out to her it was like seeing a gleaming fish leap from a murky pool. She felt somehow privileged by that.

"No, I'm clumsy," she said. "I've seen you, haven't I? At the chastel?"

Instantly he became more guarded.

"Perhaps."

"I'm Chrysanthe Nevelon," she said. "Just lately come up from Mesembria. I'm staying with the d'Othres."

"Oh," he said. "Yes. My apologies. I was unable to attend your welcome."

"Well, we meet now," she said.

"Yes," he replied. "I suppose we do." He looked down at his feet. "Well, I have further business here," he said. "Delighted."

"Oh," she said, "so do I. In the private chambers, but I'm new here, and don't know where they are. Would you happen to know where I can find them?"

He frowned a little.

"Yes," he said. "That's where I'm going. You may follow me, if you wish."

"Oh, thank you," she said. "That would be a blessing."

He led her around the bend, and then through a small maze of rooms with closed doors.

"I could not help but overhear you at the altar," he said. "You must have had a fine education. One seldom hears proper pronunciation."

"Oh," she said. "Thank you. I had a very fine teacher. Rafael de Marzement. Perhaps you've heard of him?"

"No," he said. "I fear I have not." He seemed to regret having spoken, and did not pursue the conversation further. They continued on, and a moment later he stopped and gestured at a row of doors.

"Your key will fit any of these."

"Thank you," she said.

He nodded, and then opened a door. While he entered, she began toward a portal further down, but once he was out of sight she backtracked and chose the room next to his. Once inside, she locked the door behind her, went to the altar and lit the candles.

In their light, she did a quick search of the room, hoping it was built like the ones back home. To her delight, she saw that it was. The small room required ventilation, especially since fire was involved, so small air shafts connected the thick-walled chambers. She wrapped her shawl around her bosom to protect her gown, climbed up on the altar, and from there pulled herself up enough to get her head, shoulders, and about half of her body into the shaft.

In childhood, she had often performed the same sacrilegious act to spy on the de Sarade sisters and a few others. Because she had never spoken anything that she heard, she had convinced herself no sin was involved. Now she realized that it had been a dubious assumption, and what she was up to today was even deeper into the gray.

Even before she was in the shaft she could hear Severin whispering, but could not make out his words. From her vantage point she could see part of his face, enough to make out the tears running down his cheeks. He was speaking to the candle, and although hushed sobs garbled his words, she could make out a bit of it.

"Beloved, my love, dearest little Sandra, darling cogwheel…" and more. Then he began to recite a bit more smoothly. He had something in his hand, and she realized it was a piece of paper from which he was reading.

"Dearest Ferrand," he began, then he continued. "I am adrift, a marinier with no rudder or sail. I am a swan with no sense of north or south, a tree that feels not the sun on its outstretched leaves. It is all the worse because each day we share a room, and books, and the duties of the house. I long for the day when we again can meet again beneath the Qarumalil, in our valugudil. My memory is as bright and as dark as the tolatolil in which we bathed together. I hope for happier times, my darling.

"Yours ever, your cogwheel,

"Sandrine."

He had just finished when a flare of light brightened his face, and she realized with a start that he had lit fire to the letter. He continued looking down as the light brightened, then dimmed, then faded away.

"I will bring your next letter tomorrow," he said, then he wicked out the candle. A moment later she heard the door to his prayer cell open, and then close.

Carefully, she wriggled from the air duct, her flesh all pins-and-needles. Burning letters was not an uncommon act in the basilica, but when one did so, it was to send the correspondence back to the author, where they waited in limbo.

Severin did not believe Sandrine d'Ospios had been banished or taken employment in some other house.

At the very least, he believed she was dead.

At the most, he knew it for a fact.

WHEN SHE returned to her rooms, Chrysanthe committed to writing as much of the letter as she could remember. The two words which gave her the most trouble, of course, were the most important. She believed both to be of Modjali origin.

The first part of the first word—qaru—she remembered from a children's reader her father had brought her. It meant "bridge." She also recalled that Kotai Qaril, a prominent city in Modjal meant "fortress at the bridge". She didn't know what any part of "Valugudil" mean except the ending, "il", which meant something like "at."

Whatever these places were, it seemed clear that there had been assignations there, between Severin and Sandrine, and that d'Ospios had felt compelled to disguise the names of the places even in private correspondence.

Severin's quarters and office were in a part of the chastel she could not visit without arousing suspicion, but she spent the next morning exploring the areas of the vast dwelling that were available to her. To her delight, she discovered a rather nice library. Most of the books were familiar, classical works, among which she found d'Aubry's *Lexicon of the Modjali Language*. She spent the better part of the morning lost in its pages.

It did not help that she was working from the memory of two

words pronounced by Severin, who probably could not speak Modjali, and was reading the transcription of the language by a woman fond of puns and cyphers. If she retained her conviction that "qaru" meant "bridge," though, she might be looking at Mountain Bridge, Bridge of Dying, Sleeping Bridge, Shuddering Bridge, Fertile Bridge, or any of several other possibilities.

On the other hand, "qaru" could mean black, tooth, anger, melt, or stick.

"Valugudil" was worse; it might mean big thunder, stone chapel, or small net, but it could also mean something like "love nest," toward which she gravitated for obvious reasons. Tola could mean "flow" or "tomorrow" or "dead."

Of the various maps on the walls, she found one of the local county and Roselant. Several waterways flowed through the district, and the map pictured just over a dozen bridges. Most were not named, but the few that were bore no resemblance to any etymology she had yet contrived.

Around noon, she heard a little sound at the door to the library and found that Plesance was watching her.

"I should have begun with the most boring room in the house," the young woman said. "It would have saved me some time."

"Good day, Plesance."

"Yes, isn't it?" Chrysanthe saw that she was clearly trying to suppress a grin. Did she know about the meeting with Margot? It was hard to imagine Margot telling anyone, but she and Plesance—despite their very different personalities—were clearly close. Or worse, what if the whole thing had been some conspiracy to test her virtue?

Plesance came over and glanced at the map.

"Oh dear," she said. "If you're trying to find something interesting there, I'm afraid you won't."

"I'm just curious," Chrysanthe said. "Since I'm staying here, it behooves me to learn something of the area."

"Well, then you should ask me, silly," Plesance said. "What does an old map know? It's not even a good map. Half the villages on it don't exist."

Chrysanthe realized that she had failed to wonder about the date of the map, but now that she was minded, she noticed in a notation near the compass direction that it was more than a hundred years old.

"Oh," she said. "I see."

"Anyway," Plesance said. "You must come with me. I've the most delightful surprise for you."

Chrysanthe thought that she had had quite enough of Plesance's surprises, but knew it would be rude—and worse, suspicious—if she fought too hard to remain in the library.

"Very well," she said. "Do I need any special clothes for this adventure?"

"No," Plesance said. "I think what you're wearing will do quite nicely. Now come along."

The young woman had heard about the dance her grandmother had planned, and Chrysanthe was subjected to a good bit of advice about comportment, which men to avoid, and other closely held opinions as they made their way through the corridors. At last, they came to a sunny sitting room in the far eastern wing. Someone within was playing on a harp, "Faer" by the composer Millot. It was a favorite of her sister, Phoebe, and for a moment she felt pleasantly transported to her home in Mesembria.

The emotions deepened a moment later, but without the good aspect, for a man sat in the room, listening to the music, holding a glass of wine in his hand. Like the tune, he was familiar.

It was Lucien de Delphin.

His eyes widened when he saw her. His face still had a battered look from the beating Renost had given him. Dressed in a russet jacket and lemon-colored scarf knotted at his throat, he was fashionable enough, but there was something a little careless about the way he wore it, not in keeping with the tidy appearance he had always presented before.

His eyes flicked from her to her companion.

"Plesance," he said. "What have you done?"

"I've brought an old friend from foreign shores," Plesance said. "I thought you would be pleased. You must have so much to talk about."

Belatedly, Lucien rose from his seat, upsetting his wine a little. He frowned, as his gaze darted about the room.

"Danesele Chrysanthe and I have little to discuss."

The music stopped, and the young woman playing it stood up. Chrysanthe recognized her, too. Emeline, from the sewing-room in the palace.

"Who is this, Lucien?" Emeline asked innocently, as if they had never met. Looking trapped, he blushed and appeared as if he wished to flee, but the reflex of manners took over.

"This is Chrysanthe Nevelon," he said, "of the Nevelon estate in Bellship, in Laham, Mesembria. Danesele Nevelon, this is my sister, Emeline de Delphin."

Emeline stepped forward.

"I am so pleased to meet you," she said.

Not knowing what else to do, Chrysanthe decided to go along with the charade.

"As I am pleased to meet you."

"You and my brother were friends in Mesembria, I take it?"

"We knew each other," Chrysanthe said, allowing the girl to kiss her cheek and returning it. "I did not know he was friends with the d'Othres."

"We are relatives, actually," Emeline said. "The lady here is our grandame on our mother's side."

"I was not aware of that," Chrysanthe said, feeling a little dizzy. Her placement with the d'Othres suddenly took on an entirely different dimension. Had she been sent here so the family could exact revenge? To give Lucien further excuse to claim her father's charter?

"Will you be staying long at Roselant?" she asked.

"For some time, I think," Emeline said.

"It's not safe near the cities these days," Plesance said. "The lower classes have lost their minds, it seems, and without the army here to put them down, they've become quite the nuisance."

Lucien was dithering, his mouth drawn tight.

"I am sorry to be unsociable," he suddenly said, "but I've been feeling out of sorts all morning. If you ladies will excuse me, I must retire." With that, he successfully fled the room.

"Well, that was rather rude," Plesance said. "I must apologize for my cousin."

"I think your cousin is not at fault here," Chrysanthe said.

"I am sorry, too," Emeline said, "but as you know, Danesele Chrysanthe, my brother suffered terribly in your country. He was set upon by brigands and was lucky to escape with his life."

"He was indeed fortunate," Chrysanthe said. And clearly even more so in the court of the magistrate, she reflected. He had been sent home, instead of being punished as befitted his crime. Here he was free to work his mischief.

She wondered if Lucien had a brown coat and hat.

And what was Emeline playing at? Why didn't she want her brother to know they had already met?

CHAPTER FIVE

THE WAR BEYOND
THE DAWN

TWO WEEKS after the sea battle, ships from Modjal arrived on the Zamiran waterfront, greeted by a lackluster fanfare. Cymbals and trumpets rang out, colored smokes ascended in ephemeral banners, and a ragged crowd assembled to cheer the arrival of the new veil. The ships were five in number, detached from the Modjal war fleet after communication between their strixes established the need for Modjal to reassert control over their wayward province.

Crespin did not attend the celebration that followed, but stayed with the *Leucothea*, inspecting her repairs.

It was near midnight when Saja arrived. He welcomed her guardedly.

"You weren't going to say goodbye," she accused him. When he spent too long trying to find a response, she smiled. "Yes," she said. "I know you sail with the sun. You need not assassinate me; it is an ill-kept secret."

He shrugged. "That may be," he said, "yet I am tasked with keeping it."

"Well, you know how to stop my mouth."

He did, and they spent an hour or so pleasantly.

"WHAT ARE you thinking?" she asked as clouds crept across the stars and a breeze came up. On land, the din had died almost to nothing, although the faint strains of flutes and drums still issued from the fortress. Closer by, the nasal drone of a musette accompanied a group of sailors drunkenly singing a bawdy song about shore leave, improvising the verses to reflect their own adventures, real or imaginary.

"I'm thinking I've become very fond of you," he said.

"What do you mean by that?"

"As a companion," he said. "You are more than able in almost every way I can imagine."

"That's a polite way of putting it," she replied.

"No," he said. "That's not what I mean. You're far smarter than me. Good in a fight. Independent. Fierce. I've never known anyone quite like you."

"I sound amazing," she said.

"That's it exactly."

"I can't go with you," she said. "I have things to do."

"I wasn't asking—"

"Maybe you weren't," she said. "After all, you don't love me, that much is clear, and neither do I love you, for whatever that's worth. Assuming there is such a thing as love to begin with. But we are agreeable together, are we not?"

"Yes," he replied.

"Well," she said. "Then let us part with fondness, and perhaps one day we shall meet again."

"I would like that."

"Survive Basilisk then," she said. "After that, we shall see. The world is as wide as the heavens and as small as a hamlet. And as for her, the witch—do not make a fool of yourself there."

"What?"

"Calliope," she qualified.

"Are you jealous?" he asked.

"No," she said. "Just concerned for a friend."

THE ADMIRAL called Crespin and the other officers to a meeting the first day they were underway.

"The assault on Basilisk will begin in ten days."

Crespin thought at first that he'd heard wrong. Judging by their expressions, so did some of the others.

"With the best of winds, we will be twenty-five arriving," Crespin said.

His father shrugged. "Some of you felt we did not spend enough time on repairs," he said. "I agree. Two or three months might have been adequate. More would have been ideal, but two weeks is what we had."

"And still we arrive late," Crespin said.

"We were never meant to carry the front of the fight," his father said. "We've been tasked to resupply, and by the time we arrive they'll be wanting us, there's no mistake. As it is, there is no cause for alarm. but we must make good time. All of you must see to that. In the meanwhile, I am now at liberty to speak about the disposition of the fleets.

"His Majesty's ships joined with the main body of the Velesan forces yesterday. The fleet from Modjal will reach them within perhaps three days. From there they will subdue the Drehhu south at Syleme and north at Hhark. By the time we arrive, the assault on Anvvod should be well underway, and the supplies and relief we bring will be necessary."

CRESPIN LEFT the meeting infused with a sense of urgency, but in the days that followed, he found he could not sustain it. The winds were with them, but the sea came one swell at a time, and the days stretched dreadful long. Helios was a fire in firmament, with no clouds to veil him. Each night the stars blazed so that, even without the moon, darkness seemed far away.

Many nights he saw Calliope at the rail, staring east, but he could not summon the resolve to approach her. Whatever might have grown between them now seemed poisoned at the root, and it was probably for the best. He was not yet of the disposition to take a wife, and if he were, what sort of wife would a strix make anyway?

They were already married, in a sense, to the Cryptarchia, and their lives, as far as he could tell, were not lengthy. A dalliance with her might be gratifying for a moment, but the little that had already passed between them made them bad shipmates, and as an officer he could hardly afford that sort of thing. Saja had been right to warn him against such foolishness.

So let her be: that was his watchword. And yet each time he saw her, he felt a slight lift, a moment of unguarded feeling that he did not understand.

The sky grew peculiar, a darker blue, and the sun seemed to struggle upward each morning, as if something was trying to pull him back down. Dawn was uncommonly beautiful, but she felt dangerous, as if something sinister was hiding behind her rosy gown.

Still far ahead of them, war began, and each evening he and his father met with the maps, marking the positions of the fleets and counting up the losses as the strixes reported them. The casualties were horrifying, but the fleet was advancing nonetheless. The fortress fell at Syleme, and then Hhark, and all that remained was Anvvod, a narrow passage between mountains filled with weapons carved into the living stone.

By the time they arrived, Crespin realized, it all might be over.

CHAPTER SIX

ALLIANCE

CHRYSANTHE SLOWLY stirred cream into her coffee, watching as it first formed currents and whirlpools, then eddies and curling figures that sometimes resembled writing in an elegant hand. In the end, of course, the cream and the coffee became indistinguishable and uninteresting to observe, and instead she cast her gaze out through her window at the gardens and distant line of the forest, wondering if the man in the brown coat was hiding just at the edge of sight.

More likely he is in the next room, she thought, plotting his next attack.

Her room was back in order, the mess cleaned up, but she could never view this chamber again without seeing him in it. Perhaps she should have let Margot find her other quarters.

She pushed that off. Maybe the man truly wished her harm. Maybe he only meant to scare her. Either way, she could not be distracted by him. She could only prepare herself for their next encounter, should it come. She had taken once again to carrying her bodkin with her, as she had in Mesembria. She always kept the little box her father gave her on her person, in a pocket in her undergarments. That way, if someone took it, she would either know or be in no position to care about it.

The only importance the man in the brown coat should have to her was his part in the enigma she was trying to unriddle.

CHRYSANTHE HAD always fancied herself adept at solving mysteries. Her mind seemed suited to it, to sorting out the various clues set before her and assembling them into a form that made sense. This natural ability seemed to work best in moments when she was not thinking hard at all, when she was distracted by light and sound, taste and smell.

Though she liked to take credit for the skill, secretly she had always believed it was some sort of proclivity with which she had simply been born. It was true she had practiced it since childhood, to the point that even adults sometimes had come to her when there was some mystery to be solved. She had also read broadly on the topics of logic, reason, and investigation.

In reality, she was often never sure exactly where her most important insights originated.

Whatever its source, that ability was why her father had sent her here. He believed that some secret plot or treason threatened his safety, Crespin's safety, perhaps the Ophion Empire itself. Bonaventure believed the same, and he had maneuvered her here, to Roselant, where she had almost instantly discovered a mystery buried deep in the d'Othres household.

But was it the *right* mystery? What could a boursier and his mistress have to do with the war, the emperor, or the Cryptarchia?

Had she stepped down a false road?

Maybe. And perhaps it was a road to nowhere.

The places named in d'Ospios' letter remained mysterious. Hours in the library had brought no further progress.

But...

Sandrine d'Ospios had possessed a secret. Whatever it was, it seemed as if it was connected to Ferrand Severin, who kept the books for House d'Othres. Possibly it involved something recorded in the books themselves, some activity by the house against the crown, or something similarly damning.

And Sandrine d'Ospios was dead.

Each logical exercise and every fearful dream at the edge of dozing brought her always back to the same conclusion—that d'Ospios had been murdered for what she knew.

Chrysanthe did not know what that was, but it was clear that there were those who suspected she did. The man in the brown coat, for instance. Maybe *he* had killed d'Ospios.

Her room provided no safety, that much had been proven beyond doubt. She had no one she could count on to act as her defender, including Quintent—and even if he might have been, he was mysteriously absent.

Chrysanthe was still alive—probably because she really *didn't* know what had led to d'Ospios' death. Yet here she was, working each day to discover it, and once she did, then she would probably suffer the same fate. Whatever the secret was, someone believed it worth committing murder to keep.

For the first time since meeting him, she wished that Bonaventure was here. He was a lecher, a debauch, and overall a thoroughly disgusting fellow, but her father trusted him, and he seemed to understand the treacherous world in which she found herself.

She hadn't the faintest idea how to contact him.

Feeling very alone, and very far from home, she thought that if perhaps she tried to forget—about the journal, about Severin's burnt letter, about all of it—if she devoted herself to eating, dressing, flirting, gossiping, whatever it was Plesance did when she was not inflicting her barbs on innocents, then she might yet survive.

Then she thought of Crespin, of Renost, of her father—of all the men of her town, her country, her empire, sailing into the flame and fire of the Salamandra, of war. She remembered who she was, and that death was not too much to dare. Until now, all of her little intrigues, all the mysteries against which she had set herself had been mere play. She had never been in any real danger, even from Lucien.

She had believed herself brave.

Now she had a chance to *be* brave.

THE NEXT day, she did what she had been avoiding. She arranged again for Jean to escort her to the basilica. From what she had gathered, the boursier burned a letter almost every day. Eventually he would run out of them, and any chance she had of learning more from him would be lost.

It was evening, misty and gray. A light drizzle came and went as they followed the track to town. Chrysanthe tried to conjure memories of the sun on the Laham River, of clear blue skies, and even the torrential rains, just to cheer herself. The distance between her and her homeland, however, seemed impossibly great. Her father had once told her that many sailors came to their ends by clinging to the false belief that it was possible to cross the same ocean twice, and only now was she beginning to understand what he meant.

It was better to keep her mind where her body was.

As she hoped, Severin was there, but as she approached the second circle to recite her mysteries, she noticed Emeline, looking as if she was on the verge of tears. The girl hadn't seen her yet, and Chrysanthe thought she might slip away unnoticed.

"Chrysanthe?"

She should have known better.

Severin was still in sight, but she had to deal with this first, she supposed.

"Emeline," she said, approaching the young woman. "Is this another first meeting?"

"Oh, that," Emeline said. "I'm sorry for that. My brother would have been cross if he'd known I had gone to see you in the palace. He has designs against your family, you know."

"So you know how we are… connected."

"Yes. It is one reason I wanted to meet you."

Chrysanthe took that in. "That you and he are here now is quite a coincidence," she finally said.

"For my brother it is, yes. I suggested that we leave the city and take our respite with our relatives here. I had heard you were coming but Lucien, poor thing, did not know. Had he known, he would not have accompanied me."

"I see," Chrysanthe said. "So, coming here was all your idea."

Emeline nodded, and clasped her fingers together. "I did not follow you here to the basilica, though," she said. "That really was coincidence. Lucien dragged me here, and has of course abandoned me."

"Abandoned you?"

"He is an initiate of the third circle, so he has little time for a simple like me, sister or no. I do not know this place, and... dislike being alone."

Chrysanthe was surprised. In his time in Mesembria, Lucien had spent very little time at worship. Initiation into the third circle required a fair amount of industry and conviction, neither of which she had imagined him to have.

She resisted glancing at Severin, who was half-finished with his preparations. If she did not move now, she would lose her chance. Maybe her last chance.

"Would... you accompany me?" Emeline asked.

The young woman seemed different from their first meeting. Less assured, less in control of the situation. Or perhaps she was merely adept at counterfeiting whatever demeanor most suited her needs. Either way, Chrysanthe couldn't not refuse without arousing suspicion.

"Yes," Chrysanthe said as Severin moved off. "Of course." It was too late, now. She could only hope the boursier had more than one letter left. She led Emeline to the Hall of Light, where they kindled candles together.

"Thank you," Emeline said when they were done.

"It was my pleasure."

"Lucien will be a long time," Emeline said.

"Well, may I continue to keep you company, then?"

"That would be kind of you."

They sat together in silence on the steps outside, underneath the portico. Jean stood nearby, waiting patiently. The rain had slackened off, but the sky was still overcast. Candles illuminated a few windows in the village, and passersby with lanterns formed fleeting paths of light. Other than that, night was entirely upon them, and a dark one at that.

"I heard Grandame is arranging a dance in your honor," Emeline said. "Are you excited?"

Chrysanthe shrugged. "I enjoy dancing," she said. "I'm less interested in making a match, which seems to be the reason for the whole thing."

A little frown appeared on the girl's face.

"What's the matter?"

"Is it true that you were responsible for Lucien's beating?" the girl asked.

There we are, Chrysanthe thought. It was almost a relief.

"Did he tell you that?"

"No," Emeline said. "I only heard it yesterday, in the chastel, but they are all saying it. That you tricked him, and your brothers nearly killed him."

Chrysanthe thought for a moment.

"I think it best you ask your brother about this," she said.

"I did," she said. "Now I am asking you."

Chrysanthe took a deep breath and nodded. "You must know I do not think very well of him," she said.

"You have no reason to, from what I understand," the girl replied, "but you must understand that Lucien is not really a bad man. He is driven to do dreadful things, mostly by our father and others in his life. And yet, in the deep of him, he knows he has wronged you. I can hear it in his every word when he speaks of you."

"I would like to believe that," Chrysanthe said, wondering if she believed it. "But in the end, it is his actions I must judge."

"That is a most keen observation," Emeline said, "and it applies much more generally than to my brother." She glanced up at Chrysanthe. "He *is* my brother, you know."

"Yes," Chrysanthe said. "I know all about having brothers."

Emeline nodded and unclasped her hands. Somewhere in the distance, a man bellowed a woman's name, but was answered only by laughter.

"It's not to help you make a match, you know."

"What?"

"The dance. It's meant to humiliate you."

"That had crossed my mind," Chrysanthe admitted. "It assumes I'm willing to be humiliated."

"That's very nice," Emeline said, "but it isn't to do with how you feel about it. Grandame has invited courtly notables. They intend to completely ruin you."

"How can a silly dance ruin me?" But even as she said it, a feeling a dread settled over her. Wasn't this exactly the sort of thing her mother had warned her of?

"You're very innocent," Emeline said.

"You're a year my junior, if not more," Chrysanthe said, trying to sound as if she was joking.

"How many of those extra years have you spent at the emperor's court?" Emeline asked. "Or in the High Houses?"

"None," she admitted. "You came here because I am here. Why?"

Emeline smiled a little. "It's a feeling I have about you. I may be wrong. I hope I am not. Here is what I know—they intend to make an example of you. To destroy you and your family. To take the charter for your father's estate, whether through my brother or some other agent, and leave you all without home and income. That is why you are here." She sighed and looked down at her shoes. "They're trying to ruin me too, you see. I'm not quite certain how, but I know it in my bones. We should be friends, you and I."

"And if we were friends, how would you help me?"

"They are making you out to be a bumbling bumpkin, and a loose one at that," she said. "They will attack both your comportment and your virtue."

"I know how to dance, and I know how to behave myself."

"You know how to dance?" Emeline said. "Various sorts of carole, I assume, rounds, gavottes, a low dance or two?"

"Of course," Chrysanthe said.

"And the corsacors? You are familiar with them?"

"No, I must admit," she said. "I don't know those."

"There are five dances known as corsacors," Emeline said. "The latest, the Turn, has only been in fashion for a year."

"I see. And if I do not know these dances, I will be thought provincial."

"Or far worse," the girl said. "In the corsacors, the man and woman hold each other as they dance. Not hands, mind you. You and your partner embrace, and if you hold too closely, or turn the wrong way, or let your breast graze his chest, it is considered lascivious. You become known as a wanton with no self-control, but if you dance too far apart—well, that is clumsy and shows lack of courage."

"This doesn't sound fun."

"It isn't meant to be."

"Well," Chrysanthe said. "I wonder if there is someone who could show me these dances?"

"I might do that," Emeline said. "For a friend. For an ally."

"Shall we shake hands?"

———

ON THE way back to Roselant, the rain began again, this time in earnest. Jean gave her his cloak, but she was still soaking wet before they were even out of the village. The mud sucked at the hooves of their horses, and the downpour scattered the light from Jean's lantern so much as to make it nearly useless.

Chrysanthe's resolve, to confront whatever came against her, was wavering. She began to wonder what would happen she simply turned her horse from the road and went away. Jean might not notice she was gone until it was too late, and she would be impossible to find in the dark. She could hide—perhaps ride to the mountains—or find some small port where she could hire a boat to take her home, or someplace else far away from her problems.

Her speculations were interrupted by a small curse from Jean, who reached over to take her reins.

"What?" she asked, but then she saw. A stream of water ran across the road, broader than their horses were long. It was hard to tell how deep.

"I don't remember a river here," she joked.

"Oc, not for a long time," Jean said. "It ran here when my grandfather was a boy, before the river silted up at Loel and the Cendel shifted beds."

"Loel?" She remembered the name from the map in the library, a nice little town on the ocean.

"Oc," he said. "Quite the place, back in the day. My grand had many a story of that little wycke, but when the river went north, so did everyone else, and built up Neapol. Loel, she's fast asleep now."

Chrysanthe felt a small shock go through her, and for a moment each raindrop seemed like a perfect crystal, suspended between breath and heartbeat.

"What do you mean, 'asleep'?"

"Oh," he said. "I'm sorry, miss. It's a local expression. From a story, I think. Anyway, when we say something is fast asleep, we mean it's done—run its course."

Sleeping Bridge, she thought. Wherever Severin and d'Ospios met, it couldn't be far, could it? If the river had once flowed through here to Loel, wouldn't there have been a bridge on it somewhere? A bridge that no longer served any purpose? That was "fast asleep"?

Most likely Jean could tell her, but she didn't want to ask. That might raise suspicion. Yet if she was right, it could narrow her search. She could check the map, perhaps in the morning.

Jean determined that the once-empty riverbed was not yet too deep to ford. They were soon across it, and on their way to being dry.

SHE DID not go to the library the next morning, because Emeline came for her early, with breakfast packed in a basket. They wound their way through the gardens until they reached a stone-surfaced court hedged by blackthorn.

"For dancing outside?" Chrysanthe asked of the paved area.

"For playing palm," Emeline said. "You know, with the feathered ball?"

"Oh," Chrysanthe said. "Of course, but we play it on the grass."

"I remember watching people play here when I was younger," Emeline said, "but palm has been out of fashion for five years or so, so I don't expect we'll be interrupted, unless by gardeners."

"Why here? Why not in the chastel? There are many rooms

which are little used."

"I think it would be best for both of us if my help to you goes unnoticed," Emeline replied. "Indeed, in company I intend to snub you. You understand, I hope?"

"I think I do."

"In fact, this is the last time we will be seen walking together. I will spread it about that I found you coarse and tiresome, and from this day on we will each come here by different routes."

"If that is what you wish."

"Good," Emeline said. "Now, do you know the steps for a troipé?"

"I do not," Chrysanthe said.

"Very well," Emeline said. "We'll start with that."

"Do we embrace, then?"

"Not yet. Steps first."

She watched as Emeline demonstrated, and realized almost immediately how out of her depth she was. The dances she had grown up with were lively—rarely did both feet touch the ground at the same moment. Much hopping and even the occasional leap was involved, but Emeline moved as if she was made of silk, and the floor of ice. She seemed to glide upon the stone with effortless grace, her feet making no sound at all.

"That was beautiful," Chrysanthe said when the girl came to rest.

"Now you try," she said. "Here, let me sound the tempo, so you can feel it." She clapped and hummed a tune, but Chrysanthe did not "feel it." She kept wanting to put her feet down on the wrong beat, and in general felt like a hobbled rhinoceros attempting to gambol. Never in her life had she felt clumsy, but she did now, and it was not a welcome sensation.

"I must learn this in a few weeks?" she said. "That seems impossible."

"It isn't," Emeline insisted. "You move well and have a fine figure. For you, it is more a matter of unlearning than learning. Here, let me show you how it works with a partner. I will be the man." She stepped close, put one hand in the small of Chrysanthe's back, and her other palm in hers. Then she pulled her nearer, so only the space of a thumb separated them at the belly.

"You're not serious," Chrysanthe said, stepping back a little. Emeline followed her, keeping the gap infinitesimal.

"No," she said. "Yes, I am. It's just like this."

"How can we move without, ah, rubbing against one another?"

Emeline smiled. "That is the challenge. The more so because most men will make it their business to try and accomplish exactly that. You must evade them without seeming to."

"It seems… uncouth."

"Have you never 'rubbed up' against a man?" Emeline asked. "My brother, perhaps?"

"More unseemly yet!" Chrysanthe said. "But if you must know, except on two occasions, your brother played the perfect gentleman with me. One of those incidents was not an… amorous one." She pulled away. "And you? Please tell me that at your age—"

Emeline shrugged. "I think we have different expectations, you and I."

"But that's terrible."

Emeline lifted her chin. "I didn't come here to be insulted," she said. "I came here to help you."

"Yes," Chrysanthe said. "I'm sorry. I'm ready now, if you will show me."

LATER, RESTING in the shade, Chrysanthe nursed her frustration and nibbled at a pear.

"You may not think so, but you are doing well," Emeline said.

"You are a good teacher," Chrysanthe. "Very patient, and good at explaining."

"I had a good teacher." She took a sip of her wine. "I was quite in love with him, of course."

"Oh dear."

"Yes. I was nine when we started. By the time I was thirteen, I knew I must marry him. And so, of course, he was exiled."

Chrysanthe blinked.

"I'm sorry. Did you say he was exiled?"

"As in sent away," Emeline said. "Very far away, in fact—to Nihar of the Sands. I tried to send him a letter, but my governess discovered it, and that was the end of that."

"I'm sorry to hear it."

"I know now it was inevitable," Emeline said. "I have been promised in marriage since my birth, and nothing or no one can interfere—or even appear to interfere—with that match."

"Oh," Chrysanthe said. She finished the pear and tossed the core into the hedge.

"You sound as if you pity me," Emeline said, "but you should not. I have come to know my fiancé, and he is a man of many excellent qualities. I am lucky."

"I'm sure that is so," Chrysanthe said.

"No more of that," Emeline said. "You've lazed about long enough. Let me show you the antilios."

"Of course," Chrysanthe said. She stood, dusting off her dress. Emeline faced off with her, and then once again reached around her waist. She gazed into the young woman's eyes, thinking how a few days ago there had been no hint that she existed. How this was Lucien's sister, who might well be plotting revenge for her brother's treatment? What if the girl was teaching her everything exactly *wrong*?

"I appreciate your help," Chrysanthe told her, "but you've never said how I can help you."

Emeline frowned briefly. "There are no friends at court," she said. "Everyone is always trying to get the advantage over everyone else. Here, it is no different, and may in fact be worse. If I were sinking into a swamp, any of my cousins would use my head as a stepping-stone to reach the dry bank."

She paused, and in that moment her expression faltered. She looked sad, and frightened, and very young. A girl forced into a woman's shoes.

"You are not from the court," Emeline continued. "You are not a relative. I have a sense about people, and in you I sense something I have never known. I don't trust you, exactly, and yet I do not automatically distrust you. And the little my brother has said—"

"I cannot believe Lucien would have a favorable impression of me."

"I did not say his opinion of you was favorable," she replied. "That is not the point. The point is, you seem to be a person with scruples. In my experience, that is an exceedingly rare thing. I look out for myself very well, but sometimes that is not enough. What I need is a friend to help look after me. Someone who will not push me into the swamp and step on my head. Preferably someone who will warn me before someone else does."

"That is the least I would do for you," Chrysanthe said.

"Those are words," Emeline replied. "I have heard many words in my life. Remember your comment about actions."

"It is fresh in my mind," Chrysanthe said.

CHAPTER SEVEN

THE SALAMANDRA

THE SALAMANDRA appeared first as a line of green-tinted clouds on the horizon. As the *Leucothea* drew nearer, the dark outline of the land appeared, a jumbled silhouette drawn skyward by a chain of mountains that looked as if a giant had cut off their peaks with a sword. Mist drifted up from a few of them; far to the north, Crespin could see one belching smoke in a gray cloud, reminding him of the Isles de Seismoi in another ocean more than half a world away.

Their progress slowed to a crawl as they navigated treacherous reefs. Once they were beyond the worst of those, they began to come across wrack. Beams and barrels, shattered planks. Corpses. The waters were alive with sharks and other carrion fish, and twice they sighted the immense form of a xiphodon, a shark larger than some ships. Fortunately, there seemed to be enough carrion to keep it contented.

It took almost a day to be certain of their bearing, and then they steered toward Anvvod. By noon of the next day, the strait was in sight.

Crespin had seen only engravings of the place, in which the two sides of the strait were depicted as towering cliffs guarded by colossi of steel. One of the statues was missing entirely; of the other, the legs remained to the knee. With the ships to give them scale, Crespin felt dizzied by how titanic they must once have been.

The cliffs themselves were lower than usually depicted: not the natural fortress walls he was expecting, but still more than substantial. They were riddled with dark holes which he knew to be emplacements for diabolic weapons. These remained dark and quiet. The war had been here already and passed on. He wondered how many Drehhu and their slaves lay rotting in those cliffs.

The strait was choked with wreckage, and the smell of corpses was nearly intolerable. Flocks of gulls and sea-crows feasted, squabbled, and soared above, raining their droppings upon the Mesembrian fleet.

A small contingent of ships remained between the cliffs, acting as a rearguard—proud galleys from Modjal flying the banner of the hooded serpent. The rest of the combined fleet were already beyond, laying siege to the city of Basilisk itself.

To Crespin's great frustration, their orders were to stand far from shore. While the merchant ships were excellent for making speed under sail, in the narrow confines of the Mere de Basilisk, the more maneuverable warships that had both sail and sweeps were needed, especially against the demonic Drehhu vessels.

The mercantile fleet, late as it was, could not have been allowed to come later. Some of the Navy crews had been on quarter rations for two weeks, and half the fleet was without quilaine shot or arrows. Galleys came out from Anvvod to take on supplies before returning to the fray. The men they carried had a worn, battered look about them, but with the timely arrival of the ships from Mesembria they seemed newly optimistic that the city would soon fall. Few outsiders had ever walked the streets of Basilisk, but that didn't stop sailors from speculating what they would find, be it streets paved in rubies or slave women bred for sexual characteristics that Crespin doubted existed in any variety of human being.

For the merchant ships, their lot seemed to be a boring one—or so he thought until the third day. On that day a new fleet appeared, arriving from the south. A fleet with no sails.

In good weather, with a fair wind, Crespin was sure the *Leucothea* was faster than the devil-driven ships. But wind usually blew one way at a time, and unless you desired to go in exactly that direction, full speed was impossible. The Drehhu fleet had the advantage of being able to move in a straight line, and turn in whatever direction they wanted, whenever they wanted.

Crespin watched the approaching ships impatiently as their own ships raised their sails and began to tack about. His father stood nearby, studying the oncoming fleet as one might observe an odd turn of the weather. If the Mesembrian ships had possessed oars like the galleys beyond the Anvvod gate, they might have been better at turning and assembling to face this new enemy, or taking up another position as might be required.

Calliope came on deck, already swaying, her gold-flecked eyes wandering as she tried to focus on the admiral.

"This was not expected," she said. "The siege of Basilisk is vulnerable to an attack from the sea."

His father nodded. "The Drehhu must have sent half of their fleet to Timur," he said. A small frown creased his forehead, the first sign of worry he had expressed. "Now they return, with most of our ships in the harbor, where they cannot maneuver."

"How can that be?" Crespin asked. "This has been planned for more than a year. How can our intelligence have been so faulty?"

His father shrugged slightly.

"Does it matter now?" he asked. "We must keep them on this side of the gates until the warships can arrive from the harbor, or all is lost. We'll form in columns, just as we did at Zamir."

Zamir had been good practice, at least, and despite the uncanny speed of the enemy vessels and the wind coming against them, the Mesembrians managed to sail into formation. At Zamir, however, the wind had been their friend, and most of the ships they faced had been ordinary galleys, not demon-driven craft.

Night rose up in the east, and the Drehhu ships glowed as if afire with the light of the dying sun. By the time their weapons began to speak, the stars were appearing in a cloudless sky.

"Let us hope," he heard his father murmur, as the first of their ships burst into flames. He turned to Calliope. "Begin now," he said.

She nodded and closed her eyes.

Crespin stared helplessly as the enemy's streaming balls of fire crossed the distance between the fleets, bursting on water or slamming into timber and sail. It was as if the sky itself was falling, and was in a way as beautiful as it was terrifying. They were still too far away for the merchant ships to use any of their own weapons. Anger stirred in him. Why did the Cryptarchia deny them such arms? Surely one magic was as good as another.

If they possessed weapons like the Drehhu...

Across the water, an incandescent flower bloomed, and then another, and in an instant it was nearly as bright as day. Their bowsprit glowed white, the faces of the men were lit, eyes squinting as ship after ship exploded in flame.

He looked to his father and saw the satisfaction on his face.

"They misjudged our range," Crespin said. "You were right. The sacrifice of our vanguard at Zamir was worth it."

"Maybe," his father said. "Maybe not. We will probably never know. They understand that they must enter the Mere de Basilisk before the warships collect themselves. Perhaps they are making a sacrifice of their own."

BY EARLY morning the bombardment had ceased, but it was difficult to tell what the outcome had been. The strixes were all exhausted: according to Calliope, many had died. By counting the fires and lucnograph report, they reckoned that more than half of the merchant ships were gone. The Drehhu ships, if any remained, were not to be seen.

Faltering in the dark, they turned with the wind and made their way to the Colossus Gates, forming a wall with their ships and waiting for the dawn.

Then, when Eos drew herself up in her rosy gown, they saw the enemy, half again their number, far out on the horizon, but unmistakably bearing toward them. Crespin moved about the ship, shouting for the men to be ready. He spoke with the lucnograph operator, then returned to his father.

"Our own warships will not reach us for hours yet," he said. "The Modjal galleys have arrived from Hhark and are moving to our flanks, but we're still outnumbered."

His father nodded.

"We have a little time," he said. "Come below with me and have some coffee."

––––––––––

CRESPIN WAS buttering a hard roll when the *Leucothea* trembled a bit, so that the porcelain cups and saucers rattled on the table and dust drifted down from the beams overhead.

"I guess they're nearly in range," he remarked.

Across the table, the admiral lifted his cup of coffee and took a sip. "Almost," he agreed.

"I suppose I'd best go above," Crespin said. "Make ready."

"Finish your coffee," the admiral said. "Then we'll go together." Crespin raised his cup. It was translucent, almost like glass. Not the usual ware in the mess.

The admiral noticed his expression.

"Picked these up in Li Teal," he said. "Quite nice."

Crespin nodded and sipped, savoring the dark, spiced coffee and rum. He set the cup down, just in time for another explosion to rock the ship more violently than the last. The cups and saucers jumped from the table, but were saved from breaking by the Modjal carpet that covered the floor of the mess. The remains of Crespin's coffee soaked into the intricate weave.

"Well," he said. "I'm done with that." He dithered a moment, not wanting to bring up the obvious—but he felt he had to, given his rank.

"The strixe—" he began.

"No," the admiral said. "She's finished for today."

"As you say, sir."

The admiral nodded, his blue-green eyes morning bright, his expression carefully neutral, as usual.

"Well," he said, rising and reaching for his sword belt, hung across the back of his chair. "It is time now. Thank you for your company, Crespin."

"A pleasure, sir," Crespin answered, feeling a slight lump in his throat. The admiral buckled on his weapon and sent him another half-smile.

"Let's do our best to die with a little dignity, shall we?"

Crespin returned the grin.

"I'll do my best, Father," he promised.

"Of course you will," the admiral said. "You are, after all, a Nevelon."

Crespin leaned over, picked up the cup, and put it back on the table. He felt oddly calm.

It had been a long voyage, but it was over now.

CRESPIN STRAPPED on his saber and began following his father toward deck, but hesitated and instead made his way down the hall to the door at the end. He knocked upon it.

"What is it?"

He pushed the hatch open. The room inside was large, by ship's standards. It contained a small bed, a closet, a sitting chair, and small writing desk with several drawers. Calliope was sprawled on the bed, a bottle of rum clutched in one hand. Her eyes were the color of lemons, her face pallid and slack. She wore only a shift, and the cuffs of it were stained yellow.

Her gaze seemed to go through him.

"Who is it?" she asked.

"Crespin," he replied.

"Oh," she said, a sickly smile crawling upon her face. She laughed. "Here I am," she said. "In my repose. Am I all you dreamt of?"

"I only meant to ask how you are."

Her eyes finally focused on him.

"And how am I?"

He noticed her accent was different, stronger, more akin to something one would hear in the darker streets of Ophion Magne than in a drawing room.

"I'll leave," he said.

"Wait!" she snapped, pushing herself up to take a long, hard drink that would made any turpentine-bobber seem timid in comparison. "You've never come here before," she said.

"I have not," he replied.

"What is the matter?"

"Nothing," he replied. "Rest well."

He stepped through the door, closed it, and quickly returned to deck.

CHAPTER EIGHT

THE TSAU DADAN

BY THE time Hound realized they were surrounded, it was too late. He was so shocked, he only barely managed to raise the alarm before the enemy came swarming out of the trees.

They reminded him of the apes and baboons of his homeland, but were much larger, heavier, and shaped more like men, albeit with freakishly long arms. They charged on all fours, running on their palms—they had hands for feet—or swung overhead through the trees. Covered in fur, dappled like fawns, they blended in with the jungle light. Their large, ridged heads rested directly between their shoulders, with no necks to speak of, and their jaws stuck way out.

Their teeth were large and square, save for two pointed ones that were quite prominent.

The attackers slammed into the mounted chevaliers, carrying some of them from their saddles to the ground. The horses screamed in panic, and pandemonium took rule.

Hound managed to kill the first that came at him, striking it between the eyes with his tomahawk, but before he could wrench his weapon from the beast another hit him from behind. It wrapped arms like oak tree roots around him, after which its weight crushed him to the earth.

Rose sunk her teeth into the attacker, ripping away flesh, and he was loose again. Hound fought free and scrambled up a tree, with two of the creatures following him. He kicked one under the chin. It fell and struck the other, giving him the few moments he needed to unwind his sling. Their skulls were thick, but not thick enough at the temples—he killed both and fought his way higher.

Looking down, Hound saw Martin dealing blows with his fists that sent shattered bodies spinning away from him in every direction. The chevaliers had managed to form themselves into a rough fighting square. Hound began slinging in their support.

A movement in the corner of his eye turned out to be one of the beast-men, hurling itself from branch-to-branch. Before he could even get a stone into the sling, it knocked him from his perch. Branches blurred by, then he found the ground. He tried to scramble away but felt as if he wasn't connected to his body anymore, as if the impact had knocked not just the wind from him, but his soul as well.

The monster landed next to him and raised both fists.

Two crossbow bolts appeared in its chest. Its quick eyes registered surprise, then went dull as it slumped to the ground. A moment later, Selene was there.

"Help me up," he grunted.

"It's alright," she said. "They've lost interest in us."

He sat up as feeling began to return to his limbs.

"Yes," Martin said. "They got what they came for."

At first Hound didn't know what he meant, but then he understood.

Veulkh, the ravens, and Ammolite were nowhere to be seen.

AMMOLITE LOOKED back the way they'd come, but the fight was no longer visible, hidden by the dense forest. She hoped Hound was still alive. As for the rest, she did not care.

"What are they?" she asked Veulkh, nodding at their strange escort. She, Veulkh, and the ravens were still mounted. The beasts had surrounded them but made no sign that they would attack.

"Stay your hands," he'd told his men. "If we let them lead us, they will do us no harm." And so here they were, advancing up the slopes of a mountain, led by the grotesque beast-men.

"They are called Tsau Dadan," he said, "among other things. And they are supposed to be extinct."

TWO MEN-AT-ARMS were dead, both of broken necks. One had been the man of the chevalier Ariston, and he was in a rage. Hound had learned enough of his language to follow him, although some of the expletives escaped him.

"He betrayed us," the horseman roared. "The damned sorcerer led us into a trap."

"That doesn't make sense," Selene said. "We were at his mercy back at his mountain. He could have killed us there, without going to all this trouble."

"I know what I saw," Ariston persisted. "The beasts did not touch them."

"Someone wanted to separate us from Veulkh," Martin said.

"That much is clear, and nothing else. Whether Veulkh was complicit, we cannot yet know, and it does us no good to speculate. We must follow them. Without Veulkh, our mission will fail. There is no more to say. Bind your wounds and gather your things. We move on within the hour."

"Guyote and Kyros deserve burial," Ariston said.

"They do," Martin said, "but there is no time for it now."

"Perhaps you are no longer leading this expedition," Ariston said. Martin looked at him.

"You are bound by oath to follow me," he said. "Do you renounce your oath?" Ariston locked eyes with him for a long moment. Then his gaze seemed to travel down to Martin's blood-covered fists.

"I'm no oathbreaker."

"I thought not," Martin said. He looked around at the others.

"Within the hour," he said.

THEY HAD been in the mountains for several days before the appearance of the Tsau Dadan, and the land had become stranger. Once, from a high ridge, they had seen a distant peak shaped like a great cone, belching clouds of black smoke as if it had a fire inside of it. Flecks of ash settled in their hair and on their shoulders. The earth beneath their feet trembled often, usually a little but sometimes with enough force that keeping his footing required effort.

There were no further signs of the Ngachok warriors, or indeed evidence of any human beings whatsoever. It rained every day, sometimes all day, and now this. Hound remembered Martin's comment about keeping their eyes open, but it seemed as if they had not been attentive enough.

He hadn't been attentive enough.

It was a strange thought, made even stranger by the realization that the notion of abandoning Martin and Selene was no longer easy to entertain.

Gradually the tall jungle gave way to fine-limbed laurels, delicate ferns, and lacy green strands that crept along the ground and into the trees. As they gained altitude, this in turn was replaced by scrubby, moss-like plants, clinging to what was little more than bare, black stone.

Without the trees to shorten his vision, it was clear to Hound that they were climbing the slope of a mountain, but unlike the crags and ridges of Vereshalm Mountains, this one seemed very regular in shape and inclination—like the burning cone they had seen a few days before. There was no smoke, however: instead, a white, cloudlike haze rose into the sky from somewhere ahead.

The heat of the lowlands was gone, replaced by a damp chill.

The mountain had no true summit, but instead a rim, as if some god had torn off the peak and dug out a bowl-shaped cavity. They were high above the jungle, and he saw that the mountain was part of a chain marching north and south. The nearest looked like this one, a decapitated cone. Off to the east, he saw a vast blue water that had to be the sea.

The circular valley was half-filled with water, from which rose the cloud of vapor he'd noticed earlier. No trees grew there, only scrubby bushes, moss, and ferns. In the center of the lake stood an island, and on the island a dome of black stone that looked too regular to be natural.

They followed the trail down to the bare rock of the water's edge, where Hound observed yet another smooth depression.

"That's where they went," he said.

Martin looked across at the black dome. He approached the water and dipped a finger in, then withdrew it quickly.

"It's near boiling."

"So I don't guess we'll be swimming across," Hound remarked.

ONCE AGAIN, Ammolite experienced the violent sense of dislocation. Her knees would not hold her. When she tried to open her eyes, she became so dizzy that she shut them instantly. Strong arms took hold of her and would not let her fall. Weariness brimmed in her, and she descended into strange colors and unclear voices.

SHE WOKE on a bed in room illuminated by a familiar opaline light, and for a moment thought she was back home, that the whole strange adventure had been a dream. But the bed was not familiar to her, and the coverlet on which she lay was dusty and stiff.

The room was equally unfamiliar, and rather small. Veulkh was there, standing over her.

"Quickly," he said. He took her hands and brought them to his temples.

"What's the matter?" she asked.

"Don't be thick," he said. "You've lost your seeming. It may be too late already, but if it isn't, we must hurry."

"Oh," she said, realizing it was so, that for the first time in weeks she wore only her own skin.

Orra was there waiting, however, and soon she had changed. Veulkh took her on the small, decaying bed. When he was done, he lay staring at the ceiling, as if trying to pierce it with his gaze.

Ammolite lay beside him, noticing as she did that the wall had a long, fine crack in it that separated the top of the room from the bottom. She followed it around and realized that the corners did not fit neatly, as if the chamber had been broken like a clay pot and not been put back together quite right. The door stood open.

"I expected this," Veulkh muttered. He sounded oddly subdued. "I anticipated it, and still…"

"I don't understand," she said.

"It should have been empty," he said. "The last sorcerer to reside here was Chalicon, and it killed him. My kind are nearly all dead, and the ones that survive have their own demesnes: familiar, fortified, not as fraught as this place."

"You came here," she said.

"Yes. To do a single thing, and even that so perilous…" He shook his head. "I took nothing for granted. I planned contingencies…"

"I don't understand," she said. "The Tsau Dadan. You didn't expect them? They left us alone. They allowed the ravens to keep their weapons."

"Yes," he said. "Whoever is here recognized me for what I am, and perhaps even *who*. I have been extended a sort of courtesy, I believe."

"We are safe, then?"

"No," he replied. "We are not safe at all." He sat up, put his elbows on his knees and bent his fists to his forehead. "The Tsau Dadan," he muttered.

"What are they?" she asked.

"They were here before us," he said, "or their ancestors were. Before the Drehhu. Before Ophion, Veles, Modjal, Helios, Taman, Okeanos, and all their kin arrived. In the dead city where we entered this land, Sular Bulan, they were bred as slaves. Eventually they turned on their masters. In the battle that followed, master and slave alike were destroyed, the city abandoned. Or so I was taught. Obviously some have survived, and moreover, someone remembers—or has learned—the art of commanding them."

"Who could that be?"

"No one living," he replied. "A strix might control one or two, briefly, but what we saw requires—well, something special."

"What of Martin and the rest?" she asked, eager to move from the subject. "Do you think they are dead?"

"I shouldn't give another thought to them."

"No," a new voice agreed. "You shouldn't."

The voice might have been that of a child, or a woman's voice pitched a little high. Through the open doorway, Ammolite saw the outline of someone standing in the hall, just beyond the light. She was suddenly, acutely aware of her nakedness and reached for her clothes, holding them in front of her.

The figure stepped nearer, into the dim light.

Her face was more girl than woman, pale and pretty with wide dark eyes. Her black hair flowed in curls below her waist. She was petite and dressed in a black gown that fastened up the front with little silver buckles.

"She's shy, this woman of yours?" the woman said. Ammolite wondered how long she had been standing there. Had she seen them in the act? Veulkh, for his part, actually seemed to be speechless. He stared at the woman for an uncommon length of time before finding his breath.

"Marnora."

A delighted smile stole across her face.

"Just so," she said. "You know me, then?"

"I know you," he said.

"Well, that's marvelous," she said. "I wondered. I suppose it has been a long while since we've seen each other."

"Centuries."

"Well, there you have it. You've a good memory." She beamed at them for a moment. Then she beckoned with one hand. "Come along, then," she said. "Get dressed or not, it makes no difference to me."

They did dress, while Marnora watched with a sort of guileless regard. It seemed harmless, but Ammolite found her heart racing. She felt utterly exposed in a way that she hadn't since the first night Veulkh unclothed her. When they were finished, Marnora turned and led them through the faintly glimmering halls until they reached a room with a large, round table, upon which rested a carafe of dark red wine and three goblets.

"Let us take some refreshment, shall we?"

They took seats in high-backed chairs spaced so that they faced each other in a triangle. Above, a golden light appeared, emitted by a crystal sphere scribed with the symbols of Helios Megistos, Pozdu Nalna, and Rahh Hamakurya, along with a few others she did not recognize. Now that it was illuminated, the entire chamber had a sort of autumn glow to it. The walls were leafed in gold, and the vaulting ceiling of some dark stone embellished with symbols of the night below, the journey of the sun beyond the horizon in all of its theometamorphic complexity.

The wine was dry and flowery, and reminded Ammolite of the spring breezes that lifted up from the valley below Veulkh's manse. It also brought her to a surprising realization.

She had changed into Orra without Veulkh's wine. That had never happened before. For years she had believed the wine was an essential ingredient to the magic. Now she knew it wasn't. She didn't understand what that meant, really, but the more she knew, the better the chance she would have to somehow change her fate.

The glasses on the table suddenly began to rattle and dance. Then Ammolite realized it wasn't the glasses moving, but the table, and the floor beneath their feet. Marnora did not seem to notice, and the shivering lasted for only few moments. She lifted her glass and, with her other hand, gestured so as to sweep the chamber.

"It's a little dull, isn't it," he said. "Do you remember that place, the castle of—oh, what was his name? Pleur?"

"The Sea Palace," Veulkh said. "Carved within an ancient coral reef."

"A hundred glistering pools," she said, "and the fountains. The ammolite courtyard. You remember?"

Hearing her name in so different a context was jolting, especially since the only other person to say it in years had been Hound. She remembered her kiss with the strange boy, coupling with him. It hadn't been nearly so unpleasant as it was with Veulkh. He'd been funny.

"I remember," Veulkh said.

"Whatever became of Pleur?" she asked.

"The earth shook," Veulkh said. "The sea rose up. Beautiful his palace may have been, but safe it was not."

He glanced around the chamber significantly.

"No," Marnora said, her brow slightly puckered. "I don't suppose it was. So few places are, but I have fond memories of Pleur and his castle."

"As do I," Veulkh replied.

"The past is like a large, dark cave," she said. "Lit only by a few gems scattered about. Or, no—better! A dark, endless night overseen by only a handful of stars."

Veulkh nodded, and Ammolite saw heaviness on him, as if he had just done a terrible thing in his conjury. She saw the same gravity reflected in Marnora's otherwise childlike eyes.

"So here we are," Marnora said, resting an elbow on the table, her chin in her palm. "I don't often have guests, or visitors at all. It is so… surprising when one comes my way. When it does happen, I usually forgo the pleasures of conversation. I'm glad that this time I made an exception."

"This makes me glad, as well," Veulkh said. She had never heard Veulkh behave so deferentially toward anyone. It was almost as if he was afraid of her. Silence stretched awkwardly, to the point that Ammolite felt she needed to say something.

"Are we—in a volcano?" she asked.

Marnora looked pleased. "So you have some education."

"I've read about them," she said, "and we saw one on the way here, belching flame…"

"You came from the north, I take it."

Ammolite suddenly realized she may have said too much. Marnora didn't seem to really expect an answer.

"You know what a volcano is," she said. "A synapsis of earth, fire and air, and sometimes water, as well."

"Yes," she said. "I've read that."

Marnora cocked her head, and her eyebrows lifted a bit.

"You seem familiar to me," she said. "We've met, haven't we?"

Ammolite felt a clutch in her throat. Veulkh had talked a great deal about his life with Orra. He had spoken of ancient friends and foes, but she was quite sure he had never mentioned anyone named Marnora.

"Yes," Marnora said. "I *do* remember you. The witch of Mirrordim." She snapped her fingers. "Orra. Orra Speklonduma."

Ammolite tried to keep her face neutral.

"Orra,"Veulkh said."Indeed."

"That's very odd," Marnora said."I have—for many years—been under the impression that I murdered you."

CHAPTER NINE

BASILISK

WHAT REMAINED of the merchant fleet from Mesembria now choked the strait of Anvvod, with some of the Modjal vessels already present. The *Leucothea*'s neighbors were so near that Crespin thought, with a good run, he could jump from one to the other.

The Drehhu, in contrast, had formed into a wedge and were cutting toward them like the tip of a vast spear. This wouldn't be a battle of clever maneuvers or hidden tactics.

Like the other ships, the *Leucothea* had dropped anchor and sail. They were no longer a ship, but one plank in a barricade. At the railing, the xelons crowded behind their shields while the archers prepared their first volley. Crespin hoped that the Drehhu ships would ram them, as it looked like they might. At least then they might die swinging their swords.

Instead, as feared, the ships drew up just outside of quilaine range and began to turn broadside, presenting their weapons to full advantage. For what seemed a long time, nothing happened.

Then the Drehhu fired their first volley.

Crespin watched his father, who didn't so much as flinch at the impact. Unholy screams went up and down the line as the unnatural weapons carried off arms, legs, and souls, but even that awful music was muffled by the cacophony of shattering timber. Smoke and flame seemed to erupt everywhere at once. In the pause, while his ears rang, Crespin's gaze swept the ship. He saw that a marinier named Barie and a sailor he did not recognize had fallen from the rigging and lay broken amidships. A dozen xelons were smeared across the deck in bloody pieces.

A lone gull sat on the babord rail as if nothing was amiss.

The Drehhu fired again.

This time something hit close. Crespin felt a shocking pain along his ribs and lurched forward, hand to his side, teeth gritted, trying not to cry out. He saw his father unsheathe his sword, although there was nothing at which to strike. Smoke burned his nose and throat as he drew his own weapon.

He looked down and saw his uniform growing dark with blood. Felt a sudden grip on his arm and found Renost there, grinning.

"Ready, mon vieil?" he shouted in Crespin's ear, yet he still sounded distant.

"No," Crespin said, "but here we are, nevertheless." He clapped his hand on his friend's shoulder and turned his gaze back out to the enemy fleet.

"Sacre merde," Renost swore.

At first, he assumed his friend was simply making his peace, in his own profane way, but then Calliope walked past him, heading toward the bow. Her face seemed somehow bright, although she didn't shine like the sun, or really give off any light at all. Yet he could not look at her without squinting. Tendrils of glowing mist came writhing through the air and attached to her skin, then in a second he saw that they came from the other ships, like insubstantial ropes thrown across the sea.

His father noticed her, and took a single step forward, his hand reaching for her arm, but then the strixe lifted into the air like a feather on an updraft. She vomited a golden cloud. It poured on and on, erupting also from her eyes, her nostrils, from the very pores of her skin. She suddenly twisted somehow, become something less than real, a sketch of line and color that suggested a woman but did not really depict one.

Gleaming, flowing almost like a liquid, the gold flooded out—not toward the enemy ships, but into the sea.

The Drehhu fired again.

This time the explosion caused Crespin to lose his footing, and when he fought back to it he saw that most of the ship's bow rail—where Calliope had been standing—had been blown off. Above it, however, something still drifted, a rift in the sky, a jaundiced wound in the universe, bleeding into the deep waters.

Then the deck began to tilt.

At first Crespin thought they were sinking, but it happened too quickly, and the other ships in the front of the line were inclining, too. It wasn't them going down but the sea coming up, mounting in a great swell. Something broke through the wave.

Crespin's left hand was wet with blood, his right still clutched on Renost's shoulder. Everything seemed unreal, even the pain threatening to overwhelm his senses.

It emerged from the sea, shaped something like a man but wrong in every dimension, a mockery of the human form. Dark, crusted in barnacles, its face impossible to see. It stood to its waist in water, yet towered higher than the tallest mast in the fleet.

The ancient Drehhu colossus had risen, and Crespin knew their doom was sealed.

The thing lurched away from the *Leucothea*, toward the nearest Drehhu ship, stretching out its titanic hands. More smoke billowed from the enemy fleet, and for a moment, a pall of flame and black cloud hid the monster from sight. Then he could just see it, through the haze, as it lifted a Drehhu vessel like a toy.

Up and up it went, and suddenly incandesced, a blue-white sun. Lightning struck out from the colossus, arcing from ship to ship, enmeshing the Drehhu fleet in a fulminating web. Steam boiled from the water; a hot wind burned his face, and Crespin staggered, grasping for something to steady himself and finding Renost still there.

Calliope tumbled to the deck like a broken doll. He saw the admiral rush forward and gather her up in his arms, saw the look on his father's face.

Of course, he thought. How did I not know?

Does my mother know?

He was vaguely aware as Renost lowered him to the deck. The sun dimmed as a huge cloud churned up from the sea, until he could see nothing farther than two yards away.

SOME HOURS later, he was standing again, but only by leaning heavily on the rail, which he could now hardly feel beneath his hand. His side felt as if it were aflame, and each time he closed his eyes he found it harder to open them.

Earlier, he had been able to walk. Now it was the best he could do to not collapse. He didn't think he could keep it up much longer, but with his father below, he was in charge. He took the reports of the deaths as they came, marking them off in the log, reassigning duties as necessary.

The Drehhu fleet was defeated, but there was still much to do. The *Leucothea* had again been lucky. The damage was extensive, but she had only one wound below her waterline, and temporary repairs on that were done already. More than half of the ships that had bottled up the Anvvod Gate hadn't been so lucky. Survivors were still being drawn from the water.

A ship approached from inside of the gates. She flew the banner of Ophion, and he could see uniforms, now.

"The *Karkinos*," Renost said. "That's Captain Peleas."

Aided by her sweeps, the ship soon drew within shouting distance. The man who came out to speak to them, however, was not Captain Peleas. He was young, fair-haired, and would have been taller if his back was not somewhat bent.

"Aubin, you old dog," Renost shouted at the young man. "Where is your captain?"

"My captain is cargo now," Aubin replied, "and the first lieutenant, and second. It's down to me, I'm afraid." He looked around. "Looks like a mess here, too. Is the admiral…?"

"He's fine," Crespin said. "Below."

"You've looked better, I must say."

"I'll survive," Crespin said. "What's the news?"

Aubin hesitated. "Have you taken on any flotsam from Modjal?"

Crespin shook his head. "All our flotsam is from the emperor."

"Good. Then here is the command from the arch-admiral. Bring all your ships to Basilisk, and do it now."

"We're in no shape to mount a siege," Crespin said.

"We need your supplies, not your weapons," Aubin said. "The siege is done. The Mere de Basilisk is ours. We began landing xelons an hour ago." He straightened incrementally and looked past Crespin.

"Admiral," he said.

"You're relieved, First," his father said.

"I'm fine, sir," Crespin replied.

"See the surgeon immediately."

"Sir, I'm sure Hector is busy with men who have more urgent need of him."

"Rest then, and see him as time allows."

Crespin nodded and tried to take a step. It didn't work out so well. Renost caught him—again.

"I suppose a visit to the surgeon would do me no harm," he managed. He met his father's gaze. "Will she live?" he asked.

The admiral's face showed no emotion.

"It is doubtful."

CRESPIN WAS on his fourth cup of rum before Hector managed to get to him. As Crespin had suspected, there were many men more grievously injured than he.

The surgeon looked weary and his shirt, once white, was now mostly the color of blood of various ages; some nearly brown, some as bright as if fresh from an artery.

Crespin had a double handful of splinters in his side, some about the length and breadth of a finger, a few longer. They had pinned his jacket and shirt into the meat around his ribs.

"You're lucky," Hector said. "One of these nearly reached your lung."

Crespin glanced at the patient nearest him, who was missing a leg.

"I'll take what luck I can get," he said.

"Have some more rum," Hector said. "It's going to hurt getting these out."

"Have you seen Calliope?" Crespin asked.

Hector nodded. "There's not much I can do for her. She shouldn't be alive. What she did—I've never heard of a strixe doing anything remotely that impressive and surviving."

"Impressive is one word for it," Crespin said. "She single-handedly destroyed the Drehhu fleet."

"I think she had help."

"What do you mean?"

"Sometimes one strixe can unite the powers of several. Two, three, more maybe."

"It's hard to believe even four of them, exhausted as they were, could have accomplished that."

"Indeed," Hector said. "I agree. I think she united all of them. Now, hold still." As the surgeon had promised, it hurt.

Gasping, he put his attention to drinking rum.

WHEN HE awoke the next morning, they were on the calm waters of the Mere de Basilisk, beneath an aquamarine sky. Anvvod lay far in the distance, and to the west. Much nearer stood a mountainous island, and a city unlike anything he had ever seen outside of a picture book.

The city was built on the lower slopes, with the mountain behind it. The wall surrounding Basilisk was not so unusual—its many star-shaped angles had been copied in human fortresses for decades, but the city visible behind the wall was… magnificent. Ophion and

Modjal had towers and spires, some of which were exceedingly tall, but Basilisk was all towers.

Most were cone-shaped, massive at the base, narrowing to delicate pinnacles high above, adorned with hundreds of balconies and windows. A few of the largest structures rose almost without tapering, or in a series of exceedingly steep tiers, and were surmounted by domes as large as some castles. Most astonishing were the colors, for whatever had been used to build the city resembled gems or glass. If one looked for even a short time, every color known to the eye could be discerned somewhere. And yet, they did not jar; the tints merged gradually, so that it was impossible to see the boundaries between the various hues.

As he watched, the colors of the city seemed to shift, very slowly. He had heard that this was in response to the movement of the sun.

IT TOOK days to regain his strength. Within the city the fighting raged on, but he rarely saw signs of it from the ship which had become his sickbed.

Finally, after daylight had come and gone six times, he felt hale enough for the night watch. When the moon rose, he saw the true beauty of Basilisk. Under Selene's cool gaze, the city shimmered like a phosphorescent sea, like the ember curtains of the far north, the silent play of lightning inside of a thunderhead on the horizon.

"The Drehhu were the chosen of Nyx, the ancient of night," a soft voice said, behind him.

He struggled to rise from his seat by the rail.

"No," Calliope said. "Keep your seat. I shall join you. My legs will not support me."

"You should not be up," he said as she sank onto the bench.

"I have dreamt for days," she said. "The air is what I need."

"I did not know you had waked."

"Yes," she replied. "But only this morning."

He nodded.

"Nyx?" he said. "I did not think the Drehhu recognized any god."

"They acknowledged her existence but broke from her long ago. She is one of the eldest, and weary, and long ago drifted into sleep. The Drehhu declared themselves without lords and began the task of making themselves as gods upon the face of the world, but now their time, too, has ended. Yet such beauty they made." She gestured at the city.

Calliope did not look well. Her face was gaunt, and every motion of her body suggested weakness. The proud set of her shoulders was gone, her chin tended to drift toward her chest, and her hair had turned more than half yellow, just as her eyes now seemed to contain permanent flecks of gold.

"You saved us all," he said.

"I hardly remember." She shrugged a little. "I did what I had to do."

"To save my father."

She closed her eyes. All of her former combativeness seemed to have leaked out of her.

"Yes," she said.

"How long?"

A tiny frown appeared.

"It isn't your business," she said.

"No," he said. "It isn't. I'm sorry."

She put her hand to her forehead. "Almost from the beginning," she said. "He was so restrained at first, so controlled. We spoke, you know, of many things. I knew how I felt, but I believed he returned nothing. And then, one day..." She opened her eyes and looked back out at the city. "I would die to protect him."

"You almost did," he said. "Hector told me. He said what you did has never been done before."

She lifted one hand as if to wave that away.

"I need to talk to him," she said.

"He is on the *Vanax*, with the other admirals."

"Will he return soon?"

"I can get word to him."

"I see," she said. "I shall trust you, then. You will tell him. I feel—I am still tentative. My heart makes odd motions inside of me. At times I forget to breathe. I may not last, Crespin."

He recognized the look in her eyes now. Despair.

"You are awake," he said. "You must be better."

"No," she said. "Asleep, I was protected. Awake, I must face the consequences of what I did."

"Then go back to sleep."

"I will try, but there is something—I have something more to do. So you must know, in case. That day when the colossus rose, I did not do it alone. I am always connected to the other strixes, but that day, in my desperation, in my determination—I found strength in my sisters. Each alone, we were exhausted, but bound together, I was able to raise that thing and let loose the lightning that remained within it."

Crespin nodded, remembering Hector's speculations.

"They lent you their strength."

She shook her head. "I *took* it," she said. "I didn't know it was possible, but in the moment I felt all of them, in all three fleets. And beyond. I saw the hearts of many, not just the strixes. I saw the shadows of the days that are to come."

"The future?"

"No," she said. "Not the unknown future. Only what is planned. What your father feared."

"And what is that?"

"Three fleets from three nations, all fighting against the common foe," she said. "All bound by the Accord, which has been kept for a thousand years. But soon, when Basilisk lies defeated, the Accord too will be broken."

"Who will break it?"

"Everyone," she whispered. She closed her eyes again, and he waited for her to say something else, but instead she swayed and slowly slid down to the deck.

"Calliope!" Crespin blurted. For a horrible moment he thought she had crossed into limbo, but then he saw that she was still breathing. He picked her up, sickened at how light she felt, and carried her back to her bed. He sent a mariner to find Hector.

The surgeon arrived a few minutes later. He looked exhausted, but quickly moved to Calliope's side as Crespin filled him in.

"She got up, you say?" he asked Crespin.

"Yes, she was on the deck."

"And talking?"

"Yes."

Hector sighed. "Her heartbeat is weak and irregular. She needs rest. She needs someone to keep her from getting up again."

"I'll find someone to do that," Crespin said.

He did so, then waited impatiently for his father to return from his meeting. A longboat approached, bearing the older man. Crespin went to the rail to meet him as he came up.

"A word, Admiral?"

"What is it?" As usual, his father's features didn't give much away, but Crespin thought he saw something new there. As if something at the meeting had upset him and he was barely keeping it covered.

"I think we should speak in private."

The admiral nodded. "We must anyway. My quarters, then."

CRESPIN RELATED the details of his encounter with Calliope. His father did not look surprised. When Crespin was done, Alastor took a long breath and let it out.

"She's right, of course," he said. "We just got new orders from the emperor. We are to hold Basilisk at any cost."

"The Drehhu are already defeated."

"I think you understand what I am saying."

"That we must betray the Accord with Modjal and Velesa?"

"No more so than they will betray us," his father said. "And each other." He rubbed his forehead and pushed his hair back.

"Did you know this was going to happen?" Crespin demanded. "Did you know all along?"

"No. This was not a part of the plan to which I agreed."

"But surely you had some idea," Crespin pushed on. "Calliope said you feared this." His father held his gaze for a half-dozen heartbeats, then nodded.

"I did fear it," he said.

"But you didn't see fit to tell me?"

The admiral's brow furrowed, and his eyes went sharp.

"For what reason? I hoped it would not happen. I hoped the three empires would settle this situation through reason and diplomacy. Rattling off my unfounded suspicions to my officers would have served no purpose at all."

"But—"

"Crespin, you have made much of your military background. When you served in the Navy, did you dispute your orders? Did you second-guess your superiors? Did you demand an accounting of the inner workings of their minds and insist they share their every thought with you?"

His father's words had the intended effect. Crespin felt his growing outrage suddenly cut off at the knees.

"No," he admitted.

"No," his father repeated. "Nor can you expect me to do those things. The emperor has given a command. I will obey it, regardless of my feelings in the matter. Like yours, they are of no consequence."

Merde, Crespin thought. He's right. Again.

"Understood," Crespin said. "But what now? Do we attack them right away?"

His father shook his head. "No. Thus far, no ship of the alliance has attacked any other. We are to prepare and wait until Modjal or Velesa gives us a reason to act—or until we receive further orders."

Crespin nodded. "I thought we had won," he said. "But we've only traded one war for another."

"Not yet," his father said. "There is still hope the three empires may yet see a more reasonable course. So let us hope for that. But we prepare for the worst."

CHAPTER TEN

MEETING
IN THE WOODS

CHRYSANTHE SETTLED onto a bench and watched as Emeline made her way through the gardens and eventually vanished from sight. Looking about carefully to make certain no one else was around, she slipped off her shoes and massaged her aching feet.

Emeline assured her that she was getting better at dancing. Chrysanthe was not certain she believed her. It was a part of life now that she trusted no one around her. She wondered if she would ever recover from the feeling.

If she survived at all.

So far, it seemed as if no one knew that Emeline was helping her. She hoped not. Without a doubt, if her enemies suspected that she was learning to play their game, they would change the rules.

There was a motion from the periphery of her vision, a flicker of blue, and she realized the very suspicion that she was coming to despise had alerted her. Someone was watching.

Pretending not to notice, she took up the book she had brought with her and stared at its pages, keeping whoever-it-was at the very edge of her vision. Was it a merely a spy, or someone sent to assassinate her? Was it the man in the brown coat?

After a moment, the person moved out into the open.

She dropped her right hand from the book, laying it near the little bodkin pocket in her gown where she kept her knife.

"Danesele," someone whispered.

She looked up and found a boy, perhaps eleven years of age, with flaxen hair cut to just below his ears. He wore an azure vest and looked like a groundskeeper, one of the small army of them who kept the gardens neat and trimmed.

"Yes?" she replied.

The boy looked around, carefully, then came a little closer.

"Someone wants to see you, Dan'sel," he said. "I am to take you to him." He nodded toward the woods to the west.

Follow a stranger into the woods?

"No," she said. "I'm happy right here."

"It's about your father," the boy said. "Alastor Nevelon. My master says you shouldn't fear me or him, and that this time he is respectably dressed."

Bonaventure? She wondered.

"Does this master have a name?"

The boy looked unhappy. "He said to say he might be called *abul* in a language you know." When she didn't respond, he cleared his throat. "It might have been more like *ha-bool*," he said.

"Oh!" Chrysanthe gasped. "That's… you shouldn't…" She shook her head and let it go. The word the boy was trying to pronounce was the Tamanja equivalent of Li Baud, "The Lewd One." Bonaventure's nickname, although the Tamanja word was a bit more direct, and referenced a particular item of anatomy.

"How far?" she asked.

"Not far," the boy said. "I will protect you."

She hesitated. It might be a trick. For that matter, even if it was Bonaventure, why should she trust him? But if this was really about her father, how could she refuse?

Indecision was a torture of its own. If her enemies wanted her dead, she probably already would be. She could not let fear control her every thought and movement.

"Lead on," she told the boy.

EVEN BEYOND the gardens, the woods had a tame feeling about them. The trees were spaced evenly, there was very little clutter on the ground, and no understory of bushes and vines to obscure her view for some distance. That made her feel easier.

When she saw a carriage up ahead, her misgivings returned, and she put her hand into her bodkin-pocket as she neared the conveyance. A young driver watched her come, the reins of four horses slack in his lap.

She stopped about thirty paces away.

"Go tell your master to stick his head out, please," she told the boy.

The boy nodded and started that way, but he was only halfway to the carriage when the door opened and Bonaventure stepped out. He wasn't in bedclothes, but his appearance was nevertheless one of disarray. His vest was half unbuttoned, the cuffs of his white shirt stained purple with wine, and he wore no jacket or coat at all.

"Come, come," he said. "Gererd, go stand watch."

The boy nodded and went back the way they had come. Chrysanthe walked nearer, and once more had to endure his leering gaze as it swept over her.

"You look in fine health, Danesele," he said.

"What do you want, Dam Bonaventure?" she said. "The boy said this was about my father."

"Get in the carriage," he said.

"No," she replied. "We can speak like this."

He sighed. "I don't blame you, I suppose. Let's keep this short, then. Tell me what you have discovered, if anything, since you arrived at Roselant."

"Well, they plan to make me dance," she replied.

"That is known," he said. "Even in the capital. It is one reason I am here. I hope there is more."

"I am to trust no one, yes?"

"Your father trusts me."

"News of my father is what brought me here," she said. "I will tell you nothing until I have heard it."

"Very well," Bonaventure said. "You should know that the war at Basilisk has begun, and that the Drehhu are on the verge of defeat."

She blinked. Her next breath felt lighter than those before it. Maybe her father had been wrong. Maybe there was no hidden plot, and this was all done. Yet what was Bonaventure not saying?

"And my father? Crespin?"

"They still live."

She closed her eyes for a moment in silent prayer to the Virgin. When she opened them again, Bonaventure looked bemused. "Does that mean—is this over?" she asked. "Can I return home now?"

"What?" Bonaventure said. "No, of course not. What it means is that you're running out of time."

"I don't understand."

"The war with the Drehhu is at an end, but the battle for Basilisk has not yet begun. The three empires have turned on one another."

"How can that be? The Accord—"

"Broken as an old nag, I'm afraid," Bonaventure said.

"Did Father know this would happen?"

"No. He might have guessed. Anyone might have, but the order only went out after the Drehhu were routed."

"The emperor planned this all along."

"Of course," Bonaventure said. "Although the original plan was better. Modjal and Ophion were to unite against Velesa, but Modjal has instead withdrawn from the fray at the last instant, presumably to let Ophion and Velesa deplete one another. My sources inform me that the Cryptarchia may have influenced Modjal in this decision, but I cannot prove it."

"Is that what my father hoped I would uncover?"

"I don't think so," Bonaventure said. "I think there is yet another arrow in the air. The Cryptarchia is… confident about something. Smug, almost. They seem to know something no one else does. They seem to be counting on it, but I do not know what it is. I hope that you do."

"I do not," Chrysanthe said.

"What have you been doing here, then?"

"Well, let's see," she said. "My room was searched, and I was assaulted by a man who threatened my life. Everyone I've met is possibly an enemy, planning to destroy me and my family, and now I must attend a dreadful dance that I'm told is designed to destroy my honor and good name."

"In that, at least, someone is telling you the truth," Bonaventure said. "Although you only have yourself to blame."

"What could you possibly mean by that?"

"You met the emperor, did you not? And you made a good impression. He went on for days about your obvious good character and the moral superiority of the colonials compared to the 'degenerates' at court. So someone—the Duc de Margerie, to name him—challenged the emperor to a wager. He bet that you are capable of being compromised, publicly, in a dance. That your lascivious Mesembrian nature will reveal itself.

"The emperor took that bet," he continued. "Word was passed on to Dame d'Othres—need I mention that she is cousin to the Duc de Margerie?—and now you have a dance in your honor. So, yes. If the emperor loses his bet, he will be embarrassed, and you and your family will suffer badly. This is made all the worse by your position as a hostage. You might even be imprisoned, until such time as your father can pay you out—which lacking his lands and funds, he will never be able to do."

"Such wonderful news," Chrysanthe said. "My day is improved by meeting you."

"Of course it is," Bonaventure said. "Now that you know what could await you, you will no doubt rise to this task. But this searching of your room… what were they looking for?"

Chrysanthe felt herself on the verge of tears, but she beat them back. Bonaventure was foul, but as far as she could tell he had always been truthful with her, and her father did seem to hold him in some regard. And her investigations hadn't moved forward, both because she could find no new evidence and because she was preoccupied with the upcoming dance—apparently for good reason.

Maybe Bonaventure could help.

So she related what she had learned—about the boursier, d'Ospios and her journal, and her speculations. When she was done, the man nodded slightly.

"I shall see what I can learn about this," he said. "A boursier? Perhaps it has to do with money. What have the d'Othres been spending money on—or *not* spending—that someone wishes to remain secret? I will see what I can do." He smiled, thinly. "Meanwhile, I suggest you continue your study of dance." He turned to go back into his carriage.

"A moment," she said.

"Yes?" he said without turning.

"Quintent d'Othres," she said. "What do you know of him?"

Bonaventure did not answer right away, but he faced her again. He scratched the stubble on his chin, and cast his gaze at the sky.

"That is a good question," he replied. "What of him?"

"Does he work for you?"

Again Bonaventure paused. This time, he looked a little… embarrassed?

"He does. I think."

"What do you mean, 'you think'?"

"It is complicated."

"Many things are, until they have been explained."

Bonaventure sighed and nodded. "Very well,' he said. "Quintent, you see, has something of a double life. He has long been a member of the Cryptarchia. I have known this for many years and cultivated him as a friend. I flatter myself that I have turned him to my point of view, and that he serves me as a spy in their midst. It is through Quintent that I learn much of my information about the Cryptarchia.

He is not very highly placed; he is not privy to their deepest secrets, but it was he who suggested you be placed at Roselant."

"And now you're not so sure of him."

"Indeed." Bonaventure threw up his hands. "I may have been overconfident. It may be that I was the one fooled, and that he was a spy for the Cryptarchia residing in *my* camp. In any event, he appears to have gone missing."

"I noticed," Chrysanthe said, "right after a man in a brown coat and mask threatened my life."

"I see." Bonaventure clasped his hands behind his back. "Well. There isn't much to be done about it at the moment. Not until he appears again. If he does, you should perhaps be skeptical of his advice."

"Should I?" Chrysanthe said.

"Sarcasm does not become you, my dear."

"How convenient that I do not care what you think becomes me," she snapped back.

"Be assured I am looking into this matter," Bonaventure said. "But if you do see him, let me know."

"How?"

"The boy. Gererd. He works on the grounds. Give him a note. Discreetly. He will find me."

With that, Bonaventure stepped back into the carriage and closed the door. The driver picked up his reins, and a moment later the carriage rolled off through the trees.

CHAPTER ELEVEN

THINGS WITHIN

MARNORA TOOK another sip of wine as her confession of murder hung in the air.

"It is a matter of no great consequence," she finally said. "I honestly cannot remember how you gave me offense. It's just that, usually when I murder someone, they stay murdered. So I'm curious how you're sitting here before me."

Ammolite wanted desperately to look to Veulkh, to see if there was some clue in his demeanor as to how she should answer. However, that in itself would be an admission of some kind. She didn't know anything. She opened her mouth, still unsure of what she would say.

Fortunately, Veulkh cut her off.

"She is not the same Orra, of course," Veulkh said. "As you may remember, I am at times sentimental. The woman you see before you is just a girl I saw in some village, who had a passing resemblance to the witch of Mirrordim. I bought her and changed her name, and as she grew, I applied minor somatic metamorphisms so she more resembled my old friend. Surely you sense her youth? Her lack of sorcerous power?"

Marnora's brows lowered, and suddenly she did not seem childlike at all. Her gaze was almost too much for Ammolite. It was all she could do not to look away.

Finally, Marnora's eyes slid away from her, and back to Veulkh.

"I see," she said. "but this is not sentiment. This is purest fetishism."

Veulkh shrugged. "Perhaps," he said. "Although you are an odd one to speak against that sort of thing."

"It might be best for you if this one is destroyed, as well."

"I disagree," he said. "She amuses me."

"I see." Marnora nodded. "Well, we all must have our amusements."

"Yes," he replied. "I imagine you are lonely here, with only the Tsau Dadan to keep you company."

Marnora's good spirits seemed to return. She laughed, and it sounded almost like chimes. Then she wagged a finger at him.

"You haven't thanked me yet for driving off those Cryptarchia drimpets."

"For that, you certainly have my thanks," Veulkh replied.

"And you are most certainly welcome," she said, lifting her glass. "All is understood."

"All is understood," Veulkh replied, then they all drank. After the toast, she was silent for a long moment.

"Do you want to see it then?" she suddenly asked.

"If that is your wish," he replied.

"Well, you've come a long way," she said, rising, and he followed suit. "At the very least you should get to see it." Ammolite began to stand, as well. Marnora shook her head.

"Not you," he said. "You will return to your room."

Ammolite looked to Veulkh. His expression was carefully neutral, but there was something about the set of his eyes that frightened her. He didn't speak for what seemed like too long a time.

"Go along," he said. "I will see you soon."

"Take these with you." Marnora took the flowers from the vase and held them out toward Ammolite.

HOUND WAS dozing under a tree when he heard Selene approaching. By now he knew her cadence, and although he was certain it was her, something about her step seemed off. When he opened his eyes, he saw why.

She had eschewed her heavy clothing for a light shirt and riding pants. Her eyes were yellow, as they had been after the fight in the pass. She reached out her hand to him.

"Come with me," she said.

He took it, puzzled, but also increasingly aroused. She had a scent about her he didn't recognize, a sort of musk.

She led him up from their camp on the mountain's slope to the rim, with its view of the lake and the island. With each step she seemed to go more slowly, and once they reached the edge she stopped. Her expression was almost beatific—she seemed as happy as he had ever known her. Yellow mist began drifting from the bare skin of her arms. She opened her mouth, and a thicker saffron vapor breathed forth, drifting out over the valley.

Her grip on his hand tightened, but at the same time it also felt as if it was about to slip away, as if he was squeezing an over-ripe peach. When he looked at her, she appeared strangely… flattened, and seemed no longer aware of him at all—or of anything, except whatever was going on inside of her head.

After a time, her mouth curved up in a silly smile.

"Ah," she said.

"What?"

"I found it," she said, dreamily. She turned and looked at him. Her eyes seemed unfocused. And then she kissed him. He was surprised, but not so surprised that he pulled away. Her breath was hot, and the musk even stronger.

Everything went all dizzy. He felt as if he was whirling up, like a leaf, like a spark from a campfire. The mountain, the lake, the island shrank away below him, and she was inside of him, her slippery thoughts entangled with his. He tried to pull away then, but he couldn't. His limbs, his breath—the very heart beating in his chest—no longer belonged to him. They belonged to her. It was terrifying, but at the same time a sort of unfocused, diffuse ecstasy filled him.

Then she left him, and he choked back tears, because he didn't want her to go. He wanted it to continue—forever, if possible.

She too was weeping, pollen-colored streams running down her face.

"I'm sorry," she said. "I didn't mean to do that…"

"Do it again," he said.

"No," she said. "You think you want me to. Please believe me when I say you don't."

Those words seemed to take all of her strength. She slumped, and he caught her before she could fall. He lowered her down and put the back of her head in his lap. Sat with her as her smile vanished and her eyes rolled back and little sounds of anguish crawled up her throat. He wondered if he should get Martin, but in time her breathing sorted itself out and she seemed to come to herself.

"Forgive me," she said. "I meant my touch to be much lighter, but sometimes my control…" She looked up uncertainly. "Did you get it?"

At first, Hound wasn't sure what she meant, but then he realized it was there, after all.

"Yes," he said. "I see the way in."

"And you can take us there?"

"I can," he said, "but—"

"After I recover," she said. "In the morning." She struggled to stand. Hound put his arm around her and helped pull her up.

"Don't you want to rest here a little more?" he asked.

"No," she said. "Martin should know as soon as possible, so he can prepare." A shudder ran through her body.

"Selene?" he said.

"Something I didn't show you," she said. "Veulkh and the others are there, but so is someone—or something—else. Something terrible."

"Whatever it is," Hound said, "I'll kill it for you."

HOUND WAITED until the moon was high before rising. He nudged Rose, and she came silently to her feet. Together they started back toward the rim. When they reached it, a lone figure stood waiting.

"Martin," Hound said.

"I wonder what you think you're doing."

"I'm going to find Veulkh," Hound said.

"By yourself?"

"It's the only way."

It was light enough that he could see the frown on Martin's face.

"Explain."

For a moment, Hound debated that. He probably couldn't win a fight with Martin, but he might be able to get around him. Veulkh had made him promise to tell no one, but he didn't feel that much allegiance to the sorcerer, and promises had never seemed that important to him in the first place.

"Don't you remember?" Hound said. "Veulkh refused to come along unless I came, too."

"I remember," Martin said. "He never explained why, but without you, we never would have escaped Sular Bulan. I assumed that was what he needed you for."

"I thought so, too," Hound said, "but he had a talk with me a few days ago. He told me about this place, and what I was supposed to do here."

"And what was that?"

"When I climbed up into his palace, Veulkh didn't know I was there. He's supposed to sense whenever someone enters or leaves his place—it's part of his sorcery, I guess. He knew when you were approaching his mountain, but he didn't know about me. Not until he saw me with his eyes."

"Why?" Martin asked.

"It's something about being around Grandmother for so long," Hound said. "Veulkh didn't explain, but he said he needed to know if anyone was in this place, and if so, who they were and what they were doing. The plan was for me to go alone. Anyone else would raise the alarm. Then something went wrong. He thought we had another day before anyone would notice us, and he probably *didn't* know about those ape things."

"Tsau Dadan," Martin said, absently. He looked levelly at Hound. "I trust you, I think," he said. "Go in. Discover who is there and what

357

is happening. Put yourself at no greater risk that is necessary, and if you can, find a way for the rest of us to enter without being known."

"That's what I was going to do, anyway."

Martin nodded. "We shall wait," he said. "For a while, but if you do not return in a few days at most, we must attempt to enter on our own."

AS HOUND picked his way along the rim of the mountains, the earth shook again. It caused an odd play of ripples upon the lake, and he watched a while before continuing. Was there something under there? A sleeping giant? Something like the thing at Sular Bulan?

Whatever it was, he wasn't in favor of it.

Soot landed on his shoulder.

The raven had a language of sorts, a combination of postures and gestures, clicks and croaks. Hound understood him well enough, although what Soot had to say was usually uncomplicated. Today, however, the bird had a mood about him and seemed to be trying to express something that at first eluded Hound. Then, when he began downslope, heading into the thicker forest of the mountain's flank, the raven suddenly darted in front of him, landed on a branch at eye-level, and clacked out his equivalent of a strong *no*.

Then Hound understood. For want of a better word, Soot was contrite. He had failed to warn Hound of the attack of the beast-men, and he wasn't happy about it.

"Don't worry, Soot," he said. "How many times have you warned me true? More than I can count, even taking tally. There was more to that ambush than a bunch of overgrown apes. Nothing moves that quietly. Sorcery was involved, I'm certain."

Soot regarded him for a moment, then took wing and did one

of his little aerial dances, indicating downslope.

"Yeah," Hound said. "I didn't reckon they lived underground someplace. They have to eat and drink, after all, and I doubt it's coincidence they happen to be in the same direction as our way into the mountain." He scratched Rose. "Let's go careful and quiet. It's all we can do."

Soot seemed to think there was plenty else they could do, in almost any direction, but he settled down as Hound continued on.

Whether sorcery or unnatural stealth had allowed the beast-men to creep up on him before, this time Hound had little trouble hearing them. They hooted and barked at one another—at first in the distance, and then closer—and the crack of limbs and shushing of leaves marked their passage through the trees. He wondered if they lived in houses of some sort, or just slept in the branches. Hopefully, he wouldn't have to find out. His destination wasn't far. Maybe it wasn't inside of their territory.

His goal was a very-nearly round hole in the side of the mountain, mostly covered over by hanging moss and creeping vines. It was upslope, about a quarter of the way from the bottom to the top of the mountain. The surrounding jungle was dense, composed largely of thick-boughed trees that looked to him like some variety of fig. In these, the Tsau Dadan had built platforms of bamboo lathed with branches, roofed over with strips of different-colored bark woven into elaborate patterns, usually using an existing branch as a ridgepole. Beneath these roofs hung baskets and netting, the latter of which seemed to hold mostly fruit and bundles of leaves.

More panels of plaited bark looked as if they could be lowered to form walls against wind and rain, but at present they were all pulled up, suspended by cords. Dwellings were connected by narrow rope walkways, tree to tree. More ropes dropped toward the ground, many near the cave, where water trickled out and down the mountainside.

The arboreal houses were clustered most thickly near the cave mouth. He had passed several on the way in, although he hadn't gotten close enough to see much detail. How many of the creatures lived there, he could not say, but he guessed at least a hundred, and maybe more.

Impatiently at first, but eventually with interest, he watched them as the sun climbed up and then down the sky. Their attackers, from what he could tell, had all been adult males. Here he saw the smaller, more slender females, and young ones as well. He watched them bring in food—mostly roots and a few kinds of fruit. The tubers they pounded in large, hollowed stones on the ground, adding water to make a pulp. The fruits they either simply ate or placed in the netting hung beneath their ridge poles.

In fact, most of the big males appeared to be absent, probably off hunting or something. He had been planning to wait for nightfall, but began to think that would be the worst time. All the big ones would be back by then, and probably vigilant against night-stalking predators. He began to ease closer.

He would not reach the cave mouth without being seen, and even though the females were a bit smaller, he didn't think it would go well for him if he tried to fight his way through them. Especially with the young around.

There was a series of cries—long, strange, hooting sounds that nevertheless sent shivers through him. They sounded very much like calls of alarm. In response, the apes on the ground began scrambling up the ropes.

Something was coming.

A moment later, Hound saw what it was. At first, he thought it was a lion, but it was bigger than any lion he had ever seen, and it lacked the long fangs of a knife-tooth. On second look, it was something like a cross between a hyena and a bear, its forelimbs longer than its hind legs. Below the massive bunch of its shoulders was a huge head that seemed to be mostly mouth. It was dappled on the flanks, much like the apes, but the high ridges of its spine bore stripes.

The Tsau Dadan clearly had a great deal of respect for the thing. They climbed as high as they could from its path.

"This is our chance, Rose," he said.

Moving quickly, he kept to the undergrowth. With the apes watching the giant hyena-bear, there was a good chance they wouldn't even notice him, which would be ideal. Once in the cave, he would have to find his way, which would be a lot harder with a bunch of the creatures coming after him.

He was more than halfway there when he heard the crackling of branches overhead, and something in his peripheral vision hurtled toward him. He dodged aside and heard a thud, followed by a cry of pain. He whipped out his tomahawk, certain he was under attack, but then saw it was one of the apes—a little one, probably not even half-grown. He stood transfixed for an instant as it stared up at him with wide eyes.

Then the brush parted, and all he saw was a huge maw bristling with teeth.

Without thinking he leapt up, striking at the center of the massive skull. His ax connected solidly and briefly stuck there, arresting him in mid-jump so he landed on the back of the beast. It yanked its head to the side, but the weapon was still lodged in its skull. Hanging on to it, he figured it couldn't bite him if he was on its back. How long he could stay on its back, of course, was the problem.

Hound managed to get his legs around the bulging neck and wrapped them tight as the monster rolled, nearly crushing him with its weight. If it had possessed the brains to stay on him, he probably would have been done for. Instead it rolled back to its feet and tore off through the underbrush, slamming him into a tree trunk. His grip loosened, and suddenly the ax popped free of the huge skull. He flew from the monster's back and rolled awkwardly to his feet.

Despite its mass, it was fast. He knew if he turned and ran from it the hyena-bear would be on him in a few breaths, so he faced it, ax in hand. It eyed him cautiously, then took a measured step forward.

Rose charged from the underbrush and clamped her jaws under its massive neck. It howled, shook, and raked a paw at the dog. Hound took the opportunity to dash in and hack into one of its eyes. It batted him with a massive paw and sent him hurtling into a rock. He managed to keep from breaking his neck, but only by letting go of the weapon.

When he got back up, it was charging at him. He stiffened his hand like he had seen Martin do and drove it into the beast's other eye as the monster smashed into him. Teeth sank into his shoulder. It shook him hard, and everything seemed to go white. He had a sensation of wild motion, as if falling down a series of rapids.

Then he vomited.

CHAPTER TWELVE

HISTORY TURNS

CRESPIN WOKE hours before dawn and went up onto the deck to join his father. The mariniers were already working furiously, making ready the sails, winding the quilaines, preparing for battle.

"Has something happened?" Crespin asked. Tension had been mounting for days; when night had approached, he had been watching the Velesan ships exercise in the distance, moving to and fro on the still water of the Mere de Basilisk, in and out of formation. It was nothing unusual for a fleet to rehearse in such a way—with no shore leave to occupy them, sailors often found trouble on board, and it was best to keep them busy.

Given what Calliope and his father had told him, it felt very suspicious. A fleet training was a fleet ready to fight. The Mesembrians, on the other hand, hadn't put up sails in days, and many were tied up at the great quays so cargo could be readily unloaded.

"I believe Velesa will move against us in the morning," his father said. "I do not intend to give them the chance."

"I thought they would wait at least until the land battle is won."

"It is all but won," his father informed him. "The Drehhu do not surrender, but we've breached the inner citadel."

"And Modjal?"

"I expect they will wait to see the outcome of our fight, and then take on the winner. We shall see."

"They haven't broken the truce yet," Crespin pointed out.

"They plan to," his father said. "If we wait, we shall be at their mercy. As it is, we may surprise them."

"I thought we were supposed to wait."

"Things have changed. The emperor fears our supplies may fall into Velesan hands. In this, I agree with him. We are to leave the harbor and find our way to Hhark, leaving the fight to the Navy."

"But they are everywhere. Without Calliope, what chance have we?"

His father shrugged. "The Cryptarchia will not take sides. The strixes would take no part in this."

"That makes it worse," Crespin said. "This is a merchant fleet. The Velesans are better armed than we, and they have their sweeps to maneuver. We will be chopped to pieces."

"We're running straight through them," his father said. "We'll do all the damage we can, and then keep going. While they are in disarray, His Majesty's galleys will attack."

THEY CREPT off east in the night, on a soft but favorable wind. The handful of docked ships stayed where they were, to give the appearance the fleet was still in place. The wind dropped but came back at the first glimpse of dawn's robes on the horizon, and when it revived it was blowing west, just as it did each morning.

In a light fog, sailing out of the rising sun, they came upon the Velesan ships, whose intent had been to invade the harbor and battle it out with the imperial warships. They had not yet launched that assault, however, so when the first flights of black arrows and quilaine missiles fell upon them, they were taken unawares.

Ahead, two gallavants loomed, their sweeps just coming about, dipping furiously into the water. Crespin heard the drums beating out the strokes, working up in tempo as the ships tried to turn. They managed it by half, and then the *Leucothea* scraped hard against the hull of the nearest, snapping all of the oars on that side as they bombarded the deck and sails with the issue of their war engines and archers.

The Velesans came fully awake and returned fire. Mariniers who had survived the fear and flame of the Drehhu succumbed to the weapons of their fellow humans. Crespin felt a terrible, hollow pain as he understood, in that moment, that all of history had turned. There had always been pirates, rogue cities, disputes of all manner that needed settling. Drehhu armies were largely made up of slaves, so soldiers of his race had died in plenty over the years.

But for all the centuries of modern history, no army or fleet of a human nation had turned against another. Now it had happened, and he was on the ship that fired the first shot. Whatever happened here, the *Leucothea* and her crew would be remembered—but perhaps not kindly.

In the din and maelstrom, he put those thoughts aside, and concentrated on winning.

Another vessel loomed, this one broadside, and the *Leucothea* rocked beneath its attack. After the devilish weapons of the Drehhu, familiar weapons seemed small and weak by comparison, but that was an illusion. Arrows and steel-pointed bolts took the lives of men as readily as demon shot, although the damage to the ship was not as great.

To make matters worse, the Velesan ship managed to secure grapnels faster than his mariniers could cut them. They dragged at the ship, when the intent was to break through to open ocean, where their superior sailing abilities would carry them from further danger.

The galley was half their size but carried twice the men and war engines. They managed to remain under sail, clearing the western side of the Velesan line, but the warship was still stuck to them; after a few moments, the first Velesan warriors began climbing over the *Leucothea*'s flatboards. The xelons were ready, however, and for a long time managed to keep them back, but the Velesans kept coming, climbing over the bodies of their dead until the shield wall collapsed and the *Leucothea* succumbed to general mayhem.

Grimly Crespin drew his sword. He was still weak, but at least it was his left side he favored, not his good arm. A stout fellow with a steel cap and one-edged cleaver of a sword reached him first, probably trying to get to the wheel. Crespin took a few steps out to meet him but arrested as the man leapt forward to cut. It was a terrifically powerful slash, and he assumed the man would overbalance. He did not, perhaps because of his short legs. He parried Crespin's cut to his head, and closed distance.

Crespin had only a yard to retreat, but he took it, making a quick draw-cut along the top of the man's weapon arm. It wasn't a powerful blow, but he prided himself on keeping his edge keen. The blade sliced through jacket and laid open the arm, severing tendons. The man's second attack stopped midway, giving Crespin time to moulinet, developing enough power to take his foe's head half off.

That turned out to be enough to stop him.

But there were more, and Crespin had nowhere to go but back, toward the wheel. He parried the next man's attack and stumbled, trying blindly to predict where the following blow would fall so he could deflect it.

Renost saved him the trouble by running the fellow through and, with a cry, repulsed the next several comers with one of his wild advances. That gave Crespin time to find his footing again, but he was already panting as if he had run a league.

By that time more of his men had found their way to defend the bridge, and the tide turned again. The Velesans were forced back onto their own ship. Having lost so many in their boarding, they now lacked any advantage in numbers.

Even encumbered by the Velesan ship, the *Leucothea* was free, headed once more toward the Colossus Gate and the open sea, the remainder of the Mesembrian merchant ships with her. Behind them, the war fleet of Ophion engaged with the Velesans, and this new battle for Basilisk was out of their hands.

THE VELESAN ship was named the *Kamor*. Rather than scuttle her or cut her free, the admiral decided to make a prize of her. A few hours after they passed through the gates, her captain came aboard to offer his sword. The admiral bade him keep it and invited him below for coffee. Crespin sat with them.

The captain's name was Morjebor. He was slight, and looked a little sickly, but his sun-darkened face had an intelligent aspect. His blood-spattered uniform was forest green, edged in red, with a double line of large brass buttons on the vest. His bicorn sported a plume of horsehair, a common affectation of Velesan officers and a nod to their history as an empire built upon the best cavalry in the world.

Crespin remembered a mural he had once seen in the city of Ostroh, of a massive Velesan charge on horseback into the fire and thunder of the Drehhu weapons at the battle of Wherna, where more than half of their force perished before even reaching the walls of the place. A brave people, the Velesans.

Morjebor sipped his coffee delicately and looked as if he wanted to say something, but held back. The admiral broke the uncomfortable silence.

"Your men fought well and valiantly," he said. "Your surrender was a mercy on all of us."

"Thank you," the Velesan said.

"We find ourselves on undiscovered seas," Crespin's father went on. "I am not certain what to do with you."

"I understand," Morjebor said. He hesitated. "I appreciate you allowing me to keep my sword." He leaned forward a little. "Admiral Nevelon, may I ask you a question, captain to captain?"

"You may."

"Do you agree with what is happening here? This monstrous thing we are engaged in?"

The admiral took a moment to answer. Crespin watched his blue-green eyes, realizing he wasn't able to guess what his father would say.

"I do not," his father said at last. "I believe that the Accord is law. I believe we are, and should be, bound by it, but I am also the servant of my emperor."

"As I am the servant of mine," Morjebor said, "although I feel the same. And so I fear I cannot promise you what I believe you are going to ask of me. If you let me go, I will rejoin the fight."

"I understand," the admiral said. "Therefore, I will not let you go. At least not yet. Your ship will be disarmed, along with your men, but they will not be harmed. When this ends—however it ends, whatever agreements our nations make or do not make—I will release you. Until then, you will remain with our fleet. Is that agreeable?"

"It will do," the Velesan captain said. "You are more than fair, Admiral."

"Let us hope this matter is settled soon," the admiral said.

THE SKY that night was strange. Black clouds hung low, and a pale purple lens lingered above the Salamandra.

They sailed, as instructed, for the fortress at Hhark. It was firmly in Ophion's grip, and warships lay in anchor there, needing only supplies to make them ready.

AT HHARK they discovered five ships from Modjal laying siege to the fortress, but on their arrival, they surrendered without firing a shot.

The surrender was fortunate, given the asset they had lost. They had been relying so much and for so long on the strixes that it now seemed a major handicap to not have their services. Not only would they not participate in combat, but they refused to pass messages from ship to ship. Because of that, and because ships could not be spared to form a chain long enough to correspond by lucnograph, it was impossible to know what was now happening in the Mere de Basilisk. That would hopefully be remedied soon, as various small vessels, unsuited for fighting, were being modified to create a line of communication. Until then, all they could do was maintain their position and hope that word came to them in the form of a courier ship, rather than a victorious fleet from Modjal or Velesa.

They took the Modjal ships as prizes and placed the crews—along with that of the *Kamor*—on shore, unarmed, in an empty part of the fortress. A hospital was set up, and Calliope was moved to land. The surgeons could not say if she was doing better or worse. She spent most of her days unconscious.

Hhark had once been a city unto itself, but those days were long past. What remained were ruins, and the fortress built into the cliff face. No Drehhu prisoners had been taken, but many of their slaves had survived the battle. They were still housed in the quarters the Drehhu had provided for them. Eventually they would be shipped out to slave markets, to be sold to help the empire pay for the war.

Crespin wondered how many slaves still lived in Basilisk and how many would survive. Whoever won, their fates were likely to be the same as those at Hhark. Crespin found it distasteful; he had grown up without slaves, and disliked the practice of owning them, but he had been around the empire enough to know that sometimes the life of a slave was better than that of a free man.

That hardly seem an argument in favor of the institution.

In any event, there wasn't much he could do about it.

CHAPTER THIRTEEN

A BARGAIN

WHEN EVERYTHING came back in focus, Hound was no longer on the ground, but instead on one of the woven platforms on which the Tsau Dadan lived. Three of the creatures surrounded him, one rather large, with a good deal of silver shot through its black fur.

He tried to sit up, but one of the younger ones pushed him back down. The old one barked something at him in a language he did not understand. Down below, he heard the hyena-bear, crashing around.

"Rose!" he shouted.

Even after several calls, she did not answer.

Soon there were more than a dozen of the apes gathered around, looking curiously at him, prodding him, chattering in their language. The larger, old one—a female, Hound realized—sat silently.

After a while, they brought a young female and placed her in front of him. She was given a bowl of something yellowish, and she drank, gagging once or twice as it went down. Then she sat staring at him for what seemed like a long time. Finally she reached out and took his hand. Her weird, too-long fingers were knobby with calluses.

The instant she touched him, Hound felt a sort of shock, as if something really warm had been poured into his head. He became dizzy again, but not in an altogether unpleasant way—more like he did after a few glasses of wine, and a little like he'd felt when Selene had… gone into him.

The older creature spoke again. The language sounded no different—still a strange collection of grunts, clicks, and back-of-the-throat trills. But now the words were… familiar.

"You understand?"

"Yes," he said.

"My name is Knot," the ape said.

"Hello, Knot," Hound replied.

"You killed our warriors on the mountainside," Knot said.

"They attacked me," Hound said. "What did they expect?"

Knot regarded him, then shifted her right shoulder a little. "Fair enough," she said. "Why did you save the young one from the hyena-bear?"

Hound blinked. He supposed it had looked like that.

"I saw him fall," he said. "I did not think he would survive, so I helped him."

"He is not of your people. Why should you care?"

Hound shrugged. "I do what I do," he said.

"You were trying to enter the mountain. To find your people. If you had let the young one die, we might never have seen you."

"That's probably true," Hound said. "I've done you a favor. Perhaps we can be friends."

The old ape sat back on her haunches. "You are lucky the

males are with Her," Knot said. "That it is just an old woman you have to deal with."

"Deal?" Hound said.

"Yes. The men must attack you, you see. They must do what She demands. When they return, they will kill you or give you over to Her. If you are here."

"Maybe I shouldn't be here, then."

"Maybe you shouldn't," Knot agreed. She reached up and scratched her chin, then tapped his knee with one long, hairy finger. "We could let you go," she said, "but you must do something for us."

"What's that?"

"We have been in thrall to Her for many years. We should be free."

"I don't even know who 'She' is," Hound said.

"She is the one who holds our heart," Knot told him. "Find our heart and set us free."

"Very well," Hound said. "You let me go, and I will do that for you."

"This is a bargain," Knot said. Hound wasn't sure if it was a question or a statement.

"It's a bargain," he said. Of course, he hadn't the faintest idea what Knot was talking about, and he had no intention of keeping up his end of the deal, but he was willing to say what he needed to set him on his way. "This heart. What does it look like?" he asked.

Knot lifted her shoulder again.

"She was our heart, they say. Our queen, the great mother of us all. She was changed into something, they say. My grandmother says she is an actual heart, salted and dried. Others say she appears as a pretty jewel, or a small animal. Whatever she wants her to be."

"That sounds like a challenge," Hound said, "but I will do as you ask. I will find your heart."

"Go, then," Knot said. "Before the males return."

Hound stood, carefully, testing his limbs, reassuring himself he was bruised, but not broken. Soot was watching from the safety of a tree some distance away. Of Rose, he still saw no sign.

"I had a friend with me," he said. "A dog—"

"She was injured by the hyena-bear," Knot said. "We will keep her safe and help her heal until you return."

"Oh," Hound said. "I see." His rising spirits flagged a bit. The apes weren't quite as simple or trusting as they seemed. "Well, that's nice of you."

"You saved our little one," Knot said. "So we repay you. Now go, and hurry."

THE CAVERN was not as complicated as some Hound had seen: just a long, regular tunnel that led straight back into the mountain. It turned just enough that soon there was no light, and he hadn't anything to make a fire with, so he went on, feeling his way forward. The weight of the mountain increased on all sides as he forged deeper into it.

The walls were smooth but had regular convolutions that felt to Hound like giant ribs. It made him think of Sular Bulan, and the shaking of the earth, and he wondered if he was inside the remains of an ancient serpent which had somehow become stone, instead of rotting away.

The tunnel was well used. The smell of Tsau Dadan was thick through the length of it, and here and there he encountered piles of their feces.

Eventually the cave met another, through which he could hear a stream flowing. He couldn't tell how deep or wide it was, but after feeling about for a while, he discovered that another tunnel departed there, winding upward. This one seemed distinctly unnatural, carved into regular steps that led him toward a faint, orange light and finally into a large open chamber.

The tunnel had been cool, almost cold, but here the air was warm, and had a peculiar smell that tickled his nose and itched at the back of his throat. The floor of the chamber was hot, as if someone had built a fire and then put stones over it upon which to cook. Illumination came from the walls, which contained some inner light like the walls in Veulkh's manse, although here the hues ranged mostly from red to yellow.

He passed through a vast chamber filled with vaults carved from the living stone and figured with skulls, roses, crescent moons, and other symbols that held no meaning for him. He stayed as far from them as possible.

From there he entered a maze of corridors, most of which seemed untouched, but eventually he ran across one that had known recent traffic. Among the scents of the Tsau Dadan he detected more familiar smells—Veulkh, the ravens, Ammolite. He came to a branch in the passages where Ammolite and Veulkh had gone one way, Kos and his warriors the other.

His choice didn't take long.

The scent led him to a bed on which she had lain with Veulkh, but she was no longer there.

AMMOLITE HAD not seen the Tsau Dadan waiting in the hall, but as soon as she was out of the great room, two of them took charge of her, leading her silently through the corridors.

She knew within a few paces that they were not taking her back to the room she and Veulkh had shared. Instead they went deeper, down slopes and stairs and into stone that warmed her feet through her shoes.

Now she understood the look in Veulkh's eyes. He believed he would not see her again, because he thought she was going to her death. Perhaps he feared for his own life, as well. He was afraid of Marnora, of that there could be no doubt. Ammolite knew him too well for him to hide it from her.

She wondered if she could escape the Tsau Dadan guards, but she remembered how strong they were. If only there were some magic she could perform, but for all she knew about the principles of sorcery, she did not know how to work it. Any practical application was far beyond her.

In all her searching, she had never discovered Veulkh's magical heart, or learned how to make her own. Maybe that's why the sorcerer had never become concerned about her explorations. Without the knowledge to create synapses, everything else she learned was moot. As they continued along, fear grew within her.

They're just taking me someplace else, she told herself. *Their intent may not be my death.* Maybe they would use her for ransom, to help Marnora strike some bargain with Veulkh.

Her steps faltered, but the apes would not let her slow their progress. They pushed her roughly along, unravelling any illusion she might try to spin in her mind.

This was the end of her.

Although there had been times when she longed for the peace of death, this was not one of them. She wanted out of this place. She felt she was suffocating. She needed air. Ammolite thought about fighting, but what if they killed her outright? Most likely the only reason she was still breathing was because they didn't want to carry her. They went mostly on all fours. Carrying her or dragging her would be a chore.

Far sooner than she would have liked, they reached an arched doorway with guards on either side. They appeared to be human, rather than Tsau Dadan. When they drew nearer, she saw that they once had been—probably long ago. Each was encased in armor, but between the gorgets and helmets, their faces were withered, bits of dried skin clinging to bone. Someone had placed yellow flowers in their eye-sockets.

The room within was strewn with flowers as well—some fresh, some dead, some crumbled nearly to dust. For the most part, the fresh ones were placed in the empty skulls of the room's inhabitants, of which there were many—more than she could easily count. Some sat in chairs, others reclined on coaches or small beds. They were mostly women, or were at least dressed as women, clad in whimsically weird and colorful gowns with ribbons, bows, feathers, and glittering stones, and they were arranged in life-like poses—this one playing a lute, those four gathered around a small table playing cards, a duo locked in an embrace.

The Tsau Dadan pushed and pulled her along until they reached a freshly made bed with clean linens and an embroidered coverlet. She stood, staring at it, aware that one of the creatures stood directly behind her. She turned to face him, her heart thundering.

Once, when she was fourteen, someone left apples for her on the table in Veulkh's manse. She ate a few, but found several full of worms, and amused herself by hurling them against a stone wall, enjoying the satisfying, wet explosions that resulted.

The sound she heard now was something like that.

The Tsau Dadan looked confused; she noticed one of his pupils

GREG KEYES

was huge and the other tiny. He made a little clucking sound in the back of his throat and fell over. As the other turned, his temple burst, spurting blood. He lurched forward, hands stretching out toward her, but she heard the sound again and watched the creature join its companion on the floor.

She looked past the dead Tsau Dadan.

"Hound?" Ammolite gasped. He looked bloodied and beaten up a bit, but there could be no mistaking him.

"Of course," he said, grinning.

"How did you find me?"

"I just followed the smell of flowers."

"Oh." She looked at her hands, and realized she was still holding the blooms Marnora had given her. She understood now what their purpose had been—to adorn her corpse. She looked up again. "Do you know the way out?"

"Yes," he said. He smiled. "It's nice to see you looking like you again."

She wondered what he meant by that, but then realized she was no longer Orra. She wasn't sure when she had changed.

"Yes," she said, nodding.

"But listen," he said. "What's going on?"

"No time," she said. "We must leave now, before more come. Before *she* comes. We can talk later."

"Who is 'she'?" he asked, sounding slightly irritated.

"They were going to kill me, Hound, make me like these others. Please, we have to go." But he was looking around now, distracted.

"Have you seen a heart?" he asked. "Or something *like* a heart?"

"Heart?" That reached through her terror. "What do you know of hearts?"

378

"Well, I'm supposed to find the heart of some old Tsau Dadan woman. It's how—someone—controls them. Tell me, who is *she*, and what is happening?"

Ammolite fought to push through her mortal panic get her mind working again. Hound was talking about the same sort of "heart" Veulkh was supposed to have, the thing she had been trying to find for years—a synapsis formed from a soul. He wasn't talking about Veulkh's heart, but it was her first clue in a long time.

"Marnora," she said. "That is her name. A sorceress, and I don't know what she's up to. Veulkh might be dead already."

"Wouldn't that be a shame."

She had to figure this out, but not here, not now. More of the apes might come—or worse, Marnora herself. She had to get Hound to leave. Ammolite stepped quickly to him, took him in her arms, and kissed him. Savored his surprise for the few seconds it took him to respond, and then things happened in a hurry. He kept saying things like "wait" and "hold on," but his hands and mouth never stopped moving. They removed their clothes, piece by piece, and soon they were sinking down to the floor.

"Not in here," she said. "Not here."

That motivated him, and he was willing to leave. She led him from the room, down the hall to an empty chamber. The floor was very warm, not quite hot enough to burn.

As they came together, she had a sudden, powerful image of another woman—dark skinned, with soft, tangled hair. Selene, the woman from Ophion. It angered her a little, but at the same time she felt Hound's lust redouble, so she ignored it.

Just as quickly, the image faded.

For the first time in her life, it felt good—not bearable, not vaguely pleasant, as it had been her first time with Hound, but really, really good. She quickly forgot about everything but the sensation, the tingling creeping up from her toes and fingers, a sort of melting, and then something arriving, something she was completely helpless to stop—didn't want to stop. She lost control of her body, and it was a complete, amazing surprise.

When it was over, she lay there, wondering, astonished.

Hound smiled at her. "I didn't know you could do that by yourself," he said.

"Do what?" she asked, but then she saw. Her limbs were longer and dark brown. Her hair fell in a cascade of obsidian curls.

BOOK FOUR

THE

DUES

OF

TREASON

CHAPTER ONE

THE BALL

THE DAYS tumbled by quickly—far too quickly for Chrysanthe. Her dance lessons continued, along with instruction on etiquette, but a nightmare had seeped in. One of those awful dreams where her true goal seemed ever-further out of reach. If Bonaventure was right, she had little time left to solve the mystery before something terrible happened. Something, but no one seemed to know what.

On the other hand, she now knew exactly what would happen if the dance did not go well.

TWO DAYS before the dance, Chrysanthe was awakened in the night by a faint rap at her door. She had been sleeping lightly anyway, and the sound brought her to a fully alert state. She sat on her bed, listening.

The sound repeated itself.

She withdrew her bodkin from under the mattress and went to the door. When she cracked it open, she found Emeline there, dressed in her nightclothes.

"For heaven's sake, let me in before someone sees me." Once she was in and the door was closed, she noticed the knife in Chrysanthe's hand. "What's that for?" she asked.

"Midnight visitors are not always friendly," Chrysanthe replied. "What is the matter?"

"It's your dress," Emeline said. "The one for which Ysabel had you fitted."

"What of it?"

"I snuck into the quarters of the seamstress while she was out," she said. "The dress isn't right."

"What do you mean?"

"Details," she said, "but important ones. It must have been deliberate."

"Explain them to me."

She listened as Emeline talked about the turn of the hem, the ties at the elbows, the pleats in the back.

"Perhaps we can bribe the seamstress to do it properly," Emeline suggested.

"No," Chrysanthe said. "I will collect the dress this morning and make the changes myself."

"How would you do that?"

"With my sewing kit."

Emeline looked sideways at her. "You know how to sew?"

"Of course," Chrysanthe said.

"I see," Emeline replied. "And do you also pull the dung from the asses of horses to fertilize the fields?"

"No one does that," Chrysanthe said. "It falls out all by itself, but I have shoveled it before."

"I think I may vomit," Emeline said. "Can you clean that up as well?"

"If necessary," Chrysanthe said. "And I can certainly alter the dress, so long as you instruct me in its proper appearance."

Emeline nodded. "Very well," she said. She turned to the door, but hesitated.

"Is there something else?"

"It is childish," Emeline said.

"We are alone."

"It's only…" She stopped and closed her eyes. "At home, I sleep with my old norrice," she said. "I—have difficulty…"

Chrysanthe considered her for a moment. Was this yet another trap? But Emeline genuinely seemed upset, and Chrysanthe felt obliged toward her.

"I am used to sleeping with my sister Phoebe," she said, "but Orenge will discover us in the morning. That could cause all sorts of talk, and your plan to make us seem enemies will be shown false."

"I will be gone before morning," Emeline pressed.

Still Chrysanthe paused, remembering her encounter with Margot—but the secrecy of that meeting had been due to intent, and there was none here. At home it wasn't much thought of if young ladies innocently shared a bed. Or young men for that matter.

Yet the rules here…

Well, surely Emeline knew them. If she meant to do Chrysanthe harm, there was little Chrysanthe could do about it at this point.

"I will be happy of your company."

As Emeline climbed beneath the covers, she seemed unable

to meet Chrysanthe's gaze. Once the taper was dowsed and a few moments had passed, the girl's hand crept over to lie on her shoulder. In a matter of moments, her breathing became slow and even, and Chrysanthe, feeling more secure than she had in months, soon followed her into the demesne of Hypnos. Only once did she wake, when Emeline cried out in her sleep, and mumbled nonsense before returning to slumber.

AS PROMISED, the girl was gone before first light.

Chrysanthe turned her thoughts to the mystery she was bent on solving. Where had d'Ospios and Severin trysted, and what evidence might they have left there? What was the boursier hiding, and why had d'Ospios died? The bridge was the key to the enigma, of that she was certain; although the more rational part of her mind reminded her that the evidence was very slim, based on one of many potential interpretations of a cryptographer's letter.

Once the dance was over, if all went well, she would find the bridge and discover the truth. If it was a false trail, she would search until she found the true one.

THE BALL was set for evening, but guests began arriving the night before. Chrysanthe had never seen so many carriages in one place. Emeline had spoken the truth—this was to be more than a simple country dance.

The chastel had been transformed into something from a faerie story. The grounds in front of the house were arranged with lounging couches and tables decorated with silver service and crystal goblets. Banners and gigantic vases of flowers were placed in the halls. Harpists and quartets of mixed instruments occupied the grounds and chastel corners, playing continuously.

The ballroom stood adjacent to the great hall, and was easily as large. Hundreds of candles were placed in chandeliers of gold and ivory, fastened to a ceiling of darkest blue and figured with signs of the zodiac and planets. The walls and floor were of polished white marble, with long carpets from Modjal and Codaey forming walkways at the entrances.

At one end of the room, an ensemble was playing an old chanson. It was the largest collection of musicians she had ever experienced: a viellete, two vielles, a chalamel, flaut, recorders of three sizes, viol, guitern, and granviol. What seemed lacking was any sort of percussion—not so much as a simple timbrel. This set it apart from any dance she had attended. The absence of even the smallest drum somehow underscored the strangeness of the evening.

The music was quite lovely—and *big*. It swelled to fill the ballroom, where a smaller group of musicians might have been lost.

A young man she had never seen before met her at the entrance. He was tall, emerald-eyed and chestnut-haired, dressed in a pearl jacket, long pants of watered silk and charcoal waistcoat, a fair match for her own ivory gown with its pale blue trimmings.

"Danesele Nevelon, I hope?" the young man said.

"Yes," she replied.

"I am Straton de Chalkis," he said, "and I am privileged to introduce you to the floor."

"That sounds painful."

Straton's brow wrinkled slightly in puzzlement, but then he brightened. "Ho," he said. "I see. Very good. I was told you were quite lively." He coughed. "No, it is only that I should accompany you in the first dance."

"Yes, I understand," Chrysanthe. "I look forward to the introduction."

"Will you take my arm?" he asked.

"Only temporarily," she replied.

"Ho," he said. "More wordplay."

She slipped her arm through his and went with him out onto the marble floor. Couples from around the room followed their lead until the ballroom—as large as it was—seemed to overflow.

For a moment the symphonia stopped playing, and quiet settled over the room. Then a single viellete began a plaintive melody. Straton took one of her hands in his and placed the other in the small of her back.

The dance began.

At first, she could do little but concentrate on putting her feet in the right places, but it soon became clear that Straton was an able dancer, and she began to allow herself to follow his lead. As Emeline had predicted, however, that carried with it its own peril.

As the dance progressed, Straton contrived to bring their bodies closer, exactly what Emeline had predicted. She almost missed it and by the time she had the sense to pull more distant from him, they were almost brushing together. After that his attempts became subtler; stepping forward slightly out of time, so that their thighs might touch, turning a bit too far during the volte.

Everything around them dimmed away as she gave all her attention to the contest. Stratton's expression remained fixed, as if none of it was happening. The music seemed to go on forever, and when it finally ended, she realized she was sweating. She bowed, thanked him, and then drifted from the floor as quickly as decorum allowed. The emperor had almost lost his bet on the first dance of the night.

Chrysanthe was looking for a place to be alone, but alas, Plesance appeared as if from nowhere and took her elbow.

"Well, what did you think of Straton, then?"

"He seems pleasant enough," she replied.

"If by pleasant you mean he shall inherit a grand estate, you are not far from the mark," Plesance said. "Some would set their aim higher, but there is a certain virtue in appreciating one's limitations."

"No doubt."

"Did you enjoy your dance?"

"Oh, very much," she said.

"That's good," Plesance replied. "I was afraid our northern dances might be very different from what you were used to."

"A little different," Chrysanthe said, "but Straton is a very good partner. I just followed him."

"Oh, I see," she said. "Well, here, let me introduce you to your next one."

"I had thought to take a breath—" she began, but another man looked up and acknowledged their approach. He was shorter than Straton, rather thick-lipped. His cheeks were red enough she wondered if he had powdered them.

His name was Piers de Solon, and he was neither as good a dancer as Straton nor as subtle in his attempts to compromise her. On the other hand, his conversation was better—his father was a silk merchant, and Piers had been on several sea voyages with him. Added to that, he was a reader of some appetite, so she shared two dances with him, especially as the second was a tardif, and thus very slow, making simpler the business of avoiding his clumsy attempts to clutch her.

When they were done, she left the floor, and caught Emeline watching her from a cluster of guests. The girl nodded slightly and smiled, which Chrysanthe took as approval. A moment later she was pulled aside by Ysabel, who wanted to introduce her to a young man named Andros. He was dark-haired, with an olive complexion, and his waistcoat had red roses embroidered onto it. She had noticed him already—his was by far the most colorful clothing in the room, and he sported a jaunty little cane, as some from her homeland were wont to carry.

After introducing them, Ysabel made some excuse and wandered off. Andros caught her examining his vest.

"Yes," he said. "I'm the peacock in this crowd. My apologies. I'm a colonial, and I'm afraid it shows."

"Don't apologize," Chrysanthe said. "I miss the color. I'm also from afar—from Mesembria."

"Laham?" His eyebrows raised up.

"Indeed." She smiled. "Port Bellship. Where are you from?"

"Elaph," he said.

"Oh, yes," she said. "In Gawey."

He smiled back. "Few would know where that was."

"And how did you end up here?" she asked.

He paused for a moment, then quirked a little grin.

"Same as you, I expect," he said. "My father is admiral of the fleet of the Cocytus."

She blinked. "Damon Charron is your father?"

"Oh, you've heard of him?"

"Of course. My father is Alastor Nevelon. They served together, many years ago."

His mouth hung open for a moment. "Alastor Nevelon's daughter," he said. "This is astonishing. That the two of us should meet like this."

"Not so astonishing," she said, "when you consider who introduced us. You were staying nearby?"

"Not at all," he said, looking suddenly a bit peeved. "I am quartered in Leonsmere." Then he grinned. "I see what you mean, though. Two colonial hostages, meeting on the dance floor. What amusement might result?"

"Do you know these dances?"

"By reputation only, but it is moot. I cannot dance."

"Cannot or will not?"

"Cannot," he said. "If I could dance, I would not be here, but in the fleet." He glanced down, then. She followed his gaze to the cane. "It isn't an affectation, you see."

"Oh," she said. "I'm sorry."

"Well, there's nothing to help it," he replied, "and certainly, no fault of yours. But I'm no use on a warship, so I am here instead. At least the company is pleasant."

She was trying to think what to say next when the music abruptly ended, and then started again, playing a dramatically different tune. Everyone stopped what they were doing and stared at the entrance to the hall. A man was just entering.

He was young, fair, and dressed impeccably.

"Who is that, I wonder?" she whispered.

"That," Andros said, "is my current benefactor and landlord, Prince Heron."

She recognized the music now. It wasn't a dance, but a royal fanfare. She watched, curious, as the prince stopped at the end of the carpet and waited, and she wondered what would happen next.

After what seemed a long time, nothing did.

Then Andros bent a little and whispered in her ear.

"I believe he is waiting for you."

THE PRINCE had soft hands, though his nails felt like glass. Up close he was handsome, in an almost delicate way. His eyes were pale brown with touches of green. She thought about apologizing for keeping him waiting, but thought it might only make matters worse.

Why in God's name would Ysabel invite the son of the emperor to a dance held ostensibly for her? Heron was ridiculously beyond her station. The only possible explanation was that his appearance was to do with the emperor's wager. But was Heron here to help his father win the bet, or make sure he lost it? She didn't know anything about the relationship between father and son. Did one dance differently with a prince? Had she already ruined herself by making him wait?

There was no way to know. She could only do what seemed right.

The music struck up again, a familiar old carole reformed for the corsacors. Heron began—he was adept, though not as graceful as Straton, nor as forceful as Piers. At first, they danced alone, but the second time the melody came around, others joined them, until the floor was full. By then, Heron had a little smile on his face, as if he kept a secret.

"You are Chrysanthe Nevelon, are you not?" he said as they turned upon the floor.

"I am, Your Highness" she said.

"You dance very well, for a beginner," he said. "You must have had an excellent teacher."

She felt her face flush. "You can tell, Your Highness?"

"I am perceptive," he said.

"I hope I am not too clumsy."

"By no means," he said. "I am enjoying it very much." His smile broadened. "You have met my friend Andros?"

"Yes, Your Highness."

"That is good," he said. "I am glad you are acquainted." The smile became a grin. "You made quite the impression on the court," he said. "My father was much taken with you. Although there is now a musical divertissement named for you that is all sorts of dreadful. I had to sit through it twice."

"Oh, I am so sorry, Highness."

"Be assured that I like the subject much better than its treatment."

"That's very kind of you to say."

The music ended. They bowed, he kissed her hand, and everyone in the room clapped. As the next dance began, she made her way from the floor, trying to avoid the gazes now fastened on her from every direction. The prince didn't dance again, but instead approached Andros. They spoke for a moment, then Heron left the hall.

Chrysanthe took the moment to try to work through what had just happened. The prince hadn't made any attempt to pull her close, but although he seemed candid enough, he also hadn't mentioned his father's bet. Was it possible he didn't know, and that he was here for some other reason?

Whatever the case, she seemed to have survived his presence.

As the ball continued, more people than ever stared at her, and she didn't know what it meant. Plesance was positively beaming, which couldn't be a good sign. Ysabel, too, seemed to be regarding her attentively from across the hall.

Despite her misgivings about dancing, she wished someone would ask her, but no one approached her, and the men in the hall seemed determined not to even look at her. Across the room, she saw Margot staring, but when she caught her gaze, the other woman hurried through a door.

Chrysanthe began to understand, and her heart sank. Andros began limping toward her, and she felt the stirrings of panic. When he was close enough, she saw that he looked uncomfortable, which did not help.

"Let me first say, I'm terribly sorry about this."

She smiled as well as she could, and kept her voice very low.

"Do not," she said. "I know we are not friends, but I beg of you, do not."

"Keep calm," he said. "I assure you, any discomfort will be temporary."

"I cannot," she said.

"If you refuse, it will be much worse, I assure you," he said. "I like you. I do not wish you ill. I may not be your friend, but you do *have* a friend, and she asks that you trust her. I advise you to do so."

Something seemed to turn in the music, as if she was hearing it for the first time. Around her the dancers continued, like parts in a great clockwork machine.

"Should I take your arm?" she asked.

"It will help me walk better."

SHE TRIED to ignore the glances, the expressions, the asides whispered behind flattened hands as Andros escorted her from the hall. Soon they were beyond the bustle, walking through corridors she had never seen before. Shortly they came to the door of a suite, outside of which stood two guards in the royal uniform. Just to the right of the suite, a small, open salon held several courtiers playing cards. Among them were Tristan and Marie, Plesance's parents, and a parfait she recognized from the basilica.

Their gazes flicked over her as she went by.

Her chest felt tight, as if the bodice was trying to smother her. One of the guards opened the door to the suite. She looked to Andros, who nodded slightly. Then she went in, and the door closed behind her.

She stood in the perfumed air, slowly taking in the tapestries on the walls, the statuary, the couches and chairs arranged at the fireplace—one of them occupied. There were three doorways, two of which revealed no details she could make out. Through the third was the largest bed she had ever seen. She wondered if anyone stayed here when there were no princes around.

Emeline stood from her chair by the fire and walked toward her.

"You did very well," she said. "Your dancing was not perfect, but it will not bring you to grief."

"No," Chrysanthe said. "Not my dancing. But this visit—"

The young woman came nearer and embraced her.

"I knew I could count on you," she said. "Even if you feared for yourself."

"I still fear for myself," Chrysanthe said. "Will you explain?"

"Your enemies weren't certain enough that you would fail at the dance, so they laid another trap for you. Here."

"Prince Heron."

"Of course," Emeline said. "Everyone would think you had lain with him, and would just as well know you could never be his intended."

"I see," Chrysanthe replied, struggling to keep her anger in check, "and yet that seems to be exactly my fate. You knew about this and did not warn me. Were all of your lessons and attentions to me just a ruse to make certain I fell into this snare?"

Seemingly unperturbed, Emeline stood on tiptoes and kissed her forehead. "I told you I was betrothed," she said. "I did not tell you to whom."

Suddenly Chrysanthe knew.

"The prince?"

"Yes." She smiled. "And not merely promised—we are married. But it is a secret. No one knows, and until now, it has been impossible for us to meet in private. You have made it possible."

"I don't understand," Chrysanthe said. "If you are married, why should it be secret? Why should there be any impediment to your being alone?" There was movement in the corner of her eye.

"Because my father does not approve of the match."

Heron entered the room. He had changed into a dressing gown.

"We were promised long ago, but since then the politics of our situation have changed. Yet I have spent so many years dreaming of Emeline as my bride—and I am a man of my word, even if my father is not. In time, all will be well, but for now it is not prudent to tell him—nor anyone—of our situation. You have done us a service, Danesele." He smiled. "It is funny, you know. My father sent me here to help you. Little did he know my real reason for coming."

"You knew of your father's bet?"

"Of course, and I have helped him win it, which will incline him to look more kindly on my marriage when the time comes to reveal it."

"How can your father win the bet?" Chrysanthe demanded. "The dance was meant to reveal me as a wanton. What does it matter if that fails when everyone now thinks I have slept with you? This is much worse. Your father will strip may father's estate from him."

"At the very least," Heron said. "There is every chance he will also find some pretext to have you imprisoned—or worse. My father seems an amiable sort, if you don't know him, but he is in fact rather without remorse and a bit feckless."

Chrysanthe opened her mouth, but found she did not have the words. She wanted to scream at the both of them, but she knew she couldn't. She had to find something to say that would make all of this unhappen, like the impossible happy ending of a children's story where everyone came back to life.

"Prince…" she began, without any idea what her next words would be.

"Hush," Emeline said. "You worry for no reason. You have done us a favor. And now we must do you one."

"Of course we must, my dove," Heron said, moving over to Emeline and kissing her on the lips. Then he took Chrysanthe by the arm and led her to the door. He smiled at her, took a deep breath and began shouting.

"You *dare* refuse me, you frigid *putain*? Who do you think you are? What possesses you to think so much of yourself?"

After the initial shock, she thought that he was overacting. Abruptly he yanked the door open and shoved her roughly through.

"Escort her back to whatever convent bred her," he snapped at Andros. "Then inform the master of the house that I have become fatigued, and will attend no more of what passes for festivities in this forsaken place." He slammed the door.

"Danesele," Andros said, offering her his arm.

As they passed the card players, they looked bewildered—except for Tristan d'Othres, who nodded approvingly, and she saw his lips move. She thought she could tell what he was saying.

Good girl.

Once they were alone, Chrysanthe leaned against a wall.

"Are you well?" Andros asked.

She laughed, her nerves still wound tight.

"Frigid putain?"

"Well, he's no great thespian," Andros whispered, "but it leaves no doubt as to your virtue. You have refused a prince, which few would do. This will only improve your reputation."

"You might have warned me."

"Then your own performance might have been compromised," he said. "Also, the princess thought it would be more fun this way."

"For her."

"Of course," he said.

"And so now?"

"Now you must return to the ball," he said. "It is, after all, in your honor."

"I begin to think it was contrived for a different purpose altogether," she said.

"It is possible to catch two fish with the same worm."

CRESPIN TOOK a drink from the bottle Renost proffered him. He almost spit it out.

"Merde," he gasped. "What is this?"

"Something from Velesa." Renost shrugged and took the bottle back. "I traded for it."

"That's remarkably foul," he said, as his closest friend took another drink.

"Also remarkably strong," Renost said, handing him the bottle back. Crespin nodded.

The two sat near the edge of a cliff overlooking Hhark, as the dim red rim of Helios edged into the dark distance of the horizon. The view of the coast—especially the southern approach—was excellent, and Crespin intended to recommend it as a watchpost when they returned to camp, which would be in the morning. The ascent had been treacherous enough with plenty of light. To attempt a return in the darkness would be suicide, especially given that the ground itself had a disturbing tendency to move with alarming frequency.

"Should we build a fire, do you think?" Renost asked.

"I don't think it should get too cold," Crespin said, "and the moon will give us light enough to finish this bottle."

"Another night on the ground," Renost said. "We might as well have joined the infantry."

"Or the merchant fleet," Crespin said. "Oh, wait… we did that."

Renost's eyes dropped a little.

"What is it?" Crespin asked.

"Nothing," Renost said. He took the bottle back and lifted it. "To the supply chain!" he said.

"We fought," Crespin said. "We acquitted ourselves well."

"Your girl acquitted herself well," Renost replied. "Otherwise we would all be pickled meat, floating on the tide."

That stung. Crespin tried to go around it, but the drink was indeed strong.

"You have something to say, Renost?"

"Nothing of consequence."

"No," Crespin said. "You have been in a *mood* since this expedition began. For no reason I can identify, I feel your judgement at every turn. What is provoking you?"

"I am ungrateful," Renost said. "That is all. The fault is with me."

"Renost—"

"Why did you want me along?" Renost snapped. "You left the Navy because you did not have the courage to go against your father, but why did you arrange for me to do the same?"

"Renost, it was a suggestion. You could have refused. I only thought—"

"That I would follow you to the ends of the world?" Renost said. "Yes, I know that, but why? *Why* did you think that?"

"I don't understand this question," Crespin said. "We have been fast friends almost since birth. We have done everything together. I thought you would…" He trailed off, at loss for words. He looked up at his friend.

Renost leaned in and kissed him.

The surprise lasted only an instant before familiarity washed it away. Then he returned the embrace, and for a long time, there were no words at all. He was a boy again, with no cares, no plans for the future.

NIGHT CAME, and eventually they slept. It was colder than Crespin imagined it would be, but their body heat sufficed. When he woke, he found Renost already up, watching the sunrise. A new day. The first of many.

"Good morning, mon vieil," he said.

"Good morning, Captain," Renost replied. "I think there is light enough to make our way back down."

"There is no hurry."

Renost turned toward him. "There is for me," he said. "The *Tethys* is in port, but she sails just after noon."

"The *Tethys*? A warship?"

"I spoke to your father," Renost said. "He agreed to transfer me back to the Navy."

"Renost, why? I thought—"

"Tell me anything has changed since the sun last set, and I will crawl back to your father and beg to stay on the *Leucothea*."

"Changed?"

"I love you, Crespin. I have always loved you."

"And I love you, Renost, but what is it you think? That you and I could marry? That we could raise children? Take our places in the world?"

"There are places where none of that would matter."

"It matters to *me*, Renost," Crespin said.

"I know that, Crespin." Renost sighed, and a little smile crept upon his face. "I knew it last night, and I knew how it would end."

"Then…" Crespin held up his hands, feeling helpless.

"It's all right," Renost said. "All is well. You will always be my friend. There can never be any doubt of that, but if you have a life to find, then so do I. And I will not find it following you about as if I were a lost puppy. You understand that, don't you?"

"How did this become so complicated?" Crespin asked. "It was all so simple. So easy."

"For you," Renost said. "For me, it had never been simple, or easy. Not for many years."

"I didn't know," Crespin said. "I swear to you. I always thought you had your feather set for Chrysanthe."

Renost chuckled. "I love her too, of course. I loved the three of us together, and I suppose I dreamt of a world in which we could remain together, in some fantastic fashion. You as my true love, and she as our greatest friend and champion. As you said, however, we are children no longer. For you, that means one thing. For me, another; for each of us to thrive, we must part."

Crespin approached his friend. As they embraced, Crespin fought back tears.

"You were never supposed to be the wise one, Renost."

"Nor shall I ever be."

CHAPTER TWO

TRANSFIGURATION

AS AMMOLITE raised her unfamiliar hand to examine it, she heard a light, clear, musical tone. It was the sound of the clock striking on the morning of her sixteenth birthday. It was the space between one breath and another, when everything changed.

"*I* do it," she said, very softly. She stared at her fingers, the peculiar tan color of the cuticles in the nails. "I do it. It isn't the wine. It isn't Veulkh. It's me." Her voice rose. Hound stared at her with widening eyes. "I do it!" she screamed. "*It's always been me!*"

Her breath tore itself in and out of her, now, and she felt hot. She felt a thousand feet tall.

Hound scrambled to his feet.

"Quiet," he said. "Someone will hear—"

She balled her fists and swung them at him.

"Me," she yelled, tears of fury boiling out of her eyes. "Me!"

It felt good, her fists on his flesh. It felt wonderful, despite the hurt expression on his face. Maybe because of it. He backed up a little, but didn't try to stop her—and finally, like a fever, her anger broke, and she sagged against him.

"It was always me," she sighed. "What am I, Hound? What am I?"

"You are Ammolite," he said. "That is all that matters to me."

"But you wanted *her*, Selene. Just like him. Like he wanted Orra."

"For a moment," he said. "Sort of. I feel things. Things I don't understand, but I don't want you to be Selene. I didn't wish it. Well, not exactly."

She realized as he was talking that once again her arms were light and thin. She had become herself again, if that meant anything at all. *Was* there an Ammolite? Or was that form, too, just an appearance someone had once wished on her?

"Hound," she sighed. Then she put her palms against his head.

"What?" he asked.

"Wait," she said. "Just wait." He stood still as she reached in, but then she understood that for this, she didn't actually need him.

Hound took a sharp breath and stepped back.

"I don't much care for that," he said. "Although I guess it depends on what you have in mind."

She opened her eyes, but she already felt the difference, the way her body was put together, the balance of it.

Now she was Hound, complete with—everything.

"I could have become one of the ravens—Kos! Or Veulkh. I could have… that first year…" She closed her eyes and let her body change again. "I've been so stupid."

"No, look," Hound said. "You have an advantage now. You know, and he doesn't. And…" He broke off again. "Tell me," he said. "Quickly, but everything. Who is Marnora?" She told him, and he listened, and his smile grew the entire time.

"So Veulkh thinks you're dead," he said when she was done. "That's even better. You could take the form of one of these apes and leave the way I came in. They might be confused by your smell…" He looked a little irritated. "That might not work. You would have to make your way through the jungle, find Martin—"

"But you would be with me."

He shook his head. "I can't go back out that way," he said. "Not unless I find the heart."

"Heart?" she said. "Yes, tell me about that."

It was her turn to listen, until he was done.

"I know something about this," she told him. "It could be anything. The books speak of all sorts of hearts, but they usually aren't literally hearts. They're more like something…" She trailed off, trying to think how to explain.

"They're more like keys," she said.

"Keys? Keys to what?"

"The world is built from different elements and forces," she said. "There is a language and a structure in the way it is made. What we call sorcery—what Veulkh is able to accomplish—comes from understanding that structure and making things with it." She thought back on what she had read. "The way a smith chooses metal and figures it into useful things using fire and force. Or like when someone builds a windmill by selecting wood and stone, shaping it with tools, then applying the knowledge of wind, mechanics, and friction to make an engine; something that harnesses natural properties to serve the needs of human desire.

"Wizards take the stuff of fire, earth, water, air, spirit," she continued, "and form them into physical objects, into engines that they can use for particular purposes. The synapses, for example—the places where we come and go over distances—those were shaped, long ago, from the elemental forces discovered by the first and greatest of the sorcerers. Some say they were created by even greater beings long ago, yet not everyone can use those things.

"A sorcerer must either have a key—a heart—or he must somehow make one. The Tsau Dadan once served the rulers of Sular Bulan. Those masters must have made some sort of key to keep them in thrall, but it may have been stolen or destroyed. Marnora must have found it, or made a new one. It could look like anything."

"She would probably keep it near her."

"Probably," Ammolite said.

"Or hidden in that room where I found you, with all of her trophies?"

"Why would it be there?"

"It might be. It might not." He shrugged. "It's the only place I can think to look. What could it hurt?"

"Hound, do not go back there," Ammolite said. "I'm afraid of that place."

"I entered Veulkh's manse without him knowing I was there. It seems as if I did the same here. Whatever spells these wizards use to discover intruders, I am protected from them." He grinned cockily. "I'll be alright."

As he said it, she knew it was true, but she realized something else, as well.

"She'll know where I am," she said. "When she discovers I'm not in that room, she will find me."

"I can show you the way out, then."

"No," she said. "We'll both go back. Together."

———

"OH, MY dear," a girlish voice said. "Waiting for me, I see."

Ammolite was not certain how much time had passed—hours, probably, but it could have been as long as a day. She and Hound had searched the room endlessly, and its deceased inhabitants, finding nothing that resembled a heart.

"Indeed," she replied, again in the form of Orra. She was waiting on the bed that had been prepared for her. Marnora entered with a train of her servants. They were carrying something. After a moment, she realized it was Veulkh.

"I see you've found your place," Marnora said. "What did you do to my poor servants?" she asked, gazing at the dead Tsau Dadan.

Ammolite shrugged. "They did not treat me well." She gestured at Veulkh. "Is he dead?"

"Veulkh?" Marnora said. "No. Of course not. Not yet anyway. I once was fond of him, don't you think? But I must archive him for a time. It is for his own good, and he will thank me when all is done." She smiled. One of the Tsau Dadan brought a chair over, and she took a seat. It wasn't a large chair, but still she seemed far too small for it.

Marnora sat, silently regarding Ammolite as one might an insect in the corner of one's house. Frowning slightly, she looked a little impatient. Finally one of the Tsau Dadan arrived, carrying a dark green gown trimmed in black lace and small, perfect pearls.

"You had best put that on," she said. "I will wait."

Ammolite began to unbutton the dress she wore. "I've been trying to guess what you're doing here," she said. "Veulkh thought this place would be empty. He was going to do something, some sort of magic for the benefit of the Cryptarchia. But what?"

Marnora's lips bowed faintly.

"I have been in this form for a long time," she said. "I have aged forward, I have aged backward. I have stepped in and out of time itself. Most of my debtors are dust, and yet a few remain, and I am very much a creature of habit.

"My habit—well, honestly, it is to do what I want, and I thought it would be nice to see Veulkh again. I did not know he would come, but really, there are only one or two who could accomplish what he was asked to do, and I hoped it would be him. If not, I would have found him some other way."

"What is he to you?" Ammolite asked. "Were you lovers?"

Marnora laughed. "Maybe," she said. "We have been many things. Friends, mortal enemies. I have spent many years hardly remembering him at all. If we were lovers, I suppose I have forgotten that. There is only so much one can remember without going mad."

Ammolite let the dress drop to the floor and took the other in her hands. Marnora walked a clinical gaze over every inch of her.

"I did kill you before, didn't I?"

"You haven't answered my question," Ammolite said. "So I shall not answer yours."

"Question?" Marnora said, looking a little perplexed. Then her face cleared. "Oh, dear girl," she said. "I am his mother, of course."

Stepping into the green gown, Ammolite stopped long enough to look and see if Marnora was speaking the truth. There was no telling, however. The childlike face gave nothing away.

"His mother."

"It is a matter of fact," Marnora said. "Although sometimes I forget it."

"How could you forget that?"

Marnora looked genuinely astonished. "Well, when we were young, we grew as others do. He was born, and twenty years later he was gone. I am more than seven hundred years old, so what are twenty of them to me? It's very little, I'll tell you. For two hundred years, he and I fought on opposite sides of a war. Which is more consequential?"

"I don't know," Ammolite said. "I never knew my mother."

"Well, I'm sure I had one," Marnora said, "but I don't remember her, either." She smiled. "You look quite elegant in that."

"Thank you."

"I answered your question," Marnora said.

"You did," Ammolite said. "Thank you. The answer to yours is that Veulkh told you the truth. The Orra you knew is long dead."

"You're quite sure?"

"I am."

"Very well," Marnora said. "I think we're concluded, then. Unless you have anything else."

"What was Veulkh planning on doing?"

"Waking the engines of stone," she said.

"I don't know what that means."

Marnora shrugged, ever so slightly. Then she stood and stepped near enough to bend and put her lips upon Ammolite's. She was so surprised, she didn't try to stop her. Marnora's lips were sweet, and cold, and Ammolite suddenly felt a longing deeper and stronger than she had ever known she had capacity to know. She took a quick, ragged breath and returned the kiss, even as her limbs felt suddenly warm and heavy.

There was something, like a constellation, a scattering of jewels. Marnora pulled away. Ammolite tried to follow but found she could not. She couldn't move at all.

"It will be quick," Marnora said. "There will be no pain."

CHAPTER THREE

A WIND IN
THE HALLS

EYES AND whispers followed Chrysanthe again when she returned to the ball, but soon everything was as it had been before. Various men presented themselves, led her to the dance floor, and attempted to besmirch her honor. Their attempts, however, seemed half-hearted, or perhaps it was simply that after her encounter with the prince their claws had been removed.

Her breath came easier.

She had not only avoided the trap set for her, but she seemed to have gained important allies. Tomorrow, she could return her attentions to the real reason she was here: to help her father. For the first time in weeks she felt confident that she was up to the task.

After a while the music paused, and servants circulated through the crowd with white wine. She was gesturing to one of them when Plesance arrived, bearing two glasses.

"Bravo," she said.

"I'm sorry?" Chrysanthe responded.

"Oh, come now," Plesance said. "I underestimated you. Everyone did. Let's not belabor this." She handed the drink to Chrysanthe. "To the prince," she said, lifting her glass.

"To the empire."

The wine was cool and tasted of rose petals. It burned a little in the back of her throat—obviously a bit stronger than it seemed. Deciding she would be better off not finishing the glass, she thereafter held it, only pretending to drink.

Plesance was under no such self-restriction. She finished the contents of her glass in a few gulps and signaled for more. Seeming to feel increasingly friendly, she twined her arm with Chrysanthe's.

"Truth be told," she whispered conspiratorially, "you might have done better to let the prince entertain you. Virtue is fleeting, and so may the royal favor be, but while it lasts it can take you to great heights."

"I seek no favors of any sort," Chrysanthe said.

"Oh, please," Plesance said. "Enough. You have impressed sufficiently. There's no need to become boring." She leaned over and kissed Chrysanthe on the cheek. "Go on," she said. "The music is about to start. It's all for you, of course, and here is your next partner."

She turned to find Quintent smiling at her.

It took her a moment to find her voice.

"Ah—you've returned."

"How could I miss this?" he asked. "I'm only sorry to have arrived so late. There was—trouble leaving the city."

"Nothing serious, I hope," she said.

"Nothing that bears discussing on so festive an occasion," he replied. "There's the music. Are you up to another dance?"

She stared into his eyes, looking there for the person who had broken into her rooms, but after a breath or two she waved off the notion. It could have been any of an unknown number of people, and his eyes looked on hers in such a way…

"I am entirely yours," she said.

The instant the words left her lips, she regretted them. It wasn't seemly, it was far too bold—and yet, after all that she had been through, it was very agreeable to dance with someone she liked. Moreover, she felt pleasant from the wine. Relaxed.

Quintent was more than adept, and in his firm grasp it seemed almost as if her feet had wings. She felt as one with him, and with the music, and everything else began to blend into a pleasant blur. She became keenly aware of his hand on hers, and where his other hand touched her back, a pleasant burning sensation began, spreading around her hips to her belly. She could feel his breath and wondered what it would be like if their cheeks touched, just a little, if they were to graze one another, accidentally, innocently.

It was as if the chords of the instruments were inside of her, vibrating, and the skin of their hands was mingling. Her own breath felt moist, like she was exhaling the vapor rising from the earth after a rain on a hot day. She was dizzy, as if her head were beginning to turn in impossible directions. It was becoming difficult to think. She remembered when Plesance had given her the lacrime of cinnamon, and suddenly understood that she must have been slipped something again, probably in her wine.

Looking at Quintent, she saw he was pretending not to know, but he had to understand that all she wanted was to wrap her arms around him, to sway with the music and hear his heartbeat.

In that moment, she knew he was her enemy.

Chrysanthe had believed herself safe, that she had passed every test, but Plesance had done her in, and Quintent was her confederate. He tried to tug her closer, and she knew she would be unable to resist, that it wouldn't even occur to her to struggle. She would be the object of gossip and ridicule, a colonial girl who could not hold her wine, and the emperor would lose his bet and bring his wrath down upon her and hers.

And then they stopped, and she realized the music was no longer playing. She let go of his hand and stepped back, and it felt like leaving home all over again. Yet it was a false feeling. It was the drink, the lacrime, and his insidious, lying words.

"Are you well?" Quintent asked.

She knew him now. If the music began again, it would be the end of her, and he knew it, too, damn him.

"I am a little dizzy."

"Then let me help you—"

"*No,*" she said. "I can take care of myself."

She turned and walked away, made it perhaps ten steps before she realized she didn't know where she was going. Stopping, she looked around, and found the door. Whatever Plesance had put in her drink, it was getting worse. Her entire body itched, but she could not scratch. She had no choice; she had to return to her room. To be alone. Whatever the social consequences, they could not be as grave as those which would accrue if she remained another moment at the ball.

Chrysanthe stumbled, but someone caught her, pulling her up by the hand. For an instant those fingers on hers seemed like the entire world. Looking up in terror, she saw that it was Margot.

"Chrysanthe? Are you well?"

Margot, too? It was all she could do not to scream.

"I need air," she said. "I need to leave."

She broke free and nearly ran, leaving Margot behind.

Once outside of the ballroom she ran as best she could toward her rooms, but everything looked both the same and unfamiliar. She knew she was lost, and she also knew her mind was leaving her. Soon she would forget she even had a destination, and that wouldn't do.

She didn't see the man until she bumped into him, and her legs went out from under her. He said something as he caught her, and then she was against him. She felt a sort of explosion course through her, and then her lips were touching his, and they were hot, and she remembered, remembered everything, their bodies in the dark, his caress, her guilt, the sudden shock of pain in her back.

All went dark, and she felt only cold, and the weight of the water upon her and longing—terrible, longing, loneliness, moving like a wind through the halls, searching, unable to touch, to feel, except for now, finally…

CHRYSANTHE REMEMBERED herself with a sudden judder, as if violently waking after just dropping off to sleep. For a moment, she thought someone had hit her, but then she realized she was in bed, with covers pulled to her chin.

It was not *her* bed. She pulled back the blankets to reassure herself that she was still dressed, and was relieved to see she was still in her ball gown. Sitting up, she looked about in the gloom, trying to ascertain where she was, and stifled a scream when she saw someone in a chair, staring at her.

"Do not be frightened," the man said.

The room was lit only by a single taper, so it took a moment for her to recognize him.

"Dam Severin," she said.

"I am no Dam, as you must know," he said. "Do you know who you are?"

"Yes," she said, "but I do not understand why I am here."

"I found you in the hall," he replied. "You were—not yourself. We were near my rooms, so I brought you here."

"I see," she said. Memories flashed through her, like things seen in the dark during a thunderstorm. "I do not know what happened."

He regarded her with a flat expression. After a time, she understood that it masked intense agitation.

"Don't you know?" he said. "Don't you remember?"

She did and wished desperately that she did not.

He sighed, and took a long draught from a goblet, and she realized also that he was quite drunk. Not long before she might not have understood so quickly, but now she knew far too much about the man.

"You were *her* for a moment," he said. "You were her."

"D'Ospios," she said.

He nodded and took another drink.

"Yes," he said. "I suppose I should thank you for that. I never got to tell her—" He broke off. "Do you remember all of it?"

"I'm not sure," she said.

"I thought she was dead," he said. "I was all but sure of it. Now I know."

"Do you know who killed her?"

"I went to meet her," he said. "She wasn't there. I thought she had changed her mind, and then I thought perhaps she simply fled. After all, she had taken what she came for. Destroyed me. But then, nothing happened. It became clear to me that she never left. That perhaps she did, after all, have some feeling for me."

"She loved you," Chrysanthe said. "I don't understand it all, but I know that. I felt it when"—she paused—"when her ghost…"

"Yes," he said. "I know. I know now, as I said. You have some experience with ghosts." It wasn't a question.

She nodded.

"Yes. I've met a few. One of the parfaits back home once told me she thought I was especially sensitive to them."

"So it would seem. She must have been here, the whole time, but I was blind and deaf to her." His gaze sharpened a little. "What else did you learn from her?"

"She was in agony about something. She knew she had betrayed you, and she decided not to go through with it."

"It," he murmured. "Do you know what 'it' was?"

"No," she said. But she did, at least in part. Sandrine had gone to the bridge to meet him. She had hidden something there, in a place only she knew. What it was, Chrysanthe did not remember, but she knew it was what caused them to kill d'Ospios.

He nodded.

"It was no accident that they put you in her room," he said. "Anyone could see that. Whoever sent you here did you no favors."

She took a moment to digest what he said, then made a decision.

"I feel well enough to walk," she said. "I think it best I return to my own room. My reputation—"

"Your reputation is no longer of any consequence," he said, and he smiled weakly. "They will assume what you know, and then they will murder you, just as they did my Sandrine."

"But I know nothing," she said.

"Perhaps not," he shrugged. "But it will not matter. Not if I tell them, and I must tell them."

This wasn't supposed to be happening. Everything had been going so well. She tried to control her breathing, but it was getting away from her, and she felt as if she might faint again. The lacrime in her wine, the invasion of her mind by Sandrine's spirit had shocked her numb. But she was beginning to wake—not from a nightmare, but *into* one.

"Must you?" she said, fighting for time, until she could think of something. "Why?" He stared at her, as if he was really considering her pleas.

"I could help you," he said at last. He closed his eyes. "I would, but there is a price."

"What price?"

He reached over to the table near his chair and produced a small, black vial.

"Someone recently gave you a lacrime," he said. "Probably a distillation of nutmeg and ginger, designed to inflame your passions. Mixed with wine, perhaps?"

"I believe so."

"But nutmeg has other effects," he said. "It is attractive to the dead, and Sandrine loved ginger. Still, you must have already formed a bond of some sort with her, living in her room, which made it easier for her to enter you."

Chrysanthe stared at the vial.

"You want me to do it again."

He held up the small container. "This is a lacrime of ekaton."

"I've never heard of it."

"It is a little-known spice, partly because it is forbidden. Like nutmeg, it will draw the dead, but with far greater efficiency." He looked at her, his eyes brimmed with misery. "One more night with her, do you understand? And I will do what I can to protect you."

He reached the bottle toward her. She stared at, horrified.

"Do not ask this of me," she pleaded.

"I must," he replied, "but it must be now. By morning, this house will be in a great deal of turmoil. It will make everything more difficult." His words were beginning to flow together. She could not take her eyes from the bottle he held closer to her.

In an instant, something fell into place.

The ball. The prince. Emeline.

"The house will be in turmoil because Prince Heron will be dead."

"Yes," he said. "Just so."

CHAPTER FOUR

THE HEART

THE LAST breath she had drawn remained in her lungs; Ammolite no longer remembered how to exhale. She felt the faintest panic, but she had spent so many years ignoring her body, pretending not to be there while Veulkh imposed his will upon it. She was just as able to disregard it now, as it began to die. Instead she clung to what she had seen during the kiss, trying to stretch her mind around it.

Marnora's serene face took on the slightest look of puzzlement.

"Oh!" she said. Ammolite had expected to surprise Marnora, but had not expected to be shocked herself. She could not see her own face, of course, but hair that fell down her chest was a golden brown, not black, and the instead of the straight figure of a girl, her form filled out the dress meant for Orra's curves.

Marnora stood and reached to stroke her face. Ammolite remained paralyzed, still could not breathe. She felt her heart laboring to strike time and starting to fail.

"What is this?" Marnora murmured. "How is this?" Her mouth formed a little "O", and for a heartbeat she looked very much like the little girl whose form she wore.

"Veulkh," she said. "Clever Veulkh, and to think I almost killed you, you precious thing. How he would have laughed at that." She waved her hand, and the paralysis lifted. Ammolite blew out her last breath and desperately sucked in a new one.

Marnora's smile suddenly vanished as she saw something over Ammolite's shoulder, and in the next instant, her left eye was gone, in its place a flower of blood. She staggered back, raising her hands, and Ammolite felt a prickling on her own face. Then a second hole appeared in Marnora's forehead. In the same instant, Ammolite felt something blow through her—a wind, a smoke. A thousand sparks flashed in front of her, and all her thoughts seemed to gleam like copper and bronze. Her chest felt tight, and for an instant she knew ecstasy like nothing she had ever known before, making what she had earlier experienced with Hound seem like the mere shadow of pleasure.

Then she was back to herself, watching as Marnora coughed out something that might have been a laugh. Very slowly she sank to her knees, her dress fanning out around her. She put her hands in her lap, rested her chin on her breast, and did not move again.

All was silent.

Then the Tsau Dadan howled. Hound came up from behind her, sling in hand. The creatures regarded him, then backed away.

"Well," he said. "I didn't think that was going to work."

"I didn't either," Ammolite said.

"Who are you?" he asked, looking at the form she had taken. "She's pretty."

"I think this is what she looked like, long ago," Ammolite said. "Marnora."

"She can change shapes, as well?"

"I don't know," she said. "I don't think so. She's something different."

Hound went to Marnora's corpse and started to search it.

"There's no need for that," Ammolite said. "I was wrong. The heart was never something you can hold in your hand. It's something she took, long ago, and I have it now." She looked at the Tsau Dadan. "Lead us out of here," she said. The words seemed strange and familiar, at the same time. "Back outside of the mountain."

They looked at her with anger in their eyes, but one nodded. He croaked what might have been an affirmation.

"You speak their language?" Hound said.

"I do now."

"What about Veulkh?" he asked. "They put him back there."

She thought about that, but not for long. Ammolite didn't know what Marnora had done to the sorcerer. If he was dying, paralyzed, or asleep for eternity, that was one thing. But if the spell on him—like the one Marnora had cast on her—ended with the witch's death, then he might already be coming back to his senses. Likewise, if the Tsau Dadan had merely rendered him insensible with a blow.

Alive and aware, Veulkh might yet be able to defeat Hound and all of the Tsau Dadan, and make her his slave again. As it was, he thought *she* was dead.

Best to leave things that way. For now.

"Leave him," she said. "But we'll take Marnora."

———

AMMOLITE DIDN'T need Hound to lead her from the caves—the Tsau Dadan knew the way. Soon they were back in the light, near the creatures' village.

When the rest of them saw Marnora's corpse, they rejoiced, but as Ammolite spoke to them, the celebration ended abruptly.

"What's going on?" Hound.

"They thought I would free them," she said.

"Won't you? I told them—"

"It doesn't matter what you told them," Ammolite said. "Do you know where we are? Where the nearest town or city is? I know very little of the outside world, and you know nothing of this region. What if we encounter more warriors who wish to make trophies of our heads? If we are to survive long enough to reach safety, we need them, Hound."

Hound caught Knot glaring at him. He shrugged apologetically.

"But we won't be alone," he said. "We'll be with Selene and Martin."

"I can't trust them, and neither can you," Ammolite said. "We can trust only the Tsau Dadan, because they cannot betray me."

"I suppose that's true," Hound said, "but I still have to go see Martin first, to let them know the way in is clear."

"Why?"

He opened his mouth to explain, and then realized she was right. After all this time, he still wasn't sure what their mission was or why it mattered—and he felt pretty sure that, even if they explained the whole thing, he still wouldn't care. It would be this kingdom plotting against that kingdom, or something equally unimportant.

Still, he had stayed with them through a great deal, and although it was tempting to just leave with Ammolite, he was resigned to the fact that he wanted to see things through.

"I have to at least go talk to Martin and Selene."

"I can be either one of them, if that's what you want," she said.

"No," he said. "That's not it. It's just that I told them—".

"You told me, too, Hound. You promised me."

"That was when you needed my help," he said. "You don't anymore."

She frowned, but he couldn't tell if she was angry. Couldn't tell *what* she was feeling.

"I suppose you're right," she said at last. "Do what you want, but I'm leaving this place. Veulkh might still be alive. I won't be his slave again."

"I can kill him for you."

She shook her head. "We were lucky with Marnora. She was old, and confused, and I was able to take advantage of that. Even then, we almost failed. If she had known you were there, we would have failed. Veulkh knows about you. I'm free. I'm not going to take chances. If you go now, when you return, I will be gone."

Hound studied her face. She was serious, and come to it, he didn't blame her at all.

"I'm sorry," he said. "I have to go, but I can track you. I'll catch up with you before you know it."

"If that's what you want."

"They have Rose," Hound said. "Can you ask them to let her go?"

Ammolite nodded.

They had bound and muzzled Rose. She was wounded—gashes from the hyena-bear scored her side, and she favored one of her legs. Once untied, however, she was able to walk.

As they departed, the Tsau Dadan scrambled about, making ready to follow Ammolite's orders.

CHAPTER FIVE

EMELINE

CHRYSANTHE REACHED for the bottle and took it in her fingers. It was larger than the tiny crystal container in which Plesance kept her lacrime of cinnamon.

"Must I drink it?" she asked. "Or dip it on my tongue?"

"You need not drink it," he said. "It is very potent. A few drops on your skin will suffice."

She nodded, then dashed the contents of the bottle into his face.

He gasped, clapping his hands to his eyes, then groaned in pain. She smelled nothing, but felt a sudden burning in her nostrils and threw herself back, away from him, but misjudging so that she rolled from the bed and slammed hard to the floor. She heard him shriek loudly, and floundered desperately to get to her feet.

When she came up to face him, he had a dagger in his hand, and stood between her and the door. His eyes were wild and unfocused. She looked around for something—anything—she could use as a weapon.

"Why?" he asked.

"You never intended to let me live," she said. "You would have found where she hid it, and then I would have been of no use to you."

"She cannot have died in vain," he said. "Don't you understand?"

"Besides that," she said, "I have a murder to prevent, if I still can."

He stumbled toward her, and she leapt back up upon the bed, hoping to dart past him to the door. However, she was still feeble from the lacrime, and her limbs were unwilling to obey her. She fell, and he loomed over her, knife drawn back. She threw up her arms in defense.

His already drunken eyes rolled back in his head, so she could see only the whites.

"Cogwheel," he mumbled. Again Chrysanthe felt the cold, the sense of weight and pressure, but it was not in her—only passing by, like a strange breeze. Severin slumped against the wall, a terrible little smile on his face.

"One last night, Ferrand," he said. "One last night, my love."

It was his voice, but it did not sound like him.

Gathering her wits she ran to the door, unlocked it, and left him lying there.

BY THE time Chrysanthe reached the prince's room, midnight had come and gone. The hall was deserted except for two of his guards, who were playing dice on the floor next to the entrance. They were alert, however, and both were on their feet long before she reached them. To her relief, they were the same men who had been there earlier.

"Well, Danesele," one of them said. "To what do we owe this pleasure?"

She was still having difficulty holding her thoughts together, but she knew what she had to do.

"I have an invitation to meet with the prince."

"As I recall," one of the guards said, "you made a fuss about not keeping your appointment."

"I have had a chance to reflect on the matter," she said. "I should very much like to apologize to His Royal Highness."

The guards looked at one another, and Chrysanthe felt her heart sink. Too much depended on things she did not know. Were these men aware of Emeline? Would the prince be inclined to a visit from a lady at this hour?

"We'll have to search you," one of the men said.

"That's true," the other agreed.

"Search me for what?"

"Daggers, poison, anything that might do harm."

Chrysanthe met his gaze, trying to look bold.

"Very well."

The men were much more thorough than necessary, and much of their "searching" amounted to fondling that took far too long. It was difficult to endure, and she worried that things would only become worse, and their liberties bolder.

"I've only just met the prince," she said. "I do not know him well, but suppose he takes a liking to me? Suppose we become friends?"

The smaller of the two men extricated himself from her clothing and stepped back.

"We were just being sure," he insisted, giving his partner a whack on the shoulder. "His Highness's safety comes ahead of all else."

"I'm certain he will be happy you considered him above all."

They cracked the door open, and let her in.

"Good night, Danesele," the bigger man said.

The tapers had burned down, some almost to guttering, but there was light to see by. She made her way to the bedroom. Emeline looked up as she came in, her eyes reflecting the candlelight. She had drawn the covers to her chin. The prince lay next to her, blanket covering him only to his waist. His eyes were closed.

"What in God's name?" Emeline whispered fiercely.

"Is it done?" Chrysanthe asked.

"What do you think?" Emeline said. "I've been here for hours."

Chrysanthe came closer. "That's not what I mean," she said, very softly. Emeline stared at her for a moment, then glanced at the prince. Her hand came from beneath the covers, a dagger gripped in her fingers.

"Not yet," she said. "Not yet. I have been gathering the nerve."

"He sleeps deeply," Chrysanthe said.

"Yes," Emeline said. "A tincture of lotus mixed with wine."

"Shall we go to another room, just in case?"

Emeline shook her head and moved the blade of the dagger toward his throat.

"How did you know?" Emeline asked. "I told no one of my plans. I had no confederates."

"Yet it was known," Chrysanthe replied. "You must have had correspondence with him."

"Of course," she said. "Now, let me see—in my letters, did I let slip my intention to send him to Hell in his sleep?"

"Probably not," Chrysanthe said. "Is it because of your dancing instructor?"

Her head dropped. "He was not exiled," she said. "That is only what they told me. I learned the truth."

"And if someone knew you well enough, they might guess

what you would do. Provide you the means to do it. Where did you acquire the tincture?"

"I told the lady Ysabel I had trouble sleeping. She happily…" Emeline trailed off. "Yes, I see."

"His life is not worth yours, Emeline."

"I had not intended to get caught," she said. "I planned to slip out before morning. There is a window, and I brought a rope… "

"They must know," she said. "Whoever provided you the opportunity to kill him. They will have made plans to catch you, Emeline. You said someone was trying to ruin you. This will do it; you can be quite certain."

"I do not care," Emeline said. "I will have my revenge. Then I will depart this life and wait in limbo with my beloved Remon."

Her hand moved.

"*Wait,*" Chrysanthe said. "You could have killed him an hour ago. Why did you delay?"

She sighed. "He's not so bad," she said. "That's the problem. He was very gentle and considerate. He may actually love me."

"Did he kill Remon himself?"

"I doubt it."

"Did he even know the deed was done?"

"I thought about that, too," Emeline said. "Maybe not. It might have been my father who arranged Remon's murder. That would be his way. It is possible Heron knew nothing of it."

"Give me the dagger, Emeline," she said. "Let me be your friend. Morning will come, the prince will be alive, and all their plans will be for naught. If you really must kill him, do it at another time, in another place. One which has not been designed to undo you. You will have other opportunities."

"Perhaps," Emeline said. Her eyes were wet with tears. "You *are* trying to help me, aren't you?"

"I am," Chrysanthe said.

"And if I kill him now, with you here, perhaps you will be blamed. The guards must have seen you come in."

Chrysanthe felt cold. "Yes," she said. "That might work."

For a long time, Emeline didn't say or do anything, but Chrysanthe could see that behind her eyes, the girl's mind was quite busy. Then she smiled, very faintly, and handed Chrysanthe the blade, handle first.

"As you said," she whispered. "There will be other opportunities. Tonight—this is all too complicated."

"Thank you," Chrysanthe said. She took the weapon, hid it beneath her skirt, and left the room.

"So quick?" the smaller guard said.

"He was sleeping too peacefully," she returned. "I did not wish to disturb him."

"Is that what they're calling it, now?" Bigger said. Despite everything that had happened that night, she still blushed.

Down the hall she felt less triumphant. If the guards talked, her reputation was done. And what if Emeline had another knife, or smothered the prince with a pillow? Could she trust the girl?

She could not. Besides, there was Severin, who might eventually recover from whatever delirium the lacrime had sent him into. She might not have much time.

She had to discover the secret d'Ospios was hiding.

Immediately, while she was still able.

CHAPTER SIX

WORMS OF
THE EARTH

MARTIN AND Selene listened to Hound's story without asking any questions. It wasn't a strictly true account. In Hound's version, Veulkh's companion, Orra, was slain by Marnora, who then departed with the Tsau Dadan, for reasons he did not know. Hound couldn't think of any reason anyone should know about Ammolite, or her abilities, or what had really become of her. This was especially true if Veulkh was still alive.

Martin stirred the coals of the fire. "So you don't know if Veulkh is alive or dead," he said.

"No," Hound replied. "I thought we would find out together."

"He has to be alive," Selene said. "If not, then everything has been for nothing. We will have failed."

"The way in is no longer guarded," Hound said. "It should be easy."

That was true. The Tsau Dadan were gone, their treehouses abandoned. He wondered how far Ammolite had traveled by now. It had not been a full day since she left.

The chevaliers left their horses outside, and several men to tend them, and then the rest went into the mountain. When they reached the first chamber, Kos and his ravens were there to greet them.

"Veulkh said you would come," Kos said. "He awaits you."

The sorcerer was indeed waiting for them, most specifically for Hound, whom he took alone to the grand dining chamber.

"You saw her kill Orra?" he asked, pointedly.

"Yes," Hound lied.

"And then she left. Why would she do that?"

"Because I hurt her," Hound replied. "I hit her with a sling stone. Her apes carried her off, and when I went out, they were all gone."

"You must have hurt her very badly," Veulkh said. "Or else it was some trick of hers."

"Maybe she died," Hound said.

Veulkh made a rough sound in his throat.

"She does not die easily," he said. "She has used many bodies, through the years. When one dies, she always has another prepared, usually far away, so that whatever killed her will not be close."

"She can move from one body to another?"

Veulkh frowned, as if realizing he had said too much. Hound wondered if the body Veulkh now wore was his original form. He didn't look very old, but Ammolite had revealed that his age numbered in centuries.

"It doesn't matter," Veulkh said. "What has happened has happened. I will mourn her, as I have mourned many others."

"Orra?" Hound asked.

"Both of them," Veulkh replied. He rubbed his head. "There is nothing stopping me now. I will do this damned thing for the Cryptarchia and be quit of this business. Tell Martin I need four days.

Tell him I am not to be disturbed. Perhaps you can use your time making certain that Marnora is really gone, or dead. If she remains, she can certainly still spoil our plans."

HOUND DIDN'T like the inside of the mountain, so he took to spending most of his time outside. He hunted, rested, and took care of Rose, who walked with a distinct limp but grew stronger each day.

The earth shook more than ever. Several times he climbed the mountain to its summit, and sat there with a view of the steaming lake on the one side and the long march of mountains on the other. His earlier impressions kept returning to him; the tunnel with ribs, the thing at Sular Bulan, the snake that killed the chevalier, the shaking of the earth. To his eye, the mountains seemed almost like the spine of a gigantic snake. He thought about the bodies of dead animals, the worms that infested and burrowed through their rotting flesh. Was the world the same way? All burrowed through by strange serpents?

The sky was changeable from one heartbeat to the next. The surface of the Earth altered more slowly, he mused, but noticeably even over a handful of years. Forests burned, then greened into meadow. Trees came again, shading out the grass and bushes, and meadow became forest again. A river could change course after a big flood—not a lot, but noticeably.

Hound had always imagined that the depths of the world—the hard parts of it, anyway, the stone beneath the soil, the mountains—were eternal. Now he saw that it, too, was always changing. He remembered things now that Grandmother had said, little hints she had dropped, just rambling in her way. How had the world looked when she was young? If she had ever been young. Had the mountains grown up like trees?

Several of the distant peaks he saw were smoking—some just a little, and others belching forth black clouds within which he could sometimes see fire. They looked pretty much the same as the mountain on which he was sitting. What if it started to make smoke and spit fire? Wouldn't Veulkh, Martin, Selene, and the chevaliers be burned up?

Wouldn't he, if he was sitting on the rim?

After that, he didn't rest on the edge of the mountain.

AFTER FOUR days, Selene came looking for him. He heard her calling below, and found her near the opening of the cave. The earth was shaking near constantly now, and more steam than usual seemed to be coming off the lake.

She smiled when she saw him.

"Hound," she said. "Always so quiet." She seemed nervous, somehow, fidgety. Kept glancing back, as if worried someone might be behind her.

"What's wrong?" he asked.

"Nothing," she said. "At least nothing for you to worry about, but I think—Hound, it's time for you to go."

"Go where?" he asked.

"Away."

He studied her expression.

"Martin doesn't know you're here now, does he?"

"He doesn't." She shook her head. "He wants… it doesn't matter. You've done enough for us, Hound. More than we should have asked."

"What about my reward?"

"I have nothing to give you," she said.

"That's not true," he said.

She flushed darker. "Hound, my vows—"

"You're in love with Martin," he said.

She cocked her head. "Well, I don't suppose that was too hard to put together," she said. "But even if I wasn't, it still wouldn't matter. Hound, I'm giving you the only thing I can. Take it."

"Something's about to happen," he said. "What?"

"Don't ask me that again," she said. "Just go. Please." Then she left. He watched her vanish into the mountain.

Beneath his feet, the stone shivered.

CHAPTER SEVEN

THE BRIDGE

CHRYSANTHE STOPPED in her rooms long enough to gather a few necessary things, principally her bodkin. She checked to make certain her father's silver box was still safe in the hidden pocket of her undergarments and then slipped out the window, hanging by her fingers from the sill and then dropping the remaining distance. The fall was farther than she thought, and her weight drove her to the ground. She lay there for a few moments, gathering her strength and hoping nothing was broken.

The night seemed peaceful, the air a little cool. Stars gleamed here and there through a ragged tissue of clouds as Chrysanthe climbed first to her knees, and then to her feet. She got her bearings as best she could in the fitful light and then started out, cutting northwest across the grounds, winding her way through hedges, leaping over small brooks.

Nothing seemed real, and more than once she wondered if she was moving through a dream—but then a thorn pricked her toe through the thin dancing shoes, and her body brought her back to reality.

Even so, it was difficult to keep her mind on task, to forget about what tomorrow might bring. In the course of a single night, almost every hope and comfort had deserted her. Her mother had been right, and so had Bonaventure. She could almost imagine the two of them on a couch someplace, talking about how they had warned her, as Bonaventure pulled her mother ever closer, offering her a bottle of wine and a lewd wink.

Emeline was not her friend, but her purpose in pretending was now easy to see. Quintent's motives in feigning friendship were still unknown—perhaps he was in on the plotting, or maybe he was like Plesance—merely cruel, but better at hiding it, delighting in the deception.

She had no one left. Once she had believed herself to be self-reliant, but now she knew that to be false. Whatever she had done, whatever trouble she found herself in, her family had always been there, ready to help. Now she was truly alone, with no one to rely upon. Her courage felt thin, as if only habit carried her forward, instead of courage.

She came to a wall a bit higher than she was tall, and followed it until she came to an apple tree that allowed her to climb over it. Beyond stretched a hunting park of wide-spaced trees and very little underbrush. It was dark, and the leaves blotted what little light came from the sky. She was forced to pause and unshutter her lantern, pouring light out in a reassuring pool around her, but also making the night darker beyond its limited circle.

By the time she reached the old road, she was convinced the eastern sky had started to brighten a little. A wind began to bend the trees, and the warm air seemed damp, as if rain might be coming.

Before long, the road was bounded by old buildings. Most had been built of wood and were in various stages of deliquescence. A few had stone foundations, and one or two had once been of some size.

Sure enough, she soon reached the bridge. It should have been a triumph, but by then, she had become pessimistic. The evidence was so slight, her leaps of logic so large—and luck had run so hard against her tonight. Maybe she was hunting a deer with a feather.

She stepped onto the bridge, and her doubts began to fade.

The river may have shifted its course, but there was still water beneath the span. The stream had left behind a black water lake, the sort known as a "dead arm" because it was now cut off from the living stream, and because it somewhat resembled a half-bent limb. She examined the still water, which was a mirror for the waxing light in the sky. She remembered the letter then, the mention of swimming in the "tolatolil." D'Ospios had simply translated "dead arm" into Modjali.

Tola, "dead" and tolil "arm".

The old bridge was of stone and supported by three arches, all crusted in moss and lichen. It was built wide and had been a market bridge, so funny, narrow buildings had been constructed along either side. These, like the houses she had already seen, were falling apart, but on either end of the span stood structures of stone which must have once served as gatehouses, or perhaps even guildhalls.

In the middle, just above the keystone of the central arch, stood a small stone chapel dedicated to Themis.

D'Ospios was no longer in her head, but if she let her mind drift, some of the dead woman's memories came. She followed them to one of the gatehouses, and stairs within that went down into the footings of the bridge. Those dug into the bank itself, and there she found a room, plain and empty, long ago looted of anything valuable. For a moment she stood there, puzzled, but then she went to the western wall, where she pressed first in, then to the side.

A panel moved and revealed another room.

It was not large; a small window slit let in light and air, which must have shown Severin, or d'Ospios, or someone they knew the way into this hidden place.

A bed of sorts had been made on the floor, a mattress stuffed with batting and thrown over with brocade coverlets, linen sheets, and pillows in fantastical patterns. Paper lanterns hung on colorful cords, and books of poetry were piled neatly near the bed. A vase near the window contained flowers no more than a few days old.

"The nest," d'Ospios had called it in her Modjali code. Here they had met, made love, drunk wine, read books to one another. Their secret place. And here she had died, to lie sunken in the deep, stagnant waters of the dead arm of the Cendel river.

But Chrysanthe had not just come to find the nest.

She did not believe that Severin had murdered d'Ospios. Whoever it was had probably rifled the nest. Afterward Severin came, searched, and tidied the place up to serve as a morbid memorial—the flowers suggested that he had been here recently.

What she was looking for would not be any place obvious, but she checked anyway. Underneath the bed, among the books. She felt within the mattress and pillows, and as she expected, discovered nothing. She searched for loose stones on the floor and in the walls, but that was just as fruitless.

She knew it was here. When possessed by the spirit of d'Ospios, she had known it was hidden in the valugudil, which she was sure meant "love nest." But d'Ospios liked words, didn't she? And when Chrysanthe had first tried to parse out the meaning of valugudil, there had been other possible translations.

Suddenly she understood. She left the nest and climbed back up to the bridge, to the little enclosure above the middle arch, dedicated to Themis. It was very simply made—the front was open, and it was shallow, only large enough for one person to enter. Inside stood a small altar for candles. An image of Themis was carved in bas relief on the back wall.

Stepping in, she made a sign to Themis and whispered three of her names. Then she knelt and pushed at the top of the stone altar. It moved easily.

Beneath it was a hollow.

In the hollow, a book.

Valugudil could mean "love nest," but it could also mean "stone chapel."

Removing the book, she replaced the stone lid, set the tome upon it, and opened the cover. It was, as she had suspected, an accounting book—no more and no less. She had wondered what secret it might hold that people had killed and died for it, and how subtle a secret that might be. Some small thing in the numbers that might take her a long time to unravel.

That wasn't the case.

She understood within moments of gazing at the crabbed handwriting what Severin and the d'Othres had striven so hard to keep concealed. It took longer to comprehend what it *meant*, and even when that understanding came, she first tried to deny it.

"So it was there all along," someone said behind her. "How vexing, and how unfortunate for you."

Chrysanthe turned. The speaker was still some distance away, but even through the heat of shock she knew who it was.

"Hello, Margot," she said. "Have you come to try and kiss me again?"

Margot stood a few dozen feet away. She was dressed in breeches, vest, and coat, and a thin sword dangled from her belt. A broad-brimmed hat was pulled low on her head.

"I must apologize for that," Margot said. "It was the only way I could think of to throw you off the track. Although I would not have minded if I had been successful."

"You searched my room. You and your confederate in a brown coat. Lucien, perhaps? You took the journal."

"Oh, but I did fool you, didn't I?"

"Yes," Chrysanthe admitted.

"You've done very well, otherwise. I wasn't able to figure out that damned journal. Bonaventure sent you, didn't he? Just as he sent d'Ospios."

"I know no Bonaventure," Chrysanthe said, determined to give away as little as possible. She saw then that Margot was not alone. Two more figures stood at the east end of the bridge.

She looked the other way. The west end of the bridge was still open.

"Chrysanthe," Margot said, "You must listen to me. You have seen the ledger. I do not flatter you when I assume you understand what it means. I like you quite a lot, but—how to put this?—you will not live out your natural days. Yet you can live a bit longer. I erred in killing Sandrine when I did, and I do not wish to make the same mistake with you. You can come with me now, and answer some questions truthfully, then slip from this world painlessly. Or you can spend your remaining days in agony. I really advise the former."

Chrysanthe stepped away from the book, onto the bridge. Margot, still a few yards away, drew her sword.

"Don't," she said.

Chrysanthe turned and ran. Behind her, she heard Margot curse in a most unladylike fashion.

"That's useless," the woman shouted after her. "There's nowhere to go."

Chrysanthe already knew that. What Margot did not know was that she had no intention of leaving the bridge. She no longer needed the book—even if Margot hadn't come along, there was no one she could trust to do what was needed. Her father must have known that all along. Because Margot didn't understand what she was up to, she was slow to give chase.

That gave Chrysanthe time to run back down the stairs into the nest, close the panel behind her, and throw fast the bolts that locked it. Then she shucked the gown over her head and took the little box her father had given her from the pocket in her under-skirt. She carefully unlatched it, opening the lid.

Someone thumped on the door panel. A muffled voice advised her that she was trapped, and she ignored it.

The small tin contained brownish powder. The strigas. There was also a lock of hair.

Chrysanthe brought the tin to her nose, as her father had instructed, and inhaled. At first it smelled like nothing, but just as the lacrime of cinnamon had bloomed on her tongue, this took fire inside of her skull. It was as if every flower in the world gave up its perfume all at once, and she was jolted by joy so sudden and complete that every other sensation she had ever known seemed listless, gray, incomplete.

It was if she was standing in a warm, strong wind, her hair streaming. The walls, the floor, the window, the very air itself began to shimmer with better-than-real colors. In her hand, the lock of hair began to writhe and burn, to stretch out into the infinite sky-beyond-the sky, drawing her along behind it. Her bones all pulled apart and joined in a chain, a wire, a crack in the air growing thinner, longer, more aware each second.

The huge, slow thoughts of God surrounded her like the sound of basilica bells, and everything seemed to stop. She was inside the stone of the room, inside of Margot and her men. She could feel their beating hearts, the feverish cackling of their thoughts.

And she could feel—another.

Far away, across water and land and the course of the sun and moon. At first the other did not know her, but after a moment it was as if she awoke from a dream, as if their fingers locked together, their tongues mingled, and a voice came forth. Her voice. She said what she needed to say, even as everything began to slip away, as the colors faded, and agony exploded in her chest.

Chrysanthe wasn't done. Margot and the men were still there, although they, too, were slipping from her. If she could command them, if she could do something to them…

The wind in her head became a hurricane, and all the beauty went out like an extinguished flame. Everything ended, and she felt the greatest despair she had ever known. God shut her out, was done with her.

Nothing could ever be the same.

THE DAY after Renost left, Crespin walked out to the farthest edge of the curving harbor and sat on the ancient tide-wall, gazing out at the breakers foaming against the treacherous reef to the south. He closed his eyes and conjured home—his mother, Chrysanthe,

Phoebe, his brothers, the fever trees along the banks of the Laham River. Renost.

Try as he might, the present kept pulling him back, even with his vision shadowed by his eyelids. The cries of the gulls were familiar enough, but the Salamandra Coast had seabirds in an astonishing variety, many of which he had never seen before. They gave voice to a chorus very alien to his ears.

A stone's throw along the away, a work gang of former Drehhu slaves labored under a Mesembrian supervisor, clearing a drainage channel, chanting a work song. The rhythm was not so different from what the Tamanja laborers in Mesembria might sing, but the tune was very strange, leaping about in bizarre intervals, and although he had heard many languages in his short life, none had ever sounded so peculiar.

The air itself smelled wrong—metallic and yet perfumed with odd, cloying nectars.

And then the earth itself moved.

It began as an odd sliding in the stone beneath him. The light seemed suddenly weird—brighter than it had been a moment before, yellower. In the next instant the world itself lurched, a movement somehow both small and indescribably large, as if he were a flea on a sleeping elephant that had shifted. In the distance he heard someone scream, and then a chorus of shouting from seemingly everywhere. Dust came out of every window and door of the fortress, as if it were exhaling.

Oddly, the work gang of Drehhu slaves he'd been watching seemed unperturbed.

It seemed to go on for a long time, though in reality it might have only been a few heartbeats. When the ground felt solid again beneath his feet, he dropped down from the wall and walked over to the slaves.

"You there," he said to the foreman, a navior from one of the warships that had captured the fortress.

"Sir," the man said, standing.

"Do any of them speak our language?"

"No sir," the foreman said. "I was long in Boloy, though, so I speak a bit of theirs. It's why I pulled this duty."

"Ask them what just happened."

The man sputtered out what sounded like mostly sibilants, after which one of the slaves replied. Two others interjected now and then. The foreman turned back to Crespin.

"They say it's a common thing," he replied. "I've heard the same from the fellows who have been here a while."

One of the slaves pointed and said something else.

"Oh, I see," the man said. "It's the volcanoes, sir. They make the earth shake."

Crespin followed the man's pointing finger. In the distance, a column of black smoke churned skyward to join the gray lens that had obscured the eastern skies for days. He remembered again the map of the Salamandra, dozens of mountains drawn with smoke pouring from them.

"This is a common occurrence?"

When they heard the question translated, the slaves nodded, but one of them, an older man, said something more, and there was a brief argument.

"What are they on about?" he asked.

"He says that last shaking felt different to him. The others are calling him a crazy old man."

Crespin wondered if he should speak to his father, but then remembered that the admiral had gone reconnoitering on the

Daulphin, a naval ship whose captain had died in the fight at Basilisk. Instead, he walked back to the fortress.

On the way, the earth trembled again, just a very little this time, but as he entered the inner wall, the shaking came yet again, so violently that he almost lost his footing. There was a grinding, cracking sound: he looked up in time to see part of the upper fortress, carved into the living stone, break and fall in a small avalanche.

He watched, scalp tingling, as the dust rose.

Someone said his name.

It was so quiet he was surprised he heard it at all, and at first he thought it had been whispered it in his ear. When he turned to look, no one was there. He took a deep breath to calm his nerves; clearly, he was becoming a little unhinged.

He started to take a step, when he heard it again.

This time it filled his head. He began walking, then jogging, then ran as fast as he could, his heart racing. Into the fortress, to the makeshift hospital. Everything to the sides of him darkened, while the way ahead shone with perfect clarity.

Brushing past a guard, he ignored whatever the man said, pushing through a door and into a room. It was small, with white walls, yet dark because drapes covered the windows. She lay there on a single bed, gazing listlessly at him as he entered.

"Chrysanthe!" he gasped. Impossible.

It was impossible, and yet his sister was there.

Chrysanthe nodded weakly. "Our father?"

"He's exercising the *Daulphin* up the coast," Crespin said. He dropped down by her bedside and took her hand. "How are you here?"

"Hush," she said. "Listen. She needs to tell you something. Listen."

"Yes," Crespin said. "I'm listening." But it was confusing. Who did Chrysanthe mean by "she?"

"You have been betrayed. All of you. The emperor. Velesa. Modjal. You are all meant to die here."

"I don't understand."

"There is no time. You must sail. Take the fleet as far from Basilisk as you can, and do it now."

"Chrysanthe?"

Gold was leaking from her nose, from the corners of her mouth and eyes.

"Chrysanthe!" he screamed. But then he was no longer holding his sister's hand, and she was no longer in the bed. It was, instead, Calliope who lay there. Her eyes were open, but when she moved her mouth, no sound came out.

He stayed there for a moment, by the bed, not sure what had happened. Then he turned and found the guard, a young ensign, watching him.

"Sir?" the young man said.

Crespin let go of Calliope's hand and stood.

"Fetch a surgeon," he said. "Have him accompany her to the *Leucothea* and tell them to make ready to sail immediately. The entire fleet. Everyone."

"Sir, the admiral…"

"He is not here," Crespin said. "I am assuming command. If I am at fault, I will take the consequences."

The young man nodded and turned to go, but then he stopped and made a peculiar sound. Hector was there, on the other side of him, standing in his way. Something was sticking from the ensign's back, something long and red…

Hector withdrew his sword. The marinier fell at his feet. The surgeon looked at the dying boy and shrugged.

"He wouldn't have lived much longer anyway," Hector said. Then he lunged forward, thrusting the point of his weapon at Crespin. Still stunned, Crespin was a little slow dodging aside, and the weapon stabbed him in the side, stopping on a rib. He yelped and drew his own weapon.

"What are you doing?" he demanded as Hector came after him. He tried to parry the surgeon's next thrust, but it hit him on his off-weapon arm.

"My duty," Hector replied. "I'm sorry. If I thought I could trust you, I would let you live." He attacked again, and this time Crespin managed to stop his blade and reply with his saber, but Hector was no longer there for the cut to land.

Crespin tried to back away, to put a little more space between them. Hector had an espey, a long needle-like sword made for thrusting. They weren't usually used by naviors because they were impractical in battle, but as a dueling weapon they could be grimly efficient in the hands of the right person. Crespin hadn't had much practice using his edged weapon against such swords, and Hector was a master.

Add to that the fact that he was still weak from his earlier injuries, and had already been twice stuck. Now his back was literally against the wall.

"Will you at least tell me why?"

"No," Hector replied.

"That's just as well then," Renost said as he bolted through the door. Hector almost managed to turn, but Renost's cut hit him in the neck, and the surgeon fell, blood spraying. Renost stabbed him in the back, kicked him over, and stabbed him again.

"I think that will do, Renost," Crespin said.

"You're welcome."

"I thought you sailed with the *Tethys*."

"I changed my mind," he said.

"And after such a pretty speech."

Renost shrugged. He nodded at the body of their former companion.

"Why did I just kill Hector?"

"I don't have time to explain, but we need to sail, now. All of us. Take Calliope to the *Leucothea*. If my father can be reached by lucnograph, inform him of my decision. I will meet you on the ship."

"Where are you going?"

"I have something else to do."

CHAPTER EIGHT

ASHES

HOUND WATCHED the sun move a quarter of its journey across the sky before he gave up and followed Selene back into the mountain. He was certain her advice was well-intentioned, but curiosity was driving him mad. He had also become attached to Selene and Martin, and could not brush off the suspicion that they still needed his help.

He was the best part of the way to his destination when the stone beneath him quaked so hard he fell to his hands and knees. An instant later a hot wind blew down through the tunnel, accompanied by a sound so low he heard it in his bones, rather than his ears.

Then, everything was still.

Without knowing exactly why, he got up and began to run.

MOST OF them were already dead when he got there, ravens and chevaliers mingling their blood on the concave stone. Martin was still alive, his fists striking at four ravens so rapidly that it seemed to occur all at once. Kos and Ariston were engaged in a fierce sword battle, the chevalier bearing a shield and heavy blade, the raven moving a bit more nimbly with a lighter weapon flashing in the bloody light.

To his relief he saw Selene, backed against a wall, nimbused in yellow. A few feet from her, enclosed in her golden cloud, Veulkh was frozen in the act of rising from one knee, a fist on the stone. His eyes were terrifying, red as blood and shining like lamps, black smoke pouring from his mouth. All his hair was gone, and his naked head gleamed in the firelight. Two chevaliers and four of their men lay in a rough ring around him, blackened, vapor rising from their corpses.

Hound didn't know who started the fight, nor did he care. He knew which side he was on. Taking a stone from his bag, he loaded it into his sling. Before he could finish, however, he saw Kos and Ariston come together. When they parted, Ariston took three steps and collapsed, headless. Kos turned and charged toward Martin, who had just knocked one of his opponents to the floor.

Hound whirled his sling and let loose at Veulkh. It was a fair cast, and he knew it should have hit, but nothing happened, so he raced forward, choosing another projectile as Martin savaged the last of the ravens attacking him. Kos was on him by then, and the two came together in a blur. Kos went staggering back, and Hound saw he no longer had his weapon.

Then Hound saw why. It was stuck in Martin, piercing his thigh.

Kos came back toward Martin, a dagger in his hand.

Hound was close to Veulkh now, far too close to miss. He whirled his sling. Then he saw that the sorcerer had his burning gaze fixed on him.

As he flung the stone, he heard a clap like thunder, right in his ear, and something hit him hard, knocking him backward off his feet. The wind blew out of him, and he landed roughly, but he scrambled back to his feet, drawing his tomahawk.

Veulkh was now standing, and before Hound could take another step, Selene crumpled to the floor. Despite the sword in his leg, Martin spun aside from Kos's attack and hit him with the back of his fist. From where Hound stood, the blow didn't look all that hard, but he saw a spray of blood and teeth, and Kos crumpled.

Hound ran at Veulkh, just as Martin turned on the sorcerer.

Then Veulkh shouted.

It sounded like a word, but it was more than that. Suddenly Hound felt impossibly heavy. His knees buckled, and he fell to the floor. Struggling to raise his head, he saw Martin still standing, legs bent, a look of furious determination on his face. Veulkh took a few steps toward him, raised his hand, and closed his fist.

Martin went down to one knee.

Veulkh stood there for a moment.

"I did what you asked," the sorcerer said. "It is done. Now you have slain my guards. Why?"

Martin managed to raise his head. He opened his mouth as if to speak, but instead he yelled and leapt forward.

He didn't make it. He slammed to the floor with the sound of someone who had fallen a hundred feet, instead of four.

Then Veulkh turned toward Hound.

"And you, Hound. What business have you siding with these? You have no kinship with them." He began walking forward, slowly. His eyes had returned to normal, he was limping, and his lips were red with blood. He was panting as if he had run for miles, but Hound could still feel his power and he knew he was at the sorcerer's mercy.

Hound himself was a little unclear on the concept of mercy, and he strongly suspected Veulkh had no truck with it at all.

"Veulkh."

The sorcerer turned. Hound painfully twisted his head. A woman was approaching them, a very familiar woman.

"Orra?" Veulkh said. "I thought…"

"I am well," the woman said. "There is nothing to worry about."

"I kept my part of the bargain." Veulkh swept his arms around, motioning at the corpses in the room.

"I know," she replied. "I know, my love, but you are safe, and now we can leave."

Veulkh looked puzzled. "Ammolite?"

"Orra," the woman said. "Only Orra now."

He nodded. "I am tired," he said.

She opened her arms, and he stepped into them.

Hound saw the knife the instant before she buried it in his back.

Then the air itself seemed to explode.

CRESPIN WAS with the lucnograph operator when the mariniers began shouting that the admiral was boarding. Crespin made certain his message was in order, put on his hat, and went to meet his father in the mess.

This time there was no coffee. His father did not sit.

"Explain yourself," he said. "What is happening? Why is my fleet preparing to sail? Why are the Velesans and Modjalis back on their ships?"

"I released them and gave them their parole."

"On what authority?"

"My own," he shot back. "You took me from the Navy. You made me second on your ship. You weren't here. I made a decision."

"Based on what?"

"The strixe has advised that we clear out of here."

"The strixe?"

"Yes. *Your* strixe. Calliope."

"You go too far," his father said.

"Really? Do I?"

"Crespin—"

"Never mind," Crespin said. "That was stupid of me. Just listen for a moment. I'm certain you will think I am mad, but I assure you, I have never been so certain of anything in my life." For an instant he thought he saw something, an unguarded expression on his father's face. It did not last long.

"Chrysanthe?" he said, softly. "You heard from Chrysanthe?"

Crespin felt suddenly very cold. "Wait," he said.

"Tell me," his father said. "What did she say?"

"You knew?"

"Tell me!"

For a moment, shock stopped Crespin from speaking. He had never heard his father raise his voice like that.

"What did you do to my sister?" he said. "What is happening?"

The admiral closed his eyes, took a long breath, and opened them.

"Tell me," he said.

So Crespin told him, and was not surprised that his father showed no skepticism. The admiral listened to him without comment until he was done.

"Have you contacted the war fleet?" he asked.

"Calliope is in no condition to communicate," Crespin replied, "even if she was inclined to break Cryptarchia rules. I have sent word by lucnograph relay. I can only hope it reaches them in time."

"The Velesans? The Modjali?"

"I warned them as best I could. If they can convince their strixes to break their vows, I suppose they might warn their people."

For a long moment, his father said nothing.

"You understand what you've done?" he finally said.

"I understand that it is possible I will be charged with treason, if that is what you are asking," Crespin replied.

"I understand giving alarm to our own fleet," his father said, "but why did you inform the others?"

Crespin met his father's gaze squarely, and for the first time in his life, he didn't feel even the slightest urge to flinch.

"Because I know you," Crespin said. "You would not have abandoned them to die. If I had not warned them, you would have, and it would be you standing trial for treason."

Outside, a chorus of shouts went up. The admiral turned and went on deck. The ships were nearly ready. In the east, the sky was as black as soot, although overhead the sun still shone in a blue sky. Crespin noticed that small, gray-white flakes were drifting down from above.

"Snow?" he asked.

He caught one of them on his finger. It was not cold, and when he rubbed it turned into a light smear.

"Ash," his father said. "It is ash."

"Admiral."

One the nurses had just come up from below, one who had been assigned to Calliope.

"Nurse."

"She wants to speak to you," the nurse said. "Immediately."

His father's face didn't change, but he nodded.

"I shall then," he said. "Crespin, the ship is yours."

CHAPTER NINE

ANOTHER HEART

AMMOLITE FELT the knife go in. She wasn't sure how she had expected it to feel. His flesh resisted a little, but then the point slipped through, like pushing the blade into butter. Veulkh's grip on her tightened, and he gasped, almost the way he did in the throes of passion, and she wondered if this was what it felt like when he pushed himself into her.

Around them, the cave seemed to be shaking apart, but where they stood, everything was strangely still.

She tried to pull the blade out, so she could stab him again, but it stuck. He kept holding on to her, his eyes wild.

"What?" he demanded. "What? Orra…"

She let Orra go and became Ammolite.

"It was always me," she said. "Why didn't you tell me?"

"Orra," he said.

"Ammolite!" she shrieked. "*Ammolite!*"

His eyes were like glass. He let go of her long enough to knot one hand in her hair and pull her head back.

"I was good to you," he said. "Wasn't I good to you?"

"I left," she said. "I was gone, but I need you to die. I came back to kill you. That's how good you were to me. That's how much I love you."

He coughed, and blood spilled from his mouth.

"Oh, Veulkh," she moaned in false ecstasy. "I love you so. Take me now. Make me yours!"

"Shut up," he snarled.

"You're pathetic," she said. "You're nothing. *It was always me!*"

"Shut up!" he shrieked, and he took her throat in both hands. Pulled her close. She couldn't breathe.

Her hands found the knife-hilt. This time, perhaps lubricated by blood, the blade pulled out easily. She thrust it in again. He fell, but he took her with him to the floor. She tried to stab him a third time, but the angle made it difficult. Then his grip loosened, and she was able to sit up and pull the knife around.

"Orra—"

"Hush," she said, and she pulled the blade across his throat, watching almost curiously as it yawned open like a great, red smile. She watched his breathing end, and his eyes go still, and in that instant, she saw it: the synapsis he'd made for himself, the key to his power. Like Marnora's key to controlling the Tsau Dadan, it was not a physical thing, but a part of him, like a tumor in his brain.

She took it.

Then she went to see if Hound was still alive.

The chamber was quiet now, but quickly becoming hotter.

———

CRESPIN WAS below decks when it happened. The wind was against them; they had been sailing as near to it as their rigging allowed. Some ships accomplished this better than others, and the fleet was drawn out over more than a league of ocean.

There were shouts from above, and he ran up to see what the matter was. The coastline of the Salamandra was no longer visible, although Crespin knew it was still nearby.

The darkness in the eastern sky was overwhelmed by a black cloud, expanding with such unbelievable speed it seemed like a trick of the eye. At this distance, it was impossible to tell how big it really was, but it felt somehow gigantic.

And then Crespin heard the sky break.

It resembled a sound as a zephyr resembled a hurricane. He heard it not only with his ears, but with his face, his flesh, his very bones. Everything around him suddenly became a strange language he could not interpret: the mariniers moving frantically but without purpose; the sudden tautness of the sails; the immense, boiling darkness that was the whole of the eastern horizon, mounting up to fall upon them. His father's mouth was moving, but no words came out.

Nothing remained but the endless ringing of God's great bell.

Then something else unseen hit the ship, and he was off his feet, flying, slamming into the deck, all the air punched out of him. Retching, gasping, he fought back upright. His father was a few feet away, lying on the deck. His head was bloody and his eyes were closed. A little further away, Renost clambered to his feet, pointing, shouting soundlessly.

Crespin's first instinct was to go to the admiral, but he followed Renost's gesture. The cloud had reached upward beyond sight now, but on the near horizon, something else was happening.

It resembled a wave, but it was the color of charcoal and moved more like an avalanche. At first, he thought it wasn't that big, but then his mind took in the distance.

It was immense and growing with each instant.

For a few heartbeats, all he could do was stare, but then he thought he understood. He began to yell at the helmsman, but couldn't even hear himself shouting, so he stumbled to the wheel and took it from the surprised man. Renost looked at him, puzzled, and Crespin gestured, nearly due west, straight into the wind.

"Run!" he bellowed soundlessly.

For a moment Renost didn't understand, but then he went among the crew, grabbing them, shaking them from their stupors and telling them by gestures what they had to do—put their stern directly at the black wave, as if they were running before a storm.

As Crespin made the turn, their speed dropped off to nothing, and after a moment he saw that the sails were filled, pushing them the wrong way, back toward the terror that was coming for them.

He glanced at his father again; the older man lay still, and Crespin saw blood on his lips. He wanted more than anything to rouse him, to have the admiral tell him he was doing the right thing—and if not, to tell him what he *should* do. There was no time. If he was wrong, they would all die together. If he was right, they might anyway.

The wave came. There was still no sound except the tintinnabulation within his skull. The sky overhead remained eerily blue.

It wasn't a wave, he understood, but a cloud, a churning, demonic smoke moving faster than anything natural. All over the ship, the men stopped to watch. The *Leucothea* was turned, the sails were ready. There was nothing more they could do.

In the distance, Crespin saw the winking of lucnographs from the furthest ships. One by one they went out, and then the wind came.

Everything began to break.

CHRYSANTHE WAS never certain when she truly woke. The visions stayed with her for a long time. They frayed at the edges, then pulled apart like rotting drapes, to become a gray dust that settled all around her. Followed finally by darkness.

It was in this darkness she finally decided that she must be awake. Or perhaps dead. To be sure, she did not care. She had been touched by perfection, by the blessing of the bright world beyond the limbo that encircled the mundane world, and now that was withdrawn. Whether this was some dark place in the realm of flesh or the limbo that followed death, she knew there was no going back.

When the light finally did come, she did not rejoice. She shut her eyes against it, because it hurt. The food and drink she was offered tasted like nothing, but she did take it. Her body, it seemed, still clung to some illusion of life.

They lifted her up and forced her to walk on legs she could hardly feel. Just as she thought they would give out, someone pushed her down into a chair.

"You must open your eyes now," someone said. "Or I shall be forced to cut off your eyelids." She weighed the threat without fear, but eventually did what she was told.

Margot was there, still in men's garb, although her hair was let down. They were in a parlor with large, bright windows. Across the room she made out the blurred outlines of another woman wearing a deep blue gown, sitting behind a small table. Several equally unclear figures wore dark clothes and bore swords, so she took them to be guards. The faint scent of roses drifted in on a breeze from the window.

"You said you would kill me," Chrysanthe said.

"I did say that," Margot said, "and eventually, I'm afraid I must. But you did something. With the powder in your little box. The strigas. I must know what."

"If I tell you, will you kill me?"

"Is that what you want?"

"I do not care," Chrysanthe replied.

"That is the aftermath of the strigas," Margot said. "You will feel better… eventually. Better, but from what I understand, always a little less than you were. But you know, I can probably get you more, which will make you feel a great deal better. You can leave this life in good spirits. Can you imagine?"

She wanted that, yes, but Chrysanthe forced her mind to move past that to what Margot had just said.

"You can get me more strigas?" she murmured. "Then you must, I suspect, be an instrument of the Cryptarchia."

"What a wonderful mind you have," Margot said. "What else have you guessed?"

"I do not guess," Chrysanthe said. "I infer."

"That is a very confident and fancy way of guessing," Margot said. "What did you 'infer' and to whom did you pass that inference?"

"I'm tired," Chrysanthe said, "and I am not in a cooperative mood."

Margot tilted her head and smiled a little.

"You aren't the only one who can infer things, you know. You found the ledger. You must know perfectly well what it means. You must know about our fleet, and I suspect you used the strigas to contact your father."

Chrysanthe tried to keep her expression neutral.

"Yes," Margot went on. "That is what you did. Of course, you could not speak with him. Instead, you were in contact with one of the strixes on the expedition. And yet, all of the strixe belong to us. To the Cryptarchia."

"You know so much about this," Chrysanthe said. "A wonder you need me at all."

"Her name was Calliope," Margot said. "You know that, I imagine."

Chrysanthe shrugged.

"She did as her duty dictated," Margot went on. "She reported your communication to us."

"Did she?" Chrysanthe said. "Because—" And then she stopped, realizing what was happening. That there was something in her head, something not her. "You have one here, don't you?" she said. "A strixe?" she glanced at the other woman, across the room. Her eyes still refused to focus entirely, but the woman's eyes gleamed with a yellowish light.

"Of course," Margot said. "Just to make certain. Shall I tell you? What became of your father and brother?"

Chrysanthe took a deep, shuddering breath, trying to hang on, to keep her thoughts from spiraling out of control.

"Not just the fleet, I assume?" she said.

"No," Margot said. "Our fleet—the Cryptarchia's fleet—was never meant to engage with the navy. Only to replace it. The navy is destroyed, along with all of the ships from Velesa and Modjal. The city of Basilisk and the seas around it are now quite empty of human and Drehhu life. Oh, there may be some stragglers here and there. A few survivors, but our fleet will make short work of them."

"What happened?"

"You are familiar with volcanoes? Mountains that have flame smoldering inside of them?"

"Yes, of course."

"Then you know the Salamandra is one long chain of such mountains."

Chrysanthe nodded.

"Sometimes volcanoes erupt slowly, fitfully. They spit out ash and smoke, and molten rock oozes from them. Other times they explode with unimaginable force. Force enough to raise tidal waves and wipe cities clean of their inhabitants. Such an explosion occurred a few days ago, just a short distance from Basilisk. I tell you this partly so you will understand our power and our determination. We made this happen, you see. We shattered a mountain to win this war."

"And may have killed thousands," Chrysanthe said. "Including your own people."

"You mean the fleet of Ophion? The Cryptarchia serves no empire, but they will serve us."

"I meant your strixes."

"Oh," Margot said. "Yes, them. Given, but we had a purpose, there. When the volcano erupted, all of the strixes on all of the ships went silent."

"You sacrificed them."

"Their lives belonged to the Cryptarchia," Margot said. "They served us in life, and now in death."

Chrysanthe glanced over at the strixe across the room. "You have many more to replace them, I take it. Who take no umbrage at what you've done to their sisters, and might do to them?"

"Do not think you can sway me," the seated woman said. "I am loyal, as were they."

"To the Cryptarchia? Why?"

"You met the emperor, did you not?" the strixe said. "An idiot. The rulers of Velesa and Modjal are no better. After four hundred years the Drehhu have finally been defeated, and what happens? The three empires immediately begin fighting over their scraps. They will not stop. They would be at war for another four centuries, if not for us. The Cryptarchia will control the Basilisk Throne, and in a short time, the three empires will be one."

Chrysanthe turned her eyes back to Margot.

"Bravo for you," she said. "So my father is dead, and my brother."

"And all your efforts were for naught."

"Then why are we even discussing this?" Chrysanthe asked. Margot started to answer, but Chrysanthe interrupted her. "It's a rhetorical question. The reason we're having this conversation is because you aren't sure of your facts. What if my father yet lives? What if his ships are intact, and his strixes have turned against you?"

"That is impossible," Margot said. "We would know."

"But only by questioning me, it seems."

Margot stared at her for a long moment. Then she looked to the strixe.

"Do you have what you need?"

"For now," the strixe said, "but do not kill her yet. There is more we can learn from her. Her contacts at court, and Bonaventure's stink is on her. Let her rest, and we will speak with her again tomorrow."

Someone lifted her roughly from behind, and she saw one of the other figures in the room stand. His face suddenly came into focus.

"Lucien?" she said.

"Yes," he said. "How has your little game played out this time, Chrysanthe?"

"I should have let my brothers kill you."

"Of course," he said.

"Are you satisfied?" Margot asked.

"Quite," Lucien replied. "I am now done with this, and with her." He stood, bowed slightly at the waist, and left the room.

They returned her to her cell, where she finally broke and began to cry, silently at first, but then in great, hideous wails.

HOUND REGAINED consciousness with Ammolite touching his cheek. Her fingers were wet with blood; at first, he thought it was his, but after a moment he knew it wasn't. He remembered her stabbing Veulkh. A glance showed him the sorcerer lying immobile on the cavern floor.

"Come along," she said. "We have to go."

The stone shuddered beneath them, and the floor felt hotter than it had before.

"Wait," he said.

Martin was thoroughly dead, smashed as if by a giant's heel. His blood formed a nearly circular pool around him. Hound thought Selene was dead, too, but as he drew near her eyes focused on him. The lower half of her face and her neck were slicked with yellow, and golden beads stood out all over her exposed skin.

"My hero," she said, very softly. "Is he dead?"

"Veulkh? Yes."

"Good," she sighed. "He was so strong. I thought I could hold him, if I took enough strigas, but he was too strong."

"What happened?"

"We were always supposed to kill him, afterward," she said. "Not very nice, I know, but necessary. For the good."

"I don't understand."

"I know," she said, smiling. "For all your bravado, you are an innocent in many ways, my Hound. I will miss you."

"Selene…"

"Martin is dead, isn't he?"

"Yes."

She nodded. "Then, maybe, now that we are done with our vows and obligations, when we return from limbo to the bright world…"

"Just stay here," Hound said. "For a little while."

"I knew," she said. "I knew it was a fatal dose. It was our only chance, even with Veulkh exhausted from the deed. He was so, so strong…" The last word faded to a whisper, and her eyes rolled over.

"Where is he?" she asked. "Where is Martin?"

It was the last thing she said.

Ammolite was standing just behind him.

"It's time to go, Hound," she said. "Unless you want to die, too."

THE SUN stood at midday, but it was paler than the faintest moon Crespin had ever seen, and the sky was black to every horizon. The last of the flames were quenched, and everything was unnervingly still. Most of the sails were gone, along with many of the beams and spars which had supported them. The mainmast still stood, but only because five men had died keeping it secure, replacing the cables as they snapped. The deck was covered in black ash, which continued to fall from murky heavens.

He went below to see to his father.

Alastor Nevelon tried to rise. Hector's assistant—now the ship's surgeon—pulled gently on his jacket, trying to keep him in the cot. His head was bound in bandages.

Crespin's ability to hear was gradually returning, although even the nearest voices still sounded far away. He reported as best he could, aware that he was shouting, but knowing his father would otherwise not hear him.

When he was done, his father fought off the surgeon and rose shakily to his feet. He caught Crespin's gaze and held it, then clapped him on the shoulder with one hand and with the other took Crespin's own and shook it firmly. He nodded approvingly.

"Meet me in the chart room at the next clock-strike," he said, and then he left.

CRESPIN TIDIED himself up as best he could. He went on deck to take better inventory of the repairs underway, and when the time came, went below. His father was there, coffee already poured.

Calliope was also present. She still looked unwell, but some of her color had returned. Crespin nodded at her.

"Sit," his father said.

Crespin did so, then took a sip of the coffee. It was still nearly scorching hot.

"You took a great risk, doing what you did," his father said. "Warning the other fleets." Then he added, "It was the right thing to do."

"Thank you. I believe you called it treason, earlier."

"There is little doubt you will be charged with that," his father said.

"You need only brand me a mutineer," Crespin replied. "That will solve all problems but mine."

"No," his father said. "I have greatly compounded your treason, so we are now in this together."

"How so?"

"The strixes," Calliope said. Her voice sounded raspy.

"What of them?"

"Some of us were tasked with keeping the Cryptarchia informed of events here."

"Did you know?" Crespin asked. "Did you know all along that they planned to murder the lot of us?"

"I did not," she replied. "None of us did, but I can work it out. If their plan succeeded, and the volcano killed us all, there would have been no need. Our silence would prove our deaths. Continued communications would alert the Cryptarchia that something had gone wrong."

"So you're saying the Cryptarchia did that? Made that volcano explode? Did a strixe do that?"

"No," she said. "No strixe has that kind of power. That is a different sort of magic, a very old kind, and one I know almost nothing about, but they probably arranged it somehow. At the very least, they knew it would happen, and roughly when."

"Do you think they know some of us survived?" Crespin asked.

"I do not believe so," Calliope said. "Each of us has a limited store of strigas. We use it sparingly, and communications across such vast distances is difficult. It takes more than the usual amount of the spice to accomplish." She leaned forward, putting one elbow on the table.

"Back at Basilisk," she continued. "when I raised the colossus… something happened that, to my knowledge, has never happened before. The strigas allows us to 'get into things,' we like to say. That day we 'got into' each other. A bond was formed, not just between one or two of us, but between most of us."

"In the fleet of Ophion."

"In all of the fleets," she said. "They all joined me. We strixes are not separated by nation, you know."

"No, only by the Cryptarchia," Crespin said.

She nodded. "When the eruption began, I took strigas again. I reached out once more and felt what they were feeling."

"And what was that?"

"No two the same. Some were proud to die for our masters. Many were afraid. Many felt betrayed."

"Many, but not all," Crespin said. "If even one of them took their powder and reported our survival to the Cryptarchia—"

She shook her head. "I told the admiral."

Crespin looked at his father.

"And I contacted the other captains," he said, "while we were still in lucnograph contact. The strixes have all been confined, and their strigas withheld from them."

"Until I can sort them out," Calliope said. "Until I know which ones we can trust."

Crespin stared at her for a moment. "Then this fleet, the one coming to seize control of Basilisk…"

"They believe they will find an empty sea," Calliope said.

"Instead, they will find us," his father added.

"And by us you mean—"

"All of us. Velesans, Modjali, Ophions."

"At last count, we had hardly a hundred ships combined," Crespin said. "Most of the warships were fighting over Basilisk, near where the eruption occurred, and so perished. What we have left can hardly be thought of as a fighting fleet, even if we act in concert—and we have no good idea of the size of our enemy."

His father shrugged. "We will win, or we will perish."

"And what then? Even if we beat the Cryptarchia fleet, will we not revert to war with the other empires?"

"I have, of course, been thinking about that."

WHEN NEXT Margot and the strixe came, there was no conversation. The strixe forced herself into Chrysanthe's body and dug about in her mind. The pain was like nothing Chrysanthe had ever felt before—a distillation of pain, unmediated by the weakness of her flesh. No matter how great it became, she could not faint or otherwise flee into oblivion; she was forced to watch, helpless, as every dignity was robbed from her, as every part of her was violated.

It was not all pain. There was pleasure as well, more than she could have imagined. That was worse, in many ways, than the pain.

When the strixe finally released her, she finally fell blessedly into sleep. As the darkness closed in on her, what little remained of her intellect knew she would not awaken. She had given Margot and the Strixe everything. There was no reason at all for them to keep her alive—and for that, she was grateful.

CHRYSANTHE WOKE to a familiar face, although it took several heartbeats for her to fully recognize it.

"Lucién," she managed. "You've come to kill me, I suppose."

"Quiet," he hissed. "I have not. This is a rescue, if you can believe it."

She tried to breathe. "Lucien, this is cruel."

"I never wished you dead," he said. "The ruse in your chambers—I enjoyed it, I will admit, but I would never have hurt you. Later, the kindness you showed my sister—it is no matter. There is no time to speak of this now. Can you stand?"

"I cannot feel my legs."

"I shall carry you then." From somewhere near, she heard heavy footfalls and voices. "Merde," Lucien said. "A moment, then." He brushed her brow with his hand and then stood. She heard a dull *snick* as he drew his sword. He glanced down at her.

"You will have the best of me," he said. "As little as that might be." Then he darted from sight.

There was the clash of steel, and a shriek that might have been Lucien. As she struggled to stand, night again fell across her mind.

CHAPTER TEN

THE BASILISK THRONE

CHRYSANTHE AWOKE again, this time in a small, dark room. At first, she assumed she was back in her cell, awaiting more torture, but then her eyes made out the odd shape of it, the one curved wall. Her body registered a familiar motion.

She was on a ship, at sea, lifting and falling on the swells. Her cabin was small, and neat, and she lay on a cot, clothed in a white sleeping gown.

She tried to rise, but found her legs were still too weak to hold her. She sat on the side of the bed, gathering her strength. Trying to recall what had happened. She remembered Margot and the strixe. Lucien. And then nothing—no, not nothing. Images. Faces. She had thought them dreams. It was all gray, blurry, except for one set of features.

"Hello?" she called, raising her voice as much as she could. "Is anyone there?"

After a moment the door to the cabin opened, and a young

woman wearing a headscarf peered in.

"Danesele?" she said. "How are you feeling?"

"Who are you?" she asked. "Where am I?"

"I am Alips," she said. "If you will wait, I have orders."

"What choice do I have?"

Alips didn't respond, and turned, closing the door. Before Chrysanthe took more than a few breaths, it opened again.

Bonaventure was groomed this time, dressed like a gentleman at leisure in a dark green vest and a robe of quilted off-white silk. He was clean-shaven, and there was no young girl in his grasp. He smiled, giving her time to register his presence.

"Did I do well?" she finally asked, wearily. Even her voice felt weak. "Was your faith in me justified?"

"Need you ask?" he said. "I think you know the answer to that."

"Why didn't you tell me about d'Ospios? That the last agent you sent to Roselant was murdered?"

"I wasn't sure of her fate," he said, "but if you have discerned that much, you surely know the answer."

She shrugged. "It doesn't matter," she said. "It is all done now, isn't it?"

He looked steadily at her for a moment.

"It will get better," he said. "The effects of strigas are profound, but in time your optimism will return." He crossed his arms. "That was not my idea, by the way," he said. "Your father must have somehow convinced the strix on his ship to give him a portion. A most serious offense for both of them."

"It's almost as if he didn't fully trust you," she remarked. "It was the only way for me to report to him directly. How did you know? About the strigas, and my warning to the fleet?"

"Margot told us. She told us quite a lot."

"And now?"

"She's alive, if that's what you mean. She may be of use to me someday."

She remembered something else, then.

"Lucien," she said. "I saw Lucien."

"You did," Bonaventure replied. "He sustained grave injuries, but we expect he shall live. Help arrived before Margot and her men managed to finish him off."

She nodded. "I am relieved but puzzled. About Lucien and much else."

"If I may enlighten you, please allow me to."

"Why did they do it? The Cryptarchia?"

"What do you mean?"

"The ledger. The d'Othres were supplied with enormous sums of money from various sources. They used it to finance a secret army, and a fleet to carry them."

"That much became clear, once we had the ledger," Bonaventure said, "but you uncovered more."

"The emperor's fleet—and those from Velesa and Modjal—were meant to fail," she replied. "Margot said they would be destroyed by volcanoes. The secret fleet was to move in and occupy Basilisk."

"Exactly," Bonaventure said. "I don't have to explain why it is important to control Basilisk. It is the key to the east, and the Cryptarchia covet it."

"Why would they want that? They already control three empires."

"The Cryptarchia is not without its factions. Let us just say, there is one clique that is tired of rule by proxy. They have power and are tired of working behind the scenes, cajoling emperors and councils.

They would rather make their power visible to all. To discuss it in more detail right now would be dreary, I think."

"The volcanoes? How did they do it?"

"Months ago, we learned that they were sending representatives to negotiate with a sorcerer of some ability. We did not know why, but it was worrisome, so we had them followed. Our people were never heard from again. I suspect that had something to do with all of this."

"And now?" she asked. "What happens?"

"That depends very much on whether your warning to your father was successful," he said, "and on the outcome of a war that is now sure to ensue between the crowns and the Cryptarchia."

She nodded. "How did you find me?"

"I did not, in fact. You have your friend Lucien to thank for that. He said he owed you something… for his sister. Lucien and Margot were working together, as you know. She told him you had been caught, and he asked to have his vengeance on you. She agreed, thinking Lucien would be an ideal candidate to blame for your murder."

"I should thank him, then."

"If he lives, you will have your chance."

Chrysanthe nodded. She wanted to inquire about Quintent, but she feared the answer, and was not yet ready to hear it. There were other things to ask.

"We are on a ship," she said. "Where are we bound?"

"Basilisk," Bonaventure said. "Or what is left of it. There we shall see what has become of your father." He grinned. "Though Lucien is indisposed, there is someone else here you can thank, if you wish."

"I do thank you," she said sincerely.

"What? Oh, not me. The other who rushed to your rescue." He nodded toward the hatch, where Quintent stooped to enter the room.

"Chrysanthe," he said.

She hadn't thought she could feel anything, but the sight and sound of him was almost unbearably good. That strove against her every instinct and sensibility—and anger quickly rose on the heels of her happiness.

"I'll go walk on the deck," Bonaventure said, leaving them and closing the door.

"Chrysanthe—"

"So you're an instrument of Bonaventure."

"We have an alliance, yes."

"He used me," she said. "*You* used me. Knowing what might happen."

"Not exactly," he said, "but near enough. Yet look at the outcome. Because of you, your father and brother may still be alive, along with hundreds of other men and women. Isn't that what your father sent you here for?"

"It's not the outcome I dispute," she snapped. "It is the method. Did you think if you had told me about your part in this, if you had been honest with me, I would have flinched?"

"I struggled with that," he admitted. "I flatter myself to say that I planned to tell you the truth, but I never had the chance to test my resolve. The Cryptarchia called me to another task; I now believe it was at Margot's insistence. Perhaps she suspected my alliance with Bonaventure. Or maybe she sensed my... weakness... where you are concerned. I was in a difficult situation, trying to serve two masters. Not all in the Cryptarchia are villains, and I was not yet ready to reveal myself to those that are.

"So I did their bidding," he added. "I stayed away."

"Until the dance. You could have told me then."

"I meant to. You fled from me."

She nodded. "I did," she admitted. "But you had time before that."

"I—"

"Never mind," she said. "I'm told you rescued me. Are your true allegiances now revealed to your cryptarch masters? Did you finally make the choice?"

He smiled a little. "If you were dead, how could we ever become friends?"

"I am tired of that flirtation," she snapped. "I am beyond it. What I have seen, what has been done to me—I have no interest in being clever, and far less interest in you being so."

"I am not clever," he said. "I am slow, that is all. From the moment I met you, I realized that I did not wish you to be tangled up in this mess." He looked away, as if unable to hold her gaze. "I wish I had known your plan to go to the bridge," he said. "I wish I had found you sooner. I wish… I had not let you leave the dance." He looked down. "I tried to find you that night. Margot told me she had killed you. I almost believed it, but Lucien was behaving suspiciously, and so I followed him. A good thing, too, for both of you."

"I should say so," she agreed. "But why? Why reveal your deception of the Cryptarchia to save me?"

"I think you know."

She stared at him a moment. "That is ridiculous," she said.

He nodded. "I know it is." He sighed. "This is not flirtation. It is no attempt at wit. I am forever sorry for what happened to you. I should have protected you. I meant to, but I let them call me away, and then I waited too late. For that, you may never forgive me. I cannot forgive myself. And yet, I still hope…" He broke off and looked away. "There is much that you do not know of me. Much that I wish you knew."

The world seemed to take a breath. She felt the motion of the ship, of the fathoms of water below her. She saw the flickering of candlelight on the wooden bulkheads. She saw a strand of Quintent's hair, loose from the rest of it, drifting down his face. She felt calm settle over her as everything in the world moved just a little, so everything fit in place.

He shrugged, then dropped down to one knee and took her hand in his.

"You are not a man, are you?" Chrysanthe whispered.

Quintent's gaze fixed on hers. "I was not born one," he replied. "I have had two lives, Chrysanthe. There is Helene, who served the Cryptarchia. She carried the name given me at birth. And there is Quintent, whom you know as the person you see before you."

"You think I know you?" she said. "After all of this deception?"

"Yes, and I believe you should get to know me better."

"Shall I ask you to remove your clothing, so I can see for myself?"

Looking surprised but serious, Quintent rose. He reached for the buttons of his vest. She let him undo two before lifting her hand.

"Please stop," she said. "I'm joking. I believe you. I should have known the moment I met you."

"I thought you had no wit left in you?"

"I am recovering," she said. "Does anyone else on the ship know?"

"Bonaventure."

"Is that door secure?"

"Yes."

"Then come here," she said, tugging the hand holding hers.

The kiss was small, and sweet, and filled her like a blush.

"Perhaps we can be friends, one of these days," she said.

"I should like that very much," he said.

AMMOLITE TOOK Hound by the hand and led him up a steep slope, away from the Tsau Dadan. There she found a stone slab overlooking the sea. She undressed him and then herself.

As their bodies merged, Ammolite's form altered, becoming that of Selene.

"No," he said. "Just be you."

She seemed pleased by that, but the fact was that he could not bear it. Selene was dead, her body cremated in the mountain now smoldering to their north. They had fled it for days, with ash and curiously light stone falling on them, along with fumes that threatened to burn their lungs.

Something much bigger was happening in the south. The sky was black for days, lightning flickering near constantly on the horizon. A sound like thunder so loud as to be nearly deafening had been followed by several smaller reports. Now, days later, the sun was visible only as a lemony smudge. Sometimes not even that.

When they were done, and Hound and Ammolite lay together, it began to rain. The drops were nearly hot, and had a sharp, acrid scent.

"That was nice," he said. They hadn't had sex since that time in the mountain, and he had begun to wonder if they ever would again.

She nodded and squeezed his knee.

"I'm glad you came back," he told her. "I know it was to kill Veulkh, but if you hadn't returned, I would be dead now."

"I didn't come back just to kill Veulkh."

"Oh," he said. He wasn't sure what else she might be expecting to say. "So where are we going?" he asked, after a pause.

She didn't answer at first. Then she sat up. Rain came down her hair and drops fell from her brows like a veil.

"I want to know what I am," she said. "Veulkh said he bought me in a place called Basilisk. So I'm going there."

"You know where it is?"

She pointed toward the darkness to the south.

"Veulkh knew where it was," she said. "Now I do too." She looked down, no longer meeting his eyes. "I have the Tsau Dadan to serve me," she said. "If you don't want to come, I can tell you how to get home. But it is a long way."

Hound reached over and took her hand.

"I have a feeling going with you will be more interesting."

She looked up, and her lips parted in the slightest of smiles.

ONCE MORE the *Leucothea* drew within sight of the Colossus Gates, but if Crespin hadn't known better, he might not have guessed they were in the same place as before. The remains of the second colossus were gone. The high hills flanking the straights were now charcoal, the trees and bushes that had once clothed them gone as if they had never been.

No living thing of any kind could be seen, save for the seabirds picking at the charred carrion in the noisome waters and on the broad, ebony beaches that had once been shallows. The sky above was troubled, but hints of blue showed through. The scent of ash burned his throat.

They continued into the Mere de Basilisk. The city was still there, or at least a dark shadow of it remained. Most of the tallest buildings were shattered; ash covered everything.

Two other ships lay at anchor near one of the stone quays, waiting for them. One was long, double-hulled—a Modjali kalkotay, the largest of their battle craft. The other was a Velesan galley. No other ships were visible. The remainder of the Ophion fleet was still out at sea.

The admiral stood next to him, in complete regalia. The men, likewise, were in their finest dress. As Crespin watched, the admirals from the other ships came over in smallboats.

"Are you sure this is best?" Crespin asked.

"The Cryptarchia fleet will reach us in a few weeks," his father said. "They expected to find nothing. Now they will find us."

"But the fleet originates in Ophion," Crespin said. "Even if the emperor did not send it."

"I was charged by the emperor to take the Basilisk Throne," his father said. "I will do so. This is the only way I see to accomplish that."

"Still…"

"Crespin," the admiral said, "it was you who gave me the idea. Now you argue against it?"

"How did I do that?"

"When you set free the Velesan and Modjali ships. When you gave their fleets warning. That made possible what is about to transpire."

"That's not what I was thinking at the time."

His father shrugged. "No. You acted from instinct and principle, both of which you have in abundance."

"I was not born with either," Crespin said. "I learned from you."

His father didn't answer, but something in his bearing changed.

"You'll go with me," he said. "Give the order to make port."

CRESPIN RECOGNIZED the Velesan representative—Morjebor, whose ship they had captured. The Modjali was a woman of some fifty years named Venkai with sharp eyes and an impressively hooked nose. Each came with a single attendant.

Men from the *Leucothea* brought coffee, and stools were set up so the three admirals were facing one another. Crespin and his counterparts remained standing.

"Thank you for coming," Alastor said. "I believe we have much to discuss."

"You have earned the right to say anything you wish," Venkai said. "What is your word?"

"Peace," Alastor replied.

"That hardly seems possible," Venkai said. "Not with another fleet from Ophion on its way."

"That fleet is not sent by my emperor. It is sent by the Cryptarchia, as I believe I laid out in my dispatches to you. The cryptarchs have betrayed my emperor, both of yours, and all of us. It is my suggestion we make them pay for that."

"An alliance," Morjebor said. "I thought you might suggest that. I, too, am grateful for all you have done for us, but once we defeat this fleet, what then? Your emperor will send more ships, as will mine, and Admiral Venkai's. This will all start again."

"It need not," the admiral said. "Not if we three come to an understanding."

"I'm listening," Venkai said.

"Basilisk lies empty. I sent scouts within, and they found no signs of Drehhu survivors. It is half-wrack, though many of the buildings are intact. We can fashion a port from what remains. Each of our nations wishes to control this passage to the east. So does the Cryptarchia. If we remain at each other's throats, eventually they will succeed. They control the strigas, so they control the strixes.

"I propose that the three of us rule this place, as proxies for our empires. Not one Basilisk Throne, but three. We will apportion equally whatever gains we make here, and we will defend it against any attack."

"Including attacks by Ophion?"

"Yes," Alastor replied. "And Velesa. And Modjal."

"You speak of forming a new nation," Venkai said. "A sovereign state."

"If we do not, our respective empires will fight for a thousand years," the admiral said. "I think we can make them see reason. It is my fervent hope. We shared in this victory. We should share the spoils."

The other two absorbed that silently for a moment.

"Entertaining this idea," Venkai finally said, "we would have a written agreement? One we all accept?"

"Yes."

"This all presumes we will repel the fleet bearing down on us."

"We will. They believe we perished. We will have the benefit of surprise. We have strixes loyal to us, and still enough strigas to provision them."

"And later? If they return? Or if we must beat back an attack by our own governments?"

"By then we will have learned the use of the Drehhu weapons."

"That is forbidden," Morjebor pointed out.

"Yes," the admiral replied. "*Was* forbidden—by the Cryptarchia."

"That is an excellent point," Venkai said. She looked from one to the other. "I am inclined to continue this conversation."

LATER, BACK on the *Leucothea*, Crespin looked out over the other ships.

"What if they don't agree in the end?" he asked.

"They will agree," his father said. "They will agree, and the world will be changed."

Over the ash-covered city, sunlight lanced through the clouds. A sea eagle flew through the shaft of light, its white head glowing like a miniature sun. Crespin heard a small sound behind him and turned to see Calliope emerging from below. Her fair skin seemed almost white, but she looked better, stronger. Determined.

Not far away, Renost stood in his best uniform.

Despite his father's certainty, there was no knowing what the next few weeks would bring. They might soon join the countless souls who had already perished at Basilisk.

As of that moment, it was a good day.

Everything seemed possible.

Everything.

ACKNOWLEDGEMENTS

THANKS ONCE again to Steve Saffel for editing, to Keven Eddy for the copy edit, and to Nell Keyes for early input. Many thanks to the rest of the Titan team—Nick Landau, Vivian Cheung, Laura Price, Fenton Coulthurst, Julia Lloyd, Paul Gill, Chris McLane, Katharine Carroll, and Jenny Boyce.

ABOUT THE
AUTHOR

GREG KEYES was born April 11th, 1963, in Meridian, Mississippi. His sold his first novel, *The Waterborn*, in 1995. Since that time he has had over thirty novels published. His original book series include the Chosen of the Changeling duology, the Age of Unreason tetralogy, the Kingdoms of Thorn and Bone, and the High and Faraway trilogy. Standalone works include *Footprints in the Sky* and the short story collection *The Hounds of Ash*. He has also had the privilege of writing in many shared universes, including Star Wars, *Babylon 5*, Planet of the Apes, Marvel's Avengers, the Elder Scrolls, XCOM and *Pacific Rim*. He wrote novelizations of the movies *Interstellar*, *Godzilla: King of the Monsters* and *Godzilla vs. Kong*. He also wrote the graphic novel *Godzilla: Dominion*. He lives with his family in Savannah, Georgia.

For more fantastic fiction, author events,
exclusive excerpts, competitions, limited editions and more

VISIT OUR WEBSITE
titanbooks.com

LIKE US ON FACEBOOK
facebook.com/titanbooks

FOLLOW US ON TWITTER AND INSTAGRAM
@TitanBooks

EMAIL US
readerfeedback@titanemail.com